DEDICATION

Dedicated to the WWII troops of the 150th Infantry Regiment (Powderhorns) and to the 158th Regimental Combat Team (Bushmasters), with whom I had the honor and privilege to serve during the war; to Wilma, a true and faithful partner, and friend.

ACKNOWLEDGMENT

Writing a book is a monumental task. Perhaps it is a form of self punishment the Author heaps upon himself for past sins committed or something, trying to make amends. He schemes for assistance from those who have expertise in literary technology even to cover that which is needed in the many fields to bring the manuscript to the form of an acceptable book hopefully, to be read by thousands. His literary search usually finds the best available who gladly lend their craft bringing his dream to fruition, informing the public of his adventures, hopefully in an entertaining and informative manner. My search have been successful finding the assistance needed and my appreciations are expressed, for without them this book would have not been possible.

To my daughter-in-law, Linda, for her editing; to Mich Borden, who edited parts written after Linda had initially edited the manuscript; to Scott Cravens and Louis Puster, who retrieved lost chapters that somehow I had lost in the computer, saving me many hours redoing them; and to Cathy, my daughter, and her husband, Ben Morton; Lori Deitrick who designed the cover for the book, and to my wife Wilma, the heroine of the story, for her patience, assistance, editing, and understanding. Then finally, especially to my daughter, Sandy, who often labored days and far into many nights preparing the manuscript for publication; it is through her diligence this book is made possible; she was a godsend in my time of need. To her family, who suffered through it all, and to many others, thanks.

I N D E X

APPENDIXES

INTRODUCTION

Please be advised, because of many request from readers of the book, Ben Rod Jordan of Putnam County, who realized the story of the mischievous boy and his companions were true, wanted to know what happened to him. Than this book is a sequel to the aforementioned book. It is hope the story, The Return to Glory - The Saga of Ben Rod Jordan, will be interesting, entertaining, as well as informative to the reader for it covers an important period of American history; a few years before, during, and after WWII.

The Author served with two National Guard regiments, the 150th Infantry Regiments (Powderhorns) from West Virginia, and the 158th Regimental Combat Team (Bushmasters) from Arizona. He trained with the former, going to Panama with it, and there joined the latter and traveled with it to the South West Pacific Area where the "Bushmasters" faced the oriental enemy who had made the sneak attack on Pearl Harbor. Both regiments served the country well even though having different, but equally vital missions. The "Powderhorns" and the "Bushmasters" respective states proudly records their regiment's glory that is included in the military annals of American history as well. The Author was honored to have served with both.

While writing the story, The Return to Glory, many events had to be recalled from the distant past. Even though the events are true much imagination, using non-fiction and fiction, was used to forge them into a unified, a cohesive, and a comprehensive story. For this the Author begs for understanding hoping the reader can get the feeling of young men during WWII, who were rapidly molded into combat soldiers within a few weeks of time. Later how they, their officers, and NCOs coped with the stress forced upon them on the battlefield by a fanatical oriental enemy who considered it was more honorable to die then to surrender. This forced the young soldier to kill when he really didn't want to kill; but it was kill or be killed.

To effectively portray much of the story, the Author had to refer the a few notes he had made on paper, now faded over the years; personal journals, passenger lists, company rosters, and finally, to fill the gaps, his fading memory. In view of this, and as previously mentioned, both fiction and non-fiction was used in construction the diverse story to fruition. However, in all cases the events are true but enhanced by fiction, based upon imagination, bringing the story to a logical conclusion, for the Author knew of the events, but, yet, not details that had caused the event. Example, when John Wayne, a personal friend of our affable but firm battalion commander, arrived but later disappeared, causing much anguish for us, especially so when it was found he had unauthorized had accompanied one our a combat patrol, causing much concern for the battalion commander, the commanding general of TASK FORCE DIRECTOR, perhaps even to General MacArthur; or the missing Private Maza, Company "E", during the battle of January 6, when the battalion was trying to disengage itself from battle, but because of the whereabouts of Private Maza was unknown, delayed until it was determined. Being unaware of all the details in either case, as with others, it was necessary to use fiction, or imagination if you will, to fill in the gaps making the stories logical and conclusive. In defense, all the Author can say to the reader, even though the events are all true, many of details building them up to an understandable solution, in many cases, fiction had to be used.

Hopefully, The Return to Glory - The Saga of Ben Rod Jordan will update the readers of the former book, and inform others, who will realize that the character, who is represented by Ben Rod Jordan, is alive and well even though he is in the afternoon life.

FOREWORD

Perhaps the unusual war experience had aged Ben Rod Jordan too fast. Prior to this rare experience, as a young boy, he had removed himself from the hilly austere farm life in Putnam County where, often leaning on his hoe and pitchfork handles, while working in the hot fields, and wondered what lay beyond the high steep ridges that surrounded him. His imaginations were further inflamed by the rattle of the freight trains and the lonesome whistle of the steam boats that ran beside and on the Great Kanawha River beyond the ridges - a river he seldom saw, but heard folks often talk about it. There was something majestic about the river; perhaps it was a symbol that would, someday, remove his isolation that had held him since birth. He waited for that day to come. And it did. He also heard the folks talk of the towns of Nitro, Red house, Winfield, Raymond City, etc., that leisurely nestled on its shores; they, too, became a goal for him to see.

But his source of knowledge was restricted, for he had no radio, no telephone, or even a newspaper, not even a paved road or indoor plumbing or telephone. What little current knowledge he had access was mostly by word of mouth from farmers congregated around the red hot pot bellied stove at Brady Boggess' country store on cold winter evenings; the one room school house of Mt Etna, or at the old Center Point Church with its cemetery that contained the graves of his young mother, and young sister, who had died from the flu epidemic in 1919. His motherless home, having few amenities, and farm did provided bare essentials of life for the large family, requiring them to work hard long hours, scratching these essential from the hilly and rocky earth.

It was from this environment Ben Rod Jordan sprang into a new life that he had dreamed of and wished for. He had gone to school in Charleston, later met a beautiful girl, married her, and together they began a home and became parents of two little boys. The "Great Depression Years" were coming to an end and his job at a local glass bottling plant appeared to provide a bright future for the young family; it was a family bliss. Then when his small family needed him the most he was dragged into WWII causing a separation from his loved ones for almost three years; the future was dark. The young wife would have to go it alone and shape the lives of her young sons as best as she could without her husband; a common thing during the war years.

The war would eventually move Ben Rod half way around the world. His experiences he had had during a war years would normally have been a life time for most. It was incredible and at time tragic when he observed what war did to young men who should have been home with their doting parents. Men, young in years but aged by exposure to extremely harsh and long isolation, would often become mentally unbalanced reverting to childhood, men minds became so twisted they looked forward to battle as if the vicious enemy was an opponent at a softball game: they faced death with a smile. He wondered why. How could men become so cruel blowing each others brains out with a high powered rifle and tear innocent bodies to pieces with artillery fire, or even worse, inflict lifelong suffering from horrible wounds. Ben Rod was convinced that nations without laws to govern their relations to each others were outlaws as were the gangsters of the day. Ben Rod realized that people don't make war, nations do and do it willingly regardless of the terror it brings to its people that have to fight it. In war young men become old men in a short time, an experience never to be forgotten; they loose their happy youthful life by the terror that lies forever dormant but still silently churns within. The once happy and innocent youth, removed from their parents and sent to war, will be returned having a war torn mind and often their body torn as well; they will never be the same.

He observed that by necessity the once docile youth must be made into an effective killer. From the outset the recruit is told and his training reflects, that he must kill or be killed. Survival being foremost in his mind, and having a natural instinct to live, the youth trains with this in mind. Basically, the military untrains the docile man and then retrain him to become an effective killer through harsh training methods often more demanding then even combat. Unfortunately, this is terrible fact of life and must be done surreptitiously.

Then Ben Rod would forever remember the remark by an officer of WWI vintage, as he sat with others, on the damp and cold ground in January 1941 at Camp Shelby Mississippi: "A soldier will live miserably and will die miserably." What a horrible thing to say to a new group of soldiers trying to make an adjustment from a docile civilian life to a harsh military one under war time conditions.

But the military appealed to Ben Rod Jordan, not for the terrible experience men must suffer in combat, but from the fellowship and brotherhood. He found men soon acquired an attitude: "one for all and all for one". This attitude was often demonstrated when men in combat would sacrifice themselves for the benefit of another; unfortunately, too many actions of this sort went unrecognized.

Further, Ben Rod had compassion even for the enemy who had died at the hand of the "Bushmasters" Battalion on Arawa. Standing among the enemy dead he felt they, too, had wives, sweethearts, fathers and mothers, brothers, and sisters back home and their deaths, like the next of kin of those of his own men, whose bodies, still warm, lie beside their open shallow graves, yet to be buried, would suffer terribly when notified of their great loss. He cringed, too, when he observed, because of the great number of enemy dead, a common ditch being dug by a bulldozer and their bodies unceremoniously pushed in and covered by the dozer's blade without benefit of clergy; the grave, unmarked, and perhaps to this day still contains the bodies of the brave and gallant Imperial Japanese marines of Arawa, whose families perhaps still wonder what had happened to their beloved kin.

Finally the terror over, Ben Rod, after thirty-three months, returns to his loved ones who welcomes him home with open arms. He had wondered if they would accept him in his temporarily tormented mind and weakened malarial ridden body and they did.

Eventually, after a leave at home with his family and following a visit to the cemetery where his mother, sister, and now his father, who had died in 1942, lay buried, said a silent prayer over their graves and then proceeded to his next duty station at Camp Robinson, Arkansas. There he was assigned to command a recruit training company and it was during this time he managed to come to grips with the horrible experience of Arawa placing it on a mental shelf, an experience that would serve him well in the future. Maybe, fortunately, somehow future leaders of the world will be convinced that war isn't necessary if only reasonable people would talk to each other. Otherwise, the carnage will continue even though the situations causing wars is of little importance to the people at large. Nationalism must be ended before the world is torn apart and destroyed by it. We have the means to do this; can we control it?

CHAPTER 1

THE LONG HOT SUMMERS & COLD WINTERS

The long hot summers and cold winters in Wonderful Wild West Virginia, are not enjoyable and at times most disagreeable. There are exceptions, however. Time permitting, Buss and I often go fishing over on Eighteen Mile creek, go swimming in the old mill pond down on Cherry Fork, only seven miles away; we hunt and run a trap line in winter, or just explore the forests with our dogs, Bruno and Rover. Bruno was poisoned by someone and we buried him under an apple tree down in the orchard, it was sad for us; now we have Rover; he's a better hunter than Bruno was. But we liked them both. Then we go to church, and when not doing mischief, we enjoy Preachers Morris' or Vaughn Fisher's sermons, or listen to Brade Boggess, the local store keeper and postmaster, as he leads the congregation in singing; he sings louder, above all others. Too, we pitch horseshoes, play baseball with other farm boys over on the Plez Davis' farm on Saturday afternoons or on Sundays, the only place around with ground level enough for a ballfield; we do other things, too.

Mainly, we have to work from early dawn to late at night, even until bedtime - rain or shine, except on Saturdays and Sundays, sometimes even then. Beginning early spring and until late fall we till the soil, plant seeds, work and harvest the crops. Before cold weather sets in, we begin the winter cycle of planting winter wheat and oats preparing for another harvest come late spring. We also plant turnips and mustard greens and other cold weather vegetables in late August or early September so we can have something green and fresh to eat during the cold winter months ahead - we call this our winter garden. "Green vegetables in winter, just like in summer time, are good for you", Papa says. Like everybody else living in Putnam County, if we didn't raise our own food we would starve come winter. We don't rely on welfare agencies to provide us food and clothing; this would be disgraceful. There are some welfare commodities that can be picked up in Red House, near Winfield on the Great Kanawha River, but those who use the commodities are considered lazy and good-for-nothing, and looked down upon by most people. However, we often give from our abundance to deserving people who are down on their luck for no reason of their own, such as the widows, the elderly and the sick.

We live by our work ethics, such as it is, earning our bread by the sweat of the brow, work is good for you. Papa has no use for a "lazy pup"; that's what he calls us at times, and he sees to it we do our share of the work on our hilly farm. There is little time for pleasure once we are in the fields for we work hard and long hours. We plow the soil, sow seeds, cultivate and harvest the crops, cut sprouts, cattle looked after, cut wood, coal hauled from the mines, hogs slaughtered, food stored in the root cellar. Even much of our clothing is made in the home;

our shoes are half soled by Papa, while our sisters makes patched quilts for our beds, having straw ticks instead of mattresses. Even though we grow most everything we need to eat we do buy sugar, coffee, kerosene and tobacco at Brady Boggess' store, located out on the ridge, things we cannot grow on the farm.

Even though we have little time for pleasures we enjoy working together in the fields or forest. Mischief is always going on especially if Doc, our older brother, is around. He is the ring leader when it comes to practical jokes and pranks. We make the best of it when we are lucky enough to have a Saturday afternoon or a Sunday off. Even then we have morning and evening chores to do, such as feeding the livestock, getting in coal and wood for the kitchen stove or the fireplace in the parlor, and milking the cows, taking hours.

A great responsibility rests upon Papa. He is a good planner and keeps us all busy. He gets us up about 5:30 a.m. Buss, my nephew, and I, still sleepy, round up the cows before breakfast for milking, which is usually done by our sisters. My brothers feed, curry, and harness the horses and all of us prepare for the days labor in the fields. Then we have breakfast. The large family sat around the big table loaded with platters of food; after that Papa issues instructions to us. All listen, for Papa is a man of few words and we had better know what we are to do during the day; he's not pleasant when we disappoint him. Prepared, we take off to do whatever we are assigned to do.

Even going to the field as a family is

fun. We all are in our work garb such as overalls, shoes and straw hats, except Buss and me; we go barefooted in warm weather. We carry the tools needed for the day, such as hoes, axes, pitch forks, mattocks, shovels on our shoulders. The heavy tools and equipment such as plows, cultivators, and harrows are transported in horse drawn wagons or sleds; we have no farm tractors like they do over in Teays Valley. What we do determines what kind of tools we carry. If we are to hoe corn we carry hoes, if we are to work in the hayfield, we carry pitchforks, if we are to work in the forest cutting firewood or fence posts, we takes axes and saws. We always carry a bucket of water; it is our only source of water until we are called to dinner at noon by the ringing of the dinner bell. The dinner bell is located just out side the kitchen door near the smokehouse and the henhouse.

Working the long rows of corn on the hot June days is most dreadful. The long rows, wrapping around the hillside, are not in the least encouraging, nor is the large hay field on the ridge above the cornfield. Each has to be worked in the hot sun and we pour sweat doing it - man, woman, and child. If we are working corn we pick up our hoes, put the cultivators on the sled, with horses already hitched to it, and we follow the sled down the hill using the service road. The road leads down the hill to the creek, past the old sawmill sawdust pile, then up another hill through a forest to the cornfield. The field is enclosed by a barbed wire fence to keep the cattle out; bars to a gate can be removed, permitting us to enter to work the corn.

Our trip to the field will began about 7:00AM., sometimes earlier, depending upon time of daylight or just before sun is up. We enjoy the early sun bathing God's beautiful creation; we are thrilled by the miracle of the green meadow, we pass through, damp with dew, the trees also have dew dripping from the green leaves, and the birds are singing. The rabbits and chipmunks are hopping and scurrying around us, occasionally they stop and stands on their hind legs to watch the human parade. These little fellows are part of our lives and we try to be friendly to them. The cattle are curious, too, they graze in the green meadow, lift their heads to look at us, and then continue their meal of wet green grass. Buss and I romps and play with our dog, Rover, snatching a wild blackberry or two from the vines growing by the side of the service road as Rover chases a rabbit over the hill; he soon returns, tongue and tail wagging as if to impress us. Others in the family group talk and laugh at homespun jokes while smoking their pipes and cigarettes or chewing their brown mule or twist of homegrown tobacco, I don't' like the stuff. Papa lectures us on the evils of smoking, while at the same time, he chews a big cud of tobacco himself. Both are customary in the community. Papa, for some reason, is dead set against smoking even though he chews.

We begin working the corn when the stalks are about six inches high, removing the weeds and hoeing the hills of corn. The two cultivators are tugged by horses, with one of my big brothers between the plow handles, guides the horses through the rows of new green corn. The cultivator will remove most of the weeds from the center of the row while tilling the top soil. We hoers work the corn, loosening the soil around the stalk and pulling fresh dirt to it and cutting the weeds between hills. This will increase the air circulation around the roots of the growing plant, causing its rapid growth and later, a good harvest, Papa says. While two brothers (usually Bill and Doc) cultivate the corn, the remainder of the family does the hoeing, the hardest part. Those on the cultivators kid us as we labor in the rows as they pass by, kicking up dust, for us to eat. They laugh at us as we chop weeds but we tell them we have the more desirable job; we don't have to look at the rear end of a sweating horse all day like they do - it's not a cultured thing either.

There are times when old man Bibbie, who lives up the hill from us in the old Dayton McKee place, helps us out during corn hoeing and haying season. Papa pays the old man a whole dollar for a day's work and he's worth every penny of it, too. Mr. Bibbie is the fastest corn hoer I've ever seen. He also is a man of great wisdom and I always take advantage of his knowledge.

"Mr. Bibbie, why do we have to work so much in the cornfield? Can't it just grow on its own?" I quired, trying to find reason why we should not have to work the corn.

"Now son, the Lord told Adam in the Garden of Eden that we must work and sweat to earn our keep and he put these noxious weeds and thorns here to see that we do it."

"Well, most of the weeds are killed by

the cultivator, why can't we get by with that, Mr. Bibbie?"

"Son, the cultivators will not kill all the weeds and vines, not between the hills anyway, and besides, you must hoe the corn pulling fresh soil around the stalks and air to the roots." By this time, being the fastest corn hoer in these parts, the old man is out of talking range. Later we meet him on the next row above us coming in the opposite direction quipping good-naturedly as he passes leaving a good clean corn row behind him.

Now Papa is a fast corn hoer, too, but he can't keep up with old man Bibbie. Papa said the rest of us was lagging in the corn rows and he chided us firmly.

"Look", he said, "old man Bibbie hoes twice as much corn as you", talking to Doug, my brother-in-law, being all of twenty seven years. "Why can't you do better?"

Doug unwisely gave Papa a classical reply, so to speak.

"Why Old Man", that is what he calls Papa, "he should hoe twice more than I do for he is twice older then me."

Papa thought that over for a second, but only a second, and I don't think he thought much of his son-in-law's wise reply. He told us to work faster for he wanted to finish hoeing corn by late Saturday afternoon. He planned to begin haying on Monday, the reason he was paying old man Bibbie a whole dollar a day to help us. He say if we didn't finish working the corn by late Saturday afternoon we would have to work Sunday. We work harder.

We continued to labor in the cornfield, the sun, blistering hot, climbed high while the shade of the tall trees, surrounding the cornfield, got shorter, the rows seemed to get longer, the field wider. Reaching the end of a row of corn meant a few minutes of rest under a comfortable shade of an oak tree, and a drink of the sun-warmed water from the two-gallon water bucket to wet our parched lips. Sometimes one of us, being so thirsty, will drink more than our share of water, emptying the bucket of the precious liquid. A heated discussion usually follows.

"Why you fool," the unfortunate hot and thirsty hoer of corn would say through his parched lips, while spitting wads of cotton balls, "you drank all the water!" Before blows are struck Papa sends the angry one to the creek at the bottom of the hill to drink his fill of water, returning with the water bucket filled with fresh water. If the creek is dry, and usually it is, the thirsty devil must climb the steep hill to the house to get his fill of water from the cistern, located on the back porch. He will draw water from the cistern to fill his empty bucket and return with it to the hot cornfield to continue hoeing with the others.

We continued hoeing in the long rows of corn while we baked under the hot sun. The cheerful talking, singing, and joking ceased and we choked on the dust kicked up by the cultivators. Mr. Bibbie, still leading the way, cheers us on, while the sweat poured down our faces and bodies soaking every stitch of clothing we have on. The sun continues to punish us. We work row after row resting a bit on our hoe handles at the end of each row. Finally, we hear the sharp and welcoming peal of the dinner bell calling us to dinner that Grace, Lily, and Bonnie, our sisters, has prepared for us. All efforts ceases. Leaving our hoes, marking the place to begin in the afternoon, staking the horses near the creek for grazing and watering, we head for the house to partake of the feast awaiting us. Afterwards we take a short rest under the shade of the large oak trees in the front yard.

Arriving at the house we rush to the wash-pan sitting on washstand on the back porch. Each of us takes turns, according to age, washing away the sweat and dust from our faces and hands. We dry ourselves on a single towel hanging from a nail on the outside kitchen wall near the washstand, then take our places at the big table. Buss and I, being the youngest, having last chance at the "trough", survives somehow in spite of the disadvantage.

As always, meal time is a happy time for the Jordan family. Ten or more often sits around the big table on benches and chairs while our sisters, who have already eaten, wait on us. They often replace platters of food as it is gobbled up by the hungary field hands. They keep fresh milk for Buss and me available, and even carry food from one end of the big table to the other when we are too busy eating to do it ourselves. Being the smallest, we, Buss and I, keep our eyes on the desserts, especially the apple cobbler, making sure Buck and Bill don't get more than their share of the goodies, but they usually do, anyway. We protest loudly, but it doesn't do any good.

Once we finish the big meal, we move to the front porch and yard for a short rest before returning to the hot field. The boys nap on the ground under the spreading oak trees while the elders, and Mr. Bibbie, naps in the rocking chairs on the big porch.

All too soon, our short after-dinner rest come to an end. Papa sounds work call and we arouse ourselves from our naps , stretch our tired bodies, and it's back into the cornfield. Picking up our hoes we cut the weeds and hoeing the hills of corn. The horses pull the cultivators with my brothers still between the plow handles stirring the soil and removing the weeds between the rows, still raising dust that turns to mud on our sweating faces and collects on our overalls. We pray for rain from the cloud that suddenly appears on top of the towering ridge. If it rains, the cornfield turns to mud, putting an end to working the corn for the day and we change locations to work in the barn or toolshed; we never lose time. However we would be out of the hot sun until the cornfield is dry enough to work again.

Our prayers are answered. The clouds darkened, thunder rumbled, the lightning struck, and we raced to the barn for shelter from the welcome rain. During the rain we service machinery, sharpen tools or cut wood in the woodshed. It is a welcome change but eventually, maybe the following morning, we will be back, all too soon, in the cornfield; it must be worked by Saturday afternoon, otherwise we will have to work Sunday. We don't like to do that; we worked harder. Papa wants to get into the hayfield early on

Monday morning, he says.

While we shelter in the barn or toolshed from the rain, Buss and I do minor chores. Being young boys, we are considered too small to do big things and are given things we can do, and we work with the others. Cutting tools such as axes, scythes, and mowing machine sickles, are sharpened on the hand operated grinding stone; The older boys of the family hold the cutting edge of the tool to the stone to sharpen it, while one of us turns the crank the other pours water on it; switching jobs occasionally. This tough job goes on most of the time during the rain and it is about as bad as hoeing corn in the hot sun. We are thankful when its time to chase cows; its a change.

During these thunderstorm breaks, in addition of sharpening the tools and repairing machinery, we build cabinets, shelves, or chests and other things. We even built a horse-drawn sled once. We use a horse-drawn sled instead of a wagon when snow is on the ground. We put a wagon bed on the sled, hook horses to the sled, and it is just as useful as a wagon. However, making a large sled, using hand tools, is hard work. Boring through four-inch timbers with an auger, twisting it by hand, soon brings sweat to one's brow. Our work in the barn, shed, or tool house end when the rain stopped, the ground dries, we're back hoeing corn again.

Completing the cornfield late Saturday afternoon we began cutting hay on Monday morning. This is like going from the frying pan into the fire. The haying season begins with mowing the field, using a horse-drawn mowing machine having a long sickle that is lowered to the right side of the machine. When not in use, the sickle is in an upright position for storage or while moving the machine to and from the hayfields.

Papa begins mowing the hay starting at the barn extending along McClain road, then traveling around the crooked ridge, past Center Point Church and cemetery to Uncle Will's place - a large hayfield.

While we work in the hot hayfield, Uncle Will comfortably sits in the shade of his front porch watching us. He makes his money raising and selling cattle, requiring little hard work on his part. He buys hay from Papa to feed his cattle during the winter. We can't help being a little envious of Uncle Will. Some say he is rich for he has a Model "T" Ford touring car, the only one in the community. He never let us ride in the car.

Once the hay is cut and cured the hard work really begins. It must be raked into long rows, doodled, and stacked. This must be done before the rain comes; wet hay will mold, damaging it. This is the reason Papa makes us work early to late on weekdays and on Sunday if necessary. All the farmers do this, too. The haying season ends when the hay is stacked in large stacks in the field or hauled and stored in the loft of the barn. The hay is a part of the winter food supply for our farm animals. We are glad when the haying is over; pitching and stacking hay is hard and hot work.

In late summer and early fall, the final harvesting begins with cutting corn and digging potatoes. Using a corn knife about three feet long, family members take several rows of dead corn stalks, cutting them off about two feet from the ground, leaving a stubble. The corn stalks is gathered and placed in shocks and tied around the middle, leaving a hollow space inside. The job given to Buss and me, during corn cutting, is to carry the cut stocks. They stack the corn stocks against a frame made from uncut cornstalks giving it rigidity, preventing the shocks from falling over during windstorms. The shocks, once the corn is cut and stacked, is scattered over the cornfield, give the appearance of tepees of an indian village and is a comforting sight especially once the snow falls; it is a beautiful winter scene.

Many multi-colored shocks dot the entire field that once had been the green corn we had worked during the hot days of the past summer. We often play inside the shocks, chasing away the rabbits and birds that have taken temporary possession.

The cutting of corn completed, the ears of corn cured, now golden in color, is shucked, or removed from the cornstalks, and like we do the oats after threshing, hauled and stored in the granary later to be fed to the farm animals. The tall corn stalks, now stripped of their ears of corn, becomes fodder, and are once again formed into larger shocks or stacked against the barn. The fodder along with the ears of corn, the oats, and the hay in the loft of the barn and stacked in the field out on the ridge, will be fed to the livestock during the long cold winter. Some of the ears of corn will be shelled, or stripped from the cob by hand, and taken to Joseph's grist mill in Paradise to be ground into meal. This is the main ingredient for the delicious corn bread my sisters make for us.

We have prepare well for the animals of the barnyard who have performed life long labor for the family. We, animal and man, have depended on each other and a mutual love exists between us. I've known them by name and have lived with them during my life time. We look after them as we would after each other, family members, all.

As we labor to prepare food for our livestock, we must also store food for ourselves for the coming long cold winter months that lay ahead. And it takes a lot of food for us, too.

The harvesting of vegetables, and apples, etc., begins in late August or early September. Usually we begin digging potatoes in the garden storing them in the root cellar under our house. While some are digging potatoes others pick apples from the large orchard below the house. We use long ladders to pick apples from the top of the tall apple trees. The apples, too, are stored with the potatoes, in separate bins, in the root cellar. While the men do the laborious work of gathering crops, the women of the house are busy canning fruit, pickling beans, corn, and making sour-kraut, stored in half barrels in the root cellar. The canned fruit and jelly, put in glass jars, are stored through out the house in closets or any place we have storage space. Later in November, usually after the first snow, we slaughter hogs and cure the dressed meat in the smokehouse, smoking and salting it down for preservation. Often we have an abundance of harvest having more then we have storage space. Than we bury the excess under ground. We dig several pits, lining them with straw, and place such things as apples, potatoes, turnips, on the straw, placing a top over the pit, using lumber. We complete the procedure by piling about twenty-four inches mound of earth on top of that making the pit frost proof as well as water proof. If the mound is properly formed and ditched, the winter rains and melting snows will drain off, keeping the food stored inside dry. A scuttle hole is placed in top of the pit giving access to the interior so we can get to the vegetables or fruit stored inside as needed. Cabbage, however, is buried differently; instead, we pull up the cabbage head, leaving the root intact, placing it in a shallow ditch, head down, and cover the head with dirt, the root exposed. True, the cabbage will freeze in cold weather, but it does not effect the preparation or taste of the cabbage.

Now we have sufficient food for the family and our livestock. Corn, hay and oats for the horses, hay and fodder for the cattle, corn for the chickens and turkeys, grain for the growing pigs, and scraps from the table for our hunting dogs, food stored for the family. We are now prepared for the long cold West Virginia winter, its blowing rains, its swirling deep snows, and its stinging sleet that will punish our small frame house surrounded by a rail fence on the steep hill nesting in a grove of oak trees.

Once winter arrives, we have time for some recreation. Often, on winter evenings, as the rain and snow storms howl outside, we gather as a family around the warm fireplace in the parlor (living room) for family activities. We like to listen to Grace, Lily, and Bonnie (Bon) play the organ and we sing hymns or ballads of the day; I don't like gospel songs, they make me sad, but they still sing them anyway. Adding to the family activities Doug sometimes plays the fiddle, and we square dance to his fiddlin. Often, instead of singing or dancing we engage in games, such as playing checkers (Bill, my brother, is the family champion checker player), or old maid, tell stories, or even wrestle; our dog like to wrestle with us, too. Gee! Getting ready for the winter is hard work and now we have time to play. But we are snugly prepared for the cold winter ahead - it is comforting feeling. Pappy is already planning for the spring planting.

NOTE: For further characteristics and customs of the time and place, please see Appendix 8.

CHAPTER 2

INTO THE CITY GOES BEN ROD

The long cold winter and hot summer of 1932-33 ended farm life for me. My older brothers began to look for employment in Charleston, for the pay on the farm was gratis; they felt the need of being more independent. Papa did not pay us but provided the food, clothing, and shelter we needed, a custom hereabout. If we ever had money, it was earned by our own efforts, such as trapping animals for furs which we sold to Brady Boggess for a very low price, or digging may-apple roots which we dried and sold to him. There were times we worked for other farmers in the community for fifty cents a day when Papa could spare us. In the 1932-33 school year at Mt. Etna, Buss, my nephew, and me, did the janitorial work for $17.00 for the entire year and then the county didn't even have the money to pay us. That is, until Papa made a visit to the courthouse in Winfield; somehow he wrangled the $17.00 from the County Court. We divided the money and along with Papa, we hopped a ride with Brady Boggess to Charleston riding in the truck bed of his old model "T" Ford truck, Papa rode in the cab with Brade. We each bought a suit, our first, a pair of shoes, a shirt, and a tie; boy, did we spruce up! We became "Fancy Dans" in the community and the envy of all the boys. This was during the depression years and we had to get along with very little money.

Then my oldest brother, Doc, decided to

make his fortune in Charleston, finding a job at the old Kelly Ax factory. Lily and Doug, now the parents of two beautiful daughters, Christabell and Jewell (called Boggie), had sold their farm on the hill to Willis Allen and they, too, were living in Charleston; Doug also worked at Kelly Ax Factory. The family was scattering; Grace had married John Gott, a coal miner, but later divorced him before Norma was born. She and Buss returned home to live with us; I was grateful for now we were together again, Buss and me. This was her second marriage, her first being to Cecil Landers, also divorced. Cecil and Grace were the parents of my nephew and wonderful companion, Buss. Also, Fern and Bonnie had married fine men, Sterling Bailey and Homer Kelley, and had homes of their own. Unfortunately, Sterling was accidentally killed. A street car rammed the rear of the horse-drawn ice wagon he was driving in Charleston, knocking him from the front seat of the wagon. The force had thrown him against a steel beam of the Elk River bridge breaking his neck. This was in March 1927. It was a sad time for all of us; Fern, only twenty-one, who had two lovely small daughters, Theo, age two, and Charlotte "Tincie", only a few months old, was now a young widow. She later married William Kinser, a person who easily became a member of the family. So the year of 1933 found the once large, wonderful family, in which we had enjoyed such happiness together, reduced to only five - Papa, Grace, me (Ben Rod), Buss, and Norma, age two. We were saddened, except for an occasional reunion, the family would never again be together as a group.

This was not all bad. After the marriage of Fern and Willie, they decided to buy some land from Willis Allen near our place and relocated a house they had bought from Nitro and reconstructed it on the land. The house, a prefab built during WWI, was sold to Willie for $30.00; he had to move it without delay. So Willie engaged Brade Boggess to haul the house from Nitro and Avril Casto to supervise the job of erecting it on his land. Avril's son, Guthrie, my brothers Bill, Buck; Buss, and I all worked on the house, getting it ready for the new family. After completion, Willie, Fern, and their small son, William, Theo and Charlotte "Tincie", moved in from Charleston. This was a great day for us but still we had only five remaining in the old homestead. Fern and Willie established their family there; it later consisted of many sons and daughters. They enjoyed many years of happiness in the home that began with the old house we had hauled from Nitro and erected only a short distance away from us.

However, the reduction of the original Jordan family continued. Without foreknowledge, I would be the next to leave the old homestead.

Doc, our elder brother, did something we thought he would never do. Of all things, he really got married! Previously, having little to do with women, he often spoke in disdain of the weaker sex, and vowed he would never "be tied down by any petticoat". We had given up hope that he would ever marry. But he did, and we were all happy. He married Lula, daughter of Jeptha and Barbara Casto of Charleston, a wonderful girl, much younger than he, she was the joy of his life. He had traveled some and had lived in St. Louis, ignoring the opposite sex. Doc came to Charleston to find his wife, the future mother of his fourteen children.

One day, after his marriage, and in the early fall, he brought Lou to the farm to meet the family just before Buss and I were getting ready to enter High School in Poca, which is about fifteen-miles away over on Kanawha River. That was never to be for me; Doc changed all that.

"Papa", said Doc to Papa, "Since I have to go to work early each morning at Kelly Ax, and Lou is afraid to be alone during the early hours of darkness, would you permit me to take Ben Rod to live with me. He could go to school in Charleston."

Being in hearing distance, I was astounded, for it was the first time it had ever been mentioned. Papa was surprised and remained silent while looking sternly at his elder son, picking his teeth with a match stick, his mustache twitching. The two, father and son, looked at each other as if ready to do battle for possession of their young son and little brother. My new sister-in-law, equally concerned, appeared surprised; she had no idea I was about to become a member of her new household in Charleston.

"Of all the crazy ideas, this is the worst," Papa exploded. "Here, I'm reduced to the bone for help to run this farm, and you want to take Ben Rod leaving only Buss to help me to do the work around here. Absolutely not!"

"Now look here, Papa", Doc continued,

"Ben Rod and Buss will have to walk to Paradise, a distance of three miles, to catch the school bus for Poca. They will leave before daylight in the mornings and walking from Paradise after school it will be dark before they get home. Ben Rod will be of little help to you anyway and he certainly is needed to live with me for Lou's peace of mind and security. I just don't know what I will do without him". Doc stood up to the "old man", as we affectionately call Papa, who was still picking his teeth with a match stick, now silent, mustache still twitching, eyeing his elder son with some apprehension.

Well, the argument raged but in the end my brother won.

That was in August and in early September, at age sixteen, on a hot Sunday afternoon, I found myself walking alone down Hizer Creek on a narrow dirt road, toward Poca, passing the Fisher, Goodman, Sigman farms, and other families I had known since childhood. Hopefully, from there, where the paved road would began, I would hitch a ride to Charleston and into a new life, a life I had dreamed of while leaning on a hoe or pitchfork handle while working in the hot fields. The long hot summers and the cold long winters on the farm were coming to an end for me.

While in deep thought walking down Hizer Creek near a babbling stream, I reflected on my past life on the farm. Often I would listen to the long coal trains rambling down the Kanawha or the whistle of the tug boats that were pushing barges down the river. The rattling sounds of the trains, and the whistling of the tug boats echoing over the mountains and ridges only whetted my imagination. I felt that my feet was so stuck in the mud of Putnam County that it was doubtful if ever I would find what was beyond the steep ridges and mountains that had surrounded me all the days of my life. Even though the opportunity had come, thanks to Doc, yet, I was worried. I realized I was making a great sacrifice, leaving my life long friends of Mt. Etna school as well as my life long companion, Buss; I would never find others to replace them. Also there were life long friends; Guthrie Casto, Ed Harrison, Earl Fisher and his brothers, Leonard, Denver, Aubrey and his sisters, Virginia, Marble, Virgie, and Gertrude, alone with Gaynell Casto, and Elizabeth Harrison, and Sherman Whitt, and others. We had known each other all our lives, going to school and church together. There were our teachers who had done so much for us, in spite of our mischievousness, including Evalee Leach, the beautiful redhead, with whom I had fallen in love. I was only age six, she married my first cousin, Carl, breaking my heart; Miss Ranson from Liberty, Hanley Null, Willis Allen, Willy Parkins, and finally, Professor Smith, whom we liked to pick on. And then I recalled the preachers: Preachers Morris and Vaughn Fisher, dedicated to the Lord's work, with whom I had made peace, now realizing they did not bury little boys alive and would not send us to hell by preaching hellfire and damnation sermons, trying to make decent people out us.

Many nostalgic thoughts came to mind as I walked the dusty road which rambled beside the babbling Hizer Creek and through the overhanging trees covering the steep hillsides shading me from the hot September afternoon sun. Thoughts of the small white house on the hill surrounded by large oak trees, where life and death had alternately reigned. The little house, the Jordan's nest, had brought both joy and sorrow to us. The foundation of my life had been formed there; I would never forget. My life there was ending; I would never live there, except spiritually, again. With nostalgia, and alone on the dusty road, I trudged down Hizer Creek toward Poca. From there I hoped to thumb a ride to Charleston. Maybe, with luck, I would arrive at my brother's house on Chandler's Branch on the edge of the city before nightfall in time for supper.

It was a time for change; life, perhaps, would be full of surprises and disappointments. Experiences that I never dreamed of was about to begin. In due time I would be required to make life and death decisions, some men perhaps would die because of those decisions as the threatening, dark, war clouds was gathering over Europe and Asia and getting darker. But how could I, a sixteen year old farm boy, fresh from Putnam Country, West Virginia, get involved in a war that might occur thousands of miles away beyond, and with wide oceans on each side of me? I was naive, while searching for a new life, and I would soon find it. Would it be exciting? Would it be happy? Or both? Would sadness and unhappiness be included in the package that life would deal me? Only time would tell.

CHAPTER 3

WOODROW WILSON JUNIOR HIGH SCHOOL

"Run for your life!" the women hysterically screamed, running past me. It was Sunday afternoon, shortly after my arrival at Chandlers Branch on the outskirts of Charleston to attend school. It was cloudy and raining at times.

Even though many good people lived on Chandlers Branch many thugs lived there, too, and their reputations did not include attending Sunday School. This little incident affected my reputation all the days of my school years in Charleston. Even though I always tried to be a gentlemen, I gained a reputation that afternoon of being a great fighter, a protector of women of Chandlers Branch who put me on a pedestal as their knight in shining armor. I never outlived it, but the incident was no big deal.

"He's drunk, Ben Rod, and he's threatening everyone! He's dangerous and will hurt you. You must come with us before something happens to you", they said. They continued running lickety split up the hollow on the narrow paved road criss-crossing a stream now and then, that was competing for space in the narrow valley splitting the steep ridges adjacent to the Edgewood Country Club; houses were jam-packed on both sides of the road and even up the hillsides.

Being only sixteen years of age and scared, too, I gritted my teeth and prepared to face the cursing drunkard coming up the hollow; my false pride would not let me do otherwise. Where I had come from a man would be a coward if he ran with the women who had better sense then he.

Soon the staggering form of the loudly raving, cursing drunk came into view, using such profanity that even a tough, seagoing, salty sailor would have been put to shame. Studying the wretched person from a distance, I could see the drunk was no danger to anyone, for he could hardly stand, and I prepared to counter if it was necessary. Soon his blurry eyes focused on me as he swayed from one side of the road to the other, still using language I had never heard. Coming into striking distance he swung a right which I took on my left shoulder. I countered, throwing a hard right uppercut to the drunk's chin, sending him sprawling to the hard surface of the road. He made no effort to get up and was out like a light. Dragging him off the road by his coat collar and placing him in front of a wooden frame one-car garage, I left him for others to handle, and proceeded up the creek. Many people saw this incident and from that time on I walked on water while I lived on Chandlers Branch. In reality the drunk was easy to fell because of his excessive intoxication and there was no problem subduing him. That made no difference to the good people of Chandlers Branch - I was their hero, especially with the women. Much was said about a drunk trying to beat up a sixteen-year old boy and my brother, Doc, even talked of having the culprit arrested for attacking a minor, but I talked him out of it. He was concerned about the drunk would again attack me after becoming sober but that never happened. Instead, the drunk took a liking to me never mentioning the incident; I doubt if he ever remembered it.

Consequences, however, would follow from a different angle. All this because, within a week after arriving in Charleston, I became the potential target for thugs that roamed the hollow, causing Lily and Doc some concern for my safety. They considered it prudent that I should return to the farm in Putnam County, for they knew the possible consequences should I remain in the hollow; fortunately, that never came about. Things cooled down.

Shortly, after the drunkard incident I was treated to a movie at the Sunset Theater on West Washington Street, price of admission being ten cents, but we had no ten cents. Jim Morris, my new found friend was with me, his father, Jinks, provided the twenty cents for admission. The movie, later a classic, King Kong, was so realistic making chills run up and down my spine. The great ape fighting to protect the beautiful Fay Wray, whom he held in the palm of his hand like a Barbie Doll, defending her against prehistoric animals that sought her for a tasty morsel, and from her hero who was trying to rescue her from the big ape. But beauty killed the beast; he was shot from atop the New York's Empire State building by the Army Air Corps airplanes. I literally sat spellbound, glued to the edge of my seat throughout the movie. I had flashbacks when Lily and Doug took me to the same theater to see the silent movies, a double feature, Johnstown Flood, as well as a Tom Mix movie about ten years before; then I ran down the aisle of the theater screaming for everyone to run for their lives before they were drowned by the rapidly advancing wall of water that was destroying everything in its path, and away from the bullets of Tom Mix, the cowboy hero. Everyone laughed at my innocence ignorance. My big brother-in-law, Doug, finally brought me under control and calmed me down, trying to convince me that the water and guns were only moving pictures, but I was hard to convince. Even eleven years later King Kong was so convincing I had the urge to once again run down the aisle to safety as he battled the giant reptiles trying to get Fay Wray for their evening meal and from the humans trying to rescue her. It was and is still is a wonderful movie.

The following Monday, a bright early September morning, was my first school day in the big city. What a comparison. Here I was at Woodrow Wilson Junior High School with its three floors of classrooms, hundreds of students, hallways crammed with talking and teasing kids, and having just arrived from the little one-room school house of Mt Etna, in Putnam County, with its "educated" eighth grade teachers, and its fourteen member student body. And I wondered: coming from the hills of Putnam County, where farm work was considered more important then going to school, how I could compete with all these "educated" kids and their city ways. What was I doing in a place like Woodrow Wilson when I would surely prove to be a failure and a disgrace?

Being in the ninth grade, Papa had held me back one year, saying I was too young to go to high school, I found myself much larger then the younger students with whom I was sitting during the registration; they all looked strangely at me. But as it turned out, in error, I was in the seventh grade class room instead of the ninth and the teacher sent me on my way. Eventually, after much confusion, I finally found my home room and settled down, nervously, to my strange environment. Mrs. Love, my home room teacher, seeing my fear, put me at ease among my peers. Later, Earl Rectonwald, Raymond and James Morris, became my good friends that lasted many years.

My fears of competing with the students at Woodrow Wilson was unfounded. I was accepted by the other students and academically I held my own with them. In fact there were times I even exceeded some of them in the pursuit of knowledge. This surprised me for I had expected that I would always be at the end of the class standings, but thanks to the good teachers of Mt Etna, they had taught me the three "R"s well. I was gratified when Bill Thompson, a fellow student, came to me wanting help in a mathematical problem. He said he had watched me during class and that perhaps I could tell him how to work the problem. The problem was to determine the amount of wall paper needed to paper a room considering the size, the windows and doors. I had no difficulty solving the problem; Bill was happy that I gave him some help. I did have problems with English, however, still do, but excelled in History and other subjects. I had such an urge to do good work; my teachers sensed this, so they always give me the help I needed. Again, I thought of my teachers back at Mt Etna of past years for they had, in spite of me, and other environmental considerations; managed to prepare me for what lay ahead.

The first time in gym class at Woodrow Wilson was something strange to me; I sure made a mess of things. There we were in a large room with high ceilings and with screens covering the windows standing in line for roll call. Looking around I saw a basketball court and a stage - quite a change from the school yard of Mt Etna where we played with a rag ball and a paddle-like bat made by Avril Casto from a two by four inch piece of lumber. I never had seen a basketball before, and I made a complete fool of myself. The coach threw the ball to me during practice and I ran to the far end of the gym, carrying the ball under my arm as if it was a football, placing it into the basket. The athletic instructor, patiently, took some time explaining the game to me and how to dribble the ball instead. Then we lined up to play softball in the gym and my turn came to bat. Like Mighty Casey at the bat, swinging with all my might, I not only missed the ball but the bat slipped out of my hands, just missing a man's head by inches as he watched from the stage. By that time the instructor considered me a danger to all mankind, and before we did anything further he always give me special instructions or had another student to do it. Anyway, soon I was among the others doing what they did without danger to anyone until we got on the football field and I was accused by another student of slugging him. I didn't know what he was talking about, but later I was told that I had used my arms in an illegal manner, and I still don't know what they were talking about. However, in spite of myself, I became a reasonable participant in all sports and no longer a menace to fellow students or spectators.

Every day I walked to school, rain or shine, snow or sleet. It was about a mile from the mouth of Chandlers Branch to Woodrow Wilson Junior High School on West Washington Street. There were no school-buses in those days and few had cars, so I joined many students walking to school carrying their lunches and books.

During noon hour some of us gathered at the small store on the corner near the school. The store was owned by Norman Sirk, a Lebanese; we eat our lunches there and he welcomed us. If we were so lucky to have a nickel we bought a bar of candy or ice cream or just hung around until class time.

Hanging around Sirk's store got boring and I decided to explore the area during noon hour one day. While on the farm I had listened, while leaning on a hoe handle or a pitchfork handle, as I worked in the fields, to the whistle and the rattling of train sounds echoing over the mountains - and even as I lay awake on my straw tick bed at night. Pictures of the giant locomotive with their powerful driving arms, black smoke boiling from its stack, steam blowing from both sides, and the engineer sitting majestically at the controls, fascinated me. Sirk's store was located only a short distance from the railroad yard and a shifter was always at work pushing empty railroad cars around. There I decided to learn more about the trains and their monster locomotives, so I took off for the tracks.

While watching the shifter work pushing the cars around and at times would cut the car loose permitting it to roll on the track and crashing into the end of another, making a hookup, I saw a fellow student riding the cars. Fearing that he would get hurt, I watched him as he climbed from car to car for a while. Shortly, it was time to return to class and as I was walking from the yard, I heard someone running behind me. Turning to investigate, I was immediately grabbed by the shoulders by a large man dressed in a dark suit. I was terrified, almost as bad when I imagined the leopard was chasing me on a cold winter night in Putnam County several years before.

"I've been watching you young feller riding the trains and now I'm going to arrest you.", he said. Later I found out he was what they called a railroad "bull" or policeman.

Horrified as he dragged me along the street I begged him to let me go for I was not the person he wanted, and that I did not ride his train. "Please, Mister, I did not ride the train, I just came over during lunch hour to see the engine work and I must get back to school now. Please let me go." I tearfully explained that there was a boy riding the empty cars and that he was dressed similarly to me, but to no avail. How lucky I was; during my blackest hour, (I had resigned myself to an awful fate being a prisoner in some dirty jail), here came the empty coal car with the boy hanging on the side. Releasing me, the "bull" took after the boy who saw him coming and he, too, took off running like a bat out of "somewhere", and the "bull" never came close to catching him. Then the "bull" looked at me from a distance and appeared to have changed his mind and headed my way. I don't think, had records been kept, my speed record that day could have been broken; I left the scene in great haste never to return again. I've never seen another railroad "bull" since. Believe me, I've learned my lesson.

I never told my brother Doc or sister Lily about my arrest and escape, fearing they would take some drastic action like sending me back to the farm. It had been only a short time after I had knocked out the drunk on Chandlers Branch, and I was becoming notorious and they didn't like that at all. But none of this was by design; it just happened, but nonetheless it did happen.

Similar incidents continued to happen. However, I would bluff my way out of circumstances without coming to blows with the thugs of Chandlers Branch. Again my good brother and sister had concerns, but all this happened without any planning on my part since the day I had knocked out the harmless drunk; I had become a target. One day shortly after Jim Morris and I had seen the King Kong movie, and we were walking down Chandlers Branch we met a bully by the name of Don Parsons.

"My God!", says Jim scared within an inch of his life, "There's Don Parsons, the bully in these parts, and he told my brother Raymond, that he was going to beat me up for beating his time with his girlfriend." Jim was scared and I tried to assure him that all would be well and we continued down the hollow until we met the Don head on. And sure enough, when we neared him, who was much larger than Jim, he struck him even without saying a word, landing a solid blow to Jim's head.

I was dumbfounded and realized I had to do something to save my friend from a terrible beating. Realizing I, too, could become a victim of the bully of Chandlers Branch, I stood helplessly.

"Please Don, don't hit me, again", Jim pleaded, pathetically. "You know you are much bigger then me and I don't want to fight you over the girl. You can have her and I won't bother her again. Please don't hit me again."

The bully paid no attention to his pleading and continued to land blows on poor defenseless Jim. Don actually kicked him in the groin and while Jim was bent over, unable to defend himself, and in great pain, Don continued to land blows to his sides and head. I had to do something or my friend would be beaten to a pulp. I was the only one around that could help him.

Taking position between Jim and Don, I took a blow intended for Jim doing little damage, but causing me some anger. And I gave the thug a warning.

"Now, look Don", I said, "your are beating up my defenseless friend. I guess if you intend to beat further it must be on me, but I warn you the next blow you lend will be your last." I prepared to do battle squaring off in a vigorous and threatening manner, hoping I would bluff the bully. I was concerned, that the bully, unlike the drunk I had laid low a few days earlier, would transfer his anger to me and then I would really have a fight on my hands. But the shot had been called and I had to defend Jim.

Surprisingly, Don looked at me, dropping his hand to his sides: "Look", he said, "you don't have a dog in this fight. It's between me and that SOB for what he did to me and my girl, not with you. Why don't you just get out the way and let me finish him off."

A crowd of spectators was gathering to watch the excitement, caring less who was in the right or wrong; they just wanted some action. Poor Jim was still begging for mercy and kept me between him and Don. Again, I warned Don he no longer could beat on Jim while I stood by.

"Just as I said, I'm taking his place in the fight, and you better be prepared to suffer what ever the consequences", and I moved threateningly toward him, fists rolled, ready to lead with my left, while Jim watched anxiously from the rear. More people gathered to watch and enjoy the knock down and drag out fight, they thought. Don, taking a look at me and realizing most of the people were cheering for me, decided it was a loosing game. To my great relief, he turned on his heel and left the scene, never to bother Jim again; apparently my bluff had worked. The people cheered.

This was not to be the last threat to me. Shortly after the incident with Don, and while walking in a drizzle of rain alone after dark on the unlit Sissonsville Road near the mouth of Chandlers Branch, a car stopped and a man got out.

"Hey, damn you!", he yelled, and I caught a glimpse of a jack-handle or a tool of some kind in the man's hand as the headlights of the car reflected on the culprit. Even though I could not see the face of the person with the jack handle, I thought I recognize the voice of Don Parson. Realizing others were in the car, I felt an urgent need to vacate the territory in a rapid manner; it wasn't a time to be a hero, and I prepared to break all speed records up the hollow to safety. But what luck! Just as I was about to take flight, another car came down the hollow with lights beaming on the scene. Coming to a screeching halt behind the other car and the man, with the tool, still in view, the driver quickly dismounted and said to me: "Quick, get into the car, quick!" Surprisingly, the other car, with screeching tires, left the scene with the culprit. Needless to say I never felt such relief in all my life. I felt my life had been saved by the yet unknown person, and I thanked him for being my guardian angel.

"Ben Rod, what are you doing walking alone on this dangerous road?" Then I recognized him. It was Glen Parsons, the minister of the Davis Baptist Chapel on Chandlers Branch where Lily and Doug attended. I thanked him and I felt that he really could have saved my life. Then I had flashbacks from only a few years, how I had feared the preachers in Putnam County for preaching damnation and hellfire sermons and really wanted nothing to do with them and now a preacher had possibly saved my life from a car full of thugs, a preacher of all people, had done this for me. The reverend could have passed by me, a stranger, leaving me to the mercy of the wolves, but he had exposed himself to great danger, possibly saving me from a terrible fate.

Then I received a lecture from this wonderful person, who had exposed himself to save a poor wretched soul such as me.

"Ben Rod, I've never met you before, but your reputation since arriving in Chandlers Branch makes you a target for the thugs that run about looking for mischievousness, and unless you use some common sense and quite trying to be a hero you're going to get hurt." He continued: "You didn't have to knock out the drunk the other day to save the women. He was harmless in his condition and the women were running away from him, but you had to be the hero, setting yourself up as a target for the thugs. They don't like people like you coming here being all righteous. The fight between Jim and Don the other day only added to the desire of the thugs to put you in your place and they almost did it tonight. And now they tell me you got arrested by a railroad detective for hitching rides on the empty cars. Ben Rod, wake up if you want to live. It's a dog eat dog world here in Chandlers Branch. I wouldn't like to preach your funeral soon. Take my advice if you want to live."

The Preacher was firm and seemed to scold me for trying to do what I thought was right, but I did take his advice. I will always be grateful to him.I realized that, unless I changed my self-righteous ways, and act like a boy of sixteen my life would not be worth a plug nickel. So I got to work studying, playing football, hiking about the nearby hills with friends and doing what normal boys do. Things improved, and I never found out who the thugs were that had waylaid me on that drizzling night on the dark Sissonsville road, but I do remember it well. And too, I often wonder what would have happened had Glen Parsons, the preacher, not come along just at the right moment rescuing me from certain harm or even death. The reverend had earned my gratitude, admiration, and respect.

During the year at Woodrow Wilson I enjoyed many activities and classes. Mr. Pritchard, the printing instructor, taught me, how to use the schools printing press. Never having seen anything like that before, I enjoyed operating the press. It was fascinating and I spent all my free time in the print shop with Mr. Pritchard, Robert, and Chester. I did many other things that was beyond my imagination while attending school in the little one room school house of Mt Etna. Regardless, I will never forget where I came from, and somehow the teachers of the little one room school had prepared me for what I was to endure beyond the hills of Putnam County. If I would ever amount to anything, I reasoned, I had them, the teachers of the little one room schoolhouse of Mt Etna - together, they taught me the basics of life, hopefully would take me through life's trying times. I thought of all this the day I graduated from Woodrow Wilson Junior High School, a privilege many of my friends would never have. I knew and realized my roots would forever be in Putnam County and the good people who helped to bring me up, relatives and neighbors alike - there were and are no better people.

CHAPTER 4

THE FINAL GOOD-BYE

My last summer on the farm followed graduation from Woodrow Wilson Junior High School. After having a taste of city life, while going to school in Charleston, I vowed that I could never be a farmer for there were other professions more gratifying, perhaps becoming an army officer, or even a pilot; the grass looked greener on the other side of the fence. Life on the farm, its routine and hard work in the hot fields, even though honorable, certainly did not appeal to a young man wanting to conquer the world, and who craved adventure. However, even though I had determined to conquer the world I would never forget my old friends, my former school mates at Mt Etna. Somehow I felt it would be the last time we would ever be together for any period of time and we made the best of the time we would have together during the last summer. We had grown in years, being more mature, and our antics were less mischievous. We even took Preacher Morris more seriously. He was a good man and realizing he was only trying to improve our ways, we helped him to do things around the church to show our appreciations; we even listened attentively to his hellfire and damnation type sermons.

During our last summer together, when farm work permitted, Buss and I played horseshoes on Saturday afternoons with Guthrie Casto, Ed Harrison, Earl, Leonard, and Denver Fisher. Often we played on the local baseball team, even beating a team from Dunbar. My brother, Bill, then working in the Raymond Coal Company mines over on Harmons creek, came to play for us, a good baseball player, and hit a home-run to win the game. The Dunbar team was speechless for they couldn't imagine a team from the hills, could beat them. Brade Boggess, prancing around on his club foot, yelling encouragement, was the cause of our success. Having no bleachers, the people stood around the edge of the field between first and home and third bases cheering, Brade cheering the loudest.

This game was played over at Liberty on a Sunday afternoon and Mr. Cartrell, in celebration of our victory, invited everyone over to his house to enjoy his hard cider. I think we all got drunk, at least I thought we were, for I never felt so giggly and happy before. Papa got on Mr. Cartrell for he thought I was under the influence. I acted silly, happy-go-lucky, but then it didn't take much for me to act silly, anyway.

Finally, the summer crops were laid by and it was time to return to school in Charleston. I would be entering Charleston High School on East Washington Street, not far from the new state capitol building. My departure was sad for I knew, as did the others, that our lives, as we had known, were ending and would never be the same again. As for me, except for short visits I would never be on the farm again. Unknowingly, I was about to embark upon a strange journey, a journey that, until now, was only imaginary. This journey still hasn't ended. It has taken me to many nooks and corners of the world and along the way I would find love, marriage, family, and participate in the country's wars, meet an Emperor, two Kings, a Vice President, and a future President of the United States. Added to this were movie stars, high ranking civilians and military dignitaries of many countries, often entertained by them. Now, at my advanced age, I've yet to finish my dream that began long ago while leaning on the hoe handle on the hilly farm in Putnam County, West Virginia, listening to the rattling of the unseen coal trains echoing over the ridges. This auspicious future began when I said good-bye to all of the old friends whom I would never see again for many years. Before leaving, I even visited the barnyard to see the animals that had been my lifelong companions; I would never see them again either for they would go the way of all flesh before I would return. I sought out "Old Fred" the horse, head now bowed with age, and patting his soft nose remembering the ride of my life while on his bare back during a severe thunder storm several years earlier. This old loyal horse who, in earlier years had carried me many miles, through the hot sun, rain, sleet, snow, seemed to know what was happening and nudged me with his soft velvet nose, a form of greeting that existed between us. Then I picked up my bag, waving good-bye to what was left of my family, sitting on the front porch of the house that for so long had been my home, hopped a ride with Brade Boggess and headed for Charleston. My father, now infirm by the years, watched until we were out of sight. My life changed forever.

Sadly, but ironically, the prayers I had

said as I leaned on the hoe handle in the hot cornfield only a few years before were being answered. Already I had seen some of the mysteries that lurked over the mountains and beyond, to the river and into the city, and I wasn't so sure I liked it. In less than a year I was forced to knock out a drunk, was almost arrested by a railroad "bull", bluffed a bully to keep my friend from being badly beaten, and a carload of thugs had almost waylaid me, saved only by Preacher Parsons. Things of this nature never happened in Putnam County, or if they did, I never heard about it. My love for the people of Putnam County would never falter, however, and I would never "kick" the county's dust from my shoes; my roots were planted too deep - the place of my birth.

Arriving back in Charleston, I reestablished myself, contacting my old friends. My environment changed from a peaceful farm life to that of the hubbub of the city.

"Ben Rod", said Jim Morris, "let's go down and watch the fights under the sycamore tree down near the creek. Someone got a set of boxing gloves and some hot fights are going on down there."

With my reputation I should have known better. Among the spectators was my brother Willard, affectionately called Buck. He kept a critical eye on me, for he knew the crowd would soon be clamoring for me to put on the gloves with someone. They did, and I accepted to fight an opponent then unknown. The boys of my age would not compete with me and finally a man, at least ten years older than me, said he would like to spar using only the open glove and not the fist. That was a mistake. He insisted on sparring with his cap on his head, but I knocked it off and he would put it back on. Each time I knocked his cap from his head the people would cheer. This seemed to upset him for he spent more time replacing his cap on his head than he did sparring. I was kidding and horse-playing with Anderson and not being on guard as I should have been. Then like lighting, he struck with a hard right to my mouth almost knocking me out. Blood flowed and I felt as if my teeth had been knocked out. They say I spun like a top but never lost my balance. Unable to continue, I was limp as a rag. My nose felt as if it been relocated on the side of my face. Buck, my brother, Jim Morris, and others came to my aid and finally sat me on the ground washing the blood from my face with water from the nearby creek. Even Anderson, who had delivered the terrible blow, was helping to restore me back to normal. Soon Buck spoke:

"Listen, you SOB", he said to Anderson, "this is my kid bother and we agreed to use an open hand slapping, and now look what you have done. We, you and I, will continue this fight, but without gloves, and perhaps we can settle the score right now." The crowd was furious, demanding that Anderson leave the area, saying he was not the sportsman he should have been.

Anderson, said apologetically: "Buck, I'm sorry. I never intended to hurt Ben Rod and I will make it up to him somehow."

"I want to avenge Ben Rod. You either fight me in front of these people now or you must leave the area immediately." And Buck gallantly prepared to give Anderson the beating of his life.

Anderson looked at the madly disturbed crowd and did the best thing he could. He wisely left the area, followed by jeers. I hardly remember the incident, being in a semi-conscious condition. Later, I remember Buck and Jim Morris working on my mouth removing chunks of flesh from my lips and gums. Fortunately, my teeth were still intact and the wound was superficial. However, my nose never fully recovered; it's still lopsided, they tell me.

The news traveled rapidly over Chandlers Branch that I had been knocked out by Anderson and much talk and rumors were spread around. The situation was blown out of proportion with some saying there would be a grudge rematch between us. They all said that Anderson would be the loser in a fair fight. I was not interested in a grudge fight, or any fight, but such seemed to follow me, and as Preacher Parsons stated when he saved me from the car load of thugs the year before, my self-righteousness would get me killed if I didn't stop playing the knight in shining armor.

There was another person living nearby, who was interested in what had happened to me. Bob Meadows, a former Welterweight Boxing Champion of West Virginia, offered to train me, just in case. He was a great trainer and he taught me how to cover using my elbows, how to deliver hard blows to the solar plexus and to the head. "Don't be a head hunter Ben Rod", he cautioned, "fights are won on points in the ring and the body is a much more likely target unless you can get a sure punch to the chin," he admonished. "When you throw a punch, put your weight behind it. Fights are not won by powder puff blows. Each solid hard blow weakens the opponent and, the more you deliver the more likely you will win the bout." Then he ran me up and down the hollow, building up my wind and stamina. Finally, I began to realize he intended to put me in the ring professionally, and I didn't want that. All of this training made me a target for any and all fighters who desired to fight under the sycamore tree. I was too gullible to say no. Anderson failed to accept the challenge after hearing about all the training I was receiving from the champion. This was not the end.

The successful boxing career of Joe Louis, the great black boxer, or the Brown Bomber, was hitting the sports pages, and all the black boys around were emulating him. One of these black boys was eager to meet me under the sycamore tree and a date and time were determined. I was not very enthusiastic about the possibilities, but, yet, my false pride kept me from saying no. And so the fight was arranged for a Saturday afternoon at 2:00PM.

Jim Morris and others escorted me down the hill to the Sycamore tree just up the hollow from the unimproved road leading up to the Davis Chapel Church. Lily was very concerned about the fight and felt that her little brother had no business fighting anyone, much less a black person, whose aim was beating up some white kid. But feeling that my honor was at stake, I just had to fight even though I was really concerned about the outcome. I had never yet had contact with a black person and had considered them somewhat of a mystery.

Arriving at the sycamore tree I was amazed at the number of people, all white, waiting for the fight to begin. There were many more than I could have imagined. But then I looked up the hill and I was even more surprised: there were many black people with their champion walking down toward the sycamore tree. There must have been at least a hundred; the fight then took on a different magnitude. I looked the big black fighter over as he came down the hill, and he was a magnificent specimen of a human, his size made me look like a runt. I wondered what I had gotten myself into. I thought of the preacher being chased up a tree by a bear and lacking assistance from the Supreme Being said: "Dear Lord, if you can't help me, for God's sakes please don't help that bear." I said a similar prayer, I would surely need it.

The big black boy, several feet ahead of his supporters, stopped dead in his tracks after seeing all the whites assembled under the sycamore tree. He appeared to be unnerved and kept looking back at his supporters and noting that they, too, were not about to come near the scene, he decided that he had to go it alone and continued walking toward the big sycamore tree. Again he stopped, looked back at his crowd who were still standing in their tracks, and then again he looked at the big crowd of whites below. To my great relief, he turned on his heels and melted into the crowd behind him. Nothing could have made me happier. Unlike the preacher up the tree, the bear nipping at his heels, the Lord did help me. He was the only one that saved me from this big black fighter who looked every bit a future champion.

So, once again I was the local hero but only by default. I had bluffed him as I had the thug who he tried to beat up Jim Morris. And that ended my fighting career, if I ever had one. I had learned my lesson and took Preacher Parsons' advice and became a normal seventeen year old, caring less what troubles others had. It wasn't long after that incident that Joe Louis, the Brown Bomber, became one of the greatest heavyweight fighters of all time. Displaying great sportsmanship and expertise in the ring, Joe was a credit to all, both black and white, and became an example for us all. What a fighter! Comparing my fight record with that of Joe Lewis: I had succeeded knocking out a harmless drunk, bluffed my way to victory even before any fight began, even bluffed the bully, Don Parsons, when he tried to beat up my friend, Jim Morris, over a girl; I had been almost knocked out by Anderson, who was ten years older them me; yet, they say, my boxing record did not have the shine like that of the champion's. Oh, well, one can't have everything. One thing for sure, I was the champion bluffer of Chandlers Branch. That record still stands today.

CHAPTER 5

BEN ROD IN HIGH SCHOOL

My fighting career over at the early age of seventeen, it was time for me to enter Charleston High School in the east end of the city. It was much like Woodrow Wilson, except with a larger student body, and a football team, the Mountain Lions. It was necessary to walk from Chandlers Branch over to Stockton Street, catch a streetcar to Summers Street, in the center of town, and transfer to another streetcar over on Capitol Street, completing the trip up Washington Street to the school. The fare was three cents, cheaper if you bought tokens. There were times I didn't have three cents and had to walk the entire distance of about seven miles to school. Harvey Casto, a wonderful person, my sister-in-law, Lou's, brother, kindly invited me to ride with him to his place of work located not far from the High School. I was grateful. If I waited for a while after school he would bring me back home after he had completed work.

My high school years were interesting and I graduated in the upper third of the class. Again I wondered how a person like me coming from the one room schoolhouse, Mt Etna, could have accomplished what I did. Even though I was never the outstanding student in school, I did manage to keep up by studying far into the night, still having difficulty with English. I played football for Coach Glen and ran track not excelling in either, but I did play and run. The Mountain Lions football team was often the state champions and we were a proud lot. However, the great Mountain Lions were humiliated by a small coal town school team from War, West Virginia. Coach Glen threw everything he had at the coal miners' sons on a rain soaked field, on a Saturday afternoon, but he could not keep George Cafego down. Our team would hit him from all directions but he managed to score the winning touchdown, breaking the Lion's heart. George was a magnificent player and a gentleman. He later played for The University of Tennessee, and there, like at War High School, was an outstanding football player. Following graduation from the University, he remained there as an assistant football coach.

Money was scarce in the depression years and many students looked for some type of work after school and on Saturdays. Few had luck; I didn't, even though I walked the streets asking local businessmen for jobs; even O.J. Morrison's Department store managed by my uncle, but unfortunately he had been transferred to the Pt. Pleasant store and the new manager had no sympathy for me. One day the school announced that Seigal shoe store on Capitol Street needed a shoe salesman for evenings and Saturdays. I ran from school and applied but was informed that I must have had experience selling shoes, the same story at all stores. I was discouraged. Then I got the idea of working just for experience. Perhaps, I thought, that would assist me in getting a paying job. Al, the manager of Thom McCann, a men's shoe store on Capitol Street, knew a sucker when he saw one, gave me the opportunity to work - for nothing. For almost a year I worked every day after school and even on Saturdays, at times selling more shoes than Al or his assistant manager. Enjoying my new found avocation, I found men were easy customers who only wanted comfort regardless of the style, which added to the pleasure of working at Thom McAnn's. There were times I waited on four customers at once and reported to the cash register with arms full of sold shoes. Al was grateful and complimented me for doing great work.

Selling new shoes, always in demand for the Easter season, required additional salesmen in all shoe stores, and I expected Al to pay me for working at least on Easter Saturday. To my surprise, even after many months working for nothing, he told me that he was not authorized to hire another salesman even though he said one was needed. Disappointed and not to be outdone, I returned to Seigal and he hired me for the Easter season; it was most disappointing. Siegal, being mostly a woman's store, was an entirely different experience. Women, unlike men, are different animals in more ways than one, especially concerning shoes. I found they wanted to try on every shoe in the store and more often would settle on the first pair shown. Further, many women insisted to be fitted with shoes much too small for them, but yet, painfully squeezed their big feet inside the shoes, regardless. To add to my woes at Siegel's, the shoe stock was so irregular and I had difficulty learning where certain styles of shoes were located, not being a regular salesman. It didn't take me long to learn that the women's shoe trade was not my line and I got out of the business. Gosh, women were a temperamental bunch, I thought. Occasionally women, mostly of middle age, would actually ask me to rub their tired, sweaty big feet, while, at the same time, insisting I fit them with shoes too small for them. For the week I had worked for Siegal's he paid me fifteen dollars. I was glad when the Easter season was over and I would not be selling women's shoes, ever. Later I was told that Al, the manager at Thom McCann, was angry at me for not working for him during Easter season, even though he would not pay me, saying I had left him short-handed. What a sap I had been. But I did learn something; I eliminated the shoe business from my future plans, especially the women shoe business.

However, I did find employment that paid for my textbooks and school supplies. The school announced that help was needed in the bookstore on the first floor of the high school building, and I applied. As luck would have it, Mr. Charles E. Miller, the manager, and my teacher in commercial geography, hired me for the most interesting job. I became very familiar with the bookstore's operation and soon was the student manager. I was also given the responsibility of preparing and making bank deposits and I felt proud to be trusted in doing so. Daily I made deposits at Kanawha Valley Bank located on Capitol Street. I had never done anything like this before; I was proud.

Then my life took another turn of adventure. One day during lunch hour, while standing on the steps entering the school, a friend, Robert Guthrie, mentioned that he was going down to the armory and join the National Guard.

"What's National Guard?" I asked, displaying an eager interest.

"They meet weekly and drill for two hours. Sometimes on Saturdays and Sundays they go up to Kanawha City and fire machine guns and rifles." he said, appearing to have great knowledge of the National Guard. He continued: "Than they parade downtown on special events such as Armistice Day, when the President comes to town, or during the governor's inauguration at the state capitol building."

This whetted my appetite for adventure. I was a great admirer of my two uncles, Guy and Shell Thomas, my mother's brothers, who had been in WWI. They often told me stories of their war experiences in France; I would listened spellbound.

"Man, you ought to see the uniforms they wear, just like real soldiers: riding breeches, wrapped legging, brown shoes, steel helmets, rifles, cartridge belts, and all.", Robert continued.

"A uniform?" my curiosity was up. Could anyone love the uniform more than me? It was impossible! I remembered Guthrie Casto in his Boy Scout uniform, campaign hat and all, in Putnam County riding his horse to Red House to attend scout meetings. That was the thing that got me started, and even though I could never afford to join the scouts I developed a love for any uniform just as long it looked military.

"How much does it cost to join the National Guard, Bob?" I was beyond interest, it was a demand.

"It doesn't costs anything Ben Rod, in fact they give you the uniform and your side arm. They let you fire the machine gun and even pay you a dollar for each drill. Company "D", 150th Infantry, of the West Virginia National Guard, drills each Thursday night down at the Armory. Let's go down and join, Ben Rod!"

Firing a machine gun and being paid for doing it was beyond my imagination! Let's go! I joined on February 14, 1935. My life had suddenly taken an unexpected turn and would never be the same again. Company "D" would become my second home, its members my fraternal brothers, its commander another father image.

Hitler's Nazi Germany would soon be on the march in Europe and Japanese soldiers were already taking over Asia. But who would ever think the United States, separated from both by the Atlantic and Pacific Oceans, would ever be involved? However, world politics would eventually get us involved quickly ending the depression and replacing it with false prosperity even though many good soldiers would be sacrificed.

Company "D", 150th Infantry, West Virginia National Guard, commanded by Capt. John N. Charnock, lined up for roll call and inspection on the armory floor, was very impressive. This was my first night, and I watched while waiting to sign the enlistment papers that would make me a member of the company. Sgt. Mallory, the first Sergeant, called names from the roster and each man answered "here" as his name was called. Once all were accounted for, the company was turned over to the captain who ordered the drill to begin. Lt. Paul Guthrie and lt. Walter Stone were in front of their respective platoons.

The first training conducted was close-order drill or marching in various formations. The platoons in those days were made up of four squads of eight men, each formed in two ranks. When the company was formed in line there were two ranks, one behind the other, sixteen men abreast.

The close-order drill was normally conducted by the non-commissioned officers, many of whom were veterans of WWI, who knew the army well. One of these good NCOs was Sergeant James Rhodes, who rendered firm and understanding help to me for many years. He handled the close-order-drill that night. He would later look after me as if I were his son until he was forced to retire from the army due to age while we were stationed at Camp Shelby, Mississippi six years later.

"Right by squads!" he commanded. The squad on the right gave the command "Forward March" while the other three squad leaders of the platoon, corporals, gave the command "Squad Right". Coming on line of march the succeeding squads gave the command "Squads Left", bringing the company now in line of march or with squads of the two platoons following each other in cadence, marching feet contacting the wood floor in unison, giving the feeling of a well ordered march. Rhodes performed many movements with the troops ending up in line at the end of the close-order drill session. Here the platoons were broken down for mechanical training on the

M1917AI belt fed, recoil operated, water cooled Browning Machine gun. The instructor tore down the gun to its detailed parts and I was amazed how such a machine could work. Later, one of the men, blindfolded, tore down the gun and put it back together. Another gave a verbal description of the mechanical functioning of the machine gun, not missing a word, repeating it word for word as stated in the field manual. The instructor complimented the soldier for being so well versed in the subject.

The mechanical functioning was followed by timed action or timing how long it would take the gun crew to get the gun into position after the command: "On this line action!" was given by the instructor. The well trained crew had the machine gun firing, using blank ammunition, in seconds after the command was given. Later, under field conditions, the same thing would be done but using live ammunition instead. Both live firing and blank firing was most interesting. In either case the rattle of the machine gun fire echoing throughout the armory or over the field caused the battle blood to race through our veins while watching the dust boil in the beaten zone of target area. Sergeant Rhodes said during the great war (WWI) both the Germans and the Americans feared the machine gun because of its deadly effect and took action to eliminate them once the firing began. This prompted the obvious question: How long would it take the enemy to react once a machine gun went into action? Sergeant Rhodes quickly answered the question.

"Experience during the war was three minutes,", he tartly said, "for quickly the enemy will spot the gun and would bring artillery or small arms fire to bear on the position and you must be prepared to displace or die."

It was at this time I realized I was in an outfit that could be called upon to defend our country and it was not just a parade outfit for the visiting VIPs or the governor's inauguration. My brother, Doc, once he learned that I had joined the National Guard was alarmed, not realizing what the future would be, said the National Guard was often used as strikebreakers when strikes did occur in the West Virginia coal fields. The National Guard was not a popular organization to many. Regardless, I stayed with the old Company. I've never regretted it. Luckily my outfit was never called upon to break a strike but was alerted once. I found later that the NG was used only to restore order and not to interfere with the normal strike activities of the coal miners. But coal mining strikes did get out of hand and law and order had to be reestablished. The NG did get a bad name for what they did back in 1921 while settling a coal strike in Matewan, West Virginia where the coal operators brought in thugs to break the strike. The NG ran the thugs off and the strike was settled even though not in favor of the miners, who for some reason blamed the NG after that.

Company "D", composed of peacetime strength, became a home away from home for its members; it was more of a weekly fraternity meeting. We drilled on the armory floor, and when weather permitted, we drilled outside to make combat formation more realistic. Often we would go to nearby Kanawha City and fire the 1000 inch machine gun course using live ammunition after we had "dry fired" in the armory.

At the beginning of my training Sgt Bill Pauline, my instructor, drilled me in the basics of a recruit doing facings, how to march, keeping cadence, military courtesy, and positions of a soldier at attention, parade rest, or at ease, and the general orders. Soon he passed me from the recruit stage to perform any duty of a soldier and I joined the others during the weekly drills progressing up the line. Within a year I had reached the exalted rank of private first class. My sister, Lily, sewed the single stripe on my OD shirt sleeve and I was a very proud eighteen-year-old soldier. Later I was tested to be promoted to the rank of a corporal and to my surprise, I failed. I was confused for I knew my general orders, the mechanical function of the machine gun, how to fire different types of fire, selection of gun positions, military courtesy and discipline, working hard and doing more than asked. I wondered what I had done wrong. I knew the questions on the written test were ambiguous and not very clear, and had to guess at their meaning. Years later, after WWII, while reminiscing about it with Colonel Paul Guthrie, the officer who made up the exam, informed me the test was designed to cause the applicants to fail, for there were no positions for corporals available in the company at that time. The Commander, Capt Charnock, wanted us to work harder and learn the positions of corporal, making us feel we were competing for higher rank when actually no vacancy for corporals existed in the company. Col. Guthrie laughed at the joke he had pulled on me, thinking it was funny. Well, it wasn't funny to me, for I had worked hard to become a corporal. However, years later, not to be outdone, I Ben Rod Jordan, formerly of Putnam County, even became a platoon sergeant during summer camp at Camp McCoy, Wisconsin in 1940. It was then I had the honor and privilege of conducting a live fire demonstration for the Governor, Homer "Happy" Holt, of West Virginia, during his visit at Camp McCoy, using my section of two machine gun squads. He complimented us for the good work we had done.

Following the Wisconsin maneuvers and after two years of hard work taking extension and college courses, and after a performance examination, I was commissioned a second lieutenant. The honor was extended to me by the Governor of the State of West Virginia in October 1940, in the ornate Delegate Chambers of the State Capitol, and later given command of a machine gun platoon in Company "D". Now I could take my place alone with the officers of the company as they marched forward to take over their platoons from the NCOs on drill nights or on maneuvers. To me at that time it was an extreme honor to do this. I was proud.

All of this was only a prelude preparing me for an experience I had never dreamed. Later on January 16, 1941, Company "D", along with the 150th Infantry, was inducted into active military service shipping out to Camp Shelby, Mississippi; WWII would be over before the Regiment would return to its home station. The fears of my brother, Doc, came true. The

National Guard did get me into a war much earlier than many others. It would be many years before I would ever live a normal life.

CHAPTER 6

LOVE, ACTION, FUTURE?

She was a striking beauty, Wilma, a sixteen-year-old, vivacious, brown eyed brunette. I was nineteen - would I rob the cradle? Yes, I would, and did. I met her, accidentally, while on a blind date on a Thanksgiving afternoon.

While taking a stroll down West Washington Street near the old Sunset theater in Charleston, walking off the effects of a big Thanksgiving dinner my sister, Lily, had prepared, when it all began. It was a walk that added dimensions to our worlds, changing us forever. From that time forward, and once I had staked my claim, warning other interested beaus to mind their own business, neither of us permitted others of the opposite gender to enter our lives, romantically. It was than a couple of friends of mine, Raymond and Jim Anderson drove by in their father's model "A" Ford touring car with their girlfriends, Nellie and Junaita Casdorph. They were out for an afternoon drive.

"Hey, Ben Rod", said Raymond.

"Yeah, Ray, how are you?" and in all innocence, continued my walk.

"How about going for a ride with us?", the speed of the model "A" reduced to the coincide with my pace. Not realizing a trap had been baited, I fell for it. But it was a good trap.

I became the fifth passenger in the small model "A" touring car and the girls suggested that I meet their cousin, Wilma

Guthrie, who lived nearby up the hill on Red Oak Street; she could become my seat companion during the ride. Being shy, I protested but they insisted and before I could say "scat" there we were at 811 Red Oak Street.

The two beautiful girls came walking toward us from a nice two story green house, trimmed in white, the home of C. S. and Katherine Guthrie, and their large family. Even though I had met Robert and Lt. Paul Guthrie during National Guard training, I had no idea they had a beautiful sister. They, perhaps wisely, had kept her hidden from me.

"Wilma", said Nellie, "we'd like you to meet Ben Rod Jordan, a friend of Raymond and Jim's. Would you like to go for a ride with us?"

This beautiful girl, a member of a strict Mormon family with high moral standards, hesitated, fearing the wrath of her strict parents for accepting a blind date with a person whom she had never met. With a little persuasion, and after taking a skeptical look at me, she accepted. Betty Ann Kelley, a very attractive girl was with her, a perpetual smiler, was invited to come along; they had been lifelong friends. I guess Wilma thought there was safety in numbers and decided to take the risk going for the ride with us. The small car, was crowded with human bodies, making it necessary for one of the girls to sit on my lap. Of course I made sure it would be Wilma. To this day she never got over it, I don't think.

This was the beginning of a lasting relationship that is now in its fifty-ninth year. During the course of time we have accumulated five children, eight grandchildren and six great-grandchildren. Together we have traveled over the world, often at great risk to life and limb. Wilma proved to be an even better soldier than I ever was. During our travels over the world, she has slept in splinter villages (converted troop barracks), provided by the army on the various army posts in the United States, an Ambassador's Villa, and palaces in foreign lands, with servants waiting on her, at Uncle Sam's expense. She gave birth in most unusual circumstances, almost getting us both killed during the process. She was even captured by the communists in Indochina but, fortunately, was rescued by the French Army. While we lived in Saigon, she would often put our children to bed under the sound of machine gun and artillery fire as I walked the floor of our villa worried about the possible consequences. In the meantime our cur dog, Be-O-Gee, a mixed breed, pedigree unknown, bristling, emitting low threatening growls, patrolled the fence around the yard while the French and the Communists exchanged fire. Wilma had no idea what she was getting herself into when she met me, but regardless, she weathered the difficulties, sometime completely on her own, while I served overseas caring for the boys alone. It must have been a trying time for her, and others like her, but she never complained.

Following my sophomore year of high school I was one of the lucky few that found a job. The country was approaching the end of the great depression and jobs were still a scarce commodity. In fact, I found two jobs, one of which almost cost me my life. It did take the lives of three and injured several others.

My first job, as a helper on a milk truck was with the Blossom Dairy located on Virginia Street. The first day was very eventual. Perhaps, I almost had bitten off more then I could chew. Word had reached me of a possible job opening at the dairy and I immediately took off on foot, walking the five miles to the place of business, and asked the personnel director if a vacancy did exist.

"Do you play baseball?", he asked.

"Of course I do", I said as if I were "Dizzy" Dean, Babe Ruth, Bob Feller, or School Boy Roe. I didn't tell him that I played on a scrub team from the hills or about my playing ability; our ball field was laid out on a cow pasture over on Plaz Davis' farm just over the ridge from our farm, maybe the only place in Putnam County level enough for one. Most of the team members had no gloves, often using opponents' gloves, and our bat was made by Avril Casto. If we lost the ball, that was the end of the game until we found it; we could not afford another. There was no back-stop and we used a "pig tail", usually a young boy, similar to that of a "bat boy", to chase the ball when it was fouled to the rear. We played bare-footed and our overalls served as uniforms. Opie Jeffers, a school teacher over at Liberty, our first baseman, did buy himself a fancy uniform, including shoes with cleats, and a glove; he looked real good in his new duds. It gave him prestige. Team members, Brad Boggess and team supporters, chipped in to buy our catcher, Sherman Halstead, a catcher's mitt. Catching balls behind home plate without a mitt was not appealing. I didn't tell the personnel director about my team for he might have considered it "something from the country". Maybe he wouldn't give me the good paying job enabling me to make about $15.00 a week.

"Alright, if you will play ball for us, I will hire you as a milk truck helper.", he said, pushing an application toward me for completion. "The team is playing Owens Illinois Glass this afternoon in Kanawha City. Can you play today? The team is preparing to leave now, so you had better hurry." Without completing the application, I ran to the rear of the plant and reported to the coach. He asked about my playing experience and of course I said little except that I played shortstop.

"Just what I need", he said, "we are loading now so you had better get into the truck."

I rushed for the front seat of the delivery truck, but I lost the race to Bill McCutchen and another, leaving me the last seat in rear of the vehicle. I often thanked God for being the loser in the race for the front seat that day.

The delivery truck, with two rear doors, was crowded, as team members stuffed themselves from front to rear onto the two seats that ran along each side. Some had to sit on equipment bags in the middle of the floor; I was the last to get into the truck. One of the doors of the vehicle would not close and latch properly so a mechanic had removed it since he was having difficulty repairing it. The coach was yelling to get on the way for we were already late. The driver took off in a cloud of dust almost throwing me out since I sat with one cheek of my posterior on what was left on the bench seat by the open door. I had to brace myself placing my left foot on the rear bumper to keep from falling out.

We would never reach Kanawha City, nor would the team ever play ball again. Crossing the Kanawha City bridge just east of the state capitol, we had just turned left on Kanawha Blvd that would take us to the Owens Illinois Glass plant playing field when a terrible accident happened. The driver lost control of the truck when the right front wheel ran off the berm of the road, causing it to spin and roll over once or twice, catching fire. I immediately was thrown out of the vehicle, apparently uninjured. Then I heard horrible screams coming from others who were trying to crawl through the inferno of the blazing truck as we attempted to rescue them. The two men who had beaten me in the race for the front seat of the truck, after crawling through the hot flames, even though they were still alive, were burned beyond recognition. One of the men, Bill McCutchen, came toward me appearing as if he had been roasted alive. He held his arms horizontally, screaming for someone to help him. His hair and skin were gone, displaying the bone of his scalp, I could clearly see his darkened skull; his eye lids were gone as were his lips, clearly displaying his white teeth. Nubs remained where his nose and ears once were. Cooked flesh was stringing from Bill's lower arms. His companion, who had sat in the middle of the front seat, was in about the same condition; both died by the roadside. Someone screamed that the driver was still inside the truck, injured and unable to get out. It was impossible to get to him because of the intense heat from the fire that was consuming the truck. Horrible screams were heard. Cars stopped, people came to our aid trying to help but there was little they could do. Those who could be transported was taken to the hospital in private cars even before the fire trucks and an ambulances arrived. Shortly after the fire truck arrived the terrible fire was put out and the remainder of the injured was taken by an ambulance to the hospital. The now silent body of the driver was still inside the smoldering truck. I refused to look inside the truck fearing what a terrible thing I would see.

Then someone said that I needed hospitalization, pointing to my legs and ankles. I looked and, to my surprise, it appeared that I had third degree burns just above both ankles, the first and second layers of skin appeared to be gone and fluid was streaming from the burned area. During the excitement, while trying to help others, I had felt no pain, so it never occurred to me that I, too, had been burned. Some kind person rushed me to the Mountain State Hospital where I was treated and released. I later returned for treatment on an outpatient basis. How lucky I had been!

All the ball players, except me, were seriously burned and hospitalized; three had died. It was a horrible experience and, oddly enough, I had never seen any of the men before or since. It was an episode of life that seemed just to happen and then disappear for no reason. It was a terrible never-ending nightmare; even today flashbacks occur, I can see McCutchen walking down the street with outstretched arms begging for help and hear the terrible screams coming from the burning truck. I realized, except by the grace of God, I could have been one of them. I was saved by the hands of fate, and I've often thought about losing the race for the front seat in the delivery truck. I recall the rear door of the truck that had been removed permitting me to be thrown clear of the truck as it rolled on its side. I'm sure the coincidence saved me from a horrible burning death. Furthermore, had the door on the truck been closed there may not have been a single one saved from the blazing inferno. I have a lot to ponder and to be thankful for.

Arriving back at Lily's and Doug's, I related the terrible story to them and to my brother, Doc. They were visibly upset, as they examined my burned ankles and lower leges. Doc, being hasty and having a short temper, wanted to initiate a class action suit against Blossom Dairy for the manner in which they had transported the team, causing death and injury, citing the absence of the rear door as an example of carelessness. But that was the thing that had saved my life and maybe the others. So I would not agree, especially if Blossom Dairy was paying me $15.00 a week job, as a milk truck helper.

It took a while for my legs and ankles to heal but the dairy paid me as if I was at work. My boss at Blossom Dairy, a Mr.

Humphreys, a very large man in height and girth, placed me with a Bill Crago, the truck driver with a route up in the coal fields delivering milk to the coal company stores and people living up the many creeks and hollows east of Charleston. Before beginning delivery it was necessary for the truck to be loaded and I did most of the loading, having to carry heavy crates of bottled milk from the large refrigerator and placing them in the truck. It was a backbreaking job requiring me to be at the plant very early in the mornings and getting back to the dairy about 2:00 P.M.. Then the truck had to be unloaded of its empty bottles and leftover milk crates and washed down. While the driver did the administrative work, I did the heavy work. For several days I did this and it appeared my back would break lifting the heavy crates of milk, running into the yards of people up in Cabin Creek, Paint creek, Montgomery and many other places in Raleigh and Kanawha Counties. The pay was good, I thought, so I was determined to stick it out.

However, luck came my way. Before beginning to work at the dairy I had placed several applications with businesses and factories including Illinois Glass Company in Kanawha City, just east of Charleston, a manufacturer of glass bottles. The personnel director called and wanted me to come for an interview, which I did, and was hired. Working for the glass company was much better than working for the dairy.

I reported for work and was given a job as a ware handler, stacking cartons of bottles in the shipping department, a Mr. Keller was the supervisor. I was paid sixty-five cents per hour for a six hour day and the work, like at the dairy, was very hard. Cartons of bottles had to be stacked in the warehouse, later to be shipped by rail to distillers, soft drink makers, etc. I labored all day in the dark recesses of the dimly lit place. It was as if I was working in a coal mine, but a job was a job and anyone having one was considered lucky. However, Mr. Keller took a liking to me and soon had me doing things on the dock, such as placing orders on freight cars which the loaders used while loading the railroad cars, and other flunky jobs. He even let me drive a tractor dragging small carts, in tandem, like a small train, loaded with cartons of bottles, from the machine floor, to be loaded in railroad cars or stacked in warehouse bins. August came and orders slacked off so he put me on the yard gang pushing concrete in wheelbarrows from the mixer to the new truck loading dock being built onto the rear of the plant. This was the heaviest work I had ever done, not excluding loading milk trucks at Blossom Dairy. There were times I wished I were back on the farm hoeing corn or pitching hay.

Matters even got worse. One day a high official from the company's home office came to visit the plant including the truck loading dock we were building. It was while he and Mr. Keller were observing us I pushed the heavy wheelbarrow of concrete up a ramp having to make a left turn to point of delivery. Making the turn caused me to lose control of the wheelbarrow dumping its contents of concrete at the feet of the VIP. I was sure I would be fired but the VIP was a gentleman. He laughed at my clumsiness and said: "Son, get a shovel and we will clean it up," patting me on the shoulder. I never was so grateful; he showed great compassion, restoring my confidence. Even Mr. Keller acted nice about it, too. They realized such accidents would happen and that no one was perfect, especially me.

September arrived and the hot and hard summer work was over and I happily returned to school, being relieved from the backbreaking work of pushing concrete around. But this heavy work convinced me of the importance of an education for it would keep me out of the hard labor gangs. I had disowned farm work and now I disowned common labor; it was for the birds, I thought. I had managed to save a little money, a total of about seventy dollars to buy school clothes and supplies. The high school bookstore, where I, as student manager, would work after school hours, would provide most of my school supplies. Than I had paid Lily a total of seven dollars weekly for board and room; she protested saying she expected nothing from me while going to school, but I paid her anyway.

It was a great school year and during Christmas break I visited with Uncle Bill and Aunt Bertha Thomas, and their young son "Buck", who lived in the old Thomas homestead, the birthplace of my mother, on Poca River, near Rocky Fork in Putnam County. Uncle Hershel Thomas and Aunt Ruth and another uncle, Denver Thomas, and their families lived nearby. I also met the Meltons, the McClanahans and others, all relatives through my mother's line. They treated me well.

Remembering the death of my mother when I was only eighteen months old they expressed compassion for me.

I had a delightful time with my mother's family and my short stay with them had a lasting effect. I will always remember their kindness.

It was a typical West Virginia winter, much snow and ice during the Christmas break. After helping Uncle Bill cut firewood in the nearby forest, using a two-man crosscut saw, and cleaning out his barn, hauling the manure to the field to be plowed under come spring, fertilizing the ground, I said goodby to him, Aunt Bertha, and their son, Buck. Then on a cold January morning I continued my journey on foot toward home near the Center Point Church. The seven mile journey took me across many snow covered steep hills, narrow valleys and frozen over streams, often taking short cuts through fields, and dense forests, I arrived in the middle afternoon. I was warmly greeted by Papa, my sister Grace, Buss, and Norma as I warmed my posterior standing in front of a roaring log fire in the parlor. Grace quickly prepared me a hot meal which I enjoyed for it warmed my insides as well. Here I would spend the remainder of the Christmas break with Papa, Grace, Buss, and Norma.

What a pleasure to be home with the family on the farm, and see old friends again. I also visited my sister, Fern, and her husband Willie Kinser, who lived just a short distance from our place across the road, with their growing family. Buss was attending Poca High School and we compared notes. I had missed him so much, since we had never been separated until we began high school. I often wished I had attended school in Poca for the students there were my kind of people. I wouldn't have to fight them in order to exist as I had done on Chandlers Branch. My short stay at home was filled with many activities including night hunting, parties, sleigh rides with boys and girls, using a horse-drawn sled equipped with a wagon bed filled with hay. I even enjoyed Preacher Morris's sermons and Brade Boggess' singing, as he led the congregation in song. This would be the last time I would attend Church at Center Point for many years.

When the school vacation was over, I return to Charleston; it was early January. This trip, like at Blossom Dairy, the previous summer, almost cost me my life.

Ranson Sigman, an old family friend, living down on Manila Creek near Paradise, with his wife, Lottie, and their four children, drove to Nitro early each morning to work, offered me a ride as far as Nitro. I was grateful. He worked at the Monsanto plant there. Hopefully, from Nitro, I could hitch a ride to Charleston. He said he would leave at 5:00 A.M. and I had to be on time for he could not wait; he had to be on the job at 6:00 A.M. So early on the appointed day, saying goodbye to Papa, Grace, and Buss, I made the trek, walking several miles even beyond Paradise, over the frozen rough dirt road covered by snow. At times I would walk in the snow covered fields where the ground was not rough. On my way to Paradise I passed Center Point Church and the cemetery where my mother and little sister, Alma, were buried. Their white headstones were visible in the early morning hours even before daylight; I wondered why they had to die so young. My mind was distracted from the cemetery and its occupants by a blast of the stinging cold wind nipping my ears and nose as I walked alone in the early winter morning. I pulled my coat collar up and around my freezing ears for some protection.

Arriving at Ranson's home, I was ushered inside by his wife, Lottie. She thawed me out before we departed for Nitro in Ranson's unheated Ford car.

"Ben Rod", said Ranson, before we left his house for Nitro, "there's no way you can get a ride to Charleston from Nitro in the early morning hours, and it's blue cold out there, you could freeze to death. If you can find a place in Nitro to stay until I get off work at 3:00 P.M., I will take you to Charleston." I failed to take his kind and sound advice, being sure I could hitch a ride with a kind and considerate person.

Arriving in Nitro, and after thanking Ranson for the ride, I tucked my small bundle of clothing under my arm and struck out for Charleston about fifteen miles away. I noted the temperature was below zero as I walked on the narrow snow-covered road between Nitro, Dunbar, and Charleston. Adding to the already bad condition was an icy fog covering the Kanawha River valley.

It wasn't long before the extreme cold had its effect. Several cars passed, but the drivers ignored my thumb signaling desperately for help. Time and again I signaled but with the same results. Passing by small shops, I saw the brightly glowing radiance of gas heaters inside the darkened places of business reflecting warmth and comfort, added to my concern. I thought what a wonderful thing it would be if one of those stores was open and I could get next to one of those heaters! I actually had urges to break the large plate glass window enabling me to get next to the heaters to get relief from the terrible cold, but better judgement prevailed. I continued walking in my miserable condition, and not realizing the dangerous situation I was in. Then in desperation with less reasoning power, on the lonely open country road between Nitro and Dunbar, still trying to thumb a ride, I staggered into the way of an automobile. Somehow the small bundle of clothing was knocked from my arm, bouncing across the road into the ice covered ditch; I was untouched. To this day I don't know why I was spared. How could that have happened without the car hitting me, I thought. Picking up the bundle I continued on, my body stiffening I could feel my reasoning powers still weakening; I began to pray. I realized I was in serious trouble.

Instead of using my thumb trying to hitch a ride I began desperately waving my arms at oncoming cars. Their light beams focused on me, yet they continued on without stopping. I actually prepared to die; my body seemed to be getting more rigid, my walk staggering, my legs stiff. Finally, just before entering Dunbar, a black man took mercy upon me, stopped and offered me a ride. This good man saw that I was unable to talk, and shivering from the ever-stinging cold. Pulling me inside the car he reached over and shook me, actually hitting me on the shoulders and slapping my face to arouse me from a near coma - a sign that the last stage of hypothermia or near being frozen to death. I don't remember how I got into the car. This wonderful person continued to talk to me and slap me at the same time. There was no doubt he saved my life; another few minutes and it would have been too late. Soon I was feeling better and enjoying the warmth and comfort of the black man's car. I thawed out before reaching Charleston.

Arriving at the junction of Sissonsville Road and West Washington Street, the kind gentleman dropped me off at the old Pure Oil Station just before the Littlepage mansion. After thanking the kind man, I walked the rest of the way to my sister's house; the sun was shining brightly now, its rays warming the steep hillsides, melting the ice covered water holes by the side of the road. Thankful to be alive, I enjoyed the love and comfort of my sister's warm home, while she and her small children queried me about my Christmas vacation down on the farm. I never told them about the terrible near death experience I had. I will never forget that kind black man, whose name I never knew, who took pity on me when no one else did, and without a doubt had saved my life.

Considering my two near death experiences since I had leaned on the hoe handle on the farm praying that I, someday, would find what was beyond the high ridges surrounding me, and boy did I found out. I thought, maybe I should request the Supreme Being for further considerations; like things that were not so hazardous the next time around.

CHAPTER 7

GOD LOOKS AFTER CHILDREN, DRUNKS, AND FOOLS

My life again was in jeopardy; again Providence was there and saved my neck. Since coming to Charleston to attend high school, I had been face-to-face with a hostile drunk and had to knock him out. I had stood between a bully and my friend, Jim Morris, and took some blows intended for him until I retaliated, ending the fracas. I had faced a black boy much larger than me in a boxing match, but he lost courage after looking at my gang of supporters and scooted, thank God, out of sight. I had been almost destroyed by fire in the truck accident while traveling to play a baseball game, almost frozen to death, but saved by the kind black person whose name I never knew, all in a space of one year. One would think perhaps I should return to the farm, and resume my daydreaming, enjoying my imaginations. However, even this did not awaken my sensibilities to the fact I was traveling a very dangerous road. For some reason I had to expose myself to an even far greater danger.

Glen Clark, owner of a seaplane base operating at the foot of Capitol Street on the Kanawha River, frequently flew his Aeronica Chief seaplane, pontoon (float) equipped, a two-seater with the passenger riding in front, over the city advertising his pilot training program. Since seeing a little Jenny airplane at the Dunbar Fair a few years before, I had developed a great urge to fly. This was dangerous for anyone, especially for me, for I had not yet developed enough common sense and judgment to be afraid of anything. For some reason, like a curious cat, I found it necessary, even today, to get into anything that promises adventure.

I was working at Armour and Company, meat packers, as a recap clerk for the big salary of eighteen dollars weekly. I decided to splurge and take flying lessons, which cost seven dollars per hour. Presenting myself to the instructor at the river's edge, I was readily accepted, and immediately I found myself in the front seat of the Aeronica in the middle of the river, with Glen at the stick in the rear. There was also a stick in the front but I was told never to touch it until instructed, neither was I to touch the throttle.

Climbing up to 2000 feet over the outskirts of Charleston, the instruction began. Yelling over the noise of the engine, Glen explained how to maintain level flight by paralleling the wings' under edge to the distant horizon, how to maintain altitude while making turns, using the aileron and the altimeter, in conjunction with the rudder and the turn and bank indicator. After a review we did stalls, figure eights, pylons, glides, spot landings and takeoffs on the river. Water takeoffs differs slightly than takeoffs on an airstrip. During water takeoffs the nose is high and tail low while on a landing strip takeoff, the nose is low and tail high, but once in the air the controls are the same. Then without explaining, he did a split "S" turn, a combination of a stall, a turning glide without engine power, ending in level flight with cruising engine power. I liked the maneuver very much; it was thrilling. Immediately I planned to do it someday. Glen did the turn without explanation as I watched but couldn't see how he used his feet during the maneuver. I continued to fly whenever I could and when I had the money.

Achieving solo status in four hours, a very short time, and one Saturday morning I told my Aunt Fanny Bailey, living in North Charleston, that I would be flying over her house in the afternoon.

"Why, Darlin," she said, she always called me darlin', for some reason, which I never understood, "I will be scared to death knowing you'll be in that plane. Please, why don't you give up this crazy thing you're doing before we have to bury you." I laughed at her near prophetic remarks, kidding her as I left for the hanger on the river.

The Aeronica was gassed and ready for me at the appointed hour. Climbing into the rear seat, alone, strapping myself in, I primed the engine, flipped the switch, and yelled "contact". The mechanic stepped onto the right pontoon and spun the prop; the engine coughed, then purred. The mechanic, using the wing tip, pushed the plane out into the water away from the pier, I was out in the middle of the Kanawha River, near the C&O bridge. Turning the plane's nose down river against the wind, making sure the river was clear of boats, I gunned the engine, pushing the throttle completely forward. The little plane leaped like a cat jumping on a mouse, my head was forced back against the headrest by the accelerated forward movement, the plane leaving a double wake in the rear spraying water to the sides. Pulling the stick back against my belly, forcing the tail down and the nose up, and after gaining speed, I eased the stick slightly forward leveling the plane until it was skimming on top of the water, getting buoyancy. Once I felt the craft struggling to lift itself from the suction of the water, I slightly pulled the stick to the rear gradually lifting the plane from the water's surface, achieving airborne status. I leveled the plane for a short period, getting maximum speed, then began the climb into the bright blue sky, flying over the railroad bridge near the junction of the Elk and the Kanawha rivers, the engine still purring like a kitten. People walking along the river bank waved as did the crew of a tug boat pushing a string of coal barges down the river. Feeling elated, I don't think Lindberg could have felt any better when cheered by the people of Paris after he completed his famous historic solo flight across the Atlantic ten years before, in his "Spirit of St. Louis."

Continuing a normal climb, I reached an altitude of 2500 feet near the Patrick Street bridge; I noted the sprawling Kelly Ax Factory as I flew over it. My brother-in-law, Doug Bailey, and brother, Doc, worked there. I laughed remembering how Doug had tricked me, when I was only ten years of age, into eating turnip seeds, saying they were rib seeds; they would enable me to grow ribs to hold up my britches. It never did work.

Leveling off at 2500 feet, I throttled back to 2300 RPM as I roared over Aunt Fanny's house in North Charleston, I looked down.

There she was with many of her old cronies, all pointing up and waving at her young eighteen-year-old dare-devil pilot, her great-nephew, who thought he was the Red Baron or Eddie Rickenbacker, flying aces of the Great War. They were about to get a thrill in their quiet, domestic life as I would, a novice pilot with ten hours of logged flying time to my credit.

Circling over the small village still at an altitude of 2500 feet, making sure I was over Aunt Fanny's house, I throttled back, threw the plane into a steep glide, abruptly pulling it into a powerless climb then going into a stall until the plane was hanging vertically and motionless in the sky by its nose. The plane, quivering and struggling, indicating that it was about to fall out of control, a part of the sequence of the maneuver I wanted to execute. Pushing the stick forward into a steep nose dive, rapidly regaining flying speed, the nose of the plane heading directly to the ground, I kicked the right rudder, pushing the stick to the right, and at the same time pulling it back to regain level flight, to begin the right turn the proper procedure, I thought. As I did this however, the plane's reaction was anything other than what I had expected; strange things began to happen for I was not in a split "S" turn at all. Boy, was I surprised! Instead of coming out of the split "S" turn I went into a tailspin, not realizing what was happening, since I had never been in a tailspin before. Glen had never taught me, nor had he ever said anything about the split "S" turn, or explained how it was done. I suddenly realized that I was in a heck of a fix; ground "zero" was rapidly approaching, and, as they say in flying parlance for crashed, dead pilots, "I was about to buy the farm". The hole in Aunt Fanny's chimney appeared to be getting bigger and bigger while she and her cronies began scattering like chickens chased by a red rooster. Desperately, I pushed the stick forward and applied the opposite rudder, but that only caused an increased spinning of the plane. Spinning at such speed the wings of the small fragile plane could have been torn away. By this time I was about to fly the plane right down Aunt Fanny's chimney. I prepared for the crash and, for some reason, in terror, I released the controls and the plane flew itself out of the spin, missing Aunt Fanny's chimney by inches. Poor Aunt Fanny, by this time she and her cronies were nowhere in sight; they must have run for the hills or some other place of safety.

Regaining my composure, I gunned the throttle to maximum RPM and managed, trembling like a leaf in a windstorm, to climb back to 2500 feet, and for a time, flew like a sensible person calming myself, realizing I would have been dead had it not been for some act of Providence that took hold of the plane's controls, flying me to safety.

Even that narrow escape, saving me from joining my honorable ancestors, did not deter me. While flying around after the near fatal accident, looking down at the Kanawha River behind Aunt Fanny's house, I noticed a bunch of boys, naked as jay birds, diving from a Gulf Oil Company's oil barge anchored at the river's edge. Again wanting to show off, I went into a steep turning glide making a spot landing on the river near the barge; the boys waved frantically. I gunned the plane, becoming airborne, leveling off flying just above the water's surface, watching the trees on the river bank flying by without observing to the front. Then, suddenly, I had a great urge that perhaps I had better look ahead.

Oh, my G----------d! I had done it again! Ahead only a short distance were high tension power lines crossing the river to the Carbide and Carbon plant in South Charleston right in front of me! Flying with propeller whirling at maximum RPMs, there was not enough distance for me to climb over them and the lines were too low to get under them. Frantically, I did almost a vertical sharp right turn and to my horror and disbelief, again there were power lines! I could not make a right turn; I was too close. For the second time during the morning, I almost went into the real estate business, "buying farms". To this day I don't know how I accomplished it, but I must have, somehow, for I had flown over the power lines with only inches to spare; another miracle - twice in less then thirty minutes! Had I made contact with the power lines, energized with thousands of volts of electricity, I would have been burnt to a crisp. Someone above, I realized, must have been looking out for me, two times within minutes! God must look after children, drunks and fools. Even though I wasn't drunk, I certainly acted like the other two.

Deciding I had had enough excitement for one day, I headed for the hanger on the river a few miles away, soon making a spot water landing under the C & O Bridge and taxied to the pier. A not a too friendly reception party was waiting to greet me - Glen Clark and his mechanics. I did not like the angry looks on their faces, either. Grabbing the wing, pulling the plane to anchorage, Glen opened the door of the plane and literally pulled me out of the craft.

"What in the hell have you been doing, Jordan?" Glen demanded.

I was coy: "Just flying and doing a few maneuvers," I said, pretending to be calm as a light summer breeze.

"Like hell you were! That damn phone has been ringing off the wall telling us some crazy pilot was about to crash in North Charleston." Boy, was he mad; no red rooster could have been madder.

"Now describe to me what you were doing before you kill yourself. Hopefully, I will never be crazy enough to let you fly this plane again." He was spitting fire.

"Well, I was doing the split "S" turn like you did the other day but the plane didn't do like it did for you. And-----"

"What! You did the split "S" turn? I never taught you how to do that maneuver. Damn it, Ben Rod, you could have killed yourself.", he yelled. "Explain how you did it."

"Well", I began, as the irritated Clark drilled me with a cold stare, "I put the plane in a powerless glide pulling the stick back, still without power, hanging the plane by its nose, until it began to wobble and then I shoved the stick forward going into a dive and then I applied right rudder and right aileron; the plane began doing strange things, Glen."

Clark was aghast.

"You damn fool", he yelled, so loudly even the governor in the nearby state house, could have heard him, "you were in a tailspin and didn't know it and I never taught you that either! The split "S" turn is done without engine power from a stall using the aileron only to make a right or left turn; you never use the rudder, Ben Rod. You're lucky to be alive, boy. Now get back into that plane! I'm taking you up and we are not coming down until you know how to do these crazy things before you do kill yourself and cost me my plane. Get in!"

Just what I wanted, I thought, and we climbed again up to 3000 feet and when we were over Davis Creek, away from dense population, we began the most intense period of flying instruction a novice flyer like me ever had. First, Glen did the split "S" turn. I followed and did it several times as he screamed at me until I got it perfect. Then we went into spins, loops, figure eights, turns and banks, the flip, until he was at last assured that if I killed myself it wouldn't be because he hadn't taught me how do the aerobatics.

Of all the aerobatics he taught me, the flip was most interesting. It is done at reduced speed, the nose slightly above the horizon, the RPM of the engine reduced, then suddenly, and at the same time, you pull the stick to the rear and apply right or left rudder. The reaction of the plane is immediate; it has the tendency to do a loop while the tail tries to turn the craft horizontally resulting in a horizontal or a corkscrew spin, then reverse the controls regaining level flight while applying the throttle to regain normal cruising speed.

"Now, Ben Rod", he said, "take her in. Make me a good spot landing touching the water under the C & O Bridge. Remember you could hang us on the grid work of the bridge if you come in too high!" he yelled. "Be careful, now!"

We were heading east on the north side of the Kanawha river, not too far from the C & O Depot, on the north end of the bridge, flying at 2000 feet. I throttled back and began the long glide. Soon we were opposite the West Virginia State Capitol and I did a "U" turn bringing the plane exactly over the river. Little-by-little we descended and soon we were approaching the bridge. Keeping my eyes down the river, the plane still in normal glide, it seemed my judgment was right and we would not hang ourselves on the iron work of the bridge to be scraped down by Glen Cunningham, the local undertaker. Little-by-little, the bridge neared; only a few hundred yards ahead now. The river appeared to be shortening indicating it was time to level the plane and prepare for touch down. The last thing during a landing is to pull the stick back raising the nose of the plane causing further loss of speed, the engine idles, and the plane settles to the water's surface on rear of the pontoons, just like a duck would do. Soon the rear of the pontoons, or floats, of the plane, was skimming the water's surface right under the bridge. A perfect spot landing any pilot would be proud to make.

"Atta-boy!" screamed Glen, slapping me on the back. "Take her to the pier, you've done a good job. Now be careful how you fly when doing solo. Another trick like you did over North Charleston today will be your last with me, even if you do live. You understand?" It was sound advice and I never forgot it.

Time passed, and as I accumulated "flying" money, I flew the little Aeronica cross country, using dead reckoning, "flying by the seat of my pants", as the old pilots say, using only a chart and a compass, landmarks, cities, towns, and villages. I tried to have an identifiable landmark every ten miles already marked on the charts before takeoff. Once airborne, I continued to observe from the cockpit for identifying marks along the charted path. If I got lost, I would find a railroad, a river, or a main road and follow it to my destination. Often I would encounter storms, flying above the clouds and at times wondered if I would be able to descend through the clouds without ramming into a mountainside in the hilly country of West Virginia. While climbing through the clouds visibility would be reduced to the ends of the wing tips and I was flying only by the compass and the turn-and-bank indicator, the only means of keeping the plane oriented, for I could not see terrain features or the horizon; it was a lonely feeling.

Then, again, I almost "bought the farm". While flying a triangle course with Don Snowden as a passenger, I had to land on the Ohio River near Portsmouth, Ohio when I ran out of gas. The outdated chart, I was using, indicated seaplane facilities in Portsmouth, but upon arriving even the buildings had been razed. My next stop was to be Huntington, West Virginia, but my gas gauge indicated not enough fuel to reach Huntington. Landing on the river, using the power of the engine, I pulled the plane up on the shore and struck out to a nearby airport for gas, leaving Don to guard the plane. Hopefully, they would take pity upon me, sell me five gallons of gas in a can they must provide, and then transport me and the gas back to the plane. Even this seemed to be a simple thing, but it too proved to be very hazardous. But I had to wade through a swamp, briers, and brush to get to the airport. When I arrived at the small airport my appearance was as if I had crashed in the swamps. The airport personnel, seeing the condition of my clothing, my skin torn by the briers, my shoes and pant legs wet from wading the swamp, concluded that I did crash land and all came running, asking about the "crash", if anyone was hurt and was I OK? I explained why I was there and would they please sell me some gas and take me back to the plane sitting on the shores of the Ohio River.

"Didn't you know we have no seaplane facilities here, and haven't for years?" they quired.

"I was using an old chart that said you had facilities here; that's the reason why I'm in this situation. I had one heck of a time getting here through the swamp and walking through the briers and brush that you surround yourselves with." They thought it was funny.

"Just wait until you get home. Your mother will see you and think, as we did, you had crashed, and she will never let her little boy fly again." With that they laughed again. They found a can, and filled it with fuel, charging me nothing. We got into a surplus army jeep, and after driving several miles on the hard surface road, took a dirt trail over to the river. We backtracked on the river's edge to the plane sitting on the sand, and mused at Don sitting all alone by the plane. After servicing the plane, they bid us goodby, leaving me with my problem, and did I have a big problem - it was Don.

After refueling the plane, and pushing it out into the water, I placed Don in the cockpit. While standing on the right pontoon I instructed him how to prime the engine, to crack the throttle, and telling him that he must pull the throttle to the rear once the engine came to life after I had spun the prop. If he did it right, I would crawl back into the cockpit and we would take off up the river and head over the mountains for Charleston.

Don was scared to his wit's end. He was afraid to touch anything inside the plane. Finally, I primed the engine, turned the switch, cracked the throttle and said to him: "For God's sake, Don, be sure to pull the throttle to the rear when the engine "barks" after I spin the prop." It would be dire circumstances should he push the throttle forward, causing the plane to rush up the river without a pilot at the controls. Had I told him that, he probably would have gone out of his thick head, considering his state of mind. Then I heard a loud roar. In terror I realized it was water falling over the Greenup, Kentucky dam just below us and we were heading for the eighty foot water fall.

Then I remembered the air chart indicated the Greenup Kentucky Dam was in the area, but had forgotten about it, otherwise I would have landed below the dam. The plane was floating helplessly in the rapidly flowing water; I must do something immediately for I could see the water's berm as it began its plunged eighty feet below only about two hundred feet away from us as the river's current carried us toward sure disaster. Standing on the pontoon, I spun and spun the propeller of the plane's engine as the roar of the plunging water continued to get louder and louder. Frantically, I spun the prop, yelling at Don to push the throttle slightly forward and he did. Again, frantically, I spun the propeller and the engine roared to life and Don, instead of pulling the throttle to the rear, pushed it all the way forward and the plane began to spin like a top in the middle of the river. The spinning action of the plane caused me to lose balance, almost falling into the river. Fortunately, as I was falling from the pontoon I managed to wrap my arms around the wing strut and held on for dear life. Using all the strength I could muster I was able, with great difficulty, to overcome the strong centrifugal force that held me hanging perilously on the wing strut, enabling me to climb back up on the pontoon. Frantically, I reached inside the cockpit, pulling the throttle to the rear, reducing the screaming engine's RPMs to idling speed. Quickly, getting into the cockpit, I applied right rudder, stopping the plane's spinning action, pushed the throttle all the way forward and took off up river with only seconds to spare before we would have plunged over the high dam. Easing the stick to the rear I gradually lifted the plane from the surface of the river, and as I climbed into the cloudless blue sky over the green Kentucky landscape, I said a prayer of thanksgiving, thanking Deity for our deliverance. Once again I had felt the presence of death, for we had been only seconds away from the high dam and its plunging waterfall that would have carried us into our watery graves.

Climbing to 2500 feet I circled back and took a look at the dam. Observing the water crashing over the eighty foot dam, chills rushed up my spine and I shuddered, realizing that if we had not gotten the plane's engine started when we did, instead of flying home, Don and I, along with the plane, would be at the bottom of the Ohio River. I never mentioned the life threatening danger to Don for he was about in hysterics anyway. I circled the dam for several minutes watching the boiling water as it plunged over the dam. Admittedly, my nerves were shaken as I set a cross country course for Charleston.

As we were flying to Charleston and after settling my nerves, I became madder than a wet hen at Don and the flight crew at the seaplane base; both had almost cost me my life. After landing on the river and taxing to the pier, the mechanics grabbed my wing and tied the plane to the anchorage. All noticed my roughed up clothing and the brier scratches on my hands and face. Glen again went into a tirade, something I didn't need then.

"Now don't tell me you made a forced landing!", he said.

"You're damn right, I did." I replied very angrily. "You knew I was to make a landing on the Ohio at Portsmouth and you didn't tell me there were no seaplane facilities there. It almost cost me my life."

"Didn't you check the chart before take off?"

"I sure did. And that's another thing. That damn chart you provided showed facilities at Portsmouth but there were none!", I explained how I had to get the gas, the difficulties starting the engine, how we almost went over the dam. There were other very choice words I said to him for he should have known about the lack of Portsmouth seaplane facilities. How thankful he was that his plane survived.

Forgetting the Portsmouth incident, I flew regularly, mostly alone, realizing I was living a charmed life and I think I still do. God still looks after fools, for which I'm grateful.

Somehow I had learned a good lesson in judgment the day Glen lectured me following my attempt to do the split "S" turn over Aunt Fanny's house, remembering it the rest of my life. From that lecture I learned to think things out before going off half-cocked. God knew I would need it before too many years. I was prone to danger even though not always self-imposed.

Thinking back over the years, perhaps I should have remained on the hoe handle in West Virginia, still daydreaming. Would the life I had chosen be a curse or a blessing? I should have been more careful during my wishful thinking; wishes often come true and is not always a good thing. Perhaps flying for me was one of them. However, I enjoyed flying alone over the countryside, dead reckoning, or "by the seat of one's pants," they call it. Without benefit of radio, I felt I was a part of the universe, enjoying the twisting streams and rivers meandering between the rugged mountains, across the valleys, and through the forests. I enjoyed flying over the villages, observing the ant-size people and toy-sized cars as they appeared to be from the air as they walked and moved on the street far below. I could recognize well-tended farms with crops and livestock, and enjoyed the beauty of God's creation as the plane's engine sang peacefully to me. Solo flying in a small plane is a glorious experience, and one almost feels the presence of an unseen person beside him offering advice - I'm sure I must have had.

CHAPTER 8

BEN ROD GETS SERIOUS - HE COURTS WILMA

She had other boyfriends, that is true, but they scooted or disappeared after I arrived on the scene; I wasn't playing second fiddle to anyone. Her family had hoped that some day a returned Mormon Missionary would be her companion for time and for all eternity and I certainly wasn't a returned missionary.

All parents of the Mormon faith wisely urged their children to marry within the Church for it achieves family unity and tranquility. However, there were so few eligible young men of the Mormon faith in Charleston then, so they opted for some returned missionary, who would someday answer their prayers and carry their beautiful daughters off in wedded bliss. In the meantime, during their missions, the young missionaries couldn't even look at a young girl except in the theological sense, they could shake hands with a girl, but that was the limit while they were on their two year spiritual journey.

What chance would I have against a Mormon missionary when I wasn't even a member of the Mormon Church, or any church? I was waging an uphill battle; odds seemed against me. The situation called for the highest degree of planning and strategy. Such had been the case of Wilma's older sister, Olive.

Owen Neilson, a returned missionary from Montana, did carry her off in wedded bliss. They made a wonderful couple, but unfortunately, Olive died in childbirth five years after her marriage, leaving a beautiful son she had named after her brother, Paul.

I was impressed by the high moral standards of the family, no smoking, no drinking, and the home was more sacred then the church building in which they worshiped. They spoke of the temple, a structure so sacred only the most faithful could enter. Asking questions about the temple I was informed it was a very sacred place where work for the dead was done, marriages not only for time but for all eternity, as well, were performed, and families were sealed together for the same purpose. They believe that families did exist beyond the grave; it was very important that this temple work be done even for families whose members had passed on so they could be together after the resurrection. What a wonderful thing, I thought, but yet, I was skeptical. I wanted to see what the Mormon religion was all about - a part of my strategy; knowledge is power in such matters of the heart, I reasoned. Invited to go to church with the family one Sunday evening, I accepted and went with them, riding in the Guthrie Dodge sedan. I was amazed. What strange things I heard! Preachers in Putnam County preached of hellfire and damnation but the Mormons sermons were presented in kindness, speaking only of God's love and of family life beyond the grave - no ranting or raving such as I had heard and seen at Center Point. These kind, friendly, and gentle Mormon people caused me to wonder, even though peculiar, they were good examples of living standards. They taught family basics values, be self sustaining, and idleness was a curse; never live on the eforts of another. They always looked after their own and frowned upon those who lived on welfare; the church's welfare system took care of it's own worthy members. I wanted to return and learn more about them.

Not being a Bible scholar, my mind was captured, but I wondered where they got such ideas as pre-existence, marriage for time and all eternity, and work for the dead. I was about as confused as I was while listening to the preachers during revival meetings at Center Point Church.

"Holy Mackerel, Wilma, where do you get that stuff your people preach." I asked.

"I can't explain the Mormon faith, except I know it's true", she said. "Why don't you let the Mormon missionaries teach you?" Perhaps she saw the opportunity to bring me into the church, making me more acceptable to her parents.

"Oh no, you don't! I'm not falling for that trap. I guess the Mormon Church is like all churches, trying to get people in using scare tactics." Even though I had been impressed, I was still yet skeptical.

"Our missionaries will only teach you. You must convert yourself. The Church does not force its concepts upon anyone", she said, wisely.

This was the beginning of my wonderful experience with the people of the Mormon Church. Even though I would make fun of them, laugh at their beliefs, not knowing what I was talking about, they only responded with kindness. They displayed their sincerity, and hospitality, often inviting me into their homes. I attended their social activities, and they let me play on their ball teams, act in their plays, join them in their picnics, as if I were one of them; the called me their "unbaptized Mormon boy". Their devotion to family life and all that was pure, impressed me, but I never joined until many years later. Not that I doubted their religion; I realized it contained the answers to life's greatest questions since the beginning of time: "Where did we come from, why are we here on earth, and where do we go after leaving the earth?" All of this was different from what I had previously heard in other churches. The thought of these questions and the answers they provided, provoked further search of the Mormon dogma. I found many lasting friends in the church including Oscar Patton, the Branch President of the local Church of Jesus Christ of Latter-Day Saints, commonly known as the Mormon Chruch. The church has no paid ministery, a lay ministry. The idea that families existed, not only for time, but for all eternity as well, appealed to me. And this good man, his salary as a postman, his only source of income to sustain his large family, for he received no salary from the Church, took time to answer some of my questions.

"President Patton", I said, "is it possible that I will be with my mother and sister in the resurrection? They both died when I was only a baby, and I don't even remember them." I think he detected sadness in my question.

"Brother Jordan, you will certainly be with your mother and sister, you will not be denied that joy, even though she died at an early age. And your sister will have the choice pleasure of being with you as she would have been had she lived. You will have great joy, once you go beyond the veil," he continued. "Further, all of your family, your father, your brothers and sisters, and your wife and children will also join you beyond the veil, if certain things are done here on earth."

"What are these certain things?", I asked eagerly.

"Do the temple work for them."

"Temple work?"

"Yes, Temple work, or work for the dead. You see Ben Rod, we believe we really never die, but there is a separation of the spirit from the mortal body, which returns to God who gave us life, while the mortal body is returned to the earth from which it came. The spiritual body and the mortal body will come together during the resurrection. The spiritual bodies of your mother and sister, who now resides in the spirit world, are even more alive than while on earth in their mortal bodies. Now, if you are to join your mother and sister in the hereafter, temple work must be done for them, sealing them to the family, all coming forth together during the resurrection. Ben Rod, you cannot imagine the joy that awaits you there."

I was delighted. Why wasn't this preached by other religions? For the first time religion made sense to me. There was a goal for life. Even though impressed, I continued my happy-go-lucky way of life. Perhaps, I would make the change some day, but for now I had a lot of living to do.

In spite of my non-affiliation with the Mormon Church, I was reluctantly accepted by the Guthrie family and I liked the possible prize, their daughter. Wilma was not of my family's faith, mostly Baptist, even though I was not. Liking what I saw in her, I laid fast claim. She may not have been of our spiritual blood, but I sure liked the container her's came in so I continued to hold on. I chased her up and down the Charleston High School halls, and gave her an expensive gold-plated bracelet, costing at least three dollars, maybe more. I brought her candy on date nights, eating most of it myself, and took her to the movies at the Greenbrier on Lee and Summers Street. Sometimes we even went to the Capitol or Rialto Theater, when I had the money to splurge even though the tickets there cost all of fifty cents. Wilma thought me a spendthrift. After the show, I would take her to a soda fountain, but had to have her home by 10:00 P.M. When we failed to meet the deadline, I had to face the wrath of Old C.S., her dad, as he was affectionately called, the patriarch of the Guthrie family. I did fail a few times but, after his tirade of how a young man should act, I was always forgiven. Maybe Old "C.S." did see something good in me, after all. However, I had to walk the chalk line and the family must have realized, even though I was not of their faith, it appeared that someday I would become a part of the family regardless of my agnostic religious views. Perhaps, too, they had discarded the possibility of her marrying a returned missionary; I sure wrecked that idea, somehow.

Time passed and we had wonderful times. Family and church picnics, swimming parties, dating, movies, automobile rides in the family car. One time I even took Wilma for a ride in the seaplane -being wise, she never flew with me again. I did impress her though and that was what I wanted. None of her former suitors could fly and that put me in a special status. She had a nineteen-year-old daredevil flyer for a egotistical boyfriend. None of the other suckers had a chance with her. I was admired by all the other girls, too. They wished they were as lucky as Wilma, or so I thought - again, I was egotistical. Looking back, I think, I strutted my self-importance. I was at the age when common sense was completely lacking, but somehow I got by.

Then I began to wrap my personality around the other members of the family beginning with Glendall, age eight. She thought of me as a big brother for I always paid attention to her. Then there was Helen, the oldest. I was in like Flynn with her, too, then and always thereafter. Wilma's sister, Olive, kissed me goodbye when she and Owen left for Montana after a visit home. None of us realized then but this wonderful person would die a year later in childbirth. Carl, age thirteen, paid little attention to me but Robert became a good friend. He worked for the WPA for $37.00 every two weeks and did photo work on the side. We trained together in Company "D", 150th Infantry (Powderhorns) and his brother, Paul, was a lieutenant in the company, a rank high above either of us. Paul worked as a salesman for the Lewis Hubbard Company. He was a road salesman using a company car. He was married to Della Cleek and had a daughter, Lois Ileen, age five. Finally, there was the mother, known as Kate. Now, I had to walk on eggs around her. She would cast her big, pale blue eyes upon me and perhaps wonder about the designs I had on her brown eyed beautiful daughter. I was ruining her chance to get her coveted returning Mormon Missionary for a future son-in-law. I think, by that time, I had already killed that opportunity. I reasoned now that Wilma was mine, all mine. Mother Kate surrendered, white flag and all. However, Wilma's father, old C. S. Guthrie, a local grocer, a great person, was jolly and witty, yet serious when it came to the welfare of his wife, Kate, and his family. His children, including me, adored him.

There was another member of the family whom I would never see. A younger sister, Ruby, killed at age five by an automobile as she ran across the street to her father who waited in his car to take her home from kindergarten. It was a tragedy.

The matrimonial net tightened and finally, at my sister Grace's house in Charleston, we were married by the Reverend Hobson Fisher. Only my family members were present. Feeling her parents, even though they liked me, they could have objected to the marriage on the basis we were too young. However, when told we were married, and after the shock wore off, they welcomed me into the family with open arms.

It was during this time Wilma's sister, Olive, died in Montana and Wilma's mother asked us to stay in the house while they went west to attend the funeral. She wanted us to look after Mr. Guthrie, her sister and brother, Glendall and Carl. Her father, due to business demands, could not attend the funeral. Returning from the funeral her mother insisted that we remain to enable the family to adjust and recover from the tragic loss of a loved one.

It was a this time Wilma began to look pale and feel badly in mornings. Insisting that she see a doctor, she agreed, and I took her to see Doctor Albrecht. After examining her, he announced the verdict; she had developed a disease that would take nine months to cure; in other words she was pregnant. The good doctor agreed to prenatal care and delivery of the baby for twenty-five dollars cash, paid at time of delivery, or thirty-five dollars on credit. It was during the depression years and we wanted to be thrifty, we managed to pay the doctor on the day of delivery of our son.

Errol Keith, later nicknamed "Bucky", was born at the Guthrie residence on Red Oak Street. Eighteen months later, his brother, John David arrived, calling him "Johnny". Being present at both births and after seeing Wilma going through labor, I was sure glad that I as a man, I would never experience childbirth; it was bad enough being a father. I rationalized if men had to give birth to babies it would be the end of civilization, for they don't have the guts to do it.

Our family was taking on importance now, and Wilma and I realized our responsibilities and times were hard; the depression years were still around and just before the beginning of

WWII. Life would be very uncertain for us but we would have to face it, regardless.

We wanted so much to have our own place and applied successfully for a new apartment in the nearby Littlepage Terrace, paying eighteen dollars monthly rent. I was working at the Owens Illinois Glass Company in Kanawha City, again stacking cartons of bottles in the warehouse and loading railroad cars.

Adding to our uncertainty war clouds were darkening over Europe and Asia. Germany had overrun France, and Japan was expanding and had invaded China. Sea lanes were being threatened and Russia, hard pressed by Germany, was wanting lend-lease equipment just like England was receiving from us. America, or at least the American people, wanted isolation but it appeared to be an impossibility, except there must be a reason or excuse for the United States to get directly involved in the war. President Roosevelt met Prime Minister Churchill of England aboard the US Cruiser, Augusta, in the North Atlantic. There the NATO alliance was worked out and perhaps even war plans were made to include the United States, preparing for the event that would cause our involvement. It wasn't difficult to see that it would be only a matter of time before our troops would be scattered over the world; Manifest Destiny would see to that.

With Germany and Japan on the war path, my division, the 38th National Guard Division, the 150th Infantry (Powderhorns) being a member of the 75th Brigade of that Division, was sent to Camp McCoy, Wisconsin in August 1940 for a two-week summer maneuver. I proudly held the rank of sergeant, commanding a section of machine guns, consisting of two squads. They even published my picture in the newspaper showing me boarding the train with my section for Wisconsin. That was a big event in those days.

It was miserable, rainy and cold in Wisconsin around Sparta, and in all of my army experiences that was the most miserable and difficult. It was a prelude of what was soon to come; the Regular Army wanting to test the senior commanders and staff officers of the division, brigade, and regiments, and perhaps even battalions, hoping to weed out "political officers". We marched, we maneuvered, we dug ourselves in only to move immediately to meet the "red" army and turn it around. We slept little, we ate little, nor did we rest as the cold rain pelted us. At times one of my men would hold me in the road as I walked in my sleep. Sergeant Spradling pulled me from in front of a tank during a night march. The company was on a forced road march, a column on each side of the, tanks in the center. I staggered, and he pulled me back in line just before a tank was about to run over me; I didn't even remember the incident.

The 150th Infantry (Powderhorns) performed well as did our company and we received commendations. My section of guns fired a field demonstration for Governor Holt of West Virginia during his visited in Wisconsin. I fired the demonstration using tracer ammunition; he was impressed. The demonstration was followed by a division review, an impressive sight: 18,000 troops lined up across the field, the colors of many regiments, waving and bands playing, guidons, a small unit flag, of each company size units was visible. Army Air Corps by-winged airplanes were circling overhead adding to the spirit of the occasion. This was my first time in a review of division size.

Taking part, the 150th Infantry, Company "D", passed the reviewing stand proudly and I saw the two-star general, the first general I had ever seen. He looked like the Iron Chancellor of Germany, his staff behind him. Captain Charnock, our company commander, gave the command that formed the company into two lines, sixteen men abreast, with the four hand-pulled machine guns bringing up the rear. The water jackets of the guns, surrounding the gun barrels, were glistening with polish. Captain Charnock dressed in riding breeches, OD Shirt, spit-polished boots, campaign hat, Sam Browne belt, with a diagonal strap across the right shoulder, carrying a sword waist high held at the hilt by his right hand, blade upward paralleling his body, was a magnificent specimen of an officer. He was followed by the company guidon bearer to the right rear. The platoon leaders, Second Lieutenants, Paul Guthrie and Erman Wright, dressed like the Captain, looked impressive as they, too, marched in front of their respective platoons. Sergeant Rhodes, the first Sergeant, a WWI veteran, marching in rear of the line, yelled instructions to us in front trying to keep the line dressed before passing in review. Sergeant Tillis was the right guide, against whom we formed and aligned ourselves.

"EYES RIGHT!", commanded the Captain, his voice booming above the blaring band, just before we reached the reviewing stand; the officers, dipping their swords, did eyes right, while we, in the ranks, did EYES RIGHT, dressing up the line, guiding on Sergeant Tillis, on the end of the line, before reaching the view of the commanding general, who was standing as if a statue. He returned the salute as we passed by him. The band was playing the 150th Regimental song: The Old Gray Mare Ain't What She Used to Be, as we passed. That famous song got me in trouble years later with Wilma when I suggested to the brethren we sing the song at a church Valentine party. She didn't take too kindly to that (perhaps she equated herself with the old gray mare).

Following the intensive training in Wisconsin we returned to home stations in West Virginia and surrounding states. We all had the feeling our easy fraternal days in the National Guard were over, and it would be only a matter of time until we would be called into active duty. Our personal affairs were put in order, but we continued to do our normal activities; Wilma and I enjoyed our two small boys and our small apartment. On October 18 she had a surprise birthday party for me and members of the Church sang Happy Birthday as I entered the door after working all day at the factory; I was twenty-three. Johnny, still in his play pen jumped for attention while Buck was already around my neck. It was a grand time for building lasting memories. It would be the last family birthday party for many years. My father had visited that day, but for some reason, he had left before I arrived from work. I was disappointed.

Following training at the armory on the usual Thursday night,in October 1940, Captain Charnock, summoned the officers and noncommissioned officers into his office. He had a radio tuned to WCHS, the radio station in Charleston. General Marshall, the Army Chief of Staff, was speaking. We anxiously listened. The general called up several National Guard divisions for a year long tour of active duty, but the 38th, our Division, was not one of them. However, General Marshall indicated other National Guard Divisions would be called in January. We all knew we would be called up then.

"Sergeant Jordan", Charnock solemnly said, "The regiment has approved placing you on full-time duty status effective immediately. You are to get the company ready administratively for the call to active duty. Service records will have to be made, transferring individual information to the Regular Army system, and Army Serial Numbers will be assigned to the men. You don't have too much time so you had better sever your connections with your firm and get to work here as soon as possible. Remember, too, no one knows what you will have to do for we have never used the Regular Army System in the Guard and we will be asking you the questions. Just call the Adjutant General's office if and when you have a problem. Keep me and Sergeant Rhodes informed of your progress."

I was stumped. This was the first clue that such plans had been made involving me. I knew nothing about administration. I wondered why I had been called for this important assignment. Later, I found that

Sergeant Rhodes, who felt I had the capability and could handle the job well, recommended me to Captain Charnock. This turned out to be wonderful, preparing me for more difficult assignments later.

I continued to study at nights, taking the college courses and army extension courses which I had been doing for over two years. Then passing a final examination, I was commissioned a second lieutenant in the West Virginia National Guard and I would soon be federally recognized. Later, I attended a meeting with the Regimental Officers in the delegates chamber in the West Virginia State Capitol Building, where Governor Holt presented certificates of commission to me and to others. It was a happy day. I hurried home to tell Wilma and we both were very happy. Eagerly, I went to Jaffy's Army Store on Virginia Street, and he fitted me in officer's clothing. By that time changes in officer's dress code excluded riding breeches, boots, swords, and Sam Browne Belts - the very dress that had set officers apart, and had so impressed me, but now obsolete. Now the dress included the blouse, shirt, tie, and regular trousers - I was disappointed but yet proud to be an officer.

FREDERICK R. STOFFT, Lt. General (Ret)

Hails from Third US Army, Fort Sam Houston, Texas in December 1942, taking command of the 2nd Battalion of the 158th Infantry (Bushmaster) Regiment in Panama, sailing with the Regiment to Southwest Pacific Area in January 1943. He is charismatic, a natural leader of men, who are devoted to him, and has the welfare of his battalion first of all. Is spartan in appearance, firm in determination, fearless in combat and cool in the presence of the formidable enemy on Arawa, New Britain. His excellent leadership abilities are well known by the higher command who moves him up the command ladder. Eventually, after the war and an outstanding combat experience, he becomes the Adjutant General of Arizona, retiring in grade of Lt General.

FREDERICK R. STOFFT, Lt. General (Ret)

William E. (Wild Bill) Eubanks, Colonel

Served with distinction in the West Virginia National Guard since 1898 from the grade of Private to the rank of Colonel, seeing active duty on the Mexican border in 1916 and during WWI. The state of West Virginia commissioned him a Colonel in 1923 giving him the command of the 150th Infantry, which he had organized. Both were accorded federal recognition. Firm in command, devoted to his regiment, and was respected by those that served under him. Mustered the 150th Infantry into federal active duty in January, 1941, moving it to Camp Shelby, MS. His friendly attitude and jolly mood make him the idle of everyone of his soldiers, yet his keen memory and uncanny manner of finding out things commands their unfailing respect. A firm believer of axiom: "Early to bed and early to rise...,". Colonel Eubank regularly retires early and gets up with his buglers to help some drowsy soldiers or officer get up for reveille. Because of age and permanent illness, "Wild Bill" was forced to retire on the eve of his beloved regiment's departure for Panama in December, 1941. Loss of a leg later, perhaps ushered in an early death of the great soldier in his southern West Virginia home. He taught the Author to play solitaire while both were patients together in the Camp Shelby hospital in 1941.

William E. (Wild Bill) Eubanks, Colonel

Paul G. Guthrie Colonel

A Superior commander of combat troops. His battalion was the first of allied troops to penetrate the Seigfried line defending the heartland of German for which he was highly decorated. Became a civilian after WWII but returned to military duty for opportunities offered. Served in the Pentagon, later became the G2 (Intelligence), US Eighth Army in Korea. Recommended for promotion to rank of Brigadier General by the Commanding General of Eighth Army but due to inter-service bickering the recommendation was withdrawn. Retired in grade of Colonel somewhat disappointed and discouraged for treatment received at the hands of a civilian agency. This agency, for personal reasons, recommended promotion be denied. The Army, prematurely, lost the service of this highly qualified and combat proven officer.

Dana Hamilton, Colonel

Served in WWI and later served in the West Virginia National Guard, as company and battalion commander. Marshalled the 1st Battalion, 150th Infantry (Powderhorns) into Federal Service in January 1941. Serving with the battalion at Camp Shelby, Mississippi. He demonstrated great leadership abilities while in command of the battalion in Mississippi and later in Panama Canal Department. Returning from Panama in 1945 he became advisor to the Adjutant General of West Virginia and assisted in the reactivation of the 150th Infantry (Powderhorns) and the 149th Infantry in 1946.

John N. Charnock, Lt. Colonel

A lawyer in civil life, commanded Company "D", 150th Infantry (Powderhorns) prior to WWII; marshaling the unit for Federal Service in January 1941. A father image to his men who were devoted and loyal to him. Even though determined and firm, requiring strict discipline and courtesy, he was compassionate and understanding to his officers and men who served under him. Being suave and calm has the ability to mingle with those of different level of society—wealthy or poor. Willing to help those who suffer from injustice even though it would be to his interest to ignore the situation.

Dale K. Johnson, Captain

A jovial but an efficient officer. Always was in a happy state of mind encouraging those around him when they were experiencing difficulties. Takes credit for winning the battle of the "bedbugs" Fort Clayton, C, in December 1941, recommending the Presidential Unit Citation (all in jest), but his commander denied his request. Even though he was friendly, jovial, and took events without seriousness, he was firm and demanding when the situation required. He was capable, efficient and effective both in command or when performing administrative functions. Admired by all who knew him, especially the troops who served under him.

Charles R. Fox, Brigidaire General

A second lieutenant in Company "C", 150th Infantry beginning of WWII. A smooth and efficient officer, well known for his administrative abilities. Tall and slender in build having a commanding appearance and very impressive in the West Virginia State House where he served as the State's Adjutant General. Here he further demonstrated his administrative abilities reactivating and reorganizing the 150th and the 149th Infantry Regiments of the West Virginia National Guard in 1946. Very demanding in details of those serving under him producing superior results.

Charles E. Wright, Colonel

A building contractor prior to WWII, but served in the West Virginia National Guard inducted into Federal service with Company "D", 150th Infantry (Powderhorns), January 1941. His appearance commanded attention while his personality was friendly and accommodating. Had the ability of command but at times had difficulty with superior ranking commanders who expected more personal consideration when dealing with supply and administration. Commanded the 150th Armored Regiment of the West Virginia National Guard following WWII, retiring and lived in Florida, dying there.

SENTINELS OF A LIFELINE

Colors of the 150th Infantry Jungle Regiment (Powerhorns) fly over Mariflores Locks -- the Pacific entrance of the Panama Canal. The Mountaineer regiment guarded the canal day and night. During rigid enforcement of blackout regulations, night trick guards would count their steps from end to end of the lock walls. One burly West Virginian found that any steps over 1970 would carry him into the drink. At this point, he would do an about-face--and pace his post once again. ***It was here Lt. Ben Rod Jordan, the Officer-of-the Day, held up the flag ship of a navy convoy until all seventeen ships were searched for unauthorized cameras and secured under lock and key. He had to confront a very angry navy commodore in the process. He had tweaked the navy's brass noses.

Here, I am officially welcomed to West Berlin by a British Brigidaire, while representing the 11th Airborne Division during a Soccer game between the U.S. Division and the British "Black Watch" Regiment, 1956. Score was 3 to 2, regretfully in favor of the British.

Reception For The King Of Greece

The Author (center), escorting the then exiled King Constentine of Greece (right), and major General Barnes, as the King reviewed the Honor Guard at Fort Sill, Oklahoma, in February, 1959. The young King was very complimentary and appreciative of the honor given him.

MAJOR
K.J. HONAKER
GEN BARNES
KING OF GREECE

Wilma Agnes Guthrie Honaker

A real trooper who tended the home fires while her husband participated in WWII. She added her bit to the war effort by working in a defense plant making gun barrels for the U.S. Navy. Shown here in Saigon in 1952 where she often listened to the exchange of gun fire between the French and the communist, and actually was captured by the communist but rescued by the French as they tried to slip her through a military outpost near Hanoi. Only God knows what would happened to her had they succeeded.

THE THREE GREAT SOLDIERS

Wilma with our two sons, Johnny, and Bucky, shown in 1944 just before my return from New Guinea. Wilma had to shoulder the burdens of the family alone, while I served overseas during the war for thirty-three months. However, I did return on a short leave from Panama in 1942 to attend the funeral of my father. She did a remarkable job with the boys during my long absence. Later, as adults, the boys did very well in their vocations. Both were decorated for valor on the battlefields of Vietnam. John, now is an official with a Texas Helicopter Company, while his brother Bucky (Errol Keith) retired as a Colonel from the United States Army in 1992. They, like their dad, are qualified army paratroopers; John is also a helicopter pilot.

Willard B. Honaker (Buck), my brother, and me after my arrival from New Guinea in 1944, in Charleston, West Virginia.

CHAPTER 9

THE CALL TO ARMS

On January 17, 1941, the 150th Infantry (Powderhorns), commanded by Colonel William E. Eubank, composed of units in southern West Virginia, was inducted into federal service and ordered to station at Camp Shelby, Mississippi. The Regiment was a part of the 38th Division (Cyclone), commanded by Major General Robert T. Tyndall. The General had commanded the 150th Field Artillery of the Division during WWI. Other major units of the division from Kentucky and Indiana, were also ordered to station at Camp Shelby.

These were trying times for all of us. Parts of the 1st Battalion, including Company "D" of the regiment, my outfit, assembled in the armory in Charleston for muster, and several days later we entrained at the C & O Depot for the trip to Camp Shelby. Final preparations were made including the restriction of the men to the limits of the armory, fearing some of the new men would go AWOL (absent without leave) had they been permitted to leave. We set up a lounge for families to visit their now soldier sons, husbands, and fathers, and there were many tears. We consoled ourselves with the fact we would serve only a year than return home. We really felt, however, we would be engaged in war before that, and would not return until who knew when. Germany's Hitler was practically unopposed in Europe as was Tojo, of Japan, carrying out their cruel plans to conquer Europe and Asia.

Because of the crowded conditions in the armory, and unable to do much training, we marched the men around town in an effort to combat boredom. We had no dining facilities so we marched the company to the Rose City Cafeteria on Lee Street, about a mile away, for messing. The sight of our men, dressed in uniforms, caused the people along the way to cheer as we marched, making us proud to serve our country. With the exception of individual arms and equipment, we had very little to train with for all organizational equipment had been crated and shipped to Camp Shelby.

The men marching in step through the wide hallways of the armory, their passing silhouettes reflecting through the frosted glass windows of the Orderly Room (office) door, seemed to create an omen of some kind. Corporal Millinger, the company clerk, and I watched the silhouettes of men, rifles on their shoulders, wearing campaign hats passing by the frosted window, appeared to be from another dimension of time. Taking time out, from preparing final rosters and updating service records, we observe the parade of passing images. Then we listened to the marching footsteps until they faded with distance; they could no longer be heard. The silence; it was an eerie feeling. Without comment we then continued with our work.

The journey to Camp Shelby would be a one way trip for many of our men and I tried to block out the thought; we had been together a long time, almost like brothers.

"I want you officers to take some time

to be with your families this afternoon," Captain Charnock said. "We'll need all officers and non-commissioned officers here tonight to help coordinate things. You may not have time to visit with them, otherwise. Many people will crowd into this place and I don't know how we can control them if they become extremely emotional. I'm concerned mainly about the new men for they have never experienced being away from home. When their families arrive here there may be difficulties and we must be understanding. However, once we get them aboard the train tonight they will settled down."

Lt. Dale Johnson, Lt. Woodrow Hanshaw, and I took off to be with our families. Rushing to our little apartment at Littlepage Terrace, I found Wilma, Bucky and Johnny waiting for me. The time was so short, but we made the best of it. I was so grateful to Captain Charnock for the time to visit them; it relieved the tension that had been building. I had never been away from the family, except for short time periods, and who knew when we would return from Camp Shelby. We had a lot to talk about especially arrangements for Wilma and the boys to join me in Mississippi, perhaps a month later. Coming to Mississippi would be a new experience for the family but we intended to do it when circumstances permitted. Some of the wives had already left for Hattiesburg to find places to live while their husbands mustered with their units. We planned this too, but at a later date.

My visit with Wilma and the boys was wonderful, but yet, sad. Looking at them, especially the boys, who did not realize I would be leaving them, and while they played with me, brought tears to my eyes. I tried to hide my sorrow from Wilma, but I'm sure she noticed. Leaving Wilma, then only nineteen, with the great burden alone, only caused me further depression, but I tried to be cheerful for their sake. Having to leave for the armory in the late afternoon, we said our tearful farewells, I managed to tear myself from them. I would not see the boys again until Wilma would bring them to join me in mississippi several weeks later, however Wilma would see me off at the train station later that night. Our separation was traumatic.

The short visit with Wilma completed, I reluctantly, returned to the armory late in the afternoon only to find many people already gathering for last goodbyes. Having just left my family I could feel their painful sorrows; many tears were being shed.

It was hectic; hundreds of people surrounded the armory for a last look at their boys. Because of the limited space in the lounge we could not accommodate all who were demanding to see their loved ones for the last time. Many of the new men, less disciplined, almost rioting, trying to see their loved before leaving for Mississippi. Colonel Hamilton, seeing the situation was almost out of hand, ordered the final formation and roll call early followed by the march to the railroad station.

When the rolls were called, it became evident that some men were missing even though we had all of the doors guarded.

"Lt. Johnson and Lt. Jordan!", barked

Captain Charnock, "Take some of the NCOs and search ever nook and corner of this armory. If you find a man hiding, arrest him and place him under guard. He will be court-martialed once we arrive at Shelby."

Sure enough, we found men hiding everywhere: hiding in wall lockers, under desks and behind crates. One women hid her whimpering husband under her coat. She was tearful as we gently removed him from her. The would-be deserters were dragged out and placed in line with the others, a guard hovering over them, under staring eyes. They would never live down their disgrace.

Colonel Hamilton gave the order and the march to the train station began. The long column of troops, with flags waving and bands playing, marched out of the armory into the night as relatives and friends tearfully watched for a last glimpse of a loved one marching in the long column. The streets were dimly lit, the January night was comfortable without a bite of winter, adding some cheer to the occasion. The order of march was First Battalion Headquarters Detachment, commanded by 2nd Lt. (later Major General) William W. Cobb; Company "C", commanded by Captain Robert H. Hayes, followed by Company "D", commanded by Captain John N. Charnock, with 1st Lt Dale K. Johnson, Lt Woodrow Hanshaw, and me, a 2nd. Lt., and First Sergeant, James Rhodes. Rhodes brought up the rear. My brother-in-law, Captain (later Colonel) Paul Guthrie, recently promoted, was transferred from Company "D" to take command of Company "M", 150th Infantry, located in Spencer, West Virginia, and would join us with his company after our arrival at

Camp Shelby. My other brother-in-law, Robert Guthrie, had been discharged from the company by reason of moving from the area.

Even though it was 10:00 P.M. the people had lined the streets along the way, all cheering, some crying. Wives, children, girlfriends, mothers, and dads ran beside the column of the silent marching troops, grabbing an arm, delivering a final kiss, wishing us goodbye. I saw Wilma with her sister Helen; I could see them crying, too. Bucky and Johnny remained at Grandpa and Grandma Guthrie's, too young to know what was happening to their daddy. Marching at the head of my platoon, I wept like everyone else.

Our departure from home station was painful for everyone. This sort of thing was also happening all over West Virginia; the 150th Infantry Regiment as well as was the 149th, in the northern part of the state, were both on the march. Units of the 38th Division were also marshalling in Kentucky and in Indiana and were already on the move to Camp Shelby.

Another wall of human flesh was waiting at the C & O Train Station, being enlarged by the crowed that had followed us from the armory. It was bedlam. Newspaper reporters and radio station newsmen, were trying to interview us as the people crowded around. It occurred to Captain Charnock and Colonel Hamilton that many weak hearted men, recently made soldiers, would go AWOL if something wasn't done to get the men aboard the train immediately. Some family members were seen almost dragging their loved ones away. First Sergeants began to call men's names off as they boarded their respectively assigned passenger cars, delaying the entraining.

"Disregard roll call!", the order was passed on by the battalion adjutant, 1st Lt. Alva L. Carder. "Check the men after you get them on the train. Get the men aboard the train immediately!" The men raised the windows and talked to the people standing on the depot platform and by the railroad tracks beyond. Guards watched making sure no soldier escaped through the windows. I caught a glimpse of Wilma and ran to her for a final embrace as the conductor screamed, "All aboard!" The big engine huffed and puffed, and spun its big wheels. Whistle blaring, the train began to move. The people cheered and final goodbye waves were given from the windows; I, fortunately, got a last glimpse of Wilma as we pulled out of the station. She was waving and bravely smiling as she stood by her sister, Helen. I would forever remember that smile. She was about to experience a life she had never dreamed of. Like many wives, she would have to be brave, enduring the loneliness while having full responsibility for our little family; we would have very little time together during the difficult years that lay ahead. Forcefully removing members of the Guard away from their tearful families were most difficult and I hoped that I would never have to experience this sad duty again. I know it was sad for I, like the others, suffered, too.

Initially as the train steamed through the mountains the men were silent. The rattle and the click of the train's wheels on the steel tracks, laboring of the engine, and the sound of its whistle blowing grew more pronounced as it traveled to the southwest through the night with its OD (green) clad soldiers. The worst part was over, however; now that we had left our loved ones our lives would certainly be changed forever.

Being the junior officer, I was assigned to remain with the troops while most of the senior officers enjoyed beer in the dining car. But what luck; I was given a stateroom that I would share with Sergeant Rhodes. Later Dale Johnson and Captain Charnock came to visit us during the night, bringing a few bottles of beer with them. I didn't drink beer, and told them to pour it back into the horse from which it came. They thought that funny.

"Hell, Ben Rod", said Johnson, "I'll just drink your share." and we all laughed.

The train rumbled onward. The men, aroused after the separation from their families, were now lively, talking and joking with each other, a good sign; all was well with them. Some were playing cards, others singing, while others napped. My mind reflected back to Wilma and the boys, wondering how they would fare without me. Hopefully, I could bring them to Hattiesburg, near Camp Shelby, soon.

Our arrival at Camp Shelby revealed rows and rows of tents placed on frames that would become our living quarters during our stay in Mississippi. Tent openings faced the tent openings on the opposite side while the space between formed the company street where formations would be held. Each tent was heated by a coal fired sibley stove mounted on a earth filled wooden box, metal stove pipe connected to the stove protruded through the top of the tent. Steel cots were doubled-decked around the stove to sleep a total of twelve. A wooden frame mess hall, located at the end of the company street near the orderly tent, was not only used for feeding the troops, but for entertainment, and as a classroom as well. Other frame buildings scattered throughout the area were used for battalion and regimental headquarters, infirmaries, and latrines. For the regimental commander, Colonel Eubank, the army had a small house built especially for him, while the company grade officers lived in individual unheated small wall tents. We suffered terribly from the damp and cold Mississippi winter.

After a shakedown period, we began an intensive training cycle in all branches of modern warfare. The cold rain and mud of the Mississippi winter was very discomforting and many became sick and were hospitalized, but the morale of the men was high and training proceeded rapidly and satisfactorily. After training hours and having no heat in my small wall tent, I worked in the company orderly tent late every night, enjoying Sergeant Rhodes' heat, and helped him in administrative matters. Completing our work, I would run to my cold tent, dress for bed, and crawl between the sheets of my cot; a refrigerator could not have been colder. It was miserable. Then, next morning, still suffering from the cold Mississippi winter, I ran, partly dressed, to the latrine to shave and prepare for training with the company. The latrine was one place we had a coal-fired heater, and the orderly would usually have it red hot, so I partook of the comforts it offered. There I would complete my dress, lace up my boots, shave, put on my field jacket and head for the company area. The troops, standing in reveille formation in the cold early morning darkness, were coughing all through the ranks. Each day we had a large sick call due to severe colds and bronchitis. Reporting all were present or accounted for, Sergeant Rhodes, then marched the men to the mess hall for breakfast where they ate in order of platoons, rotating at meals. Training formation occurred at 7:30 A.M. All formations were signaled by the bugle call from first call to taps.

There was no let up in training. We trained from early morning and at times far into the night. NCO schools were held each evening in the mess hall, going over the next day's training schedules. We all studied after that. Regiment held officers training schools teaching us new techniques and weapons and often on tactics used by the German and Japanese armies. We had been training with the old Springfield, 1917, Model 03-A3 rifle and later it was replaced by the new M1, Caliber 30 rifle. Everyone had to be retrained on the new machine guns, and the 81mm mortar, that had replaced the old WWI Stokes mortar. The new 60mm mortar soon arrived and we had to learn that, too. We had no tanks or anti-tank guns, but we simulated each. Using trucks with a sign, with big letters on it, saying the truck was a "TANK", so we could respond to simulated "tank" attack. We had no anti-tank guns, we concocted some by making wheels by sawing off slices from logs, and placing the "wheels" on axles made of wood while others used discarded automoble wheels scrounged from auto maintenance shops in Hattiessburg. We completed our "anti-tank" gun by nailing or bolting a small trimmed tree or a two by two piece of lumber between the wheels. We would aimed this contraption at the attacking trucks tagged "TANKs", calling the gun simulated anti-tank gun. The word "simulated" became a joke and when we needed something and couldn't get it, we simulated. We "simulated" men when we didn't have them, guns, tanks and ammunition, etc, when we didn't have them either. Finally, we realized that Hitler and Tojo weren't "simulating" anything and that we had better be getting some real equipment for our trucks with a sign "TANK' on them or our wooden anti-tank guns certainly would not stop their tiger tanks.

This were the status of our equipment when we were about half wartime strength. Soon we were joined by draftees authorized by the Selective Service Act of 1940, filling the company up to full strength. Prior to receiving these fillers, all of the personnel of the company were from the same communities and localities, but the new men made us a cross-section of soldiers from the eastern part of the United States. The new men learned quickly, and with their energy and rapid conversion to military knowledge, they were soon a credit to our company. With them we forged the company into a first-rate combat outfit capable of performing long and difficult operations, whether it be on the rifle or machine gun ranges or on extended field maneuvers. Later we would participate in the Third Army maneuvers in the Sabine River Valley of Louisiana ("loosy-anne") and Texas in August and September, the largest peacetime army maneuver ever held before or since.

It was during these maneuvers that General Eisenhower, then a colonel, became the Chief of Staff for General Walter Krueger, commander of the Third Army. Eisenhower would later command Operation Torch in North Africa, and "Operation Overlord", or the invasion of Europe, subsequently bringing Germany to her knees. It has been said that General Marshall, the brilliant Army Chief of Staff, directed that the Louisiana maneuvers be held to determined the leaders of WWII, producing Eisenhower, Bradley, Patton, and Clark, among others. Many general officers who were expected to be the leaders failed in their supreme test and had to take a back seat or forced to resign.

The Third Army had as its opposition, during the maneuvers, the Second Army, commanded by General Ben "Yoo Hoo" Lear. The maneuver was so lopsided that it had to be stopped at times to give the Second Army a chance to regroup only to be stopped again for the same reason. Colonel Eisenhower, the Chief of Staff of the Third Army, because of his military acumen, was given much credit for the Third Army's success. However, General Krueger, the commanding general of the Third Army, born in Germany, was a great field commander and later commanded the Sixth US Army in the Pacific. Krueger was in reality the architect of General MacArthur's success in the Pacific, but was never given credit for it by the egotistic MacArthur.

During the Louisiana maneuvers, I was an umpire for the 126th Infantry, 32nd Infantry Division from Wisconsin. My job was to control the action when opposing troops faced each other. Even though all were American soldiers, the situation was about the same as when actual enemies faced each other. The spirit of competition was strong. Even though blank ammunition was used, the troops would fix bayonets, at times, as if they were to be used. Using a series of flags carried by an orderly, I managed to keep anything serious under control: red to stop the maneuver, blue to advance, or white to withdraw. There were times when I had to stop the maneuver in my area, call the commanders from opposite sides and through them regain control. As a first lieutenant I had the authority of the maneuver director behind me and so, when dealing with officers of higher rank, who were eager to continue their advantage, I had to make a ruling in order to control the situation. They had to adhere to my decision or else they would have a Lt. General facing them instead of me, and their argument would cease immediately. All commanders had orders never to argue with an umpire but to obey the umpire's decision regardless of their opinion. I did have some serious encounters with high ranking officers however, but I held my ground and won the confrontation.

Early one morning I was alerted through umpire channel to expect a tank attack in my sector. I was to be mindful of the intelligence flowing through tactical channels and to be especially watchful when the attack occurred. Tanks had been reported rumbling in front of the 126th Infantry, the unit I was assigned to by umpire control, the night before, and since we had never faced an armored attack so far during the maneuvers, nor had the aggressor tankers made an attack, things could easily get out of hand and people could be hurt. I was to report any anti-tank protection by the company and battalion commanders. Shortly, the Captain commanding Company "L" yelled:

"Lt. Wells, battalion has reported the possibilities of a tank attack in your front. Get the land mines out immediately, quick." This was the first intelligence received of the pending tank attack flowing through the tactical channels. I already had been alerted by umpire control and was expecting it; the flag orderly standing near nervously watching me. Everyone was excited. I made a note of the time element which would be used later in the subsequent critique.

Lt. Wells responded immediately. His men scattered simulated anti-tank mines, made of two blocks of wood with chemicals in two bottles strapped between the blocks, all along the front. The chemical, when mixed by the tanks crushing them, caused smoke, and the tank would be declared out of action by the umpire. The chief umpire arrived on the scene to watch the maneuver and encouraged me to be brave and not let the "crazy commander" of the tanks push me around. Later, I knew what he meant when he said the "crazy commander". A tank attack was a novelty to the American army then and the brass had gathered to observe the pending action. We did experienced a tank attack in Wisconsin in 1940, but it would be minuscule compared to what was about to happen in my sector, they said.

The early morning sun shone brightly and the men of the 32nd were alert. Suddenly, we heard the roar of many tank engines, the roar became louder, and sirens started screaming for some reason, having a profound effect; cold chills raced up our spines. The men of the 126th Infantry took positions rapidly and their wooden anti-tank guns were aimed in the direction of the loud roar; I braced, control flags ready. Here came the many tanks; first in single file, fanning out right and left across the front. They began their frontal attack, machine guns flaming, surprisingly without any infantry protection. Soon the area was obscured by smoke from the crushed chemicals, and the wooden anti-tanks guns were pointing at the attacking tanks, gunners verbally "booming", claiming victory each time they yelled "boom"! Vigorously, I waved my red flag, but the tanks continued to advance on Company "L". Luckily, the chief umpire was near and in communication with Colonel Ike Eisenhower, or his G-3 Operation section, Third Army Headquarters. He demanded the attack be stopped and it was, but not before the lead tank had actually touched my belt buckle while I frantically waved the red flag. We had some difficulty keeping the men of Company "L" from boarding the tanks and dragging the tankers out from inside their armor. Only God knew what would have happened had that occurred. The fact that the tankers were Regular Army while the 126nd Infantry Regiment was Wisconsin National Guard, didn't help matters since a mutual distrust existed between the RAs and the NGs at that time.

Then the hatch of the tank opened and out popped the head of the driver; the name PATTON, with a single star above the name. In a gravelly voice, demanded:

"What in the hell are you doing stopping my attack, lieutenant? I'm trying to train my tankers in making a proper tank attack and you have prevented that."

A general driving a tank!?

"General Patton, Sir," (I was scared. More of him than of the tank touching my belly button). "Your tanks in this sector are all declared out-of-action; they have been blown up in theory. Now sir, would you be so kind as to withdraw from here before the infantrymen get out of control. They're upset for your men ignored the anti-tank mines they had laid. They played the game fairly and I'm sure they expect you to do the same, sir. Please move your men and tanks, immediately."

Surprisingly, he responded: "Lieutenant, you have done a good job this morning. We have accomplished our mission by performing the maneuver. We will withdraw." The tanks formed in a single line and withdrew across the bridge in front of us.

The very much concerned Chief Umpire arrived on scene: "Lieutenant Jordan, are you OK?", he had seen the tank touch me. "That's the 'crazy commander' you've just met; perhaps you will hear more of him." And the world did hear more of him as he put the fear into the Germans in North Africa and in western Europe during WWII. He was a little crazy but then all daring military men are, to some degree.

Even though less daring, members of the 150th Powderhorn Regiment had their opportunity for notoriety during the Louisiana maneuvers, too. While maneuvering in the swamps two of the West Virginia's finest ran across a cow. For some reason they didn't think their bayonets would work so they decided to try them out on the cow, not realizing their efforts would hurt the gentle bovine as she grazed peacefully nearby. So one of the soldiers fixed his bayonet, went on guard, and cautiously approached, bayonet pointed threateningly at the curious cow, as if she were a vicious German or Japanese soldier. With a grunt and a mighty thrust, he plunged the bayonet into the cow, and to his surprise, killed her.

Time passed and one fine day a distraught farmer appeared demanding damages for the loss of one of his "finest" cows. The "culprits" were found, court-martialed, found guilty, fined, punished and forced to pay the farmer for the loss of his cow. At the conclusion of the trial the president of the court asked the two soldiers just why they had bayoneted the cow?

"Just wanted to see if the bayonet really would work before meeting the enemy." they said.

"Are you privates satisfied the bayonet will work now?" inquired the president of the court.

"I guess so, sir." one replied, "But to be sure, maybe we should try it out on another cow."

Even the farmer, who was present for the

trial, had to laugh at that, but requested that the Mountaineers Powderhorns try their experiment on cows other then his. The farmer was well-paid for the loss of his cow, the pay coming from the fines levied by the court and the extra duty the "culprits" had to perform as punishment. To the best of my knowledge, the "culprits" never experimented on cows again.

NOTE: In our early days at Camp Shelby, the troops had to undergo what was then known in army parlance as "short arm inspections" - a dreaded a monthly event. The "short arm inspection" was an effort by the army to effectively control venereal diseases, such could be contracted from infected female camp-followers by wayward soldiers. Unfortunately, the camp followers were always present in towns near any military installation, a threat to the health of some soldiers, who when found to be infected, were hospitalized for treatment, and severely disciplined after returning to duty.

Sergeant Rhodes whistled Company "D" into formation one afternoon, every one, all dressed in shoes, campaign hats, and raincoats, nothing else. They were then marched to the infirmary to undergo a "short arm inspection" by the regimental doctors.

During the inspection, the genitals of the men were inspected by the regimental doctors. Understandingly, the men didn't like this procedure at all for it was an "invasion of their privacy" according to one Private Peacock Jones, a smart soldier. So Peacock Jones decided to show his displeasure during one of these "short arm inspections". While standing in front of Doctor Britt, with raincoat open, Peacock laid his genitals on a small table in front of the good doctor:

"Hey Doc", said Peacock Jones, "take a look at that." The doctor, professionally like, put on his rubber gloves, and glasses, using his tweezers, turned Peacock Jones genital from one side to the other, observing it very closely, performing a very thorough examination.

"I see nothing wrong with that, Jones."

"I know Doc, but isn't she a beaut?"

Poor Private Peacock Jones, the higher powers of the military immediately descended on him like a rooster on a june bug and he received two weeks restriction to the company area with hard labor during his restriction. Peacock, during future "short arm inspections", cooperated fully without saying anything about the army's "invasion of his privacy".

But Jones had medical problems too, which gave the good doctor a chance to get his revenge. Jones had a phobia and the piles (hemorrhoids), the two together almost did him in. He could not stand anyone pointing a finger toward him. The men knew this and often pointed their fingers at him to see him go into hysterics. The officers of the company had to step in, forbidding further finger pointing at Peacock Jones, thus restoring his sanity. But one day Peacock Jones had to go to the infirmary to have his piles (hemorrhoids) treated and who did he see, but Doctor Britt. The doctor remembered the "short arm inspection" the month before, had Peacock Jones where he wanted him. He had the opportunity to settle the score, for sure. The doctor put on his rubber glove, while Private Peacock Jones carefully watched his every move, then holding his finger up for Jones to see, Dr. Britt told him to bend over for a rectal examination. This threatening finger put Peacock Jones into a hysterical state, but the doctor went to work anyway. Poor Peacock Jones tried to cooperate, but when the good doctor inserted his finger into the soldier's rectum it produced a sight that never has been seen before or since. Peacock Jones jumped across the floor of the dispensary as if he were a jack rabbit. With the doctor's finger still inserted in his rectum, Peacock Jones ended up in a corner of the infirmary. Here the doctor completed his rectal examination while Peacock Jones almost butted out the corner of the building. Doctor Britt had his revenge and Peacock Jones never again displayed his genital in such a rude manner during future "short arm inspections". This story became a company legend.

CHAPTER 10

HOSPITALIZATION AND COURTS MARTIAL

During a break in the Louisiana maneuvers, all tactical commanders, including commanding generals to majors, and all ranks in between, plus umpire control, met at a theater at Camp Polk, near Alexandria to critique past actions of the maneuvers. Wanting to brief my immediate superior officer, Lt Col Hamilton, preparing him for the critique, I searched through the crowd of officers looking for him. In doing so I wandered backstage, for some reason that now escapes me, continuing to search. Suddenly, I became aware of someone standing behind me. Turning, I faced a tall, gangling brigadire general, having a hooked nose like an eagle's beak, and cold black hair, sternly looking at me.

"Lieutenant", he said in a low pitched voice, "can I be of some help to you?"

Stammering: "Sir, I'm looking for Colonel Hamilton. Do you know him?"

"Don't believe I do. Let us see if we can find him for you." He led the way as if I were a peer.

We entered a small office and there sat a three star general - a lieutenant general! Being in tow by a brigadier general, now here I was faced with a lieutenant general! I was traveling in strange and almost forbidden territory. I froze.

"General", the tall brigadire general

began, calmly, "this is Lt. Jordan and he's looking for Colonel Hamilton. Have you seen Colonel Hamilton?"

"Don't believe I have, General." His tone, too, was as calm as a soft summer breeze. "Let's see if we can find Colonel Hamilton for him."

By this time I was as stiff as a cold poker with fright as if in the morgue with advanced rigor mortis. The three of us went on the stage in front of at least two thousands senior officers.

"A-tten-chun!" someone called loudly out in the audience.

"At ease, please." responded the lt. general. "Gentlemen, is there a Colonel Hamilton here?"

From the rear of the theater a squeaky voice replied: "Here, sir." Colonel Hamilton held up his hand.

"This lieutenant wants to see you, Colonel." and the two generals retired to the small office while I stood to receive the wrath of Colonel Hamilton and the cold icy stares of hundreds of other senior officers.

"What in the hell are you doing with the two generals embarrassing me like that?" Golly, he was mad.

"Just wanted to give you my notes before the critique today, sir." I said. I think he was afraid of me since I had hobnobbed with the two generals. He said nothing about it afterwards.

The two generals were then, and even later, very important to the victory of WWII. Even though they were of very high rank, especially the Lt. General, they displayed humility and consideration for others. Lower ranking officers would have probably ignored me or even scolded me for being on the stage where I had no business. However, I often found that the higher the rank of officers, the more considerate they were; a contrast to the overbearing attitude of many lower ranking officers.

Who were the generals?

The brigadier general was Mark W. Clark, later, a lt. general, Commander of the Fifth US Army in Italy during WWII and still later, a four star or full general, Commander of the Eighth US Army in Korea. I had the pleasure of meeting General Clark for the second time when he and Mrs. Clark came to Indochina from Korea in 1952. While Mrs. Clark, Mrs Heath, wife of the American Ambassador to Indochina; Wilma, and a group of other American ladies visited the Vietnamese hospitals, the General visited the US MAAG (Military Assistance Advisory Group) of Indochina in Saigon; I was a staff member of the MAAG. With the exception of having a little gray in his hair, the general looked about the same as when I last saw him a Camp Polk, Louisiana in 1941, eleven years earlier.

The lieutenant general: he was Leslie J. McNair, responsible for training of all ground troops of the Army in 1941 at the time I met him at Camp Polk. Both generals were observing the Louisiana maneuvers to determine the effectiveness of the army's training doctrine for which they were responsible.

General McNair was killed on July 23, 1944, while observing the Air Corps pattern bombing, a new technique, during the St.Lo breakout in France. The US Army Air Corps dropped a stick of bombs short making a direct hit on his fox-hole. General McNair's death was a blow to General Marshall, causing him to have to reorganize his forces for planning and training.

The Louisiana maneuvers was a time of woe for many, even me. I was almost court-martialed. Wearing the white arm band of an umpire probably saved my neck, but not before I was relieved of command while suffering from malarial fever in the Camp Shelby hospital.

General Krueger, the commander of the US Third Army, had issued written orders that no kitchen or water trucks would be captured, for he wanted the men to eat and have plenty of water during the maneuvers. Each umpire carried a copy of this order in his satchel hooked to his pistol belt. He was to show the culprits when they captured a mess or water truck belonging to the opposition, making sure the vehicles were released to us to be returned to unit to which they belonged.

Late one night, after the troops of the 126th Infantry, 32nd Infantry Division had been pressing the "Red" Army for three days, eating out of grocery stores along the way, the kitchen and water trucks came forward and before they could be stopped found themselves in the "Red" Army area and were captured. Being an umpire, I had the authority to travel on either side and I went forward to return the trucks to the Third Battalion of the 126th Infantry whose men were very hungry, thirsty, tired, and very angry. Finding the trucks in a deep forest in the darkness, the officer in charge said he was aware of the Army order and suggested I return to the 126th and the trucks would follow. Instead, the trucks never were returned and I had a dickens of a time explaining this to the Third Battalion commander, a lt. colonel, a Pollack from Detroit, who was mad as hell. He ordered up three trucks loading them with soldiers with bayonets fixed. I finally stopped him by tracking down and contacting my chief umpire who had the regimental commander order the Third Battalion commander to cease and desist. Tempers flared, but were controlled. Taking a senior umpire with me, riding in a jeep over into the "Red" Army area, we found the officer who had promised to return the trucks to the 126th. He denied that he knew anything about the situation and said that I had lied about him. After standing in the dark forest, I walked up to the officer and declared him a walking casualty. At the same time, I told him he wasn't fit to be an officer. I didn't know his rank nor could I tell in the darkness what his rank was.

"I'll have you court-martialed for insubordination and disrespect of a superior officer!", he said.

"Yes, lieutenant", I said, "now get your butt down the road to the nearest aid station. You are declared a walking casualty and out of action for twenty-four hours."

"Don't call me a lieutenant! I'll have you know I'm a colonel."

Then I knew I was in big trouble, but the colonel obeyed my instructions, and after turning his command over to another officer, began walking down the road, disappearing in the darkness of the early morning hours.

The large maneuvers ended. After returning to Camp Shelby, I became deathly ill with malaria fever. In fact, my brother, Doc, heard about my sickness and called the Camp Shelby Hospital inquiring of me. He was informed my recovery was doubtful and if he wanted to see me alive perhaps he had better come soon. I must have been in a coma from the extreme fever; I would wake up occasionally and my bed would be surrounded by doctors and nurses. Wilma came to see me and I never knew she was there. When I was conscious, the pain was so excruciating that I would passed out again for I couldn't stand the terrible suffering. Eating nothing, my body weakened and chills shook the bed - no amount of covering would lessen the chills. Before it was over I was down from 170 pounds to 140, almost a walking skeleton.

It was then, being at my worst, Colonel Hamilton and Major Charnock, the commander and the executive officer of the battalion, visited me. I remember little about their visit, but I was jarred back to reality by Colonel Hamilton's remarks.

"Ben Rod", he said, "I have a most disagreeable message for you. I'm sorry I must give you such information while you are so sick. You are hereby relieved of your duties pending court-martial for insubordination and disrespect of a superior officer." I'm sure I saw tears in Colonel Hamilton's eyes.

Then I remembered what had happened about the kitchen truck heist during Louisiana maneuvers. The colonel from the 36th Texas National Guard Division had done what he said he would do, and I was being court-martialed.

Without any further conversation, Colonel Hamilton and Major Charnock departed and I remember little after that drifting in and out of reality. In my condition, what would happen to me in the future was of no concern to me. Luckily, others did care, especially Charnock.

In civilian life Charnock, a great lawyer, handled legal problems for members of the guard without charge. This good man armed himself with all information about the incident in Louisiana, taking a copy of the Third Army orders specifying no kitchen or water trucks would be captured and held, and headed for Ft. Sam Houston, headquarters of the Third Army. He demanded and did see General Walter Krueger personally. He was successful in explaining my situation to the General. Charnock produced a copy of the orders forbidding the capturing of kitchen and water trucks, and shared the fact that I was gravely ill in the Camp Shelby Hospital. General Krueger was furious, something unusual for him; he normally was calm, a peaceful, and quiet man.

Calling in his trial judge advocate, the general requested my file, wherein he learned that the officer preferring charges against me was a Colonel Britain of the 36th Infantry Division. The TGA explained the case to him and determined I had shown Colonel Britain, the order forbidding the capture of kitchen and water trucks. General Krueger ordered all charges against me dropped and charges preferred against Colonel Britain for disobeying his orders. I often wondered what happened to Britain, for I was never called as a witness in his courtmartial, even had there been one. Perhaps a written reprimand was used instead.

After Charnock had returned to Camp Shelby the elated pair, he and Colonel Hamilton, hastened to the hospital to informed me of the good news. Again I saw tears in Colonel Hamilton's eyes, but this time they were tears of joy.

"Ben Rod, Son," he said, as if he were my father, "I'm so happy you are now back on full duty status. Now you get well, do you hear, we need you badly back in Company "D", and they departed from the hospital. I heard nothing further about it.

What luck! Almost kicked out of the army in disgrace! Had not Major Charnock and Col Hamilton put their necks on the chopping block, this would have happened, too.

A week later, having sufficiently recovered, I took a pass to visit Wilma and our sons in nearby Petal, Mississippi. What joy to be able to be with my family once again! Even though I was still weak as a kitten, I managed to rough it up with the boys a bit, wrestling on the living room floor under the watchful eyes of Wilma. It had been some time since I had such pleasure and Bucky and Johnny both enjoyed the rough play.

All too soon it was late in the afternoon, and I was due back to the hospital by 9:00 P.M. Wanting to visit my friends of Company "D" back at camp, Captain Guthrie, Wilma's brother, drove me to Shelby, arriving in the late afternoon, almost dusk. In the twilight, I walked down the company street passing several members of the company whom I had known for years, and surprisingly, they paid little attention me as if I were a stranger. Up the street I saw Sergeant Rhodes entering the orderly tent. He gave me a strange look, and disappeared inside. Then, like a cork, his head popped back out from under the tent flap:

"Is that you, Lieutenant Jordan?"

"Of course it's me, Sergeant Rhodes. After all the years you have known me, you don't even recognize me?"

"Ben Rod, you are so pale and you've lost so much weight, your sickness must have been terrible for you. I'm sorry I didn't recognize you. Please forgive me, son." There, in my weakened condition, I felt like a son whose father was tenderly talking to him. I've never forgotten those kind words, ever. Unfortunately, Sergeant Rhodes, the old WWI soldier, left us a few days after I had returned to duty, by reason of being over age to further serve in the army. We had a tearful goodbye as I called Company "D" to attention.

"PRESENT, ARMS!", I ordered, and, doing an about face myself, I presented arms to him personally. The old sergeant returned the courtesy, tears streaming down his thin wrinkled face, without saying a word. Already dressed in a civilian suit, he picked up his duffle bag, and left the company area for the last time. We would never see him again, but we would never forget him, either.

The hard life at Camp Shelby was eased by the arrival of Wilma and the boys in March. They had traveled from Charleston with Della Guthrie, wife of Wilma's brother, Paul, then a Captain, in their 1940 Chevrolet. In the car were Lois, their daughter, and their adopted son, Steve, age one, along with our two sons, Buck and John, ages three and one. The trip had been trying for them. Wilma cared for the children while Della drove, and the fact that Buck had the measles didn't add joy to the trip. Since quarters were unavailable in nearby Hattiesburg or the surrounding area, we went to Biloxi on the Gulf of Mexico coast where the two families lived for a while. Fortunately, I found quarters consisting of only two rooms for us in Petal, Mississippi, adjacent to Hattiesburg and near the camp. Now I could see my small family on weekends and Wilma could bring the boys to have dinner at the officers mess at times through the week.

These were trying times and money was scarce. The pay of a 2nd lieutenant was only $167.00 monthly, but Wilma was skillful in money matters and made every penney go a long way. She still laughs when she tells the story of sending Buck to the nearby grocery store to buy a loaf of bread and a can of soup for lunch with a dollar. Since he had change left over, Buck decided to buy some candy for himself and his brother, John. Buck arrived home with the bread, soup, and the candy and seeing he had purchased the candy without permission, and his mother wanting to teach him a lesson, she said: "You take that candy back and return the money or get a whipping, do you hear?"

The little three-year-old boy sadly looked at his candy and then at his lovely, young, but irritated mother and said, "whip me."

On another occasion, while I was engaged in displaying our company's kitchen equipment and tentage, along with all other companies of the regiment, in the training area, the Regimental Charge of Quarters, appeared in a command car and rushing to me reported: "Sir, your son, Johnny, is dead and you must go home immediately." I had no idea anything was wrong at home and I was shocked.

"Lt Jordan", said Colonel Hamilton hearing the report, "here are the keys to the my car; get home to Wilma, immediately."

Dazed, I got into the command car, driven by the Charge of Quarters. Silently, we headed for the company area and, without changing to civilian clothes, I headed for Petal and my family. I was thankful for the use of the battalion commander's car. Arriving at our apartment in Petal, happily, I found Johnny very much alive cradled in the arms of his mother sitting in the porch swing. He must have had a seizure, she said. What a wonder relief to know my son was alright. Wilma had called the regiment to inform me of Johnny seizure, but the message was garbled by the Charge of Quarters, causing me an extreme emotional strain. What a relief to know our son was all right.

CHAPTER 11

CENTRAL AMERICA AND PANAMA

Shortly after the Louisiana Maneuvers and while working on reports of survey in the orderly tent, justifying the losses and damages of equipment during the recent maneuvers, Sergeant Rhodes said to me: "Lt, I heard at the First Sergeants' meeting today the Regiment will be shipping out to Panama before the end of the year."

"Why would we be going to Panama, Sergeant?"

"Well, they say a good regiment must be sent to Panama to beef up the security there. You know our regiment did well during the Louisiana maneuvers, even out maneuvering the Regular Army, so the powers that be must feel we could do the job well."

"I suppose, with Hitler loose in Europe and Tojo in the Far East, the Panama Canal is a critical installation because it reduces ship travel by thousands of miles and it could be a prime target for sabotage." I interjected.

"Yeah, and with all the Germans and Japanese in South America you know the Panama Canal could be a hot target. Germany may even have a secluded airfield in South America somewhere making it possible for an air strike upon the canal." said Rhodes. We continued making Reports of Survey using the list of property losses or damages provided by Sergeant Garland Painter, the company supply sergeant.

Very little else was said about Panama;

we shelved the subject placing it into the dark recesses of our mines for later discussion. It was an exotic thought, however. Most of us had never been in the tropics, but we had dreamed up a picture of palm trees, trade winds, sandy beaches, pretty girls in grass skirts with flowers in their hair, and the easy life we had seen portrayed on the movie screens. Duty in Panama would certainly be a change from the hard life we had experienced in Camp Shelby and in the swamps of Louisiana. But we questioned the idea. Why would they take a regiment like the 150th (Powderhorns), combat ready, and send it to the Panama Canal Zone to do guard duty when any outfit could do the job? If we had to leave the Cyclone, or the 38th Division, why couldn't we become part of a new division being formed using other regiments available from other divisions being streamlined from four infantry regiments to three? We felt we were ready to face Hitler and Tojo and did not want to be relegated to doing guard duty in Panama.

However, the Panama Canal was an extremely important installation. When studying a map of the canal which connects the Atlantic and the Pacific Oceans through the narrow isthmus of Panama, where the Continental Divide dips to one of its lowest points, one realizes why it is so strategic. A ship departing New Orleans for San Francisco via the canal instead of rounding the tip of South America, would save 8,868 miles, or about twenty-four days at sea.

Naturally, the Germans and the Japanese would be interested in destroying the canal.

To prevent the canal's destruction, heavy fortifications were built at both entrances to it where the army and the navy had airfields, submarines, and combat troops alerted and ready. To further add to the security of the canal, airfields were being built in Central and South America, which had to be secured to prevent sabotage by lurking spies and Axis sympathizers. Added to this, two earthen dams had been constructed, blocking up the former Chagres River. These dams formed the Gatun Lake through which ships had to travel between the Atlantic and Pacific Oceans after being raised and lowered 85 feet by the locks to continue their course of travel. Should either of these dams be blown the lake would be drained, bringing an end to the Panama Canal. Than the Panama Canal was extremely important; the best troops available must be used to guard it. If the 150th (Powderhorns) was chosen for the job, then our mission would be more important than that of any regiment on the firing line. As yet, we were only thinking; who knows what the future would bring.

Regimental activities began to change in September. Unit training reflected jungle survival, protection against tropical diseases and counter intelligence. In early October the regiment was alerted for movement to the Panama Canal Zone, departing New Orleans Port of Embarkation (NOPE) in December. Tropical clothing was issued and special health preventative measures taken.

Being alerted for duty in Panama, and since I had not been home to Charleston since January, Wilma and I decided to take the boys for a leave during the period of December 1st through the 10th, arriving in Charleston by train late in the evening, Tuesday, December 2. The week was filled with the usual visits to relatives, dinners, and parties. On Sunday, December 7, we visited my father, my brother, Doc, and his wife, Lou and their family. While taking a nap, following the big dinner Lou had prepared for us, Doc rushed in to the bedroom: "Ben Rod", he excitedly said, "the Japanese have bombed Pearl Harbor!"

Rushing to the radio, I heard the announcer say that the all military on leave must return to duty immediately. This was our "Day of Infamy" that President Roosevelt spoke of while addressing Congress, declaring war on Japan the next day. "The sleeping tiger had been awakened", said the Japanese admiral who had lead the sneak attack on Pearl Harbor. Later Germany declared war on the United States, too.

We quickly ended our visit with my brother's family and my father, returning to Wilma's parents home, where we had been staying, and packed for the return trip to Camp Shelby. However, before leaving for Wilma's family home, my father wanted to have his picture taken with me, asking Doc to take the picture. It would be the last picture of us together; my father would die the next August.

The departure from Charleston was most difficult for me. We left the boys with Wilma's parents and sister, Helen, until Wilma could return from New Orleans. When we boarded the train, the little boys thinking they were going with us, were terrified when realizing we were leaving them behind. Tearfully, they held out their little hands, begging us to take them, crying, "Daddy, Mommy", as their Aunt Helen and Grandma Guthrie tearfully held them in their arms. Sitting in the coach seat, like my sons, I cried like a baby, too, ignoring the conductor demands to see my tickets. The conductor, punching and collecting tickets, seeing my emotional trauma left, returning after I had regained my composure. Wilma tearfully comforted me as the train pulled away from the station while the little boys stood there, still crying and holding out their little arms for us. It was a lonely and forlorn feeling; a feeling I would never forget. With the exception of returning from Panama for my father's funeral, this would be the last time I would see Wilma and the boys until I had returned from the Southwest Pacific area, New Guinea, in July 1944, or thirty-three months later.

The trip to Camp Shelby was uneventful but there was evidence the country was on a war alert. Troops were posted on all bridges and soldiers returning to camp filled all available space on the train. A hushed silence prevailed, perhaps caused by the uncertainty of the future. The people could not understand why Japan would stage a sneak attack on Pearl Harbor, nor why we were caught so unprepared. Others said the leadership in Washington were aware of the large Japanese naval task force departure from Tokyo Bay, but ignored its whereabouts thereafter. Even Admiral Kimmel and General Short, the naval and army commanders of Hawaii, were never notified by the War Department of the Japanese navy was on the prowl, even though the War Department did know. Had they known, there would have been no battleships on battleship row when the Japanese surprise attack came, saving many lives and ships. Fortunately, our aircraft carriers were out to sea or they, too, would have be sitting on the muddy bottom of Pearl Harbor. The navy and army pilots were still in their officers clubs following a Saturday night binge instead of being in their cockpits. Some did manage to get off the ground, still in their dress blues uniforms, and did shoot a few of the Jap Zeroes out of the sky. Furthermore, a very critical warning did occur but was ignored by our leaders in Hawaii. A radar operator stationed at the Cola Pass, through which the Japanese Imperial Air Force flew an hour later, reported strange blips on the radar screen in the early morning of December 7th. His superior told him the blips were probably birds and to come on down to breakfast. The sergeant gathered his men and equipment, and in his truck, returned to quarters for breakfast. This warning was reported about an hour before the attack. This was not much warning, but had it been heeded, possibly it could have resulted in getting more of our pilots into the air, and the crews on battleship row could have been at battle stations when the Japs attacked. Many lives and ships could have been saved. It has been said the attack on Pearl Harbor was staged to put America on a war footing or an excuse to get into the war. Prime Minister Churchill, of England, jumped for joy when told of the attack. People on America's west coast prepared for an enemy invasion and an enemy sub was sunk near San Francisco, they said, increasing the people's fear. But "The sleeping tiger had been awakened," as the Japanese Admiral said, and would eventually bring the war to the Japanese shores.

Returning to the regiment in Camp Shelby, I was given an assignment to move a large convoy of vehicles to the New Orleans Port of Embarkation (NOPOE), which later would be loaded aboard an army ship to be transported to Panama. I would be accompanied by Sergeant Frank Corley, who later would became an officer. He was killed on "D" Day in Normandy. Sergeant Corley brought up the rear of the convoy while I led the way. We arrived at NOPOE on schedule. In the meantime, Wilma took the bus for New Orleans from Hattiesburg; she would meet me at the Jung Hotel on Canal Street.

While the convoy was moving to New Orleans, troops of the regiment were also on their way by various means of transportation, making camp near the port. Field kitchens were set up and the men were fed as if we were on field maneuvers. I stayed with Wilma at the Jung Hotel reporting daily for company duty. Captain Thompson, my company commander, did not have his wife with him, but was very considerate and gave me time off to be with Wilma.

Since our departure from New Orleans was supposed to be secret, I was unable to tell Wilma when I would leave for Panama aboard the "USAT Shawnee". Fortunately, the carpenters had work yet to do aboard the ship before receiving troops, delaying our departure. She knew it was only a short time until I would leave her. Should I not return after a reasonable time, after reporting for duty, it would be the signal for her own departure for Charleston. I would be on my way with Company "D" to Panama. This was a trying time for a young wife of nineteen traveling alone. Her sad and difficult story to Charleston follows:

* * * *

WILMA TELLS HER HEARTBREAKING STORY

Arriving in New Orleans, Ben Rod and I registered at the Jung Hotel on Canal Street for a few days. When we realized we would have more time together, we rented a sparsely-furnished room on Canal Street, closer to the downtown area. His regiment was encamped on the outskirts of the city while his ship, the USAT Shawnee, was being converted into a troop transport. Daily he, along with other officers of the regiment, who had their wives with them, reported to their units and if no duties were required of them, would return to be with us. We knew one day soon our husbands would leave us, and without a final goodbye, would depart from New Orleans without telling us when and where, for the move was Top Secret. We were told what to expect if they didn't show up after a reasonable length of time. This was the signal that the Shawnee had departed. Daily, anxiously, we waited for our husbands to return once again. And it was wonderful when they did, for we knew we would have another few hours together. However, we knew the dreadful day would eventually come and we would have to return home without them. Depression set in, but we tried to be brave and cheerful for our husbands' benefit realizing they, too, were suffering an emotional trauma. After they departed the worst part would come; we would have to explain to our children what had happened to their daddies.

The awful reality of war, the departure and long separation, was upon us. I tried to hide the terrible thought that maybe some of them would never return. While they were with us, we had time for long talks, long walks, rides on the ferry over to Algiers, window shopping, an occasional movie, and sitting in the park feeding the birds. We listened to our favorite song on the radio in our room, Red Sails in the Sunset ("way out on the sea, oh carry my loved one home safely to me").

That dreadful day finally came when Ben Rod didn't return. I tried to reason why this terrible thing had to happen just before Christmas. How was I to explain to our two young sons, Bucky and Johnny, that Daddy wouldn't be home for Christmas? Ben Rod had left us at a time when our little boys needed him the most. "Oh, God how long will it be? Please tell me", I prayed. Wiping away tears, I tried to be brave and courageous. Hearing the distant blast of the whistle of the big ship, Shawnee, we felt our husbands were on their way to some unknown place. It was about 2:00 P.M. on 23 December. Very depressed I realized that if I hurried I could at least be home with the boys on Christmas Eve. Sadly, and through tears, I packed my things and a few Christmas gifts we had bought for the boys and family. A good friend of mine, whose husband was on the ship with Ben Rod, offered me a ride to Birmingham in her car. I left the modest room for the last time with fond memories of Ben Rod and our last few hours together.

The long drive to Birmingham was made mostly in silence for we were in deep thought about our future lives without our now sea-bound soldier husbands; life would be so difficult without them. Arriving in Birmingham, I was lucky to get a seat on a crowded train for Lexington, Kentucky. The train was filled with soldiers who were sleeping in seats, on the floors, and in all the nooks and corners of the train. The train, delayed several hours in Chattanooga, making my arrival in Lexington late and missing my connection for Charleston I had to spend Christmas Eve in Lexington. It was cold, dark, very depressing and, having little money, I spent the night at the YWCA in Lexington for a dollar. With the exception of the receptionist, the dark lobby was deserted. There was a small partially decorated Christmas tree in the corner of the lobby and for some reason that added to my already deepening sadness and loneliness. Registering, I telephoned home and made arrangements for my dad to pick me up at the bus station at 5:00 P.M. in Charleston, on Christmas Day. The bus was the fastest means of getting home.

My room, being upstairs at the "Y", was small and dark, lit only with a single light bulb dangling from the high ceiling. The atmosphere did little to improve my depressive feelings. I was all alone in a strange town on Christmas Eve, without Ben Rod; I missed him so much. Finally, after many sleepless hours, the terrible night ended when I received my wake-up call. Eagerly I dressed and prepared to catch the bus that would take me home; it was Christmas Day. It would be the most unforgettable Christmas I would ever have.

The bus seemed to take forever traveling through the mountains of Kentucky and West Virginia, stopping at every little town. My unhappiness increased and I became more restless as the bus took its time traveling on the crooked roads and stopping at all the stations along the way. Finally, almost dark and with snow falling, I arrived at the Greyhound Bus Station in Charleston. Seeing my dear Dad standing there alone waiting for me raised my spirits. I ran to him and he put his fatherly, comforting arms around me, giving me the security and love I so badly needed. When I asked about Bucky and Johnny, he said they were well and at home playing with their Christmas toys and with my younger sister, Glendall. My mom and my sister, Helen, delayed the Christmas dinner until Dad and I arrived.

Finally, after the terrible experience that I had coming from New Orleans, I felt the security that I had not had since Ben Rod left.

When I arrived at my parents' home on Park Avenue, my little boys ran to me and said: "Where's my Daddy?". I could not answer them; I could only hold them in my arms and cry as if my heart would break. It was the saddest of Christmases. I did not know it then, but it would be two more Christmases before we would see my husband and their daddy again. During the long separation I never let the boys forget their daddy. I talked of him often showed them pictures of him, read his letters to them, and told them of the plans he had for our great reunion some day. Tearfully, I wondered how long it would be?

* * * * * *

We boarded the <u>USAT SHAWNEE</u> at 2:00 P.M., on December 23, 1941. the men of Company "D", were quartered in the deep part of the ship. The carpenters had not cleaned up their mess leaving this for the troops. Only one door served the troop compartment and Corporal Blake was worried: "Gosh, Lt., if a German sub sends a torpedo through us there's no way of getting out of here. This is a death trap." I had to agree. We had heard of many ships being sunk by German submarines in the Caribbean and with all the troops aboard, we would be a good target. I hoped spies would not report our departure from NOPOE.

Claustrophobia seized the troops; they were jammed almost shoulder to shoulder into the dark recesses of the ship. Lt. Dale Johnson, the Executive Officer, called the officers and NCOs together and organized a method for getting out of the hellhole in case of an emergency.

"Look, men", he said, "we are in a hell of a mess. Our men are jammed in here like sardines and they will not be able to take this very long. They are very reasonable about it now, but how long can we expect them to bear these terrible circumstances? Something has got to be done and done quickly."

Lieutenant Hanshaw and I, along with First Sergeant Knowles and the other senior NCOs went to work, showing great concern for the men. We gave encouragement as we assigned them to their bunks, and posted guards throughout the ship to keep men from entering restricted areas. The other officers returned to their own quarters while I took the first shift as an officer on duty. The men were grateful that I stayed with them. Later, after Lt. Hanshaw relieved me and I went to my own quarters, stateroom #206, I had a guilty feeling, when comparing my luxury with the crowded unventilated limited space the men down in the dark bowels of the ship. I vowed that I would be with the men as much as possible in spite of the luxury afforded me. My cabin-mates were Lt. Daniel D. Holliday from Beckley, West Virginia, and Lt. R. A. Holoday, a former Illinois state trooper. I noted the similarity of names of my cabin-mates. However, Holliday, was later moved to the cabin occupied by Lt. O. C. Thompson of Bluefield, West Virginia, who was temporarily commanding Company "H", during the absence of Captain Erman Wright.

After getting squared away in my quarters, I returned to the troop area finding the men very uncomfortable for lack of ventilation; it was stifling hot. Bringing the matter to Captain Thompson's attention, he authorized taking a few men at a time up on deck for a breath of fresh air and continued doing so until all of them had their turn. The men were grateful. We were still moored to the pier and the lights of New Orleans beckoned. Later, returning to my cabin, I played cards until dinner with Holiday using the top of a foot locker as a card table, retiring early, after once again visiting the men. My last thoughts were of Wilma and the boys before sleep; I realized I would soon be at sea far away from my loved ones. The future ahead was questionable. However on, December 24th at 8:00AM we were still moored to the pier and some of the ship's provisions were sitting on the dock. Shortly, the provisions were on board and the ship came to life, the crew active. A tug hooked onto the Shawnee, her engines turned, and her screws churned, leaving a wake of swirling water behind. We headed down the great Mississippi, or "Old Man River", as the ballad says, and out into the Gulf of Mexico. At dusk we were on deck watching the dear old United States disappear over the horizon. Soon it was dark, and the ship's captain ordered a complete "blackout". We were in the Caribbean known to be infested by German submarines, so an attack was possible. Again, I thought of the men jammed in the dark, unventilated hole and how vulnerable they would be if we were hit by an enemy torpedo. Returning to my quarters with Lt. Hanshaw, I found a Christmas Card on my bunk from my brother, "Buck" and his wife, "Boots." It was good to know someone had thought of me. Then I thought of Wilma, all alone on her way to Charleston, not aware of her extreme stress and difficulties she was experiencing. I must have had a premonition: silently, I said a prayer for her; there was no other way I could have helped her now.

Christmas day on the high seas was hardly noticed, but I thought often of Wilma. I didn't know if she had arrived safely in Charleston to be with our boys for Christmas. Later I found she had difficulty and did not arrive as expected because of a mixup in the train schedule. I felt helpless not being able to look after my family. It would be almost three years before I could as it turned out. It was comforting she and the boys would be near family and friends, however.

Having had breakfast, I strolled out on the deck to enjoy the tropical sun; it appeared we were heading directly east. Were we headed for North Africa? Then on "C" deck I heard Corporal Thomas singing Nearer, My God to Thee giving me the chills for the great ship Titanic went down while the passengers were singing that hymn. More and more of the men joined in singing and, finally, I sang, too. Chaplain Williams, the regimental chaplain, read from the Bible. Later in the day we had boat drills and test fired our anti-aircraft guns and the anti-submarine deck gun. We changed from winter to cotton tropical clothing. It would be years before we would don the wools again. After dark, we watched a movie, all wearing life jackets. Life Jackets were the order of the day. We had to wear them except when we were in our bunks and then they must be near us. Lights could be seen in the east - could it be the Cuban coast?

On December 26, I had a good shower. Hot water was available from 7:00 - 8:00 A.M. daily. My daily routine was a four-hour shift with the men in the hole of the ship. First Sergeant Darley Knowles had established a company headquarters, the nerve center of the company. Lt. Hanshaw inspected the troop compartment for policing and cleanness. Pfcs Buckland and Fizer had not eaten in two days and were unable to walk, having bad cases of seasickness. Corporal Blake had the men carry them up on the deck for fresh air and medical attention. Meanwhile, we managed to get some ice water for the men to drink and hot water for shaving and washing; they appreciated this. Later we took them up on deck where they joined Buckland and Fizer for fresh air, sharing the insufficient deck space with other troops organizations, who also were suffering from the stifling heat; we rotated to deck from quarters for all could not be on deck at the same time. I was relieved by Lt. Hanshaw later in the day.

Early on the morning of December 27, while enjoying the tropical breeze on "A" deck, a ship was spotted on the horizon. Was it friendly or was it a German pocket battleship capable of cutting us into? Nervously, we watched as its outline revealed it to be a freighter. We were aware, too, that the Germans did use freighters, outfitted with concealed navy guns, that could very well sink us. Nervously, we still watched. Using binoculars, ship's officers watched the ship for any aggressive signs as the two ships narrowed the distance. Was the ship friend or foe? - no national colors were displayed. Our deck gun crew prepared for action if it became necessary to return fire at the mystery ship. Sergeant Knowles carefully watched the ship through his binoculars. He said it was heavily armed. The ships passed within a mile of each other but no aggressive action occurred.

The lights of Cristobal were observed at 7:45 P.M; we were nearing the entrance to the Panama Canal and safety from the German subs. The Shawnee took a position behind the breakwater wall and dropped anchor. We would stay there for the night enjoying the warm tropical night the bright stars twinkling over us.

After breakfast the Shawnee headed for the canal at 8:35 A.M., entering the Gatun locks at 8:55. Six electrical "mules" hooked onto the big ship, two pulling, two in the rear, and one on each side giving the ship stability preventing scrapping the sides of the locks. Passing through the locks, the electrical "mules" were cut loose and we were eighty-five feet above sea level, riding the surface of Gatun Lake, heading for the Piedro Miquil and Miraflores locks for Balboa on the Pacific side of the Canal. In between we passed through the Culebra or Giallard Cut. What a marvel of engineering! It was a "big ditch" cut through hills and jungle permitting big ships to be raised and lowered through the canal amid strange birds and tropical growth seen from the ship's deck. We were agog, for many of us had never been on a ship and now, we were in the Panama Canal, the construction of which exceeded our imagination. Dale Johnson said it for all of us: "And we don't have to pay a damn cent for the trip", commenting on the beauty of the tropics. We laughed at his comment.

Finally, we were gently lifted down to the Pacific Ocean by the Piedra Miguel and the Miraflores locks, having enjoyed the canal trip ending at Balboa, near Fort Clayton in the early evening.

Fort Clayton's buildings were stucco, painted white, with red tiled roofs, and surrounded by glistening palm trees. Its spacious parade grounds, post exchanges, golf courses and clubs would be our home, could be seen as we passed through Pedro Miguel locks. For an outfit who had never lived in anything but tents, and after the maneuvers in the swamps of Louisiana, Fort Clayton looked like a haven, for the "Powderhorns".

Disembarking at Balboa, hundreds of troops waited on the piers and streets, being shuttled back to Fort Clayton by the antiquated Panama Railroad which was built between 1850-65. Finally, about 11:00 P.M., Company "D" detrained in front of Fort Clayton. The full tropical moonlight reflecting from the palm trees surrounding the white buildings of the fort portrayed a dream world. What tropical beauty! What splendor! A tropical paradise! We stood in amazement, wondering why we were being favored so well by the Regular Army, who had evacuated the place to accommodate us. A quartering party, consisting of Lt Dale Johnson and NCOs from the platoons of the company, who had left the ship at Miraflores locks to survey Fort Clayton, met us and led the company to its quarters. Marching into the interior of the fort, stopping at our buildings inside the quartel, the full moon still bathing us in its tropical splendor, we could not believe what was happening to us. Here we were from the hills of wonderful wild West Virginia, the tents of Camp Shelby, and the swamps of Louisiana-unbelievable! We wondered what price, if any, we would have to pay for our tropical haven we had inherited from the RAs.

Getting the men squared away in their "heavenly rest", the company officers, Captain

Thompson, Dale Johnson, Hanshaw, Hager, and I, took off for our quarters in a dwelling recently occupied by an officer and his family. All dependents had been returned to the United States because the canal was being placed on war footing. Our quarters was sparsely furnished, each officer having a steel folding cot, a dresser, a table and chairs, two officers to a room. The officer's row was on the edge of the golf course, near the country club and a swimming pool. We were getting a glimpse of what the peacetime army was all about. Even though we would live in splendor at Fort Clayton, our duties would be long and hard, but for an outfit fresh from the Louisiana swamps, we knew nothing but long hours and hard work with little recreation facilities, living in tents, with insects of all types chewing on us.

The Commander of the Panama Canal Department had things for us to do preventing sabotage of the canal, its airfields, locks and dams. Our work had already been cut out for us.

So, delighted we went to bed shortly after midnight, thinking of our newly acquired haven of rest. However, returning to check on the men after breakfast the following morning, we were met by many complaints.

"What the hell's the matter with you guys?" inquired Lt. Johnson.

"Hell, Lt.", said Knowles, the First Sergeant, "it's the damn bedbugs. They picked us up and threw us out last night. Really, the men took their blankets, left this bug-infested place and slept out on the parade ground. Something must be done quickly. We cannot live under these conditions."

Immediately, we had a meeting with Captain Thompson, the company commander, to remedy the terrible situation. We inspected the men's quarters and found bedbugs hanging in globs on all of the mattresses.

"Now we know why the Regular Army gave us this barracks", said Rabel. "Hell, they couldn't live here themselves."

We called Colonel Charnock, at Battalion Headquarters, and he said the entire area was infested, which necessitated a call to post Headquarters to correct the situation.

Thus our first "overseas battle" was with the bedbugs. We forgot about the Germans, the Japanese, the spies, and the saboteurs, as we tried to save our necks from the bedbugs. The battle raged back and forth and little-by-little we became the victor, leaving millions of the bastards dead throughout the battle area. Once again we resumed the normal duties required to get ready for what lay ahead. Dale Johnson had to put a cap on the battle by suggesting to Captain Thompson that maybe the War Department would issue us a ribbon for winning the battle against the bedbugs. "Captain," he said, "maybe we could call the ribbon for devoted service above and beyond the call of duty during the battle against the bedbugs of Panama." Thompson grinned, but did little else; he wasn't much for levity.

CHAPTER 12

SECURING THE PANAMA CANAL

Having won the battle of the bedbugs, we got the men back into the barracks and settled into a routine, but in a strange environment. Within a short time we, the "Powderhorns" had the responsibility of securing the vital Panama Canal, performing transit guard duty, and securing the airfields in Central and South America, a type of duty foreign to anything that we had ever done before. This would be the lot for the famous "Powderhorns", the 150th Infantry, during WWII; the regiment would never hear a shot fired in anger. Even though the regiment itself would never see combat, many of the men did, having been transferred to units in Europe or the Southwest Pacific Area. A few even became generals and many to field grade and lesser rank officers.

Daily, we were awakened by the bugle at 5:30 A.M., formed for reveille at 5:45 and had breakfast at 6:30. Our first day, December 29, 1941, was very informative. All of the officers attended a meeting at Theater #1, conducted by senior officers from the Panama Canal Department, updating us on the world situation.

The war was going badly for the Allies. Rommel, the great German Field Marshall, called the Desert Fox, was on the loose in North Africa, hammering the British at Tobruk. Concurrently with the defense of Tubruk, the British Eighth Army was regrouping in Egypt under General Claude Auchinleck, preparing to counterattack "the Fox". Lieutenant General Masaharu Homma, the vicious Japanese Army commander, had landed his 14th Army on the northern and southern shores of Luzon in the Philippines and was driving on Manila, and would capture the city three days later on January 2, 1942. As the United States reeled from these savage blows in Asia, the British Army, under General Sir Arthur Percival, would later find itself out-flanked on the Malayan peninsula, surrendering seventy thousand men to the Japanese in the worst military disaster ever suffered by any European nation in the Orient. Making matters worse, we were told that we had lost eighteen of the thirty-five B-17 Flying Fortresses at Clark Field in the Philippines as well as fifty-six fighters and twenty-five other planes during another sneak raid while the Japanese lost only seven aircraft. Further, the briefing officer stated, the British Navy had lost two capital ships, the Prince of Wales and the Repulse, on December 10 north of Singapore, leaving the Japanese navy almost unopposed in the Pacific. This would possibly make the Panama Canal a lucrative target for the Japanese. It would be our job to help defend the canal already surrounded by airfields in South and Central America and in the canal zone itself. We would be placed on a wartime footing just as though we were going into battle in North Africa or even the Philippines. To prepare us for the tropics we were told that we would get some jungle training immediately. Dale Johnson whispered to me with his usual wit: "Hell, Jordan, don't they even know we have already won the battle of the bedbugs; we're not neophytes." Dale could cheer us up under all circumstances, and we certainly needed cheering up that day.

There was no doubt about it. Panama Canal was considered a prime target by the Germans and the Japanese, and we would be in the center of any attack that enemy launched. If the Panama Canal was blown, draining Gatun Lake, the canal would become a forty mile long useless dry ditch. Our war effort would be set back many years so every means must be contrived to defend it - in conjunction with other military units this would be the "Powderhorns" wartime mission. The defense of the canal was even more critical than any combat mission assigned to any other military unit during WWII. The 150th Infantry, the "Powderhorns", who had performed so well during the 1941 Louisiana Maneuvers, would be split up and assigned to guarding airfields in South and Central America, as well as the dams and locks of the Panama Canal Zone. In addition the Canal Zone proper had to be secured against sabotage from within, a great concern of the Commanding General of the Panama Canal Department, and authorities in Washington. There were two other infantry regiments, the 5th and the 14th of the regular army, in the PCD even before our arrival, as well as the 2nd Field Pack Artillery, and coast artillery units.

Among the possible avenues of sabotage were from the ships passing through the canal. A German or Japanese agent, placed aboard a ship, regardless of the flag, could easily blow up the ship while it was in one of the chambers of the locks or in the Gaillard Cut, closing the canal indefinitely. To preclude this possibility, a military guard detail, the Transit Guard, was placed aboard all non-military ships using the canal, including American ships. Soldiers were placed throughout the bowels of the ships to keep a critical eye on the crew, any one of which might or could sabotage the ship. A guard was even placed on the bridge to insure that the orders of the pilot were carried out even if the captain should refuse. Furthermore, except for performing inspections, the officer of the guard was always on the bridge of the ship.

Under these circumstances, relations between the military personnel and ships' crews were often strained, especially when we were aboard American ships. Even though we were often invited to have lunch with the crew, the invitation had to be declined by orders from the PCD. The men brought their own sack lunches prepared by their respective unit kitchens. There was a time when ship's food was accepted by guard members, but this was forbidden after the captain of an American ship, showing his displeasure, billed the PCD for the cost of the food he gave to the members of the guard even though an invitation had been issued by him.

Members of the Transit Guard aboard ship were on a high alert during passage of the locks or through the narrow Gaillard cut, the critical spots of the canal. Once through the locks and the cut, and having entering Gatun Lake, members of the guard could relax, for sabotaging the ship in the lake would have little effect on the canal. However, once the ship approached either of the locks, members of the guard resumed their posts and went back on high alert until reaching the breakwaters either on the Atlantic or Pacific side of the canal.

Ship Transit Guard duty was very boring, but the men of the 150th Infantry "Powderhorn" Regiment, were dedicated, knowing the importance of their worked and performed in an excellent manner. Not being permitted to speak to a member of the ship's crew or the passengers for fear that the guard would be distracted and an act of sabotage could occur during the discussion, they were obedient. This was difficult for the passengers to understand, especially the American passengers. Usually, the "Powderhorn" soldiers were the first Americans seen by the passengers returning from overseas assignments. So they were overjoyed to see any American, especially a soldier. Naturally they wanted to talk to the American boys. American servicemen had recently died at Pearl Harbor and were now dying in the Philippines, so the feeling of patriotism among the passengers was high. Thinking that any soldier could be sent to the Philippines, the passengers felt sympathy and concern for the young Americans, whose future was in doubt.

The members of the Transit Guard, dressed in a starched cotton, form-fitting uniform, standing at parade rest at his post, shoes spit-shined, clean as a pin, weapon glistening in the bright sunshine, was the epitome of what a soldier should be; the American women were so proud of them, especially the older women. They assumed a motherly attitude toward the young homesick soldiers. They liked to think that the boys could be their very own, most of whom were about 23 years of age. This kind attention had to be ignored, the soldier apologizing, "Sorry ma'am, I'm on duty and unable to talk to you now." The passengers just couldn't understand why the American soldier could not talk to another American. It was difficult for both the soldiers and the American passengers. However, when we reached the Gatun Lake, this restriction was lifted and the men could talk to the passengers, but only a short time; they needed rest before entering the locks or the deep cut.

Escorting ships through the canal, one learns much about the crews and their country of origin. The Scandinavian and Dutch freighters were the cleanest, while the British, American, and Grecian ships were the filthiest. All the ships' masters were polite and hospitable, except for some Americans. The American ship masters failed to understand the need of the security guard aboard their ships saying: "We are Americans; why do you have to treat us like foreigners?" They did not realize that, any one member of their ship's crew, could be an enemy agent and sabotage the ship while in transit or could drop an explosive device in one of the locks exploding after the ship had left the locks. On one occasion it was necessary for the soldier on the bridge to actually aim his rifle at a group of sailors, aboard an American ship, who almost rioted, disobeying the captain's orders while in Gaillard Cut. Once they saw the rifle aimed in their direction, the unruly crowd departed which brought an end to the riot. The guard had orders to fire at will, should he feel that an act of sabotage was about to happen. He had no time to investigate; he would have to fire first and ask questions later. To my knowledge this was the only time anything like this happened to the Transit Guard and I was grateful such an incident never happened during my watch.

The Greek ships were most interesting, their sailors having a custom, even though revolting to a queasy American, was acceptable to them. While escorting the Greek ship, Aspasia, through the canal, a trip lasting almost twelve hours, an unusual thing happened. While observing from the bridge, I noticed group of Greek sailors assembled forward around a bunch of tethered goats or sheep. The Greek sailors, having empty tin cups, were sitting around as if waiting for something to happen. The guard, alerted, kept his eye on the group as I did, but the Greek captain, nearby, appeared to be calm and collected, putting me at ease. Than a sailor, perhaps a ship's cook, joined the assembled crew members. Taking a butcher's knife the man slashed the throat of one of the animals, and blood began to flow. Each of the men took turn filling his tin cup with warm blood and drank it down as an American would a cup of coffee. Soon the struggling animal was dead. Later it was explained that this was the custom aboard ship, the men drank the blood instead letting it drench the deck. The dead lamb or goat, would later be dressed out and become a part of the fare aboard ship. This was a practical thing for the deck would not have to be swabbed, and the men could have their tin cup of warm blood. I would soon have my opportunity to participate. Shortly, a neat and clean waiter, in his white apron, appeared with a silver tray holding three goblets of blood, one for the captain, one for the pilot, and one for me. As a representative of the United States Government, I was served first, but I readily declined - it was revolting, drinking warm goat's blood! I made an excuse saying "Blood doesn't agree with me." The captain, knowing full well what I meant, laughed. The pilot also refused, but the captain drank his cup of blood with gusto.

During the transit duty, escorting ships through the canal, it was necessary to stay overnight either at Fort Davis on the Atlantic side or Fort Clayton on the Pacific side of the canal, and then return the next morning to our respective stations via the Panama Railroad. The railroad extends between Colon and Panama City, a distance of 47.61 miles. Built in 1850-65, it follows the course of the Chagres river from Gatun to Gamboa and took fourteen years to complete; it was the first transcontinental railroad in the United States. It was an essential factor during the construction of the canal, and an important adjunct to its operation. It was equipped with 90 lb rails, rock-ballasted track, and automatic signals, using antique American rolling stock.

Crossing the isthmus on the railroad was very interesting. The railroad bed cut a narrow track through the green primeval jungle, making it a tourist paradise where one could observe wildlife and vegetation with an occasional view of Gatun Lake. The scenes were very primitive as seen through the windows of an old 1876 coach still having suspended kerosene lamps swaying from the ceiling. The engine was very small and of a vintage type; we dubbed the train the "Tunnerville Trolley." Even though it took over twelve hours to escort a ship through the canal, the "Tunnerville Trolley" took only an hour and a half to travel the same distance back.

When we were not performing transit guard duty, the officers had other functions to perform - such as Officer of the Guard or Officer of the Day. This duty was in conjunction with the interior guard of the Canal and other critical military installations. The Officer of the Guard directly commanded the interior guard under the direction of the Officer of the Day who in turn was responsible to the Regimental Commander. It was a large guard with sentry posts scattered throughout the Pacific side of the Canal Zone. Each relief had a corporal and a sergeant. The Sergeant of the Guard remained at the guard house, organized the guard detail into reliefs and handled the administrative functions. The men were highly alert, and even nervous, as they walked their lonely lengthy posts, especially during the hours of darkness. They took extreme precautions, and officers inspections had to be very cautious when approaching the posts. When doing so they had to properly identify themselves, or they would be arrested until they were properly identified. Once I found myself in a precarious position and almost was shot by the alert guard.

While inspecting the guard late one

night, I had the driver take me to an outlying area near the tank farm, where millions of gallons of fuel were stored. The tank farm was located high on a hill overlooking the canal. Riding in an open command car with a noisy engine, we began our approach. I was not aware of the exact location of the post nor was the driver. As we followed a gravel road into the hill, I wondered how insecure the poor guard occupying that lonely post felt in this out-of-the-way place. I was thinking how exposed the one-man posts were and that perhaps we should have two men instead of only one on the outlying posts. While thinking about this, not realizing what danger we were getting ourselves into, the driver came to a screeching halt. "Lieutenant Jordan, did you hear a challenge?" His eyes bulging with fright, looking ahead toward the darkened jungle. I did not hear that challenge, but I sure did hear the one that followed, and quickly dismounted.

"Halt!", the guard screamed! "Who are you?"

"Officer of the Guard, here, Lt. Jordan." I quickly replied hearing the bolt of the guard's M1 rifle slam forward, chambering a round in weapon.

"Advance to be recognized, sir." I could see the form of Private First Class F. L. Vermillion, Company "D", a silhouette between me and the horizon, with his rifle at the ready.

Cautiously, I made my approach and stopped at his command: "Halt! Advance to be recognized. Stop, please! Place your ID on the ground in front of you, sir." Removing my identification card from my wallet, I placed it on the ground in front of me and awaited further instructions from the alert sentry. "Now, sir", he said politely, "please step back three paces leaving your ID on the ground." Wordlessly, I did. Vermillion came forward with his lit flashlight focused on me as he stooped to pick up my ID and compared the photograph with my features: "Identified, sir", he said and presented arms to me.

Congratulating Vermillion for his alertness and courtesy, I apologized for racing into his post area and thanked him for not firing when he could have (Frank Vermillion was a member of my wife's church, the Mormon Church in Charleston, and I often had attended with him before we came to Panama).

"Lt. Jordan, your rapid approach to my post was most unusual and I felt, not realizing it was you, that someone was attempting to crash into the tank farm and I really was prepared to fire. I'm thankful you stopped when you did."

"So am I, Vermillion." And we laughed about the incident, even though it was a life and death situation. He could have shot both of us and would have been exonerated for doing so; the tank farm, like the locks below, was a critical installation and took precedence over human life if it had to be that way.

Later, a new second lieutenant joined us fresh from the states. While he was performing an inspection of the guard as Officer of the Guard, and I was Officer of the Day, accompanying him, and perhaps wanting to impress everyone, he grilled each sentry on post asking about his general and special orders and made a fool of himself, attempting to impress the soldier. We were on the north end of the Pedro Miguel locks which protruded far into the dark Gatun Lake. The sentry performed as Vermillion had on the tank farm post, halted us, identified and advanced us. His courtesy was the best.

After all of the preliminaries had been completed and we should have departed the post, the new lieutenant continued to ask silly questions.

"Soldier", he said, "what would you have done had I not stopped when challenged?"

"I would have called the corporal of the guard, sir." said the irritated sentinel.

"Then", the shave-tail continued, "what would you have done had I not stopped on your second challenge, soldier?"

"I would have called the corporal of the Guard, again, sir?

At this the lieutenant appeared to be angered. "Why in the h_____would you call the corporal of the guard after the second challenge when I could have killed you before he arrived?"

Mustering all courtesy he could, the sentinel, Pfc King, said: "Just to haul your dead butt out of here, sir."

The lieutenant then realized there was much for him to learn and, to my knowledge, he never made another inspection of the guard except when subordinated to the Officer of the Day, who made occasional inspections of his own.

The "Powderhorns" of 150th Infantry meant business; if they were exposed to great danger from possible lurking saboteurs they shot first and asked questions later.

While performing duty as Officer of the Day it was necessary to be on the locks while a ship was passing through. On one particular day, a Navy convoy consisting of seventeen ships, under the command of a commodore, a rank abolished in 1899, but temporarily restored during WWII, was beginning its passage through the Pedro Miguel locks. As I was observing from the control tower, and after the six "mules" had tied onto the ship and had towed it into the first chamber, water rapidly raising the navy ship to the level of the lake, I noted navy personnel taking pictures; an act FORBIDDEN!

Calling the Regimental Headquarters at Fort Clayton, I reported the unauthorized picture-taking: "Unless instructed otherwise", I said to the operations officer, "I intend to detain the navy ships until all cameras are collected, film removed, and placed under lock and key."

"That is normal procedures", said the operations officer."Go aboard and inform the senior navy officer that his ships are in violation of PCD regulations, but apologize for the necessary delay. Remember, be diplomatic while dealing with a sister service," I was instructed. "You may be dealing with an admiral and he won't take kindly to an army lieutenant telling him how to run his navy." Then we laughed. Quickly, I had a flashback of an incident that happened during the Louisiana Maneuvers the year before when I was almost court-martialed, being accused of insubordination and disrespect to a superior officer. I reasoned that I was about to embark upon a similar situation and that I had better be careful. I resolved to be ever so polite to the navy commander, whoever he was. He was sure to explode when I would tell him I was detaining his ships.

Instructing the civilian operator of the lock to hold the ship in the chamber until I had made satisfactory arrangements with the Navy, I proceeded down the stairs to the ship and requested permission to come aboard the flag ship presently in the chamber. Once aboard I was escorted to a commodore, the convoy commander.

Reporting, saluting, giving my name and official position, I said: "Sir, Lt Jordan, Officer of the Day, desires to report that personnel of your ships has been observed taking pictures of the canal installation, a violation of PCD regulations."

The incensed commodore tartly replied: "Lieutenant, we are on a wartime mission, and being Americans, we do not intend to sabotage the canal by taking a few pictures. Now please give the tower instruction to continue getting us through this canal. We do not have time to discuss such a trivial matter."

"I'm sorry, sir, your ship and the others waiting for passage through the canal will not move until the cameras are impounded and placed under lock and key in a central location."

The irritated commodore demanded that someone of higher rank give him the order before he complied, saying I was overstepping my authority.

"As you wish, sir, but your ship will

not leave the chamber until all the cameras are collected and under lock. However, if you wish, I will have an officer of your equal or higher rank tell you what I have been telling you." Then I invited the commodore to accompany me off the ship and together, in silence, we headed for the control tower. Calling operations at Fort Clayton informing the officer on duty of the Commodore's desire and action was initiated immediately.

"Lt. Jordan, hang up the receiver and stand by." came a terse reply from the operations officer. Soon the telephone rang and the tower operator answered and handed it to me.

I don't recall the name but I definitely remember the rank. "Lt Jordan, this is General __________, deputy commander of the PCD. Explain the situation to me, would you please." I gave him a blow by blow description of what had occurred.

"Thank you, lieutenant. You did a good job today. Please let me speak to the commodore, if I may." The general was as calm as a cucumber. I handed the telephone to the commodore and, from what I heard, it appeared the navy commodore was having his rear end chewed out by the army general, for his answers were: "Yes, Yes, Yes, General. I will comply General." The Commodore handed me the phone saying, "The General wants to speak to you, Lieutenant."

"This is Lt Jordan, sir."

"Lt Jordan, the commodore assures me he will have all cameras collected from his ships and placed under lock and key aboard his flagship. Please board his ship and remain until he assures you that all cameras have been collected and secured. Then, before you release his ships, please call me here at PCD and inform me that the commodore has complied with PCD regulations. I know you will not have personal knowledge that all ships have been searched and cameras removed, but you will just have to take his word for it, and I don't think you will have any problems enforcing the PCD regulations. Thanks again for what you have done."

Thanking the general, I followed the now very polite commodore aboard his flag ship. He issued instructions to all ships to collect and bring all cameras to the flagship for storage: they would be returned to the owners once the ships were on the high seas. It took a while, so I stood in silence on the bridge among navy officers whose stern unwelcome looks spoke their silent anger toward the army lieutenant who had the brass to hold up a navy convoy. Eventually, I was tersely and officially informed that all cameras were safely aboard the flagship. Ending my vigilance, extending my appreciations for navy's cooperation, I left the flagship and signaled the control tower to continue lock operations. Just once, as an army lieutenant, I held power over the sister service for a few minutes, anyway, tweaking the navy's salty noses, maybe causing its brass to blush.

Since high priority duty was required of the "powderhorns", we were restricted to the confines of Fort Clayton. There were movies, post exchanges, and, of course, the beer joints provided so the soldiers could relieve their pentup tension.

Because of this restriction, going to church was one of the more popular things to do. Each Sunday morning, church call was sounded by the bugler and the Regimental Band would play under the direction of CWO Dick Ramage. One beautiful Sunday morning at Fort Clayton, the bugle sounded church call and the band began to play ONWARD, CHRISTIAN SOLDIERS. The music rumbled through the quartel and over the parade ground; the "Powderhorns" soldiers, all dressed in their best cotton khaki uniforms, came running from all directions, forming in four ranks. Once formed, they did a right face, and with the band leading and still playing ONWARD CHRISTIANS SOLDIERS, we marched to the post chapel. Marching to the hymn was an experience in Panama that I still pleasantly remember. The hymn was a good marching tune and the men looked proud as they entered the chapel in single file while the band continue to play outside the chapel. The band ceased playing and Chaplain Williams, once everyone was settled, began the service. Some of the toughest soldiers I had ever seen were in the bunch. Some had never seen the inside of a church before, but they attended diligently thereafter, even Peacock Jones of the "short arms inspection" fame.

During the sermon, Chaplain Williams prayed for the United Sates Navy, which was about to engage the Japanese Navy in the Battle of Coral Sea. It was May of 1942; the aircraft carrier, being relative new in naval warfare, was about to receive its baptism of fire. The Japanese had sent an invasion fleet down past the Solomon Islands and into the Coral Sea. It would soon be met by Australian and American warships under the command of Rear Admiral Frank Fletcher. Fletcher had at his disposal the two big flattops, the Yorktown and the Lexington. The result of this navel engagement the first of many sea-air confrontations that became a phenomenon peculiar to the Pacific war between 1942 and 1945.

The engagement began between the two naval powers, but out of range of naval guns because the ships never came close enough to exchange fire. As naval aircraft swarmed overhead, anti-aircraft guns blazed, bombs fell and torpedoes came flashing out of the tropical sky and from below the surface of the blue Pacific. The Japanese navy, after two days of battle, was forced to turn back and Australia was saved from the Japanese. Later, Port Moresby, in southwestern New Guinea, became the advanced base for MacArthur, the starting point for the long, island-hopping campaign that took him back to the Philippines and onward to Japan four years later. The battle was even in ship losses; the Japanese lost their carrier, Shoho and we lost the Lexington.

NOTE: Years later, following the battle of the Coral Sea, Bob Lawson, of Johnson City, Tennessee, a friend of mine, a crew member of the Lexington, told me of the great ship's death throws. His remarks are paraphrased: "We were badly damaged, listing exceedingly, and on fire. We were beset by interior explosions and finally the order to abandon ship was given. Leaving a ship, knowing it was sinking, was like loosing a close family member; the Lexington had been our home, our security, and her crew, our family. The great ship had hovered over us as a mother hen would over her baby chicks, protecting us, and we loved her as one would his mother; we knew we were loosing the home and family we had grown to love, even that was terrible. But the worst was yet to come. While standing on the deck of the Yorktown, tearfully watching the great ship slowly slip into her watery grave, unbelievingly, I watched in tears. It appeared she was telling us, her children, to continue serving our country well, and finally, she disappeared. But then as we continue to watch, even after she had "went below", sea water boiling over her grave, a miracle happened; one of the seaman screamed in agony: 'O! my God!' Before our eyes, the great ship slowly resurfaced as if to beg for life. We were on deck of the Yorktown, all were audibly crying as if our hearts would break. The great ship lingered, still on its side, there were no hope for her recovery, and would be a menace to other ships. The battle was still raging and the outcome still in doubt; the Japanese pilots were pounding us while the Americans pilots were trying to drive them from the sky.

'Sink the Lexington!'. "Ordered Admiral Fletcher."

"The crew member were informed, and we prayed, tears still drenching our faces. Then the escorting destroyers and cruisers, using their deck guns and torpedoes, blasted holes in our beloved ship, and we watched as she once again slowly slipped to her final grave, stern first. Seeing our ship go down and then returning to the surface, as if giving us a final farewell, was more then we could hardly take. Our own navy was dealing the final death to our loved one, the Lexington. She was a proud ship. Even though we served on other ships the remainder of the war it was never like being on the Lexington. I will never forget her."

During a tour as Officer of the Day, I had a very interesting experience in August, 1942. The aircraft carrier, Hornet, passed through the canal. Since I had never seem a carrier before, it was something to behold; it was the largest ship to pass through the locks. It was an impressive sight since its flight deck, extending over the sides of the locks, had knocked down a light-post, causing the "mules", or the six tractors, to adjust the lines bringing the Hornet more to the center of the locks' chambers. It will be recalled that Colonel Doolittle, (later a general), launched his famous raid on Tokyo from the deck of the Hornet in April 1942. The pilot could be heard issuing instructions to the crew over the carrier's communications system. Had the vessel been only a few inches wider the canal could not have been used, forcing the vessel to round the horn of South America instead. The life of the Hornet, however would be short. It went down with its sister ship, the Wasp, in the Naval Battle of Guadalcanal on November 12-15, 1942.

Our troops suffered from isolation and boredom. They had to be on duty two out of every six hours while maintaining the security of the canal. I had to endure the same treatment; this constant duty made us all weary and very homesick. One day I received a letter from my brother, Doc, telling me that our father was very ill and not expected to live suggesting that I return to Charleston as soon as possible. Immediately I requested, and received approval, for an emergency leave. Quickly, I packed and headed for the airfield. Taking a civilian contract plane, a freight plane, a DC 3 aircraft, of the Banriff airline, having only a plane engine aboard and another officer as a passenger, we began the flight through the high mountains of Central America. The plane was not insulated, without heat, and I was wearing only a thin cotton uniform in temperatures well below freezing, the trip was most miserable. I was glad when the plane arrived in Brownsville, Texas. After thawing out a bit, and after refueling the plane, we took off for Cincinnati and from there I completed the trip to Charleston by train.

It was a joyous occasion to see my little family again, but sadly, my father died shortly after my arrival, passing away on August 2. After the burial, I called Colonel Monroe, the new Regimental Commander, requesting an extension of time and, surprisingly, he granted me two additional weeks leave. I never was so grateful for such kindness. Even though I had lost my father, I did have time with my family. I would not see Wilma or the boys again until July 1944. I would spend a total of thirty three-months overseas serving in the jungles of Panama and in New Guinea under conditions almost unimaginable.

After returning to Panama, I was given command of the Madden Dam. Like the locks, it, too, was a very critical installation. Should the dam be blown, Gatun Lake would be drained, making the canal a muddy ditch and useless. In addition to our manning the machine guns posts, we also walked sentries, and had listening posts. Anti-aircraft batteries were near to prevent an air attack. We were all members of Company "D", 150th, Infantry, the "Powderhorn", numbering a total forty people. As they had been on the locks, the men were always in a high state of alert and, if necessary, shoot first and asked questions later. The following are some of the incidents that happened while I was there:

One morning a sentry found a civilian in an area that required special permission or clearance to be there. The civilian was an employee of a contractor doing work on the dam, but without clearance from the guardhouse. However, the civilian employee wearing an identification tag probably saved his life. The sentry instead of shooting him, marched the "culprit" at the point of his bayonet, to guard headquarters for questioning. As it turned out the "culprit" had been ordered by his boss to do whatever he was supposed to do, and after a lecture of possible consequences of future violations, released the poor scared man to his boss, to continue doing what he what he had been doing. We were thankful that nothing, except the dignity of the "culprit", was injured. I often wondered who this well meaning "culprit" was and it wasn't until forty seven-years later that I found out. In recent years past in Knoxville, Tennessee, a friend, LaRue Styles, and I were discussing my assignment in Panama as Commander of Madden Dam and he suddenly interrupted me.

"Did you say you commanded Maddan Dam in 1942?"

I assured him that I had.

"So, you're the guy that had my butt punctured with a bayonet when I was found in a restricted area of the dam without permission from the officer in charge of the guard."

"Holy Mackerel, Styles, was that you?"

"It sure was, and I was only doing what the boss told me to do. That soldier almost shot me that morning, and from what he said, he could have shot me and nothing would have been done to him for shooting me either. Instead, he stuck his bayonet in my rear end and marched me, with my hands overhead, to the guardhouse, where I was released to my boss."

What a coincidence! Here, years later, a friend and a fellow church member, was the "culprit!". One of the finest men I have known could have been shot by a member of my guard command. We laughed, but, at the time it really was a serious situation; the common sense of the West Virginia soldier probably spared Styles' life.

Another occasion, a drunken off duty sailor, almost lost his life at Madden Dam, but saved by the unauthorized action of the Sergeant of the Guard, Frank Corley. It was a Sunday morning when the sailor, driving a civilian car, came to the barrier across the road over the dam. Only official vehicles were permitted to cross the dam because the road was dead end. The guard explained the situation to the drunken sailor, but the man took his life in his own hands, gave full throttle, crashed through the barrier and headed over the long dam. There were two manned water cooled machine guns, one on each end of the dam. They lined up their sights on the speeding vehicle and were prepared to open fire when into the gunners' view came a jeep following the car. Sergeant Corley was standing up in the passenger side of the jeep, using his pistol, taking pot shots at the speeding car in front of him. Again, thanks to the level-headed West Virginia machine gunners, who withheld their fire, Frank did not join his honorable ancestors along with the drunken sailor. Frank did chase down the sailor, arrested him, brought him to the guardhouse and called the navy headquarters in Balboa. Later, a shore patrol came to take the drunken sailor to the brig. Frank was overzealous. He had saved the man's life, but he could have easily died while trying to be a hero. He knew the machine guns had orders to fire on anyone forcing their way across the dam, yet, he had placed himself in dire circumstances that could have very well cost him his life.

Following my tour at Maddan Dam, which I enjoyed very much, I was called to be the Adjutant of the 1st Battalion, commanded by Lt. Col. John N. Charnock, stationed at Fort Clayton, near Pedro Miguel Locks. The post had all the conveniences, such as the post exchange, officers club, golf club, swimming pool, and nice quarters. It was also the site of the "Battle of the Bedbugs" which we had so valiantly fought after arriving there in December before. My good friend, Dale Johnson, and other officers were stationed there, too. We could look over and see the ships passing through the locks while sipping our soft drinks in our quarters, or watch the parade performed by units stationed at Fort Clayton. We had become accustomed to the routine and, when not on duty, we did what we wanted with our time. The only requirement was that we be available in case of an emergency. Usually the schedule was two hours on and four hours off, so we had little time do anything.

As the adjutant, I had more flexibility while carrying out the orders of Colonel Charnock, the now first battalion commander, which he issued through me to the battalion at an early morning conference in his office.

Every morning, following breakfast at the Officer's Club, I would find the Colonel in his office reading the paper, ready to fill my day with every detail he could think of. Then he would continue to read his paper, twisting his moustache, with his feet still propped up on his desk while the sergeant major and I labored in the outer office to carry out his orders of the day. Since we had an almost father-son relationship, I often had personal conversations with him, some of them quite humorous, he liked that, but I never took advantage of our relationship. One morning, he had written several sheets of work to be done during the day, I kidded him:

"Colonel, why is it every morning I come into your office, you have your feet propped up on the desk, reading the paper, while twisting your moustache, and you still continue to read your paper, and I end up doing all the work around here?" I would normally have never said that to anyone of his rank, but he liked to kid me and I gave him my share in return. Here he saw a teaching situation and he taught me a lesson that I use even to this day.

"Lieutenant, remember this." he said. "While in a position of authority, commanding men, never do anything when you have others around that can do it. If you do otherwise, you are not doing your job. You must think, plan the course of action and delegate to others. Give them the tools, keep them pointed in the right direction: check and double check: and you will always be successful as a leader. If you do this, you will not have time to do a subordinate's work. Remember this!" And he continued to twist his moustache, with his feet still propped up on his desk, peering at me over his paper, and then continued reading. From that day on, I have followed his wisdom and it works. I'm thankful to him, who has since passed on to his reward, for the knowledge and example he imparted to me over the years that we had served together. Unfortunately, the army never had enough of this kind of leadership during the war.

What a remarkable person!

CHAPTER 13

THE BUSHMASTERS

It was December 7, 1942, a year after the disaster at Pearl Harbor. I was having breakfast at the regimental officers' mess at Fort Clayton when the Regimental Adjutant, Captain Elmer C. Newman, took a chair near me. Ordering from the menu he then focused his firm attention on me.

"Ben Rod", he said, "your are being transferred to the 158th Regimental Combat Team (Bushmasters), and must report there tomorrow morning. Furthermore," he continued, "you are being promoted to the rank of Captain, effective immediately. The new regimental commander, Colonel Stackpole, extends his compliments to you for the long and honorable service you have rendered the regiment. I personally would like to express my appreciations for having the pleasure of serving with you." He further said I had been relieved of my duties as the Adjutant and Intelligence Officer of the first battalion and that I should began preparing to travel to join the "Bushmasters", who were stationed at Camp Chorrera, located several miles outside the Canal Zone in the Republic of Panama. Newman suddenly changed the subject as if my move to the "Bushmasters" wasn't a big thing even though I had been with the First Battalion of the "Powderhorn" regiment since February 1935 and knew practically everyone in the regiment. Many of them were like brothers to me, while Colonel Charnock, the commander of the battalion, was almost like a father. I was speechless for I realized I would now be among others who were complete strangers to me.

Once settling down I realized my transfer to the "Bushmasters" would be a welcomed change. It was evident that the 150th (Powderhorns), even though performing a vital war duty guarding the canal, would only do just that. They would continue to perform guard duty throughout the war. Nothing is more boring, but the "Powderhorns", as the Regiment was known, would be safe from war's harm. They would fight no battles with bullets. Most soldiers wanted to get into the big show and now my chance had come; the "Bushmasters" had been alerted for shipment to the South West Pacific Area (SWPA). Colonel Charnock remarked:

"If it's combat you want, you're going to the right place."

I spent the day visiting friends realizing it could be the last time I would see them for the "Bushmaster" Regiment was involved in an intense jungle training in the interior of Panama; I would have little opportunity to see my comrades before departing for the south West Pacific Area. The "Bushmasters", were also undergoing reorganizing and re-fitting in preparation for the move to the SWPA. Many of the "Bushmasters" officers and men, who were considered physically unfit, were being transferred out and replaced by the likes of me.

Along with 1st Lt. Garland C. Brady, an old friend, and also a longtime member of the 150th, I reported to the 158th Regimental headquarters on Monday at Camp Chorrera. Brady was later killed in North Africa in 1943. I don't recall when or why he had left the "Bushmasters", but his departure must have occurred shortly after we had reported for duty at Camp Chorrera. His presence was never noted after that and I often wondered why he had left the regiment.

I reported to Captain Ross Allen, the Regimental Adjutant, and he in turn reported my presence to the Executive Officer, Lt. Col. Wilson B. Wood. The Regimental Commander, Colonel J. Prugh Herndon, was in Washington on official business. Colonel Wood, a tall, large person, very friendly and cordial, put me at ease as we sat in his office and talked about the future. He said that the "Bushmasters" had been alerted for duty in the SWPA based on a request from General MacArthur; we would depart for Australia in a matters of days and there was much work and training to be done before our departure. Furthermore, he continued, hundreds of replacements were reporting from the 5th and 14th Infantry Regiments, many of whom were very dissatisfied with their new assignments. He said the men from the 5th and 14th had been looking forward to going home since they had been in Panama many years, even before the war, and had not seen their families since leaving the states. Later on this situation would create serious morale and discipline problems with the RAs (Regular Army). These poor devils, many of whom had already been alerted for shipment back to the states, had their orders changed for combat duty in the SWPA instead, and transferred to the "Bushmasters". Sadly, they came to us with morale and spirit deflated. Many, like others of the "Bushmasters", would die in the jungles of New Guinea, New Britain, Kiriwina. Wakde-Sarmi, and the Philippines without ever seeing their loved ones again. These men were good soldiers in combat, but I've always felt the army did them a disservice in not allowing them to go home for a short leave before sending them to fight in the SWPA. One of these men reported that he had just boarded the ship when he was suddenly taken off and sent to the "Bushmasters". He never forgot this, but he later proved to be a good combat soldier.

Since the regimental commander was away, Colonel Wood did not issue me a permanent assignment, temporarily sent me to join the Headquarters and Headquarters Company, 1st Battalion, commanded by 1st Lt. Joseph R. Welke, the acting company commander. While there I assisted him in the preparation for shipment of their organizational equipment and training of new personnel received from the 5th and 14th Regiments. His outfit was undergoing growing pains for it had been a small detachment having only a few men before, but was now a full-blown company, having a communications platoon, an anti-tank platoon, and an ammunition and a pioneer platoon. The latter two were the result of a new type of organization now included in an infantry battalion.

While watching Welke struggle, I opted to be given command of a rifle company for here I would have more flexibility in command. In a Headquarters Company, the company commander, in a tactical situation, was not only the battalion adjutant, handling the administrative affairs of the battalion, but had to disperse units of his command at the directions of the battalion commander. such as communications out to the companies, the dispersal of the anti-tank platoon, and utilization of the ammunition and pioneer platoon to operate the battalion ammunition dumps, and doing minor construction as needed, and building small bridges, etc. Each of the platoon leaders actually became a special battalion staff officer working under the direction of the battalion commander. However, this was as it should have been since the Headquarters Company Commander, as adjutant, was responsible for the arrangements, security and the interior operation of the Battalion Command Post (CP) while in combat, had enough responsibility. If he did his job well, the entire battalion would be more combat efficient, relieving the Battalion Commander of many details so he could devote his time and attention to the combat needs of the operations at hand. In addition to receiving filler personnel from all over the Canal Zone, new equipment was dumped upon Lt Welke, all of which had to be checked, crated, and prepared for overseas shipment. Since Regimental Operations wanted us to be combat effective, they directed special training, day and night, for us, which was in total conflict with the demands of the Regimental Supply Officer, Major George Colvin. He wanted progress reports of our readiness for he had received word that the ships to transport us to the SWPA, were entering the canal on the Atlantic side, and we must be prepared to load within a few days. It was almost a mass confusion, trying to train while at the same time preparing our equipment for shipment. The confusion continued; the operations officer required special training while the supply officer required supply functions. Each countered the other; there were no evidence of staff coordination and we wondered about the regiment's staff functions in SWPA where the bullets would fly in both directions. Would divine intervention be available when we would make our first contact with the "Sons of Nippon" in New Guinea? We would need it if regimental staff functions weren't coordinated better. Luckily, things got better once the new and the old got acquainted.

A few days later the regimental commander returned from Washington and I was notified to report to him. The Adjutant, Captain Allen, had me take a seat and wait while the regimental commander was interviewing another newly arrived officer. Shortly, thereafter I was ushered into the presence of the "Bushmaster" commander of whom I had heard so much. He had a reputation for being a strict disciplinarian, often inflicting group punishment for the unsoldierly acts of a few. Since I had to wait a few minutes while he shuffled papers, I recalled what I had heard about him:

Since the regiment was an Arizona National Guard Unit, it had many Indians and Mexicans in its ranks. The Indians called him "the old sunnatabichi" while the Mexicans called him viejo soldado in Spanish, or "the old soldier", according to Anthony Arthur in his book about the "Bushmasters". An example:

when a few men of the regiment went on a drunken spree in Camp Barkley, Texas, he forced 3000 of his them, in full field packs to march many miles without water, as punishment. Arthur further stated: "Prugh Herndon's approach to military leadership was discipline, not friendship, charm, persuasion, or logic." What a comparison to that of Colonel Eubank, the former commander of the 150th Infantry Regiment (Powderhorns), who, even though firm, saw to it that we received due recognition and absolutely never permitted group punishment, but God help the culprit who did commit a breach of military discipline and courtesy. We knew how we stood with Eubank but never with Herndon. We had a fatherly respect for Eubank, but only fear of Herndon. Herndon showed no respect for rank when it came to mass punishment. My battalion commander, and other senior officers, including me, and 3300 men of the regiment, would soon become a victim of one of Colonel Herndon's group punishment for the sins of a few.

A group of the Indians "Bushmasters" went on their usual payday sprees shortly after I had arrived at the regiment. Our punishment for their behavior was a twenty-mile march without water in our canteens and with full field packs. Only one command car was permitted - Colonel Herndon's. Halfway though the march, he stood up in his command car drinking ice water as we passed by "spitting cotton balls"; we were suffering from extreme thirst. One of the Indians in "F" Company said in a whispered voice, "the old sunnatabichi"; a Mexican nearby called him "the old soldado", while a caucasian called him "the old son-of-a-bitch". All laughed at the deserved expletives. My opinion was ambivalent.

The colonel's idea was to have members of the regiment to keep each other in line to avoid group punishment. He would later be unfairly relieved of command by General Patrick at the Battle of Lone Tree Hill, the battle for Wadke-Sarmi island.

The colonel by this time, as I waited, had completed shuffling papers, had me move to a chair near his desk. The stockily built, graying commander, coldly began the interview, emphasizing his words with frequent waves of his hands, a half grin on his face with an icy cold stare that seemed to bore right through me.

"Captain Jordan", he began, "we have been designated for the SWPA and this conversation must be considered confidential. We are to spearhead an offensive in the Pacific perhaps someplace in the Solomon Islands." He jabbed at a map of the SWPA behind his desk as he updated me on the military situation there, stressing the high degree of leadership he expected from the officers and non-commissioned officers of the regiment. I felt his coolness as others had had before me.

Then the conversation centered on me. What about my experience? I informed him that I had been trained on heavy weapons and communications, and had been in command of Madden Dam Guard, lock security, and transit security, and my last assignment had been as Battalion Adjutant and Intelligence officer of the 1st Battalion, 150th (Powderhorns)

Infantry. Surprisingly, he offered me command of Cannon Company, being redesignated as the Mortar and Anti-Tank Company. Since I had no previous experience with this type of organization, I requested he reconsider and give me command of a rifle company instead. He did reconsider, and because of my experience as adjutant of an infantry battalion and as an intelligence officer, he assigned me to take command of the Headquarters and Headquarters Company of the 2nd Battalion. I was to report to the Battalion Commander, Lt Col Wilson B. Woods, the acting Regimental Executive officer, who was nearby in the building.

Colonel Woods, a likeable fellow, was again very cordial and our conversation was pleasant. After a few minutes of briefing concerning the 2nd Battalion, he instructed me to report to the battalion executive officer, Major Henry C. Hornhorst, a potato farmer from Idaho. Immediately, I reported to the Major, a very stockily built, ruddy-faced, but friendly officer, who welcomed me to the battalion. Lt. John Pavlich was the acting commander of Headquarters Company, and was glad when I showed up to relieve him of all the same details that Lt. Welke was undergoing in the 1st Battalion Headquarters Company. Pavlich would become my executive officer and, as such, I would delegate to him the responsibility of preparing all company equipment and vehicles for shipment overseas with the assistance of Lt Allen, the company supply officer. With this delegation of responsibility, Pavlich went from the skillet into the fire, so to speak. His duties, previously easy, would become the center of major effort, while I rode over him and Allen with a firm hand.

"Holy Mackerel, Captain", he quipped, "I thought when you came I could take it easy."

"Delegation is the key John, delegation.", I said, "Delegation is the name of the game and I suggest you do more of it. I will only delegate and supervise, but you, as the executive officer, will see to it that the work is done. Just make sure the men understand what they are to do while you do the planning and supervision. That will be your job." That was all Lt Pavlich needed. Once I pointed him in the right direction and gave him the tools and personnel for a project, John carried it out to the best of his ability. Preparing the organizational equipment for overseas shipment was a good example.

The delegation technique was something Col. Charnock had taught me: "As a commander", he admonished, "never do anything when you have others to do it. To plan well and supervise will be your job. You'll be a failure if you don't". He was a wise man.

The excellent work of Pavlich and his crew, preparing the organizational equipment for shipment for overseas, relieved me of a major effort enabling me and the First Sergeant, Spencer D. Dixon, to prepare the men for the pending embarkation. In the meantime we made sure the men got the necessary shots and dental surveys, assigned them to positions in which they were more capable to serve, reorganize the detachment into a full-blown company, and doing whatever training we could do. It was made clear that Pavlich and Allen, with their supply crew, were never to be assigned to any type of duty other then preparing the equipment for overseas shipment.

When I reported to Major Hornhorst in the company mess hall just before lunch, I had the pleasure of meeting other officers of the battalion and company staff. In addition to Pavlich and Allen, there were Capt Pursley, the Operations and Training Officer (S-3), from Safford, Arizona (later replaced by Robert C. Caffey also from Arizona) and 1st Lt. Jennings B. Whitten, the Intelligence officer (S-2), from Quinimont, West Virginia, my home state. Also in attendance was 1st Lt Robert R. Feagan, Supply Officer (S-4), from Louisa, Virginia. While we were having lunch together in my company's mess hall, and the officers were kidding me about the big job I had just inherited, I reminded them they were my guests even though I had assumed my position only minutes before, and I expected them to assist me in the many administrative details facing me. They all laughed at my trite remark, and agreed they would assist. We would be together for many months to come and be like brothers.

After lunch I called a meeting of all company officers and non-commissioned officers. Requesting a status of incoming personnel from the 5th and 14th Infantry Regiments, I found that little had been done to assign them to compatible positions. When I asked why, Lt. Pavlich said they thought it best that this should wait until after I had arrived to make the assignments permanent. Asking about the status of readiness of equipment for shipment overseas, again Pavlich said he lacked information from the regimental supply officer. It appeared all I was getting were excuses and I realized I was going to have a major problem on my hands unless something was done immediately. So I made the immediate assignment to Pavlich and Allen, and representative, from the Communications, the anti-tank, and the pioneer and ammunition, and headquarters platoons, to get on with the preparation of equipment for overseas shipment, working night and day, if necessary. Lumber for crating, saws, hammers and nails were to be procured immediately so work could begin. Furthermore, I directed the First Sergeant to form the company so I could meet each individual man, check him as to his appearance and assign him to an appropriate position within the company. Later when the First Sergeant formed the company in the company street, I was amazed at the sloppy manner in which the men fell into ranks. Instead of running into ranks and coming rigidly to the position of attention, as we did in the old 150th (Powderhorns), they moped into ranks, some even having cigarettes in hand, as if to say "well, here I am, what do you want?". Sergeant Dixon, after receiving reports from the platoons reported: "All present and accounted for, sir."

Sergeant Dixon, who himself, had reported for duty only a few days before, appeared to be as dissatisfied with the formation as I was.

"Sergeant Dixon, are you satisfied with this formation?"

"No, sir, I'm not."

"Sergeant, what do you think is the

matter?"

"Captain, sir, these men have never served together and many have low morale, especially the new men from the 5th and 14th Infantry Regiments. Some of the men have been in the jungle so long they have forgotten how to form quickly when the whistle is blown."

"Sergeant", I said in a low voice, "that is a good summation. What do you think about doing it right beginning now?"

"How so, Captain?"

"Sergeant, you know how to form the company before reporting to the commander. Now instruct them, then dismiss them and then immediately reform them and see to it that it is done properly."

The sergeant smiled, saluted, and did about face as I walked away, giving him a free hand.

"Now listen to this!" he said to the men, who perhaps were wondering what the conversation between the company commander and the first sergeant was all about.

"You guys walked into formation like a bunch of old washer-women. From now on when I blow this whistle, all I want to hear is the patter of little feet and see a cloud of dust in front of me. Don't you ever forget. Company dismissed!"

I watched, with glee, from a distance as the Sergeant blew his whistle. The formation, even though much better than before, did not satisfy the stern sergeant. Several more times he dismissed the company and reformed it. Finally, he did an about face and reported to me as I took my position in front of the company, and he said: "All present and accounted for, sir."

From that day on First Sergeant Dixon, like Sergeant Rhodes in Old Company "D", had good soldierly formations in a timely manner and the men gained pride in their unit.

After the First Sergeant gave his report, he took his post and the officers took positions in front of their respective platoons, while the platoon sergeants took their positions in the right rear.

"Prepare for Inspection," I ordered, and the platoon leaders gave the command "Open Ranks, March!" This command formed the company with space between ranks permitting the command party to pass between the ranks for the inspection of each man, his weapon, his person, and his uniform. The men did not have their weapons with them, but I had another purpose in doing this.

Accompanied by the First Sergeant, who took notes, and Lt. Pavlich, the Executive Officer, I wanted to meet each man individually, to inquire of his welfare, his family, his problems, and if he had his assignment within the organization. Furthermore, I wanted to assure each man that the army did care about him. It was then we began to become a family, for the men knew their welfare would be my personal concern. I asked many questions specifically about writing home, how long had the man been in the company, and if he had any questions. I singled out the men recently transferred from the 5th and 14th Infantry Regiments; the regular army men often called the National Guard "tinhorn soldiers" or "weekend warriors", and now were a part of the NGs.

Feeling my initial appearance and attitude would effect their future attitude toward me as their commander, and the company, I wanted to be firm but understanding with them; unlike the Regular Army officer who felt that familiarity between officers and enlisted men only breeds contempt, remaining aloof from their men. I did not agree with such an attitude, but instead, strived to create an attitude of "one for all and all for one", working together as a team; it had always worked for me.

The RAs, mostly from New England, stood out from the rest of us, for they spoke a dialect different from the men of the Arizona NG or the filler personnel drafted and sent to us were from the midwest. Also RA's bearing were more military as well as their military courtesy toward officers, while the NGs were less formal, but yet acceptable. The RAs, such as Sergeants Bauters and Abbott, and Corporals Bergeron, Crum, and others, seemed to respond favorably to their strange environment, and from that time on were some of the best soldiers. They felt that the company was now their home and family, accepting their responsibilities as good soldiers should. Like all organizations, there were a few rotten apples that remained with us and had to be dealt with occasionally for breaches of discipline.

From that time on the morale of the men climbed, training effective, men were assigned to appropriate positions, and completion of our reorganization from a detachment to a full-blown company was accomplished. We became the best, whether in garrison or in combat.

Often, even in Australia since we were a company with the responsibilities for the battalion's communications, ammunition supply, operating the ammunition dumps and transporting same to the front, and for the battalion's anti-tank defense, we trained even while the rest of the battalion rested in Camp Cable near Brisbane. The executive officer, Major Hornhorst, took great interest in what we were doing often accompanied us in these concentrated training exercises. It was a splendid organization, and would later prove itself so in the presence of the enemy.

We progressed very rapidly. Lt. Beane's communications platoon, the battalion's nerve center, had great enthusiasm, and the platoon sergeant, Sidney Cochran, implemented his ideas, expediting the platoon's progress. All units of the company acted on their own initiative without being goaded, accomplishing much. All subordinate leaders kept abreast of the situation and were ready to fulfill their duty.

Shortly after our reorganization, training had to become secondary, for embarkation for the SWPA was close at hand. More pressure from Colvin; "Get ready, get ready, time is short! Get your equipment manifests in!", he implored, so we worked day and night, Pavlich screaming orders and instructions. Allen procured lumber, nails, and wire while the men built the crates, packed the equipment, prepared the vehicles, switchboards, and communication wire. What little training was done was conducted by Lt. Tompkins, the P&A Platoon leader. Soon the pressure was lifted and Pavlich handed me a copy of the manifests listing all of the box numbers and their contents. He, Allen, and their crew, did a remarkable job preparing the organizational equipment for overseas shipment. Everything was packed and created and deadlines were met. In fact, John had the manifests in the hands of the Regimental Supply Officer, before any other company. To their credit they did it primarily on their own, requiring little supervision from me.

Now that the pressure was off, we planned a big party for the men. The party was to be held in the mess hall with beer, sandwiches, and candy, the Regimental orchestra playing for our entertainment; we even had a magician, a "Bushmaster", from Company "H". In accordance with regimental policy, all of the men had to be dressed in freshly laundered cotton uniforms and be clean-shaven. They had to conduct themselves in a military manner. All battalion headquarters officers were invited as well as Colonel Herndon, the Regimental Commander, and Lt. Col. Wood, the Regimental Executive Officer and our former Battalion Commander. Also, in attendance was Major, later Lt. General Frederick R. Stofft, from Tucson, Arizona, who had just arrived from Third Army, Fort Sam Houston, Texas. He was to serve as our new battalion commander. We had a wonderful time and Colonel Herndon, the victorian, the disciplinarian, the stickler for detail, who insisted everything must be done properly, requested my permission to speak to the men. He was very complimentary, saying that if the company was as good as the party, we would win over the Japs hands down.

This was unusual for him since he seldom ever said such complimentary things; we were very happy.

During the party we learned that Major Stofft was a pal of John Wayne, the movie star, had attended UCLA and had played football there together, and that he had played bit parts in some of John's movies. We would later meet the famous actor on New Britain island a year later.

Shortly after the company party I participated in the twenty-mile water-less march, as previously described; our last training activity in Panama. Two days later, on January 2, 1943 the ships that would take us to the SWPA entered Gatun Locks on the Atlantic side of the Canal Zone. Again we went into action checking men and other last minute preparations. Surprisingly, more equipment was dumped on us at the last minute, all of which had to be crated and manifested. While Pavlich and his crew worked crating the new equipment, I had to transfer money in the company fund from currency to money orders at the Chase National Bank in Balboa. The long line at the bank kept me from attending to very important company functions. However, the unit performed well during my absence working under the direction of the Executive Officer, Lt Pavlich, and First Sergeant Dixon. When I returned we were prepared to load on trucks, move to Belboa, and embark on the waiting ships.

The "Bushmaster" Regiment began loading aboard ships on January 5 at 8:30AM. While leading my convoy of troops from Camp Chorrera to Balboa for loading aboard the Dickman, I experienced a lonely feeling thinking of the past, especially of Wilma, Bucky and Johnny, back in Charleston, who had no idea I was heading for combat in the SWPA. I thought, too, of the men of the 150th with whom I had served since 1935. I was now with others I hardly knew, but we had forged a tight bond of brotherhood during the short time we had been together.

When would we return home? Or would we ever return home? And what would happen to our families in the meantime? Even though I was riding with several hundred troops I felt all alone as I listened to the monotonous hum of the truck's engine.

Arriving at Balboa, I returned to reality. Many troops of previous convoys were being lined up and checked aboard their respective ships. Soon it was time for my company to be checked aboard the Dickman. By late afternoon all "Bushmaster" troops were aboard ships. A guard was placed at the gangway and no one, officer or enlisted, was permitted to leave the ship unless on written official business.

Then I had surprised visitors. Colonels Charnock and Hamilton, Major Paul Guthrie, Captains Dale Johnson, Lts Hagar and Hanshaw, Sergeant Knowles, "Tac" Jones and others of the old 150th came aboard to see me. Major, later Colonel Guthrie, my wife's brother, informed me he had been given command of an infantry battalion in the 14th Infantry Regiment. Perhaps he would soon become a Lt. Colonel, the normal rank for a battalion commander. I kidded him about members of his battalion being transferred to my unit and in jest I said, perhaps I could make good "Bushmasters" of them.

Colonel Guthrie became the commander of one of the finest combat infantry battalions of WWII, the first American unit to penetrate the celebrated Siegfried line, opening the way to the heart of Nazi Germany. For his heroic effort he received a high decoration and later would be assigned as the G-2 of the United States Eighth Army in Korea.

After a time of joviality, my "Powderhorn" friends said their goodbys. We of the old 150th Infantry, had come a long way together and now realized we faced a long separation. I would not see them again until the end of the war and we were back in Charleston as civilians. A long, war torn road still lay beyond the Pacific horizon. The ravaging enemy soldiers of Nippon must be defeated. MacArthur had stopped them in the Solomons and in New Guinea, but the issue was still very much in doubt. What part would we, the "Bushmasters", play in this drama? How many of us would die, making our wives and small children widows and orphans?

NOTE: Many years later Colonel Guthrie's recommendation for promotion to Brigadier General was sidetracked by inter-service bickering. Colonel Guthrie, as G-2, United States Eighth Army, refused to alter his procedures for reporting of critical information given to him by highly reliable sources within the South Korean Government. A certain federal agency did not accept that, feeling the colonel had additional resources beyond their means and so blacked balled him. As a result of pressure from this agency the

Department of the Army withdrew its recommendation to the United States Senate for confirmation, denying him the promotion he so rightly deserved. Guthrie, a most capable officer, retired from the army, somewhat disappointed and perhaps disenchanted. The army lost a very capable officer who could have given many more years of superior service.

CHAPTER 14

FROM POLLIWOGS TO SHELLBACKS

Leaving the breakwaters of the Canal Zone the following morning, we were joined by several other ships, and a naval escort, taking a southwesterly course across the Pacific Ocean. Hopefully, in less then thirty days we would have joined MacArthur on the other side of the world. The large convoy, scattered over a large area of the ocean, often changing directions to confuse any lurking Japanese submarines. Men lined the rails of the Dickman watching the land mass of Central America disappear over the horizon leaving us only the blue Pacific waters to enjoy; it was a lonely feeling. Four days out, we passed some very beautiful islands with large green mountains in the background. Whitecaps of water peacefully lapped the sandy shorelines, and coconuts trees, gently swaying in the trade winds, decorated the island's edges. It was very picturesque. Using binoculars, we watched the young natives girls in their sarongs, all who looked as though they had no worries of the world, and seemed to be happy meandering on the beach and between their grass shacks, and paddling their outrigger canoes. I was reminded of Dorothy Lamour, the movie star, who often played the part of a beautiful South Sea native girl, with a flower in her long black flowing hair, wearing a sarong, teasing Bob Hope and Bing Crosby. We wondered if the natives on the island even knew a war was raging over the world.

The islands, like Central America, disappeared over the horizon; once more we had the deep blue waters of the Pacific as our only companion. Often we lined the rail of the Dickman and watched the ships zig zag from time to time attempting to escape from any enemy submarines that may be chasing or lurking to ambush us. The Hermitage, a captured Italian ship, much larger than the Dickman, would be on one side of us than shortly be on the opposite side. It was marvelous just how the navy could control so many ships avoiding collusion during the zig zagging maneuvers. This being our only diversion, it too became boring. But the navy had other plans for us, that for a time, would replace boredom.

Crossing the equator the Navy initiated us into the Society of "Shellbacks." Until that time we had been known as "Polliwogs" (those of us who had never crossed the equator).The name change was made by the mythical King Neptune who came aboard to administer an initiation, a mandatory ritual, for all who had never crossed the equator; a time honored event.

King Neptune and his royal court came aboard after much preparation. The ship's captain played the part of Neptune, while navy officers made up his court. As navy officers, they intended to see the army "polliwogs" were initiated properly, and that they did, in our opinion, too well. It was brutal. They used a wide paddle, applying it enthusiastically to the rump of the unfortunate "polliwog" as he crawled through a large flexible hose while water was being shot into both ends from a five inch high pressure water hose. They had constructed a "jail" of steel wire, built to prevent a man from either sitting or standing incarcerating a "polliwog" who was foolish enough to refuse the initiation. The high-pressure water hose was trained on him while confined to "jail" until he agreed to go through the ritual. Many of the soldiers hid, attempting to escape from the torment, but were hunted down and forced to participate or go to "jail" for the water treatment. Once he "agreed" to crawled through the two-foot flexible hose, and survived the high-pressure water treatment coming from both ends, being paddled on the rump while doing so, he was about ready for the undertaker.

There were more. A large vat, with three chairs hinged to the top and filled with water, was placed before King Neptune's throne. The three occupied chairs were hinged on the edge of the vat so they could be tipped backwards, dumping the "polliwogs", head first into the water upon the decree of King Neptune. The dip into the water did not occur until after the "polliwog" had his hair nicked by untrained navy barbers, cutting a strip of hair from the center of his forehead to the nape of his neck and then from ear to ear, plus having few jolts of electricity administered to his rear end than pushed backwards into the water filled vat head first. Once we "polliwogs" were in the tank burly sailors would duck us until we said, "Shellback", then having said the secret word, we were unceremoniously thrown out of the tank onto the deck. We then, thanks be to Deity, became crusty "Shellbacks."

The problem was, we didn't know what to say, and the navy men would keep yelling: "Say it, damn it, say it!". We were unable to say what they wanted us to say. So down we would go time and time again. Finally, after continuous dunking, nearly drowning us, the "polliwog", they whispered ever so tenderly: "Say, Shellback", and we gladly complied; then they threw us out the vat onto the deck. Here, King Neptune, Roman God of the sea, crowned us "Shellbacks". The navy had finally gotten its licks in for my tweaking their salty noses in Panama the year before. Like elephants, the navy never forgets. Later we were issued certificates, indicating we had crossed the briny deep at the equator. This would prevent us from having to undergo another initiation at some other time. Nor would I ever again tweak the navy's salty noses, either.

Even though we were crusty "Shellback", our hair was a mess. Captain Barnes and I visited the ship's barbershop for remedial action by the ship's barbers, but there no barbers. Even though we had never cut hair we decided to try our luck, cutting each others hair. That was a bad mistake; we only added to the already terrible condition of the head of hair we carried on our shoulders. Even the Navy could not have done worse. That evening, during dinner in the ward room with fellow officers, who, also, had had their hair nicked during the initiation, we were judged to have the worst hair nicking job aboard the ship; all laughed at the comic condition of our barbering results. Colonel Herndon, seeing the butchering we had done to each other's hair, issued an edict that, hence forth, no unqualified barber would cut the hair of another.

With little activity of an entertainment nature, boredom became a major factor for us to contend, since the initiation. Now that we were "Shellbacks", we still had a long way to go before we would arrived at Brisbane Australia. Hopefully, our hair would recover from the butchering it had received at the hands of the Navy so that we would be spared any further humiliation when we met our Australian brothers of war. They liked to poke fun at us "Yanks". Hopefully, our posteriors would be healed by then enabling us to take a seat without experiencing pain in, well, you know where. All of us complained about the black and blue bruises on the unmentionable parts of our body, and the pain we had received in graduating from "Polliwogs" to "Shellbacks". We wondered if it had been worth it. One thing for sure we intended to keep the little cards in our billfolds showing our status as "Shellbacks" if ever we had to cross the equator again on a Navy ship! Hoo Wee! We wondered if the Japs would treat us as badly.

We had been on the high seas many days now and the men were becoming restless. We were fed twice daily, which served as a welcome break - not that we were all that hungry it did help pass the time. We scheduled an hour of physical training and an hour of school each day. I was assigned to instruct the officers in Japanese aircraft identification, comparing the enemy's planes to those of American. Movies were shown on the deck at night and the chaplain conducted services on Sundays. We crossed the

International Date Line on a Saturday, so we lost Sunday and the chaplain conducted no service; we complained. He then had church call sounded and we attended church on Monday.

On January 24, nineteen days after leaving Panama, we entered the harbor of Gnome, a seaport on the island of New Caledonia, a French possession. We looked forward to visiting Gnome, but unfortunately, all personnel, except the Regimental Commander and staff, were restricted and unable to leave the crowded ships. We were informed that the colonel had to make a courtesy call on the French Governor General or High Commissioner, and would return soon.

We departed Gnome the next morning for Brisbane, Australia, with our scheduled date of arrival being January 31. Leaving Gnome harbor, we met a large US naval task force consisting of battleships, aircraft carriers, cruisers and destroyers, that seemed to reach from horizon to horizon. It was most impressive; the thought of such a powerful force engaging an opposing force of equal strength would be overwhelming. Should this occur, the battle would be fought without the opposing ships ever seeing one another, due to extreme range of naval guns and naval aircraft.

Australia was now just over the horizon, so we became anxious and wondered if we would have rubber legs once we stood again on solid ground. We played cards in the ward room, sang songs, told jokes and listened to Australian radio and learned the Australian National Anthem, Waltzing Matilda. We learned of the fall of Buna and Gona to the 32nd and the 41st Infantry Divisions after many days of battle; Americans suffering a great loss of men to enemy action and malarial fever. I had made a lot of friends in the 32nd while I umpired for them during the Louisiana maneuvers in 1941, and I wondered how many had survived the strange battle. We heard that General MacArthur ordered General Eickelburger to Buna and Gona and stay until the battle was won or not come back alive. Until General Eickelberger arrived, the battle was going very badly for the Americans. The General relieved the division commander and many senior officers, including many battalion commanders, then again the attack was made and the battle was finally won.

Early Sunday, January 31, while strolling on deck in the bright sun light and the blue sky before breakfast, after twenty-six days at sea, I saw the mountaintops of eastern Australia, surrounded by white puffy clouds. What a magnificent scene! Herein lies some of the oldest land mass of the world, with remnants of prehistoric animals, and populated by friendly people called "Aussies". I pictured it with great admiration and felt that an objective of my life had been achieved, for I had always wanted to see this land. I was joined by others and soon the whole deck was covered by men gawking at the beautiful sight. Many men crowded the port, or left side of the ship, and the vessel began to list. The loud-speaker blared, warning us to move to the center of the big ship before it capsized and guards was placed to keep us dispersed. My curiosity satisfied, I went to the ward room for breakfast, and later to my cabin to pack. We were preparing to disembark later in the day and a lot of work had to be done to get the men ready. I called an officer's and NCO's meeting to discuss the procedures for leaving the ship, even though we were still several hours away. With preparations started and time still on my hands, I joined Pavlich, Allen, Beane, Sgt Dixon, and others, on deck, binoculars in hand, to observe the distant coast line. It was rumored that General MacArthur would welcome us upon our arrival; we were even more anxious.

Arriving at the confluence of the Pacific Ocean and the Brisbane river, we dropped anchor and waited for the signal to enter the Brisbane River on our way to Hamilton Pier in Brisbane. Soon a small cabin boat approached and a pilot boarded the Dickman to guide us up the river. It was six miles to the pier, we were told. It was an anxious trip, for the river's depth at this point was thirty-six feet, while the Dickman drew twenty-six feet, very shallow for the ship of the Dickman's size. The Hermitage, a captured Italian ship, entered the Brisbane river followed by the Dickman 600 yards behind; other ships of the convoy followed in line. We noticed that the water of the river was brown and asked why. We were told that the river was filled with jellyfish which often clogged up the vents of ships. It was peculiar sight.

The Australians lined the river waving at us as we sailed by. "Welcome, Yanks", they would yell. "Come this way to see us while in

Brisbane." It was wonderful to be greeted in such a manner.

We arrived at the Hamilton Pier in the early evening. Col Herndon, his staff, and the battalion commanders, dressed in their best bib and tucker, were on deck to meet General MacArthur. However, to our disappointment, the general was not there to meet the famed "Bushmasters". In fact, no one except officers of the port authorities met us. Only the Australian stevedores, who wanted a handout of American cigarettes, were eager to see the "Bushmasters". The "Bushmasters", caring less about MacArthur, were more interested in teasing the Aussies, threw single cigarettes to them from the ship to the pier while we waited to disembark. The Aussies, dressed in knee length pants, knee-length stockings, and broad-brimmed hats, would scramble like little boys after toys to get the "coffin nails" - the American cigarettes.

At 5:00 P.M., several official sedans arrived, with female drivers, to transport the commanders and staff to the Doombin race track. We would be quartered there for a few days. They returned about 6:00 P.M. with instructions for disembarking the troops. Lt. Pavlich, with a detail from each company, was to clean up the troop's quarters after debarking the ship.

By 6:30 P.M., my company was marching down the ship's gangway, with Colonel Stofft and the battalion staff leading the 2nd Battalion on the march to Camp Doombin, in parade order. We were cheered on by the friendly Australians as we marched along the way. They crowded the streets, waved to us from their front porches or yards, and cheered us with words of welcome. "Hello, Digger", or "This is a bloody hot day, isn't it, cobber", or "We're bloody well glad to see you Yanks here." Teenage girls and boys, riding their bicycles along the line of march, cheered and talked to the men as we marched. It was much like when the people cheered us in Charleston as we marched from the armory to the C & O Depot across the Kanawha River to entrain for Camp Shelby two years before.

However, the men were concerned, for they didn't know if we were being greeted or cursed by the Australian slang. So I explained to them what the words "digger", "cobber" or "bloody" meant, having read from the book of Australian slang words. "Digger", meant soldier, "cobber" meant pal, while "bloody" was the equivalent to "damn". Other words I also explained to them, such as "outback" which means in the country, or "dingy" a dog; "boofhead", a fool; "boozer", a bar; "cop shop", a police station; "dinkum", an honest person; "knackard", a tired person; "wowser", a party pooper; "pisswacker", an animal or insect that had urinated on you; a "prigger", a pregnant woman; "mate", a pal; etc; Already, we were beginning to feel we were home in Brisbane. General MacArthur's headquarters, we were told, were in the nearby Lenin Hotel in downtown Brisbane.

Arriving at the Doombin racetrack about 7:45 P.M., we were disappointed at the facilities available to us. There was a tent city placed on the dustiest spot in all of Australia! Tents were pitched so close together that only a single file of men could be marched between them. The dusty race track was the floor of the tents and there was no dunnage or straw for the men to sleep on or to place their equipment. Thousands of "Bushmasters" were filling the tent city, all facing the same problems. Leaving the company in command of Lt. Allen, I took a detail of men and scouted around. I soon found a pile of tent floors and straw ticks that should have been placed in the tents before our arrival. Quickly, I sent a scout back to inform Allen to bring the men to the lumber pile to carry the tent floors back to our assigned company area before other "Bushmaster" units found the lumber pile. First Sergeant Dixon and several of the men returned with arms full of empty straw ticks that could be placed on the floors to serve as beds and a place for individual equipment. The beds would be uncomfortable, but at least we would not have to sleep in the dust.

Having done everything possible for the comfort of the men, and leaving Lt. Allen still in charge, I searched for and found the camp headquarters, which was in a state of mass confusion. I inquired about messing the troops and was informed that breakfast would be served at the casual mess at 7:00 A.M. I was also told that the officers would sleep in the barn where we could enjoy whatever comforts we could find there. We realized the state of mind of the men, who expected and deserved more than sleeping on a hard board, so the company officers elected to remain with them during our short stay at Doombin. Later, we would move to Camp Cable (named in honor of the first American soldier killed in SWPA) located several miles outside Brisbane.

The following morning, 1 February 1943, I found things even worse than the conditions we had found the night before. Standing reveille at 6:30 A.M., we marched to the casual mess for breakfast, provided by personnel from camp headquarters. There was a line of soldiers ahead of us, mess kits in hand, about a quarter of a mile long, waiting to be served. Hundreds of other soldiers were lining up behind us. It was mass confusion. Walking to the head of the mess line and finding the mess officer, I asked about the confusion and delay.

"Captain", he said angrily; "this is the damndest mess I have ever been in. This is the first time we have served troops at Doombin and I do not have sufficient mess personnel to operate the kitchen and feed all these men. Can you help me in some way?"

For the first time since arriving at Doombin I had sympathy for someone who had been given a difficult task at the very last minute, using untrained personnel and trying diligently to fill hundreds of empty stomachs. Returning to my company, waiting hundred yards away, I searched for and found our company mess sergeant, Sergeant Russell T. Raybourne, and asked him if he would take our own kitchen personnel to assist feeding all the men.

"Captain, sir, this is the best news I've heard since arriving in Australia. Give me a few minutes to get organized and we will have these men fed quicker than the shake of a dead sheep's tail." I wondered how he had arrived at the remark of "the shake of dead sheep's tail", but asked no questions.

Sergeant Raybourne called for his kitchen personnel, asked for volunteers, and they went forward to help out. The line began to move and soon the men were fed. The Doombin mess officer was so grateful.

While at Doombin we went to explore Brisbane and found it to be something like a very large southern country town in the United States. The bars closed at 6:00 P.M. for which we were grateful, for it prevented many hangovers of men who had money to burn after a month aboard ship. Everything closed on Saturday afternoon and all day Sunday except for restaurants and milk bars. Theaters opened at 7:00 P.M. with only one showing; what a contrast to Panama City, Panama, and army towns in the United States, who were all after the soldier's money. Luckily, there was a USO recreational area that operated longer hours. At one time the USO facility in Brisbane was restricted only to American soldiers and their guests until an Aussie soldier, who had very little money, had his girl taken over by a highly-paid American GI. He and some of his pals came one night and wrecked the place. This event had happened before we arrived. General MacArthur wisely ordered the place to accommodate all military personnel regardless of nationality.

The Japanese took advantage of the disparity between the well-paid American GI and the poorly paid Aussie soldier. They dropped leaflets over the Aussies soldiers in New Guinea, depicting them with long beards and ragged uniforms, chasing the black, unlovable female "fuzzy wuzzies" while the well-dressed, clean-shaven, overpaid American

GI was making time with the pretty Aussiettes back in Australia. And this was partially true. The Aussiettes did favor the well-paid Americans, who showered them with gifts, candy and food - something the Aussie soldier could not do on his small pay. The Auzzie soldier was forced to participate in a government saving plan where most of his money was withheld to enable him to have money in the bank when his term of service ended. This is something the American government should have done, too, because of his temporary affluency, the American soldiers affected the morale of soldiers of other countries and at times affected the local economy. The host country often said about the free-spending American GIs, "that they were overpaid, over sexed, and over here", when they complained about the American GIs buying things they urgently needed. Furthermore, scarce commodities that the indigenous people needed were bought up by the Americans. The young girls preferred the GIs and slighted their own low paid soldiers. This caused much contention between our soldiers and soldiers of host countries in which we served. Even though the U. S. Army did encourage the soldiers to save their money by making allotments to banks and families back home, it never forced them to participate. The riot at the Brisbane USO club did cause a change in the use of the facilities but, otherwise, had little affect on the relationships between the soldiers. However, once we were on the field of battle, the animosity disappeared and was replaced by a spirit of brotherhood.

CHAPTER 15

THE BUSHMASTERS MOVE NORTH

Thankfully, our stay at Doombin was short; we moved to Camp Cable about forty miles from Brisbane, a wonderful training site. While at Doombin our equipment, vehicles, and heavy weapons, had not, as yet, reached us, limiting our training to road marches, physical training, and lectures. During road marches, on the outskirts of the city, we were always accompanied by local children and dogs making the marches most interesting. Not only were we cheered by the local people along the way, but the children were fascinated by our friendly soldiers. The men enjoyed giving them and to the adults, candy, chewing gum, and other food they carried in their packs; such items were scarce in Australia because of rationing. Friendly dogs were always present on the marches regardless of where we marched, be it in jungles, on open roads, or in the city. They loved to be with soldiers and soldiers liked dogs; once in New Guinea they made good mutual companions until the bullets began to fly. Then the smart canines scooted to the rear to escort another group of soldiers to the front, something not an option for the dogs' two-footed pals.

The move to Camp Cable via Australian Army trucks was welcomed, for we could not stretch our muscles in the city, so to speak, and Camp Cable would give us the opportunity to whip the "Bushmasters" back into shape after a month at sea.

As at Doombin, our stay at Cable would be short. Finally, receiving our organizational equipment, our vehicles, and heavy weapons, etc., we, wasted no time getting back into shape, both physically and tactically. The "Bushmasters", eager to take on the enemy, prepared diligently for the job we had come to do - sending the Japanese back to the land of the rising sun.

The time spent crossing the Pacific had taken its toll upon our combat effectiveness so we engaged day and night in small unit, company, and battalion size training to regain the sharpness we once had while in the jungles of Panama.

The camp was a good training area with good bivouac areas, kitchens, headquarters building, and latrines already built; the men slept in "pup" tents. Wearing two hats, so to speak, I had to establish two headquarters; one for the battalion and the other for the company. Fortunately, both headquarters could be in one building with Sergeant Sitz being the battalion sergeant major and Sergeant Dixon the company first sergeant, both experts in their field of administration. I was the battalion adjutant as well as the commanding officer of headquarters company, having little time for things other than duty. The battalion commander's office, the executive officer and the adjutant office was in one end of the building, while the remaining staff officers, their enlisted assistants, and company officers shared space in the opposite end of the building, using mess tables as their desks. We were a gregarious bunch. Col Stofft being cheerful, friendly, but a firm commander, was admired and respected; he was a very inspiring officer and because of his gregarious personality, we had an excellent working conditions. The mess sergeant, Sergeant Raybourne, had set up a table in the mess hall for the officers and we could eat with the men. Meal time was most enjoyable, even though we did not like Australian mutton, always a part of the evening meal. Joke telling, talking and laughing, was the order of the meal and often the Colonel would hold a short staff meeting at the conclusion. The friendly relationship which existed between the officers and the men made for efficiency in our administration and training both in the battalion and in the company. We had little time for administrative functions because of heavy training and operational demands.

We lived by the calls of the bugle. Our day would begin when Pfc Anthony Ricciardi, Brooklyn, NY, the company bugler, blew reveille, arousing us all from sound sleep. Grunts and groans could be heard throughout the camp, with a few curse words for Ricciardi, followed by a broadside of rocks thrown in his direction. Ricciardi would always get behind a tree to shield himself from an ill aimed projectile. The rock throwing was in friendly jest for the men would never hurt the company jokester, who always was cheerful "bucking" us up times when it was needed. The rock throwing, was only a friendly jester, aimed several feet away from the bugler's post.

Ricciardi, in jest, would complain in his Brooklynite dialect using his well known Brooklyn accent when giving his home address,

333, 33rd Street, Brooklyn, NY. He would say: "Tree hoindred thoity-thoid, thoity-thoid tweet, Brooklyn, adding more native slang to his comedic act.

"Captain", he would say to me, "Dees guys don't like me, they trow rocks at me like that every time I blow dis hone. They are going to kill me one of dees days. I have to get behind twees when I blow else I woid already be daid."

First Sergeant Dixon who, like everyone else in the company, would have given his life for the bugler, picked upon his remark, joined in: "That would be good riddance. Then we would not have you around to pester us in the early mornings."

"Now is that the way to talk to yo boigler. Just fo that I will not blow this hone again, and yo will be soirry."

"Just for that I can sleep too, Pvt Ricciardi."

"There yo go demotin me agin! I have you know, according to Company Order Number 10, dated December 10, 1942, Panama Canal, effective that date, I'm a Pfc., Poivet Foist Class, thank yo. Doin't yo ever forget that, not even the date.", pointing to the single stripe on his jacket emphasizing his mark of distinction, adding to the humor.

To add further to his "distinction" I dubbed him the company "jester".

Quickly he countered: "Captain, whoit's a 'joister'?"

"That's for me to know and you to find out, Riccairdi."

"If I'm to be the company 'Joister', captain, I have to know whoit 'joisters' do.

Is thoir a field manual or Army regulation I can read hoiw to be a good 'joister'? He knew what a "jester" was but he still pretended ignorance of the meaning of the term, for he was well educated. From that day on he told everyone he had been promoted to the high and exalted rank of company "joister", and that he expected more respect due a "poison" of his stature. Furthermore, because he was such an important person, no rock should be thown at his "poisonage" when he blew his "hone" in early mornings.

Ricciardi was worth his weight in gold; he was always a walking entertainment center. Later, in New Britain, he would prove himself even better as a combat soldier.

The bugler, always had the last comedic word, which caused all around him to be in a happier frame of mind. Frequently, he was engaged in a verbal "combat" with a group of men and after having achieved victory, would take off to perform other mischievous word battles with another group. What a wonderful person to have around in camp or even in battle!

Ricciardi met his equal however, when he joined up with Clark Bower of Tucson, Arizona. Clark, a very large man, over six feet tall, broad in the shoulders, friendly and likable. Ricciardi, not much over five feet tall, was small in stature and together they gave a "Mutt and Jeff" like appearance. They were always together and trying to get each other's goats. They were very close, perhaps even closer than blood brothers. They would have given their lives for each other. In fact one later did just that. They were very protective of each other's welfare.

Training never ceased while at Camp Cable. Our training progressed to regimental level. The "Bushmaster" Regiment consisted of a Hq & Hq Company, a Service company, Medical Company, a Mortar Company, and three infantry battalions, each commanded by a lt. colonel. Each battalion had about 800 men, divided into five companies, including a Hq & Hq Company, three rifle companies, and a heavy weapons company. This made a total of about 3300 men in the regiment. The "Bushmasters", a Regimental Combat Team (RCT), also had special troops attached, such as engineers, artillery, and medical field hospital troops, all of which brought the total strength well over 6000. After we had honed our combat effectiveness at Camp Cable, the RCT was in good shape to face the Sons of Nippon in New Guinea or wherever. Our mixed races, consisting of Indians, Mexicans, and Caucasians, were ready and willing to show their stuff, and for some strange reason, looked forward to that day.

About the first of March, at the end of a three-day regimental field exercise, Major Hohnhorst, rushed out to the training area from regimental headquarters, informing us that we had been alerted for movement to Port Moresby, New Guinea. Immediately, the regiment formed and began the march back to the camping area, several miles distant. Company and battalion commanders were to turn their respective commands over to their executive officers, using available organic transportation, and report to Regimental Headquarters in Camp Cable, without delay.

Placing Lt. Pavlich in command of the company, I immediately joined the battalion commander and other company commanders and we hastily departed. Major Henry C. Hohnhorst, the battalion executive Officer, would command the battalion on the march back to Camp Cable.

Arriving back in camp, we received our movement orders, our destination being Port Moresby, located at the foot of the Owens Stanley Mountains in the southeastern part of New Guinea. The next day, the "Bushmaster" Regiment was at the Pinkenbaugh Pier in Brisbane prepared to embark ships for Port Moresby. After much effort, delayed by confusion, originating from the Army transportation personnel operating the Pinkenbaugh Pier, the battalion was loaded aboard the Dutch ship, Creamer. The ship, a tramp steamer, which operated during peace time in the China Sea, was dirty from stem to stern, had to be cleaned by our own troops. After checking the troops into their cramped accommodations we established the company and battalion headquarters, and instructions were issued concerning the conduct of troops aboard ship. The ship's engine began to vibrate as tugs hooked onto the Creamer, moving her into the channel of the Brisbane River and out to sea. We would travel between the Great Barrier Reef and the eastern coast of Australia as a protection against Japanese submarines; we would travel without naval escorts until we emerged from the north end of the Great Barrier Reef. Our main concern, however, would be the possibility of lurking submarines when we emerged from behind the reef; many ships had been lost there. Then we would head northeast across the Coral Sea toward Port Moresby. It will be recalled that the first battle between the US navel force and the Japanese Navy had occurred in the Coral Sea the year before, forcing the enemy to withdraw from action, and giving the allies a much needed victory, even though we had lost the carrier Lexington. The first baptism of fire for the aircraft carrier, changing the concept of naval warfare forever, had taken place here, too. The great and prestigious battleship suddenly found itself obsolete heading for the mothball fleet after the war had ended, becoming museums pieces displaying the great history of the juggernauts of the sea; the carrier and the airplane had made them relics. That great sea victory gave MacArthur the needed success to turn the war effort in allied favor and he would never cease hammering the enemy until the war's end in 1945. That sea victory had also saved Australia from the Japanese Army's cruel greedy hands. This victory also made it possible for us to cross the Coral Sea to Port Moresby with the Australian Navy providing a few combat ships to protect us against the submarine threat. They did a good job of it, too.

The "Bushmasters" took to sea travel behind the Great Barrier Reef as if they were spending a leisure Sunday afternoon back in Arizona. Games of chance were going on and at night we would sing the songs we usually sang back home. Some of the songs were risque however. For example:

O the girl who gets a kiss
And runs to tell her mother

Does a very foolish thing
Does a very foolish thing
She'll never get another
She'll never get another

But the girl who gets a kiss
and stays to get another
Is a boon to all mankind
Is a boon to all mankind
For she's bound to be a mother
She's bound to be a mother

The men also turned to ring making using Australian shillings. By boring a hole in the center of the large copper coin and pushing a rod thought it, then hammering it around the edges, a ring could be fashioned. Then it was polished to brilliancy, a piece of mother-of-pearl was set in it, the artist jeweler would be able to send it back home to his mother, girlfriend, or wife. The entire ship echoed with constant hammering. The ship's Dutch officers called us a bunch of playboys, saying other troops they had transported to Port Moresby never made rings, but instead appeared to be very nervous, thinking about the serious combat that awaited them in New Guinea. The "Bushmasters" were a special breed for they had been trained and motivated in Panama to kill and they planned to do that. In the meantime, ring making for loved ones back home came first and the worries of combat would just have to wait.

There was a delay by orders from Port Moresby's port authorities. The Creamer put in at Townsville on the northeast coast of Australia to await available docking space in

New Guinea. Three days passed on the crowded steamer before we were given authority to continue our move north, but the hammering of ring making continued without letup. On the 22nd of March, we hauled anchor, and with two other ships, a corvette and a PT boat of the Australian Navy for escort, we again headed for Port Moresby, the "Bushmasters" still in the ring making business. One of the men had an appendicitis attack and Captain Moulton, the battalion surgeon, performed the operation in the ship's small sick bay. Later Doctor Moulton performed what seemed to be miracles as he operated on wounded men as they lay on the battlefield still exposed to the dangers. Until I saw the medics in operation under combat conditions, I never realized how important they were saving the lives of men who otherwise would have died, had they been evacuated without Moulton's attention. This would be unheard of back in civilian life, where everything had to be sterile and well-lighted operating rooms with all medical personnel dressed in gowns, scrubbed, and gloved. The unsung heros of battle so often were the medics, but were given little credit for a job well done under fire, leaving the glory, if any, to the men on the front line.

CHAPTER 16

NEW GUINEA, THE FORBIDDEN LAND

On the 23rd of March the three ships, loaded with over 6000 "Bushmaster" troops, protected by a small Australian corvette and a PT boat, emerged from behind the Great Barrier Reef, heading east for Port Moresby. Hopefully, we prayed, the small Australian corvette and the PT Boat could defend us from any lurking Japanese sub. The small Australian naval escort continually patrolled our front and flanks, giving us protection, even though not sufficient, but they gave all it had to offer, under the circumstances. Knowing, many ships had been sunk in this region, by waiting enemy subs, we were apprehensive. Since the Creamer was leading the way we reasoned it would be the target. Sometimes we spotted American fighter planes circling above, giving us some courage, but over 400 miles of the Coral Sea yet lay ahead before we would reach safety in the Gulf of Papua, and then Port Moresby. Even though we were traveling in treacherous waters, the hammering of the Australian copper coins into rings by the "Bushmasters" continued, and the ship's officers shook their heads in disbelief. "Do your men realize where they are going, Captain?", the ship's captain asked.

"They not only know where they are going, but are looking forward to it.", I answered, with a bit of bragging, although I, too, shared some of the concerns reflected by the ship's Dutch captain. We were sitting ducks on the Coral Sea, but the men still ignored the possible submarine danger and the hammering continued.

With great relief, on the morning of March 24th we spotted the Owens Stanley Mountains on the southeast coast of Papua, New Guinea, appearing to be hanging from the dense clouds. The towering mountains formed the background for Port Moresby nestling at their toes; our danger at sea was about over.

The Japanese had suffered a major defeat at the hands of American and Australian armies when they attempted to cross the rugged Owen Stanley Mountains in their bid to capture Port Moresby the year before. Their defeat thwarted their grand design for establishing bases in the northern part of Australia. Having had already landed at Buna and Gona on the north coast of New Guinea and heavily engaged with the American and Australian troop there, the Japanese began the campaign to cross the rugged Owens Stanley Range to capture Port Moresby. Such an adventure was thought to be impossible by the American and Australian strategists. However, on their drive on Port Moresby, climbing the jagged, jungle-covered Kokoda Trail that shot up two miles in the blue sky, the Japanese came within thirty miles of their objective. The experienced Japanese jungle fighters under General Horii paid no attention to this obstruction and crossed the rugged mountains.

Then disaster struck. The Australian and American troops counterattacked, driving the Japanese back over the Owen Stanleys. The enemy soldiers suffering from disease and starvation, died by the thousands, and General Horii drowned in a river crossing. Had they been successful, Port Moresby would have served as a base to provide airfields from which the Japanese could operate against Australia and prey on American supply lines.

Following the victory over the Japanese in the Owen Stanleys, General MacArthur established his forward headquarters at Port Moresby.

The first jolt of combat grabbed the "Bushmasters"; the ring making stopped and they calmly began preparing to disembark from the Creamer. We had received word that the Australians were hard pressed at the airstrip on Wau and Americans had already been flown directly into combat there. Some of them died from enemy bullets fired at the plane just as they were about to land, the remaining troops going into immediate combat at the edge of the airstrip. Rumors ran fast; would the "Bushmasters" receive their baptism of fire at Wau? Then we saw our first evidence of combat. A large Australian transport ship lay haplessly on its side in the harbor, sunk by the Japanese Imperial Air Force when the battle had raged in the high mountains above the small town the year before. To the "Bushmasters", it was a sickening sight. It reminded us of a large grounded whale that had floundered and died.

We anchored in the afternoon, and while we were still aboard the Creamer, Colonel Herndon and Colonel Woods came aboard and gave instructions how to get to Camp Carleu, our new temporary home, located about eighteen miles from Port Moresby. We would be transported over the dusty roads to Carleu by US and Australian Army trucks.

Port Moresby was a small town with few hard-surfaced streets, a small hotel and some business houses. It was all but deserted with no civilian activity. All civilians had been evacuated during the battle of the Owen Stanleys the year before, leaving the military as the town's only residents. Being the main forward base as well as General MacArthur's forward command post, Port Moresby showed much evidence of military activity. The Army had established officer and enlisted messes for our conveniences during official visits into town. The amenities were even better than we expected considering the circumstances. Several airstrips surrounded the town, which gave us a feeling of security.

Arriving at Camp Carleu, we found only an open field, located off the main road, without plumbing, showers, or even latrines. Should nature call, and until latrines were dug, the men followed the normal sanitary procedures, performing the "cat" act using their entrenching tool (small shovel) to dig a small hole and covering up their business as a cat would. Since we had personnel trained for such situations, things began to change. The RCT engineer company built roads and company streets, laid out water lines and built latrines and showers. The shower was made using two 55-gallons drums atop 6" X 6" uprights with a platform on top, then affixed shower heads. They also built athletics fields and strung lines connected to electrical generators, giving us power. Battalion and regimental wire sections tied into all headquarters so we soon had radio and telephone contact between us. The ammunition and pioneer platoons improved the interior company streets and even built small bridges over streams. In nothing flat, we had the equivalent of a small town in operation. Security was established around the perimeter with regiment, battalion, company and platoon headquarters and we were fully operational. Shortly, after arrival at Carleu, all company kitchens were functioning and a hot meal was served to the men a short time afterwards. Sergeant Raybourne, the mess sergeant, actually pitched a mess fly and a make-shift table for the officers where we were served by Privates Bandsuch and Richards, orderlies, whose services were paid for from personal funds.

Even though our main objective was to acclimate the men and conduct rigorous training during our stay at Carleu, we also planned athletic games for the men. Each company had a softball and a volleyball team. Even the officers had teams and they played against the men often. Colonel Stofft, a great sportsman and very athletic, also engaged with the rest of us in sport activities. Even though he was serious at official functions, he wanted to have fun when he could, at times kidding us, telling stories of his antics with John Wayne during their college days together.

The "Bushmasters" never forgot that our main purpose at Carleu was to prepare the troops for the confrontation that was bound to come with the "Sons of Nippon". We found the climate very disagreeable. Even though we had trained in Panama, the frequent rains and the subsequent hot sunshine turned the jungles into a virtual steaming spa. At the beginning, our strength was easily sapped and we drank excessive amount of water. Instead of one canteen per man per day, we issued a second canteen, for lack of potable water in the steaming jungle will disable soldiers in a short time. After many men suffered sunstrokes during training marches and field exercises, we finally realized that a much easier pace was necessary until we had adapted to the environment. Changing our schedule we trained in early mornings, late afternoons and evenings, we soon accomplished the mission of getting the men into shape for combat in SWPA, we thought.

Unfortunately and inadvertently, I almost disabled my company during a foolish cross-country march for which the men were not physically ready. Further, adding to our woe, we marched many extra miles during the rugged trek, due to the Australian maps having errors. I was able to return the company, minus volunteers, to Carleu not by foot, but by trucks provided by an Australian army officer who called me a boofhead (fool) for doing what I had done to my men. How lucky we were to have found the Australian truck company camped nearby.

"Yank", he said to me very strongly, "what are you bloody well trying to do? Kill your men? Even though we have been in this bloody place for years, I would never do that to my men. This climate will kill you if you don't abide by its rules."

I showed him the separate routes and march objectives on the east coast of the Solomon Sea, one for each platoon, that I had drawn on an Australian Army map. This only added further to his anger.

"Yank", he said, "that bloody map is not correct. It shows only two mountain ranges where there are three. Furthermore, the water your men thought was fresh at Austin Springs was salt water seeped up the stream from the sea. Yes, you are bloody well lucky to have recovered your men from the terrible ordeal you have put them through. It will take them some time to regain their strength so I suggest you put them to bed for a rest before you decide to do another crazy thing. Again, in a friendly sort of way, he called me a "boofhead", then provided trucks to haul part of my exhausted company back to Camp Carleu twenty miles away, using a road that circled the mountains. Now I understood why the men of the 32nd and 41st Infantry Divisions had suffered so much during their ordeal at Buna and Gona the year before. They had gone directly into combat and a steaming hot New Guinea jungle without a period of time to acclimate, or get accustomed to the environment. That problem, together with malarial fever, almost lost them the campaign. On the other hand the Japanese, being jungle wise and climatic adjusted, suffered little from the ordeal during the battle, which we, fortunately, with luck, won, but at a terrible price.

Because of an urgent last minute assignment, I had been unable to accompany the men on their terrible ordeal over the mountains, but did join them at their objectives in the late afternoon. Completing what I had to do, I loaded the jeep with "J" rations and fresh water, and along with

Colonel Stofft, the battalion commander, headed for the platoons' separate objectives situated on the coast of the Solomon Sea. Going through Port Moresby, passing the Gili Gili airstrip, turning north and following the sea coast, we were pleased to find Lt. Beane at his command post by the sea. He was already in radio contact with battalion beyond the mountains. His exhausted men had bedded down for the night and appeared to be in excellent spirits. Beane indicated that the Anti-Tank and the P & A platoons, who had marched together, had reached their objectives also and that he was in communication with their respective commanders, Lts. Allen and Tompkins. However, a further inspection of the his men revealed my worst fears. Private Charles Springle, a large man, had his jungle boots worn right off his feet during the march. I ordered him into the jeep but he begged to stay. He requested someone bring him boots so he could return with the platoon the following morning. Since he was in very bad physical shape, and with the recommendation of Lt. Beane, Springle had to return to camp by means other than by foot. Beane, said most of his men appeared to be in good shape and were ready for the return trip the next day.

Wanting to check the other men, we proceeded to Pari Village to visit the men of the AT and A & P Platoons. Col Stofft, like me, was proud of what the men had accomplished and congratulated them for a job well done. I noticed a different spirit in Lt. Allen than what I had seen in Lt. Beane for he appeared to be doubtful if his men could make it back to Carleu. Chaplain Mathews Imrie, one of the battalion chaplains, who had accompanied this part of the company, reported that the march had been murder for the men. Forced to climb mountains that were not shown on the map, through headhigh kuni grass under the scorching hot sun, wading through swamps between mountains, and worst of all, had filled their canteens at Austin's Springs Crossing, with what they thought was fresh water, but was brackish water from the sea instead. They were in a terribly desperate situation until they found water at an Australian outpost, and were able to refill their canteens. After a brief rest at the Australian outpost, Imrie said, Lt. Allen gave the order to continue this most difficult march.

Allen, Tompkins, and their men were at the very end of their resistance: they were laying on the ground as if dead. I felt badly about what I had ordered them to do and that I was not able to accompany them.

Colonel Stofft and I made an inspection of the exhausted men, who appeared to be lifeless on the ground. There were men who, like Springle, had shoes worn from their feet while others developed malarial fever. Since Colonel Stofft had to return to Carleu in the jeep, I had two of Allen's men join Springel and return with him, for they were almost unconscious from the ordeal. I instructed the driver, Pfc. Daniel M. Woolridge, to return with hot coffee and food for the men, which hopefully would cheer them up. Col. Stofft, very concerned about the company's condition, cautioned me about the return march, suggesting using trucks to haul the men back to camp would be cogent. I assured him that I would think about it during the night. The colonel, taking the jeep with the three disabled men, departed for Carleu.

The exhausted men of Headquarters Company were soon fast asleep, as the ocean waves lapped the sandy shore of the Solomon Sea. The natives of Pari Village nearby, who lived in thatched-roof huts built on the sea's edge with floors about four feet above the water, chanted as Allen and I discussed the possibilities of the return march the following day. The challenge of a security guard was heard, otherwise the night, with its moonlit and starry sky, was silent, except the gentle lapping waves that crawled up the sandy beaches, and reluctantly returned from whence they came. I was fitful and got little sleep.

The security detail got us up at 5:30 A.M. Hurriedly, we had our "J" rations for breakfast and prepared for the return march over the route used the day before. Departing at 6:30 A.M. we tried to get a start before the hot New Guinea sun rose as we headed due west for Camp Carleu. The men appeared to be in good spirits, laughing and joking as soldiers usually do, and, for a while, they looked fit for the rugged march that lay ahead. However, after crossing the first mountain and coming to a dirt road in the valley that ran between the two towering mountains, I placed the men under trees for a rest period. Making an inspection, going from the head to the foot of the column, it was evident that the company was not able to continue the rugged march. An officer and NCO meeting was called and reports were received;

it was determined the move back to camp must be accomplished by truck. Lt. Beane's platoon, traveling on a different route several miles south of us, was contacted by radio. We suggested he join us and wait for truck transportation back to Carleu. Beane, a fine officer, checked with his men and found that they wanted to continue the march. He requested they be permitted to do so and his request was granted. Then we started the search for the Australian camp we knew was nearby.

Fortunately, we found the camp and requested vehicles to haul Allen's and Tomkins' platoons back to camp. The "Aussie" commander, an army captain, who had already called me a "boofhead", provided the trucks needed and we were grateful. Soon several trucks arrived, and the exhausted men formed into truck groups and began to load. However, once loaded, several of the NCOs, the platoon sergeants; Sgt Higginbotham of the AT Platoon; Sgt Jose M. Mendez of the A & P Platoon; Sgt Kenneth A. Stokesberry, the Battalion Intelligence Section; and First Sergeant Dixon, all requested that they be permitted to return by foot to Carleu. Their request, too, was granted and, after turning the command of the company over to Lt Allen, I joined them on the rugged trek across the mountain.

The ruggedness of the terrain exceeded my expectations. As the officers had stated in our meeting, many of the existing hills, streams, and mountains did not appear on the outdated Australian maps we had been given. Climbing the steep slopes covered with head-high kuni grass, with only a little breeze, we soon felt our strength being sapped. We had frequent rest periods and a long break during lunch on "J" rations. Then we continued on our way over the mountains through the tall kuni grass, the sun's heat punishing us without mercy. Between the mountains, we came to Austin Springs Crossing where Allen's men had filled their canteens with saltwater the day before. Nearby were the remains of a Japanese Zero fighter plane that had been shot down by an Australian pilot during the battle of the Owen Stanleys. We observed the skeletal remains of the plane with curiosity and then continued the rugged march to Carleu, arriving about 4:00 P.M.

The troops under Allen and Tompkins had arrived by truck about 11:00 A.M. Because of the extreme exertion I had put forth on the hot march I developed a severe case of leg cramps. Sergeant Dixon, seeing my extreme suffering, called Captain Moulton, the battalion surgeon, who administered some kind of a shot that eased the terrible cramps; I joined the many disabled men of the company, and I learned a well-deserved lesson. Had we received an emergency combat mission, we could not have performed. I resolved to never be caught in a similar situation again.

Where was Beane and his men? It was late and far beyond the time he should have returned to camp. I was concerned about him and his communicators, the nerve center of the battalion. The battalion commander would be helpless without them for they were the battalion key communication personnel enabling him to control the units of the battalion and attached units once in combat. Realizing the possible consequence should a urgent combat mission be given us I really sweated blood, for I, inadvertently, had tied the battalion's commander's hands. I prayed we would have enough time to refit and regain our physical condition before being committed to combat. I hoped that Beane would return before the ax fell. Maybe the situation at Wau was such that we would be sent to assist the hard-pressed Americans and Australians there. The cross-country training march, on what I thought would be a simple exercise, could have been disastrous.

It would be some time, as we anxiously waited, before we would hear from Beane and his gallant men; the battalion message center had lost radio contact with them. We wondered if they had run into a rogue Japanese Army unit still wandering around from the Owens Stanleys battle. If they had, what could have happened to them? This thought should have occurred to me before I ordered the men on that hot, rugged march, almost putting them in the hospital. Pacing between the battalion communication center and my command post like an expectant father in the lounge of a hospital while his wife labors during the delivery of his child, I was on pins and needles waiting for some word. Finally, at 6:00 P.M., realizing Beane and his men only had enough rations for their noon meal and a limited supply of water, I had the cooks load hot food and water into a jeep and trailer. We, Woolridge, the driver, and I, headed for the other side of the mountain in a downpour of rain. Hopefully we would find the platoon resting beside the road well and alive.

Even this effort failed, adding to my anxiety. When we turned off the gravel road beyond Gili Gili airstrip onto a dirt road, the jeep became stuck in the slimy mud. We worked unsuccessfully for some time to free the jeep, and I realized I had to do something. Buckling on my Cal..45 pistol, which I carried in the jeep, and leaving Woolridge alone with the vehicle, I headed back toward camp several miles away. As I trudged down the muddy road cut through the dense jungle in the dark rainy night, the thoughts of the rogue Japanese raced up my spine. It was a very lonely feeling.

My fears were relieved when I came upon a well-lighted US Army motor pool. I saw the mechanics and drivers working on their vehicles. After pouring out my worried request for assistance, the maintenance sergeant agreed to send his wrecker to extract my jeep from the mud. I was grateful when the big wrecker lifted the vehicle as if it were a toy, placing it once again on solid ground, towing it back to the gravel road. Gratefully, I expressed my thanks and appreciations to the driver.

Returning to Camp Carleu about 9:00 P.M. and, happily, there, I found Beane and his men, wet, muddy, and tired, had returned just before I had arrived. Sergeant Raybourne and his mess personnel were already serving them a good hot meal. Battalion had already been notified of Beane's arrival and Colonel Stofft and Major Hohnhorst were enjoying a cup of coffee with the very tired men, as they ate their late evening meal. With relief, I happily joined them. We were all proud of Lt.

Beane and his communicators and they, most of all, were the proudest. For many days the communicators ribbed the AT and A&P Platoons, for they had done something the others could not do.

The march caused all of us to take notice and let the climate dictate our training until a proper physical adjustment occurred. As the Australian officer had reminded me, "abide by the climatic rules until you have conquered it, else it will conquer you." For four days after the march, I had the men rest and only perform equipment maintenance. They conducted physical training in the early morning and late afternoons, including tactical road marches. Soon we became masters of the New Guinea jungle and performed similar marches without undo hardships.

NOT: During the battle of Buna and Gona, which fell to the Americans and Australians in January 1943, a battle was fought that was just as important as Guadacanal. The fighting was every bit as savage and the cost in dead and wounded even higher, but there was less publicity then the marines had received in Guadacanal campaign the year before.

The term "shack commandos" was coined by the veterans of the 32nd and 41st Infantry Divisions. The "shack commandos" were those senior officers on General MacArthur's staff with comfortable offices and living quarters in Brisbane, Australia. Having all the comforts and safety of civilians back home, they would visit the front-line regiments and immediately scoot back to Brisbane in their planes. Returning to safety and comfort they would received a high decoration for their "brave" visits to the front lines, usually a Silver Star. In contrast to this was the heroism of Staff Sergeant Herman J. Boettcher, a naturalized German and a fine combat soldier, who, with eighteen men, broke the Japanese hold on Buna. By infiltrating the enemy's communications trenches and destroying several machine guns, thus creating a breach in the enemy's final protective fires through which the Americans and Australians stormed, Boettcher and his brave men caused the once impregnable fortress to fall and the battle of Buna and Gona was over after many months of fighting. Boettcher was awarded the coveted Silver Star and given a battlefield commission to captain for his heroic feat. Boettcher was quite happy to have received the coveted Silver Star, but he was most disturbed when he heard of the same decorations received by the "shack commandos", on MacArthur's staff.

CHAPTER 17

BUSHMASTERS, EAGER AND READY, FOR WHAT?

The famous "Bushmasters", had been in New Guinea for six weeks and had not yet received the call to combat. We continued to train to prepare for whatever mission we would be asked to do. The men wondered why after they had been told by the Regimental Commander, while still in Panama, that we were to spearhead an offensive in the Pacific. All the combat we had seen was an occasional aerial show between the US and Japanese fighter pilots, and air raids on our supply dumps and the Gili Gili airstrip near Port Moresby. They wanted action. They did find it most interesting to listen in on the conversations between the young American pilots as they engaged the enemy above us on the short wave radio. These young pilots sounded as if they were in a hotly contested softball game as they roared to the attack: "Hey, Joe", one would say, "that was a good shot you made." The answer would be a calm reply: "Thanks, old pal for the compliment and for the wing protection you gave me." Another would say, in an excited voice: "Look out, Bill! There's a Zero on your tail. Quick! Somebody do something!" Then the conversation was silent only to continue vigorously later. Afterward, I was informed the silence probably indicated Bill had been shot down by a Jap Zero. "Hey, there goes a Zero down in flames! Now that's a good Jap, fellahs", or Boy, that was a close call!", or, There's a bogey at two o'clock, let me have him!", or "That Zero almost fanned my tail, but you saved me, thanks!" Death was all around these young American kids and yet they acted as if they were in a game of sport.

Once we were alerted for a possible Japanese invasion east of Port Moresby and we went into defensive positions but nothing happened.

We did, however, perform a most interesting duty while we were at Carlieu; we guarded General MacArthur's personal living quarters at his advance base in Port Moresby during one of his command visits. The general only occasionally visited his forward base but when he did, the army took the most rigorous precautions to protect him. Realizing that the enemy probably knew of the presence of the famous general, and probably would take action to kill him, especially since our Army Air Corps had shot the Japanese theater commander, Admiral Isoroku Yamamoto, the architect and leader of the sneak attack on Pearl Harbor, out of the sky. The Japanese would certainly like to return the honor by knocking off our theater commander as well.

The death of the Japanese Admiral would be the equivalent of the death of MacArthur, Commander-in-Chief-C of SWPA, or Commander-in-Chief of the Southwest Pacific, Admiral Nimitiz, or even General Eisenhower in the European Theater of Operations. It was impossible for the Japanese to replace Admiral Yamamoto with a leader of like abilities. Thanks was due the US Navy intelligence in Honolulu for breaking the Japanese code making it possible for the Navy to know every move of the Japanese after that.

The admiral made the mistake of scheduling an inspection tour and sent word of his schedule, in code, over the air. This schedule was intercepted in Honolulu and quickly decoded. Interestingly enough, approval had to be granted from President Roosevelt personally before the aerial ambush of the great Japanese leader could be carried out. Before the attack on Pearl Harbor Admiral Yamamoto warned his pilots: "The Americans are adversaries worthy of you."

The plan to ambush the Admiral was prepared, using eight P-38s under command of Major John Mitchell. On the morning of April 15, 1943, Mitchell and his eight P-38s stationed at Bruin in the Solomon chain, met up with two bombers carrying Yamamoto and his staff, escorted by several Zeros, and shot them out of the sky. Mitchell had no idea he had removed the highest ranking Japanese commander from the Pacific war, second only in importance to the Emperor himself. Fearing the Japanese would learn we had compromised their code, Admiral Nimitiz only authorized information needed for Mitchell and his pilots to accomplish their mission. Yamamoto's death had an extreme moral affect both on the field of battle and back in Japan. It was a great victory for the United States. The sneak attack on Pearl Harbor had been partially avenged.

The death of the Japanese Admiral had a lasting effect throughout the war, even on the allied command. It caused us to take special precautionary measures for the security of high ranking brass when they visited our area. When General MacArthur came to his forward base in Port Moresby, even though enemy units were several hundred miles away, we were aware that they had the capability of staging a commando-type raid to eliminate him if we became careless. It was under these circumstances the 2nd Battalion of the "Bushmasters" was ordered to secure his headquarters in Port Moresby. We were not told General MacArthur would be present, but yet, we saw evidence that he was. A small building was designated to receive special attention and we ringed it with armed guards a few feet apart. Machine guns were placed in strategic places, primed and ready for instant action. Officers and NCOs were constantly in observance. While I was inspecting the guard and machine gun posts in the vicinity of the small building, my attention was called to it by one of the sentries.

"Look, Captain Jordan!"

Observing the small, dimly lit building from a short distance, I could see the famous profile of MacArthur passing the small window as he paced back and forth, back and forth. The men were as excited at his presence as was I. All night this went on until the sun appeared over the Owen Stanley Mountains. Then a command car, with two officers, appeared in front of the small building, and the general, without saying a word to the officers or to us, left the area. It was pompous but, yet, quite regal. Shortly after that, the 2nd Battalion was relieved and returned to Camp Carlieu. We supposed he had departed for Gili Gili airstrip, taking his plane, the Bataan, back to Brisbane where his wife and son lived in the Lenen Hotel.

MacArthur often meditated, throughout the night, as described above, before arriving at important command decisions relative to the war against the Japanese. Later, I was informed, that prior to his lonely vigil within the walls of his small room, the general had already picked the brains of his subordinates and staff concerning an upcoming operation. Then, turning all the information over and over in his brilliant mind until arriving at a decision, he left the small building, called for his principal staff officers, and issued the combat order. Not once, however, did he give credit to anyone for their input. Everything was done under the "I" concept as if he were the only person doing the thinking. Example: not many have heard of General Walter Krueger, Commanding General of the Sixth US Army, who really was the father of the leap-frog method of waging war in the Pacific. Using a small force, Krueger would cut off a large enemy force from his bases of supply causing starvation and death; as a result the Americans found evidence of the horrible Japanese practice of cannibalization of their own dead as well as that of Americans they had killed. The recovered bodies had muscles of the arms, legs, and the buttocks surgically removed, sufficient evidence that cannibalization was going on, perhaps the only food source available to the starving enemy. Until General Krueger arrived in the Pacific, MacArthur, as he did at Buna and Gona, was trying to fight a European type of open warfare, which was impossible in the jungle. Krueger was never given the credit due him, but he contributed to victory in the Pacific and with greatly reduced casualties. MacArthur knew how to get the best from his people, implementing their knowledge to produce the best of results and ultimately winning the war in the Pacific.

MacArthur's egotism was characterized in a cartoon by Bill Maulden, the famous cartoonist, in Yank Magazine in Europe, during WWII. Maulden's two characters, Ernie and Joe, the unshaven, dirty GIs, who were his cartoon heros, had returned home after the war was over in Europe. They were lounging on a street corner in New York, still unshaven and in their dirty combat fatigues, overcoats and beat up steel helmets; Ernie was still smoking a stub of a cigar. They were listening to the radio blaring about the greatness of MacArthur and Ernie said: "You know, Joe, Eisenhower must have been a piker, he had to have an army to help him".

MacArthur, regardless of what we think of him, won battles, campaigns, and wars, with minimum loss of life. In spite of his egotism and self-imposed isolation, he was one of the most brilliant military leaders of all time. He was not as popular as Eisenhower, nor was he liked by the politicians, but they realized his greatness. The American people would not have stood for his removal from command. He was a thorn in the presidential side of Roosevelt and the Army Chief of Staff, General Marshall, but they had to put up with his unreasonable demands, ignoring them at times.

On May 15, the 2nd Battalion was alerted for movement to Milne Bay located on the eastern tip of New Guinea where we would operate as a separate unit from the regiment and would have both administrative and tactical responsibilities. As the adjutant of the battalion, my duties tripled. Here, in addition to commanding the Headquarters and Headquarters company, I had the administrative functions of the battalion and attached units with a troop strength of about 1100 men. Perhaps our move was at the order of General Krueger, the Commanding General of the newly-organized Sixth US Army, and we would be under his direct command, separate from the regiment. It will be recalled that our Battalion Commander, Lt. Colonel Frederick R. Stofft, had been an Aide to General Krueger, when Krueger commanded the Third Army at Fort Sam Houston, Texas. Col Stofft, then a major, was very dynamic, personable, extremely intelligent, and well-liked by Krueger. This accounted for our change of location to Milne Bay, a place with the highest rainfall in the world. We only had six days of sunshine during our stay of eight weeks there, constantly raining day and night.

In preparation for our move to Milne Bay, we sent Lt. Tompkins with his Pioneer and Ammunition platoon seven days in advance, to prepare a campsite for the battalion. His mission was to locate and prepare sites for the battalion command post and company locations. This certainly would be a great help having the campsite ready for the 1100 men when the battalion would arrive during the hours of darkness. Tompkins and his men did their job well, but to our disappointment, we never saw the area that he had so well prepared for us.

On the day of our scheduled arrival the Milne Bay base commander told Tompkins that a newly-arrived unit from the states would occupy the site instead of the 2nd Battalion. The young second lieutenant protested to the colonel, but to no avail. Again Tompkins protested but was then threatened with court-martial for insubordination if he continued to protest.

The remainder of the battalion arrived in Milne Bay 11:00 PM aboard a Liberty ship, anchoring several hundred feet off shore. There were no port facilities. A heavy rain was falling. The company commanders and battalion staff were assembled in the ship's ward-room to receive the base commander and to have Tompkins tell us about the area he had prepared for us. It was important to disembark the ship before daylight for it would then become a sitting duck for enemy planes. This presented us with the horrendous task of unloading hundreds of men and the thousands of rations and pieces of equipment we had aboard.

Finally, a small harbor boat arrived and a Jacob's ladder was thrown over the side of the ship for the visiting party to climb up to the deck. The drenching rain was still falling. First up the ladder was the base commander, a tall, slim, bespectacled colonel. When everyone had left the small harbor boat and were still on the rain drenched deck, Tompkins looked at me, being unable to explain verbally, then threw both hands up, shaking his head. I knew then things were not good for us. The party moved back into the wardroom where the base commander informed Colonel

Stofft we would not be going to the camp area Tompkins had prepared for us but another one that might prove as acceptable as the other. I was alerted when he said "another camp- site that might prove as well as the other." Then I realized what Tompkins was trying to tell me by the disgusted wave of his hands as he came aboard the Liberty ship: no place had yet been determined where we would place the 1100 men, the thousands of rations, and equipment we had aboard. We were in a mess and I noted Colonel Stofft and the company commanders had the same feeling I had.

"Colonel", said Colonel Stofft, "I sent Lt. Tomkins here in advance to prepare a place for us to camp, and I understand he has done so, now at this late hour we learn we are not going there. I hope you have a place equally prepared for us to go. We must get off this ship before daylight and already it is 11:30 PM."

"Colonel, we are in a war here, and we must expect changes from time to time. Perhaps the place your battalion will go may not be the best in the world, but it will have to do until something better is found." It was evident we would occupy an area in the downpour of rain that had not been seen by Tompkins, the base commander, or anyone. Hopefully, Providence would look out for us. Only months before the Auzzies had defeated the Japanese at the edges of the nearby airstrip. Perhaps Jap rogues were still around and could do harm to us while we were trying to get organized again.

"For God's sake, Colonel, are you telling us you have not yet selected the area where we are supposed to place the 1100 men aboard this ship and the other ship following us?", Colonel Stofft was exploding; the company commanders shook their heads in disbelief.

Then Colonel Stofft turned to Tompkins. "Tompkins, I sent you here in advance to prepare a place for us and I understand you did that. Now tell me what happened. Why did you not inform me of the change and why did you not select another place for us once you were told of the change?" Everyone in the wardroom looked questioningly at the small 2nd Lieutenant; Tompkins was feeling the pressure.

"Colonel, sir", Tompkins began, "I was just informed of the change by the colonel as I got into the boat tonight. I did not have the time until now to tell you. Please forgive me, sir." He was almost pleading for understanding.

"Tompkins, you and your men did a good job and you certainly don't have to apologize for something that's beyond your control. I thank you and your men for doing something good for us but unfortunately it will be used by other people." I felt the sarcasm directed at the base commander.

"I tentatively have selected another place for you, Colonel. I suggest we quit this bickering and get off the ship so I can take you there," said the tall bespectacled colonel, waving his hand toward the small harbor boat bobbing on the rain soaked Milne Bay below.

Leaving the comforts of the ship's wardroom and stepping onto the rain-swept deck, the group of disappointed officers climbed down the unsteady Jacob's ladder to the small harbor boat. Once all was aboard, the helmsman gassed the engine and steered for the shore which was obscured by rain and fog, several hundred yards away. What would we find there?

The small harbor boat touched the sandy bottom a few feet from the shore. Wordlessly, the "Bushmaster" officers went over the side of the small vessel into knee-deep water and waded to the shore as the rain seemed to increase in intensity. The base commander led the small group up the bank to a trail that paralleled the coastline. He stopped and motioned for us to gather around him. Here he tried to designate the boundaries of our camp by pointing in various directions in the almost inky blackness of the drenching night. Then he led us off the trail stepping into calf deep swamp water, an area that had been the battlefield between the Japanese and Australians the previous August. Wading a short distance from the trail, still standing in swamp water, the base commander stopped, turned and said: "This is not much of place but you can find something better tomorrow morning after you have unloaded your men and equipment."

This was too much for the already stressed "Bushmaster" Colonel Stofft; he exploded: "Sir", he said in a raging voice, "may I say: whoever selected this place for us must be crazy to think I would ever put my men in a place like this; it's not fit even for cattle. Furthermore, I suspect not you or anyone, until tonight, ever set eyes on this damn swamp. Colonel, no, I wouldn't even put cattle in this damn swamp, much less my men!"

And the verbal battle raged between the two senior officers as we stood in the drenching rain in the swamp. The blackness of the night obscured even the forms of the participants and the small group of officer around them.

"Why", the commander of the "Bushmasters" continued, "was the change made since the Sixth Army had already selected the site for my battalion? I want General Krueger informed of this change if the situation is unknown to him."

Then the base commander, in his height of anger replied:

"Colonel, one more word from you and I will prefer charges against you for insubordination. Now this is it and you must accept it until something better can be arranged in the morning."

"Court-martial all you want Colonel, but I'm not putting my men in this dirty swamp!"

Realizing something must be done immediately, while the argument raged, I returned alone to the trail, the only place not drowned by the deluge of rain. I actually ran several hundred yards on it and found it to be about thirty feet wide and it seemed to extend the length of the bay. Perhaps, I reasoned, we could scatter the men north and south on the trail. In case of an air attack, which we knew was a good possibility, we could scatter into the swamp. The men had to be removed from the Liberty ship, still anchored on the dark waters of the Milne Bay, before daylight for it was a perfect target for high-flying Japanese bombers.

Returning to the still-battling colonels, I finally got the battalion commander's attention and reported to him what I had found. I recommended disembarking operations be initiated immediately and completed before daylight, feeling we had no other course possible under the circumstances.

"Captain Jordan, do you think we can do this?"

"Colonel Stofft, under the circumstances, I don't know of any other thing we can do. However, dispersion will be a problem putting 1100 men on the small trail. We can scatter them but it would take miles on the trail to accommodate the battalion and our attached units. Another alternative would be to bunch them shoulder to shoulder and then scatter them, come daylight, in order to expedite the off-loading procedures."

"Captain Jordan", he said, "this is the most sensible thing I've heard since arriving in Milne Bay." Then he coolly addressed the base commander: "Colonel, I suppose you have arranged for barges for disembarking the troops, or are they to swim ashore?" Silently and anxiously we awaited the base commander's reply to the battalions commander's pointed, almost accusing question.

"Yes, Colonel Stofft, the barges should be approaching the ship now." I detected a cooling of tempers between the two colonels, perhaps because a decision had been made, even though it was bad, resolving the terrible, but yet unacceptable, situation.

The small group of officers returned to the only high ground on which the trail ran, a levee of sorts. Col Stofft, after consulting with the company commanders, issued disembarkation orders. Captain Robert C.

Caffee, the Battalion's Operations Officer, became the beach-master, while Major Henry Hohnhorst, the executive officer, assisted by Lt. Fagen, the battalion supply officer, would be in charge of off-loading troops onto the barges that would ply between ship and shore in the continuous downpour of rain and in the darkness; it would be a race with daylight and the Japanese recon planes. Lights were not to be used for fear of the possibility of being spotted by enemy aircraft. This would have been impossible since we were covered by low-hanging rain-laden clouds; it was more like following established procedure than being practical.

The disembarking went smoothly under direction of Hohnhorst and Fagan and the men, even though wet from stem to stern, were cheerful and kidded each other. This was a good sign that all was well with them and they understood the situation.

"What's all the griping about, this is nothing. We've had worse in Panama," said a "Bushmaster" from "E" Company. Another one of my men recalled: "If we took what Captain Jordan dished out to us on the cross country over three mountains to reach the Solomon Sea, we certainly can take this." I was proud to hear him say that, realizing the march to the sea the previous month did have its favorable physical and psychological effects.

The remainder of the night was filled with activity. Ship to shore, shore to ship, the barges disgorged men and equipment. Capt Caffee was busy trying to keep things organized on the beachhead under the most trying conditions as men, mingled with equipment, were packed shoulder to shoulder on the narrow space available to us. The company commanders, trying to scatter their men, shuddered to think what would happen should the Japanese discover our plight. Should their planes attack us it would be slaughter of helpless men. Colonel Stofft, realizing our dangerous exposure, called for a company commanders' meeting to discuss and remedy the situation. From this meeting it was determined the units were to extend further to the south and the north on the narrow trail. My Company, Headquarters and Headquarters Company, because of the involvement of battalion command and communications personnel in controlling the off-loading procedures operating the command post, was to remain in the center near the big tree used for the meeting. The other companies would scatter to the south and north of the tree. The tree became the reference for command control. Reports from Major Hohnhorst indicated we were progressing well and the men would be off the ship before daylight. The battalion commander knew our plight would only be heightened with dawn. The Japanese recon planes were sure to be over us, if the rain stopped and the sun shined. For once we prayed the rain would continue but it didn't. The early sun, in a land usually drenched in downpours of rain, peeked over the high mountain at us sending its rays to dry out the "Bushmasters", as they slept on the narrow trail. The Japs pilots were sure to find us.

Daylight offered no solace to the commander of the "Bushmasters", as he stood among the sleeping forms of men, some of whom even slept in hammocks strung in the tall tree. How in the world, he wondered, could they have strung a hammock in the tree. He dismissed this thought for he had other more important things to deal with. Sick reports came in indicating some of the men had malaria fever and had to be sent back to Moresby to the hospital. Even Sgt. Bauters, the platoon sergeant of the Anti-Tank Platoon, had to be evacuated. I regretted this for Bauters was a good man, who had come to us from the 5th Infantry, and had helped to reduce the ill feeling of the men from the Regular Army toward the "Bushmasters", a National Guard Regiment from Arizona; he was like oil on troubled waters. It will be recalled the RAs were scheduled to go home from Panama but were transferred instead to the "Bushmasters", resulting in some disciplinary problems. This good sergeant would later return to us.

We were successful unloading the men from the ship before dawn, but we still had one million "C" rations, about a hundred tons, consigned to the base, yet to be unloaded. Even worse, these rations had to placed among the sleeping men on the already crowded narrow beach trail on shore. Our position was becoming more untenable and we could suffer a terrible loss of many men should the enemy launch an air attack once the terrible downpour of rain ended.

The commander acted immediately. He ordered Lt. Jennings Whitten, the Battalion Intelligence officer, using his intelligence section, on a scouting mission to find suitable camping areas. He was to report back to battalion before 10:00 AM. Since I was the adjutant and responsible for the exact location for each company once the site was selected, Colonel Stofft suggested I accompany Whitten. Taking our individual weapons and machetes, we marched up the muddy trail until we came to some high ground. Inspecting the area we found skeletons of Japanese soldier, some still with wrist watches around the skinless wrists. The watches, to our surprise, after winding, still ran. Many of the skeletons were located in fox-holes at the base of palm trees. The bones had crumpled and the grinning skulls peeked out from under the helmets. We found unexploded grenades on the former battlefield. We waded streams as the birds called to us. We found a good area but it was so isolated that it would be impossible to get vehicles and equipment to it. We returned to the big tree and reported our findings to the battalion commander; he directed further exploring. After a lunch of cold "C" rations we would try again, this time in the opposite direction but still with nil results.

While still unloading the ship and shifting the men on the trail, it happened. We spotted an enemy recon plane high in the sky over us. It was an assurance we would receive an attack during the coming night. The ship's captain demanded faster action for he wanted out of the bay before nightfall. The anchored ship would be like a sitting duck in the bay while rations and equipment were being lightered from it to shore, and was sure to have been seen. We knew the enemy aerial photos would uncover the hundreds of men jammed together on the trail, making them a good target. Human chains were formed to unload the rations from the barges to shore and piled them along the trail without dispersion. Feverishly, they worked to enable the ship to leave Milne Bay before darkness. Three human chains were formed to unload an overloaded barge from front to rear. The men didn't notice but the rear of the barge began to sink as the weight shifted as they unloaded the rations from the front. Quickly, the men reformed their lines from the front to the rear of the barge. Standing in chest deep water, they began the unloading procedures again causing the center of gravity to change from the rear of the barge and saving the rations that could have been ruined by the salt water had they fallen into the briny deep. Subsequently, the ship was unloaded and it left the bay and headed to safety. The "Bushmasters", however, would just have to suffer the consequences if the attack occurred. There were no escape for us.

The recon party returned in the afternoon and unfortunately, reported no likely place we could move to. Again, we would have to spend the night, scattered for miles, on the narrow dirt strip on the levee by Milne Bay and take what the Japs had to offer. Dusk was approaching and we expected company in the form of the Mitsubishi bombers from New Britain. The operations officer, Captain Caffee, at the direction of the battalion commander, issued orders to all commanders to have the men dig in; all other activity stopped and the men vigorously prepared fox-holes along the trail or at the water's edge. Officers and NCOs checked each man to see if he had prepared his individual fox-hole properly to give him protection should an air attack come.

Under the circumstances that the "Bushmasters" had found themselves in they could not help but wonder why the base commander had changed our camping site and dumped us in the swamp the night before. His negligence was criminal. We could lose many men because of his negligence and inefficiency.

The claxon sounded at 9:30PM - RED ALERT! Enemy bombers were on their way! This would be our first air attack! Where were the friendly attack planes? Why were they not swarming above us? But there were none! Our fox-holes would have to be our only protection and we hunkered down in them. We knew, even though we were in our fox-holes, because of the crowded conditions our men were in, if the bombs fell on the narrow strip some of us would become victims due to the cratering effect the bombs would have.

"Put out that damn cigarette, or I will shoot it out!", someone yelled to a careless soldier who did not realizing he was in violation of our non-smoking policy at night unless one was under cover. "Get into your fox-hole, soldier!", Lt Allen screamed at one of the men in his AT platoon, who had become careless and wanted to talk to a buddy for he was nervous. Johnson, my orderly, nervously continued digging his fox-hole deeper adding more depth for additional security. He sat on the bottom of his already deep hole pitching the soggy dirt out around the top. I laughed at his extra precautions as he continued to pile the dirt higher on the edges of his fox-hole. All of us should have been as cautious.

"Here they come!" someone yelled. Silently, we listened. The throbbing engines of enemy bombers could be heard in the distance. We hunkered deeper, head between our knees, in our fox-holes. Chaplain Emerie prayed.

Our anti-aircraft guns, positioned further up the bay, began firing. The projectiles exploded far above and puffs of brilliant red light could be seen followed by delayed sound of explosions. Happily our fighter pilots from Gili Gili arrived and immediately responded to the challenge. Eerie red tracer bullets could be seen fired from friend and foe alike. Several planes were shot down, made visible by bright flames as they plunged rapidly for earth. Again, friend or foe? On came the bombers, perhaps fewer than before the engagement of our anti-aircraft artillery and the arrival of friendly planes, but there they were above us. The sound of air rushing into the bomb bays caused an explosive sound. The bombs were on the way. We clawed the bottoms of our fox-holes. The swishing sound of the falling bombs was louder as they streaked toward us; louder and louder the screams. In terror, we felt helpless. Hopefully, the shallow fox-holes would save us; they were our only defense, for the bombs were upon us. Then came the terrible explosions, several, then another string in succession, then another! The ground shook as if we were in an earthquake. The shock waves caused the palms to sway above us so that the coconuts fell. Then, suddenly, it was over. Chaplain Emerie breathed with relief and expressed thankfulness to the Supreme Being for saving us. We were grateful the chaplain was with us.

Immediately the company and attached units made a bomb damage survey while Captain Caffee, the Battalion Operations Officer, called on the field phone requesting the same information from the units. He called the companies in order:

Headquarters Company, Captain Jordan
None

Company "E", 1st Lt Overmeyer
None

Company "F", Captain McGlothlan
None

Company "G", Captain Cochran
None

Company "H", Captain Francis
1 minor injury

Engineer Company
None

Medical Detachment, Captain Moulton None

Field hospital, Captain Raney
None

Apparently the enemy bombers' target was the nearby airstrip. Their bombs caused considerable damages there. Fortunately, only one of the "Bushmasters" from "H" Company was injured during the raid by a falling coconut blown from the tree. Except for being scared, we escaped damages and casualties in our first experience with an enemy air attack. The purple heart was awarded the soldier injured by the falling coconut causing a small blood flow, for it was from enemy action. This was a source of embarrassment to the "Bushmasters".

The soldier from Company "H" was proud of his purple heart. Later when comparing his minor wound with that of others who had suffered life-threatening wounds received in combat, he felt unworthy to have received the coveted medal. He, however, was worthy to have received it for his injury was due to enemy action, and blood did flow from it.

Gratefully, morning came, and with it, another day of rare sunshine. Sgt Stokesberry, the Battalion Intelligence Sergeant, reported he had found a suitable location for the battalion to bivouac located about five miles away. With further recon, Stokesberry's report was considered sufficient. A quartering party was sent ahead and the battalion moved to the new site. A perimeter defense was organized with all command, administrative, and supporting weapons in its center. We were now prepared to defend ourselves should a Japanese rogue unit attack. The "Bushmasters" were ready to meet the sons of Nippon, if they dared to challenge us.

CHAPTER 18

ENGINEERS, ROAD BUILDERS, STEVEDORES

Arriving at our new campsite in the jungle near the waters of Milne Bay, we were inspired by stories the Australians told of the battle between the Aussies and the Sons of Nippon at Milne Bay the previous August. I recalled the skeletal remains of the Japs that we found in the swamp. It had been a nip and tuck battle for the airstrip with adversaries firing at each other at point blank range making the airstrip between them a "no mans" land, or eyeball-to-eyeball confrontation, so to speak. The gallant and resourceful Auzzies "from down under" prevailed. The famous "Bushmasters" were now in the hellhole called Milne Bay, soaked to the skin by the constant rain. We all felt we would have been better off had the Australians just let the Japs have the place without contest.

The "Bushmasters" were willing to fight the Japs anywhere just to get out of the rain. Even though we had the kitchens under canvas, the men standing in the mess line were pelted constantly by the deluge. Once they were through the line, they would run to their "pup tents" to eat only to find their mess kits filled with water, diluting their terrible-tasting dehydrated food. Since the P & A (Pioneer and Ammunition) platoon, under direction of Lt. Tompkins and Sergeant Thomas, was trained in the construction of crude buildings, they built us a mess hall. We were so fortunate to have such expertise among us.

In building the mess hall they used logs from coconut trees as uprights and framed it with small bamboo poles cut and tied together with jungle vines. They managed to get canvas tarpaulins for the roof and, using scrap lumber they built waist-high narrow tables around which the men stood as they ate. Now they could eat their terrible-tasting dehydrated food protected from the rain which continued unabated. The P & A platoon became our heros. We still had to wade inundated by water while going to our headquarters, the kitchen, latrine, or sick call. We held formations and marched in it. Vehicles became stuck in the mire it had created. We even played ball in the continuing rain. Anxiously, we waited for orders to meet the enemy; we wanted to see sunshine, somewhere, someplace again. We were becoming paranoid with a grand delusion that meeting the enemy was better than drowning, a complex that continued throughout the Pacific campaign. Perhaps our terrible experience at Milne Bay caused the "Bushmasters" to have such hate for the enemy that their later ferocity would even exceed that of the Japanese themselves.

Combat for the "Bushmasters" would have to wait, however. The Allied Joint Chiefs of Staff had given priority to the war effort in Europe to defeat Hitler; then they planned to turn the allied might upon Japan. Therefore, very few service troops and limited combat materials were sent to SWPA. In spite of this disadvantage, MacArthur won the Pacific war with what little he had using strategy and tactics baffling to the minds of the Japanese and even to the Allied Joint Chiefs in

Washington. Furthermore, he suffered fewer casualties in comparison to those of European Theater of Operations (ETO).

So the famous "Bushmasters", instead of spearheading a big offensive in the Pacific, as we were told we would be doing before leaving Panama, temporarily became service troops, engineers, stevedores, carpenters, road builders, laid pipelines, built staging areas, camp sites, etc. We found ourselves in a very deplorable condition doing things combat soldiers were never expected to do; troop morale plummeted.

The constant torrent of rain continued; everything was soaked and moldy, vehicles stuck in the deep muddy roads, we slept in it, we ate in it, and we were delighted when the sun rarely peeked and smiled over the high steep mountains at us, but then for only a short time. We still had to occupy defensive positions to protect ourselves in the event that a fanatical rogue Jap unit decided to attack us. The troops occupied water-filled fox-holes wearing ponchos, steel helmets, with rifles at the ready for an attack that never came. Even so, some of the Japs who were still in the area often raided kitchens for something to eat for they had no way of getting food, otherwise. Even though this did happen to other units the "Bushmasters" were spared this experience while at Milne Bay. It was a sufficient threat, however, to keep us on the alert, for they would kill before starving to death.

While suffering under these conditions we were visited by the Base Engineer giving us further service troops projects. He spoke to

Col Stofft, the battalion commander:

"Colonel, we must prepare an area here in Milne Bay to accommodate a division-size unit that is to arrive here in two weeks. Even though we have an engineer regiment arriving shortly, they won't have time to build the camp, build roads, and lay pipelines. Your battalion is the only unit that can be used as service troops for this monumental task."

Hesitating, once he saw the unbelieving look on the battalion commander's face, he continued. "Colonel, please try to understand your troops are the only troops available to prepare the site for the division."

"By what authority must I continue using my combat troops as service personnel? Do you realize this sort of thing could ruin our combat effectiveness, perhaps could ruin morale as well?" Colonel Stofft was very upset.

"By the authority of the commanding general, Sixth Army, sir."

"I suppose you mean General Krueger?"

"The one and only, sir." A bit of sarcasm added.

General Krueger had recently moved his headquarters to Milne Bay and had ordered the 2nd Battalion of the "Bushmasters" to become directly under his command.

The "Bushmasters" launched into the work at hand, while still maintaining their defensive perimeter in the pouring rain. Since we had little engineering equipment, we were issued machetes, brush hooks, picks and shovels to cut the underbrush. Again, we laid pipe, installed water pumps, built roads, vehicle parking lots, etc.

To aid in our effort, seventy natives (Fuzzy Wuzzies) were included in the work force under the supervision of an Australian Army Warrant Officer. Also a Mr. Kane, an Australian civil engineer, was very helpful in our effort to prepare for the division coming from the states, a unit we would never see.

Kane described the battle of Milne Bay that had been fought the previous August and the character and habits of the aboriginal natives. We learned from both stories: first; we had greater respect for the Australian Army, and second: to have little to do with the natives, for their presence was a health hazard.

Pfc Ricciardi, Brooklyn, NY, had a way with the native small fry. When there was work they could do, he would round up a bunch of the kids and see to it that they were busy. The small native boys considered Ricciardi to be a "big wheel" in the framework of things, and worked their little heads off for him. They dug garbage pits, latrines (they didn't understand why Americans had to have latrine when a big open field was nearby), and a path through the forest. It was a show just to watch Ricciardi and his diminutive "Fuzzy Wuzzies" work force; entertainment was going on most of the time. He could not understand what it was they said, but somehow he got them to do what he told them. Gleefully, they complied with the "big wheel's" commands.

The "Bushmaster" men got a big kick out of observing the unlovable looking "Fuzzy Wuzzie" women, naked from the waist up, wearing grass skirts. Once the army took over an area, for sanitary reasons, the natives living nearby had to be relocated. This was usually done under the supervision of the Australians. Moving in groups, everything they owned carried on their backs, often moving in sight of the "Bushmasters" working on roads or pipelines, etc. The half - naked women caused the Indians, the Mexicans, and the Caucasians alike, to take a second look and all work ceased when the "Fuzzy Wuzzies" were passing under control of the Australians. Their comments were very interesting as they observed the bare breasts of the women, the young, the middle age, and old, they compared them all. The length and shape of the breast changed drastically between age groups ranging from a firm half-grapefruit size of a young girl to empty bags of rice, hanging to the waist of an old lady, swaying from side to side as she struggled under her burden of family possessions.

"Look at that!", said Ricciardi, as he stood by the roadside with his attention diverted from the supervision of the small fry work-force. He had bribed them with GI candy to do his work. He said to Boyer, his constant companion: "You know Pfc, I think I finally found out today just what a woman's breast looks like. Is that really what our girlfriends, sisters, and other girls look like back home?"

"Don't know, Bugler." Boyer said, in a voice of dignity, "The girls we know are always dressed up in their fine dresses and we never see them as we see these "Fuzzy Wuzzies". The two Pfcs continued to observe with curiosity as the natives passed silently by. "I imagine", Clark continued, "if they moved a bunch of American women by us as are the natives here today, it would be about the same. Don't you think, Bugler?"

Then Riccairdi, after glancing at his small fry work detail, and yelling for them to get to work, replied: "Its questionable, Pfc, I imagine there are some difference. Maybe I will find out once I get married."

"That I doubt, Bugler. What girl would ever want a runt like you for a husband?" The giant of a man from Tucson laughed as he dodged the make-believe threat of a flying fist from the diminutive five-foot five-inch "Bushmaster" bugler from Brooklyn.

"I would have you to know, Pfc Boyer, that I'm a popular man back home and my mommy has to protect me from all the girls in Brooklyn."

"Yeah, Bugler. That figures, you have a face only a mother could love."

With that the bugler from Brooklyn let loose a verbal barrage that put the man from Tucson to shame, but he soon recovered.

Then from another source nearby: "So that's the way a woman looks with her clothes off!" said Pvt Allen, as he leaned on his pick handle, rain drenching his young face.

"Yeah, there is a resemblance, but it's not the same thing.", said a well-seasoned sergeant of many years in the service in Panama, observing intently as the native parade continued.

"Really, a woman back home cannot look like that! What a horrible thought. My Gosh!. What a sight!" Roupa, said disgustedly.
"Look, smart guy", said Pvt Taylor, standing

in the deep pit he was digging, "You would be surprised to know what the women back home hide inside those fancy clothes and girdles they wear."

By the time the parade of partially dressed women passed, the men got back to work with the final comment from the well-seasoned sergeant of many years in Panama that clinched the conversation: "Well, fellahs, as for me, you can talk all you want about how the women back home dress to conceal their features, I sure wish they were here to cheer me up now and maybe I would enjoy this damn rain."

Listening to the "Bushmasters" conversation mingled with GI slang and humor was even better than listening to Eddie Cantor, Jack Benny, Fred Allen, or even Bob Hope, radio comedians of the time. One could not help but laugh with the men who somehow managed to be cheerful under the most horrible conditions. The parade of the half-naked natives through our area, moving to their new homes, convinced the leadership that the men did not crave sexual liaison with the "Fuzzy Wuzzies", for the sight certainly did not arouse the erotic desires of the loved-starved "Bushmasters". This was important to us, for we knew the women carried venereal diseases for which there were no known medication for treating the diseases they might transmit. The parade helped us to discourage the men from ever having anything to do with the native opposite sex. The parade certainly killed any "Bushmaster's" erotic desire, even if they had one.

Shortly after preparing the area for the new division coming from the States, we were moved to KB Mission to prepare an area for General Krueger's Sixth Army Headquarters. Lt. Whitten, our very efficient intelligence officer, quipped: "Captain Jordan, you know Colonel Herndon was right. You remember he said to us in Panama we were to be the spearhead of an attack on a large force in the Pacific. And now here we are in the Pacific spearheading the advance of the Sixth Army." He caused an uproar of laughter among the men with his candid but humorous remark as they continued cutting their way through the jungle clearing the site for the Sixth US Army Headquarters.

During our stay near the Sixth Army, we met most of the personnel as they came to their new area. Col Jones, the Headquarters Commandant, responsible for the interior layout of Army Headquarters, was old, considering others around him, but he had been with General Krueger, the Army Commander, even at Fort Sam Houston, Texas. He was very meticulous, but friendly to us. Lt. Col. Lee, Assistant G-4 (Logistics), a slim fellow, about 35 years of age, adopted us and visited often. Col Lee had a wife and two small children in Philadelphia, and often spoke of them, showing us their pictures while having coffee with the men at our company mess tent. He was very devoted to his small family.

Then tragedy struck. On may 15, 1943, Colonel Lee with four other officers and an NCO, all from Sixth Army Headquarters, boarded an antique Australian Dehaviland bi-wing, an underpowered airplane we called "Dragonfly", and took off for Goodenough Island located a few miles to the northeast of Milne Bay in the

Pacific Ocean. The young Australian pilot, named Alexander, after taking off, and while making a turn at 3000 feet between the rugged high mountains, had one of the engines of the small plane quit. Alexander, because of loss of power, could not continue the flight and the plane crashed into the mountain top. Later, about noon, two passengers, an American major and an Australian major, very fatigued and injured, staggered into my headquarters tent, telling us the story. Surprisingly, the Australian major died right in my orderly tent. We immediately called the battalion medical detachment and the dead and injured majors were taken to the base hospital.

Colonel Stofft, a very good friend of Colonel Lee from their Fort Sam Houston days, organized a rescue party and directed Lt. Whitten to proceed immediately with his intelligence section to search for the downed plane; I was a member of the main party. The area of search was determined by the American and Australian majors before the Australian's death, who had pointed to the spot on the map of the local area. Colonel Stofft was to lead the main party and would meet Whitten at 4:00PM at a spot designated on the map. If and when Whitten found the crash site, he was to fire three rounds from a rifle and we would home in on subsequent shots.

Lt. Whitten and his party departed as we continued to organize the main body that would effect the rescue, consisting of medical personnel headed by Capt (Doctor) Moulton, the Battalion Surgeon, and his assistant, Lt. (Doctor) Beatty, led by two Australian sergeants, who knew the area, as guides.

Several other personnel who would act as stretcher bearers followed. Hopefully, the natives in the area, who, because of their curiosity, usually surrounded crash sites, could also act as stretcher bearers. Later we were joined by Captain Cochran, Commander of Company "G", and Lt. Livison. When all were ready, having established radio contact with Whitten and base camp in Milne Bay, we took off marching by the rugged streams and steep waterfalls that would lead us up the precipitous jungle covered mountain that hid the downed plane and its injured passengers.

Arriving at the agreed meeting place at the time designated, we found Sgt. Stokesberry from Whitten's scouting party waiting for us; he would guide us in to the crash site. Since Stokesberry met us after finding the site, it was not necessary for Whitten to fire the three shots, for the sergeant could lead us to the downed plane.

Stokesberry gave a report on the conditions found at the site: Col. Lee, Alexander, the Australian pilot, and the American NCO, name unknown, were badly injured. He did not know the extent of the injuries, but one of the pilot's legs had been severed below the knee. Whitten had already radioed a message to base camp telling us of the condition of the injured, and appeared concerned about the pilot, who had lost much blood. We had the necessary medical personnel with us to handle minor medical problems. Looking at the rugged mountain, that appeared to hang vertically from the overhanging clouds, we began the sad and very difficult journey, hoping to find all of the men alive when we arrived at the crash site. Before starting the steep climb we established a base camp at the foot of the mountain. Col. Stofft would remain there to coordinate further assistance as needed for the evacuation of the injured. Capt Cochran and a few additional personnel would also stay at base camp.

We, the advance rescue party, caught by nightfall, crawled along the ledges of the rugged mountain. Even though the moon was full with a clear sky and stars shining in the heavens, the dense jungle forbid their light to reach us. Rocks would be dislodged from the narrow trail and it appeared to be minutes before they crashed far below; it must have been two hundred feet or more. Some of the party was terrified and I worried about the possibility of someone falling over the steep, precipitous mountain side. Hours passed as we struggled up the high mountain, which had less vegetation than far below at its base. Even though we were now traveling under bright moonlight our route was shrouded in doubt. Stokesberry had become disoriented so he decided to fire his rifle three times hoping Whitten would be able to respond using his own firearm. Immediately, confirming shots were heard and we continued in his direction, again occasionally firing shots, confirmed by Whitten. The subsequent shots now being louder proved we were getting closer. Soon, two natives appeared and they guided us the rest of the way.

We arrived at the crash site at 11:00PM. It was a forlorn sight. The plane, its wings torn off, its fuselage reflecting the moonlight, had an eerie appearance similar to a beached, floundered whale - a grim sight.

Col. Lee was in great pain, and the American sergeant, who apparently had only a minor but painful back injury, lay by the plane. Doctors Moulton and Beatty administered morphine to them to ease their pain. The young pilot, Alexander, was out of site. Whitten had moved him away from the others for his death was imminent, he said. Whitten took me and the doctors to the pilot, lying a short distance away from the plane. Whitten had done everything possible for the brave young pilot, still in his early twenties. He had made him as comfortable as could be. His leg, severed just below the knee, lay nearby. He was weakening rapidly and Whitten became alarmed as we looked on, helplessly. Alexander was about to expire. Dr. Moulton shook his head. Whitten, cradling the pilot's head in his arms, became emotional and cried "Oh God!". Then the brave pilot opened his eyes, weakly said his last words: "Mother! Mother!" breathing his last. It was heartbreaking. Tears drenched our cheeks. It was 11:45PM., May 15, 1943. Whitten's brotherly vigil was over. He had attended to Alexander before we arrived, caring for him and trying to ease his pain. The young pilot had been cheerful, and in the short time he had left on earth, expressed his appreciation for Whitten's kind attention. At 5:00PM, Whitten said, the pilot had taken a turn for the worse, but talked until he had lost consciousness. He had said to Whitten: "Yank, I cannot fathom it out. The bloody plane was working perfectly when I took off today." We could do no more for this brave young man, whose eyes were now closed in death. Dr. Moulton covered the body with a blanket retrieved from the wrecked plane and placed the severed leg on top of the blanket across the pilot's chest,then we departed to visit with Lee. Before leaving the death scene I placed the severed leg, glistened like a piece of white chalk in the moonlight, under the blanket out of sight. It was so grotesque.

We returned to Colonel Lee and the injured sergeant who lay in great pain near the wrecked plane.

Doctor Moulton gave Colonel Lee a thorough examination and called me and Doctor Beatty off to the side. His face told us that all was not well with Lee.

"Colonel Lee's right side has been crushed and his broken ribs have punctured his lungs; air is escaping into the cavities around his heart causing his chest area to swell,", he said, shaking his head and waving his hands in desperation. "The escaping air is pressuring his heart; he will not leave here alive. He probably will be dead before sunrise." We glanced toward the colonel who appeared to be rational and was, in fact, showing pictures of his young wife and babies to Whitten. He had shown these same pictures to us before he took the ill-fated flight the morning before.

We had just witnessed the death of the young Australian pilot and now we would see another death as we hovered around the downed plane. The high mountains showed us no mercy for it was very cold in this extremely high altitude. Feeling we would not get any rest, someone suggested we take the injured colonel and sergeant down the mountain, perhaps to the hospital at Gili near Port Moresby. Moulton said any movement would only hasten his death and cause additional pain, but possibly we could make him comfortable. Then they Moulton, Whitten, and most of the advance party departed for base camp to report the situation to Colonel Stofft. They would return with the evacuation party after daylight. Doctor Beatty and I, with a few aid men, remained behind to care for the injured. Following Whitten's and Moulton's departure, Doctor Beatty told me: "Had we brought an instrument, which we have at the aid station, we could have punctured the outer wall of Col Lee's chest, relieving the pressure, and maybe he could have survived." With that Beatty, the aid men and the Australian sergeants, found a place near the plane to lie down and soon were fast asleep, leaving me to attend to Colonel Lee and the injured sergeant.

At times the colonel was restless and then quieted down a bit. He talked of his wife and children, saying he had great plans when he returned home. Then he asked me to get his bag from which he retrieved his wallet. As he had before, again, he proudly showed the pictures of his young wife and children.

"You know, Captain Jordan," he said with a halting voice, "once I get back to Philadelphia I will never leave them again."

Then Captain Moulton's predictions flashed painfully through my mind:... "The colonel will not live until sunrise."... Even then I could tell that he was losing the fight by the minute.

About 2:00AM, Lee went into a coma. His

lips became parched and I applied a damp cloth using water from my canteen. His breathing became labored and the native bearers, standing nearby, began to chant as I continued to work with the dying colonel. It was eerie. I yelled at the number 1 boy (the boss) in pidgin English, to quiet the group but he said it was useless for they wanted to keep the evil spirits away. This added to my already uneasy feeling. I woke Beatty and he made another quick examination of Lee. "If only we had brought that instrument, we could have saved him," he said sadly.

Still keeping the death watch I suffered from the cold, miserable, early morning as it passed slowly. Beatty returned occasionally to observe Lee's rapidly deteriorating condition only to return to his aid men to continue his sleep. Daylight was most welcome; the terrible cold night of terror was over; it was about 6:00AM and the rising sun began to warm the high, sparsely-vegetated mountain top and its unwelcome guests. Frost shone on the fuselage of the downed plane as the aid men began to stir, wakening the Australians. The natives continued to chant their song of death. The colonel, eyes cloudy and staring, breathing laboriously, was beyond help; hopefully, death would come soon. It would be a blessing and a relief to this kind and gracious man who had longed to be with his small family in Philadelphia. He had suffered terribly.

Immediately, preparations were made to evacuate the dying colonel, the injured sergeant, and the body of the dead pilot up the trail to the top of the mountain. Hopefully, Colonel Stofft would have additional personnel there to make the difficult trip down the rugged, steep mountain side. It was 6:30AM, May 17. Using crude stretchers made from the wood of the downed plane, we placed the dead, the dying, and the injured sergeant on them. Again, I discussed the effect the move would have on the dying colonel with Beatty, the medical authority on the spot. He was noncommittal, making it more difficult to make a decision. I hesitated, fearing the move would hasten Lee's death, but then I gave the order to begin the move up the steep mountain side, using the still chanting natives as stretcher bearers.

"Look, Captain Jordan!"; an alarmed cry came from an aid man. Turning toward the sound he pointed to Lee. There was no life visible. His cloudy eyes were staring into the bright sunlit sky, and his once labored breathing had stopped. No longer could the rattle of death be heard as the natives chanted. Beatty rushed to Lee's side, listening to his heart and felt his pulse.

"Captain Jordan, the colonel is dead!", Beatty said with the relief we all felt, for we knew there was no hope for him. With the native bearers struggling with the sergeant and the bodies of the colonel and the Australian warrant officer on the crude stretchers, we headed up the steep trail for the top of the mountain.

Arriving, we were overjoyed to see Colonel Stofft, Captain Moulton, Captain Cochran and Lt Whitten, with twenty-five additional natives carriers, waiting for us. I informed them of Colonel Lee's death. Silently, they bowed their heads in sorrow.

Colonel Stofft walked a few feet away to be alone, for Lee had been a very close friend. Composing himself, he returned to us and tried to be cheerful.

It became necessary to construct new stretchers as the ones made from the wood of the plane were too weak for the difficult and extremely hazardous trip down the rugged mountain side. The native number-one boy gave orders, and his crew took off into the jungle returning soon with materials gathered for the fabrication of the stretchers. What jungle craftsmanship! Within fifteen minutes the natives had constructed three stretchers using bamboo poles and jungle vines laced between two poles to form the stretchers. Once completed, the native craftsmen laid the stretchers by the two dead bodies and the injured sergeant and stood by, making no effort to place them on the stretchers.

The Australians answered our silent questions. "The natives will do almost anything except touch a dead body. You must put the bodies on and lash them to the stretchers and then they will carry them down the mountain for you."

Quickly, we loaded and lashed the bodies of the dead warrant officer, the colonel, and the injured sergeant on the stretchers. The native bearers came forward, picked them up, and we started the difficult, dangerous, and sad journey down the rugged mountain side for the base camp far below. It was 9:30AM.

When we had climbed the mountain the night before we could not see how hazardous it had been for us. Indeed, it had been a miracle that we arrived at the crash site without someone falling over the steep, precipitous mountain that appeared to hang from the clouds. And now here we were with two dead bodies and the injured NCO, each carried by six screaming and chanting natives, trying to get to safety. While the rest of us held on to vines and trees and at time, crawled down the trail, we watched in awe as the native bearers carried their heavy burdens, still screaming and chanting to each other. One mistake and the natives, with their dead or injured human burdens, would plummet down the mountain, impacting on the rocky creek bed hundreds of feet below. We kept a constant watch over the cringing sergeant as he peeked over the side of his stretcher only to cover his eyes in terror. The number one boy constantly screamed orders to his subordinates and they chanted in return. The Australians, calm as a summer breeze, assured us that all would be well and we would arrive at base camp without further injury.

Finally, and with thankfulness for our deliverance, we arrived intact at base camp. No further death or injury had incurred to our tired and exhausted party. We were met by a waiting army ambulance and medical personnel that relieved us of our burdens.

It had been one of the most trying times of my life. Exhausted from lack of sleep, suffering from the cold night, the terrible climb up and the return down the steep mountain, we finally reached our battalion area. The mess personnel were serving the noon meal and once we were seen approaching the area, we were greeted by First Sergeant Dixon and Mess Sergeant Reybourne. Quickly, Bandsuch and Richards, our orderlies, spread our table with food and drink and attended to our every need; they knew about our terrible ordeal, both physical and emotional. The officers and NCOs crowded around asking questions and we tried to explain to them in spite of our exhausted condition. They expressed concern and suggested we get needed rest. Completing our meal, we headed for a shower made from two fifty-five gallon oil drums with a shower head attached, placed upon uprights surrounded by canvas for privacy. The cool water invigorated our bodies as we washed away the accumulated dirt and sweat. We clothed ourselves in clean underwear and fatigues and proceeded to get much needed rest and sleep. We were thankful the heavens had provided bright sun-light instead of the usual downpour of rain for the terrible ordeal we had undergone.

We attended funeral services for Colonel Lee and Warrant Office Alexander the following day at the base thatch-made chapel. Many military brass of all ranks were there, even General Krueger. I don't remember the program; I thought of the colonel's wife and two small children, and the warrant officer's mother was on my mind throughout the service. I wondered if they had been notified by their respective governments. Perhaps they were already grief-stricken.

The evacuation of the dead and injured from the rugged mountain was a dream of terror from the beginning to the end, an event that will forever haunt me as a terrible memory. Still to this day, I wonder what has happened to Colonel Lee's family to which he was so devoted.

CHAPTER 19

IT'S GOODENOUGH FOR ME

Sinhass, the private, could have compromised the grand strategy of MacArthur, the General. "It's good enough for me", he wrote to his girlfriend in Boston, but the company censor cut it out. Lt. Pavlich, being the company censor, read all of the company's outgoing mail, scanning each letter to prevent disclosure of possible military secrets that could fall into the hands of the enemy. Daily the company mail orderly would pile the men's outgoing personal letters on First Sergeant Dixon's folding field table in the orderly tent to be examined before he mailed them. Even though Pavlich detested doing the censoring, feeling he had no business reading other people's mail. It was a very necessary duty, and a distasteful job, but because of his position as company executive officer, it fell on his broad shoulders. Yet, if effective censuring was not done, military information could inadvertently be circulated back home and perhaps, eventually, the spies could forward it to the enemy, resulting in possibly compromising some of our secret operations plans to the enemy; many lives could be lost. Such information had to be cut from the letters, often leaving little for the writer's family to read.

Pvt Singhass could see no reason why he shouldn't let his girlfriend and family know where he was by writing "it's good enough for me." To the untrained eye the phrase, "it's good enough for me", only stated a satisfactory place to be or something pleasing to the eye. In Singhass' case, however, he tried to slip one by Pavlich, only to be called in and lectured about his carelessness, intended or otherwise. He was trying to tell his girlfriend that he was heading for Goodenough Island, located just north of Milne Bay, a few miles off the coast of New Guinea in the calm Pacific Ocean. Should Pvt. Singhass' information been innocently circulated by his girlfriend in Boston that he was going to Goodenough, have gotten into the hands of the Japanese, they would have known a large American force, consisting of Army and Marines, could be heading for Goodenough Island. Using such military information, even as innocent as it may seem, a smart enemy intelligence-gathering officer would know something was afoot and could take countermeasures, perhaps sinking some of the troop ships on their way to Goodenough Island. Then, too, such a troop movement would indicate to the Japanese high command that a possible major offensive was heading their way.

Goodenough was to become a staging area for an offensive against New Britain, an effort of General MacArthur to isolate Rabaul located on the northeast tip of New Britain Island. Rabaul was the Japanese' major naval base, aircraft and troop staging area for launching offensive operations against the allies. The "Bushmasters" would be a part of the invasion force, in conjunction with the 1st Marine Division, which would land on Cape Glouster, the western-most part of New Britain, staging from Goodenough Island. While the leathernecks were to land at Cape Glouster, the "Bushmasters" and the 112th Cavalry would land at Arawa, located on the underbelly of the island. Pvt. Singhass, a very devoted soldier, had no intention of giving such vital information to the enemy, even if he knew, but he inadvertently could have, had his letter telling his girlfriend that "it's good enough for me" gotten into enemy's hands. So Lt. Pavlich, being alert, cut out the passage "it's good enough for me" from the letter and Private Singhass' girlfriend never knew of his whereabouts until after the war.

We were alerted about July 1 to dispatch two infantry companies to Goodenough Island, mission unknown. However, judging from past experience, we just knew it would be a continuation of unloading ships, building roads, and laying pipelines in staging areas as we had been doing in Milne Bay. Major Hohnhorst, the battalion executive officer, would accompany the two infantry companies. In the meantime, the rest of the battalion was to train on LCIs (Landing Craft Infantry) performing combat loading and unloading with individual combat gear.

The LCIs (Landing Craft Infantry) had the capability of ramming into shore and lowering two ramps, which enabled combat troops to offload in minutes and effectively engage the enemy. Such maneuvers would be preceded by air and naval bombardment hopefully keeping the enemy bottled up in his fox-holes until we had established a beachhead. The "Bushmasters" eagerly and gleefully trained until we could disembarked the LCIs in less than three minutes and take positions on the beach, ready to meet the enemy's counterattack. We were confident and eagerly looked forward to our first taste of combat with the Sons of Nippon, but it was as if we were playing them a game of softball. The officers discussed the attitude of the "Bushmasters", for it was in that light the men were going to engage the Japanese in such a game. They needed an attitude change that would breed in them more respect for the tenacious enemy and take proper protective measures or we would suffer excessive casualties. More training was done with this in mind and we successfully ingrained into our men that invasion of enemy territory was not a game of sport, but rather one of life and death. Hopefully, the eager red man from Arizona, the Mexican from the southwest, and the Caucasian from anywhere USA, got the idea that war was a serious business. Some of them would be killed or wounded regardless of how careful we were, but we could reduce our casualties if we took precautionary measures, mainly by not unduly exposing ourselves to the enemy's deadly fire.

The remainder of the battalion was alerted on July 10 for a possible move to Goodenough Island, later confirmed to be July 15. Loading onto three LCIs in the late evening of July 14 in the usual downpour of rain, we spent the night crowded aboard the small LCIs anchored in the bay. At 4:00AM the next morning, the powerful engines throbbed and the three LCIs headed for the east end of New Guinea, turning to the northwest for Goodenough Island. The rain lifted for the first time in ten days and we enjoyed the blue waters of the Pacific as we passed Ferguson and Nornby Islands, leisurely cruising along the north coast of New Guinea. Hopefully, we would never see that dreadful place - Milne Bay - again.

Goodenough Island, devoid of human habitation, was a typical tropical island, having trade winds, palm trees, beautiful sandy beaches, and good swimming and fishing, if and when we would have time to enjoy these luxuries. After arriving, we relieved an Australian Infantry Battalion which was sent into action around Lae, New Guinea, and assumed their housekeeping duties on the island. In addition to defending the island against possible Japanese invasion, we, as usual, had the duties of a port and an engineer battalion. Captain Caffee, the battalion Operation Officer, responsible for any combat or training operations, organized a mobile force to move anywhere on the island to repel an enemy invasion if such became necessary. However, through our intense patrol reconnaissance, the only enemy troops on the island were half dead from starvation and thirst. Goodenough Island was barren of food except for water, and we controlled that. The starving Japanese were the remnants of a troop convoy sunk by General Kenny's 5th Air Force during the past February. Using a skip bombing method, they sunk six troop transports as they sneaked along the northern coast of New Guinea. General Kenny's planes also sank all the enemy's naval ships accompanying the convoy of troops. Winston Churchill said of the air victory, "It was a textbook on the use of planes in combat."

Then cargo ships began to arrive and we had to unload them. Tactical requirements demanded we constantly patrol the island on foot and by boat. Fortifications had to be built and bridges and roads were needed to reach the recently established staging area for the Marine and Army troops that would soon arrive. It looked like Milne Bay all over again, or even worse. We had given up hope of ever seeing combat. As adjutant, I was responsible for administrative details, getting troops out to unload boats, build roads, and lay pipelines, etc. To be more effective, in conjunction with Lt. Fagan, the battalion supply officer, we organized our respective sections into a twenty-four hour operation. Sergeant Sitz, the battalion sergeant major, was instrumental in working with the five company first sergeants, and was very effective getting details out to the many work places. In spite of all the details, we managed to get in some tactical training, but yet the "Bushmaster" morale and pride was injured. We were doing something we hadn't been trained to do. Even though we were told what we were doing was more important than any combat operations, our morale dropped. Adding to this, malaria fever continued to take its toll; we resigned ourselves to the fact that the Pacific war was bypassing us without our having seen combat.

When we had time, we tried to play softball we had only a few bats, gloves, and balls available, but we managed to play anyway. The Red Cross had only one copy of Life Magazine for hundreds to read and no recreational equipment. We did have a radio and enjoyed "Tokyo Rose" broadcasting American music followed by her very sultry, seductive voice, telling us how wonderful it would be for us to be home with our sweet wives or girlfriends. Her program was really the high point of our day for we had nothing else to enjoy.

Some men became mentally deranged requiring their evacuation. Lt. Pavlich and others had to be evacuated due to a fungus growth covering their entire chests area with painful, boil-like, infections. Severe disciplinary problems occurred. The dehydrated food was so terrible the men refused to eat it. The mess sergeant traded it to the natives on a nearby island for taro, a root plant something like a potato, and for bananas. For some reason the natives loved the "stuff" the army called food.

Late one evening, while at my field table planning for the next day's activities, I heard a blood-curdling cry. Quickly, pistol in hand, I jumped to my feet, heading out of the tent and grabbing a flashlight on the way. Using my flashlight I spotted two men running, one behind the other. Could this be a Japanese ready to pounce on one of the "Bushmasters"? I rushed forward to see what was happening. The rear runner finally tackled the forward runner, bringing him down. As they wrestled, I pulled the slide of the Cal..45 pistol, it slammed forward placing a round in the chamber, cocking it. Being unable to tell friend from foe, still holding the pistol muzzle upward, then I heard one of them say in a deep southern drawl: "Keep praying, mothah, I'll get home some day, yet." I cleared my pistol, replaced it in the holster and asked about the matter.

"Captain Jordan," said one, "he's been despondent for several days and just now he began crying like a baby for his mother. Then he started screaming and running, wanting to return home located someplace in Georgia."

Instructing the man to take his buddy to the battalion aid station, I returned to my table to continue the next day's troop labor requirements. The poor man was evacuated to Australia the following day. He never returned to us. I thought of the young Australian pilot who had died in Whitten's arms in the steep mountains near Milne Bay, and he, too, had cried for his mother seconds before his death. Many of the men were just young kids and had never been away from home before they were drafted into the service. Some could not break the attachment for their mothers, especially under the circumstances and the isolation we had found ourselves. I often wondered how heartbreaking it would be if their mothers only knew their sons had cried for them during such times.

"Captain Jordan", said Sgt. Reybourne, one day while discussing the possible improvement of the menu, "I have a lot of flour stacked up in the mess tent. If only I had some yeast I could have the bakers make hot rolls for the men."

What a wonderful thing to have hot rolls like Wilma had made for me while we still lived in Charleston! What a morale builder it would be for the men to have hot rolls smothered in melting butter! Something had to be done to get yeast for the sergeant's bakers. I made it known to everyone to scour the island for surely, someone had yeast. The men scattered to search, for they wanted to smell the hot rolls the baker would make them. The Japanese threat was forgotten, road and bridge-building took a nose dive, the ships stood idle; the great hunt for yeast had begun. Then it happened - a miracle!

Someone had found some yeast! A GI whiskey maker, a boot-legger, had his still snuggled among the high mountains by a rapidly running stream, doing great business they said. He had many customers.

"Captain Jordan," said Ruiz, Sergeant, Grade IV, "I have found where you can get the yeast so the bakers can bake hot rolls for us to eat."

"Ruiz, if you have done that I will petition the Congress of the United States to hang the Congressional Medal of Honor around your sweaty neck. Where did you find the yeast? Tell me, quick!"

"That's just it, Captain. I can't tell you where you can get the yeast to make the hot rolls for us to eat."

"But you just said you knew where I could get some yeast so the bakers could make hot rolls, smothered in butter, for us to eat. Another remark like that and I will have you boiled in oil." And he thought that was funny.

"Captain, I can get the yeast so the cooks can bake hot rolls for us to eat, but you cannot get the yeast from the person so we can have hot rolls for us to eat."

It appeared we were getting into a jargon of a monologue of some kind "getting hot rolls for us to eat" so I changed my plan of attack to have the crafty Sergeant Ruiz tell me where someone could get the yeast so we could have hot rolls for us to eat.

"All right Ruiz, just tell me, even whisper, if you like, where we can get the damn yeast so we... damn it Ruiz, tell me where can get the stuff so we can have, ...whatever it is we are saying, for us to eat." In the meantime First Sergeant Dixon was on his knees, his sides splitting with laughter while we wrestled the matter to the floor trying to get yeast so we could have hot "rolls for us to eat."

Then he told me. "Captain, there is this GI bootlegger from the hills of West Virginia, up in the nearby mountains who has the yeast. He has promised he would give me the yeast if you will not interfere with his whiskey making. If you cannot do that, then the deal is off."

Now these conditions put to me by the emissary of the bootlegger from West Virginia had to have some cogitation, but it didn't take long for I, too, wanted some of the hot rolls soaked in butter.

"Ruiz, I promised you the Congressional Medal of Honor, but instead I will give you even greater recognition and let you have the first hot roll to eat. Your courageous effort is above and beyond the call of duty."

Still laughing, the First Sergeant said: "What in the h... are you two trying to do? Both of you should join the circus or something. The Army has no use for the likes of you. Maybe you should join a USO show or something." He walked out the orderly tent, his sides still bursting with laughter.

Ruiz left immediately for the whiskey still in the mountains and returned with the yeast. Our bakers went to work immediately and at 11:30PM Ruiz, Sgt Dixon, and I were standing in line at the mess tent for the treat that awaited us. Ruiz was first to receive hot rolls smothered in melted butter, while First Sergeant Dixon, still laughing, was third in line. The aroma from the mess tent permeated the company area and soon two hundred men were in the line to receive the rolls. The cooks had pans and pans of the brown hot rolls "for us to eat". Then a surprise. While enjoying our rolls and butter, a Marine Corps brigadier general and his driver, whom we had never seen before, appeared as if by magic. I called attention and all stood, as is the custom of the service.

"At ease, please", the general replied. Then meekly, he said to me.

"Captain, may I, please, have permission to speak to your mess sergeant?"

"By all means general", and Sergeant Reybourne appeared, and stood at attention before the Marine general.

The general introduced himself, and said, almost begging: "Sergeant, I smelled the aroma of the fresh rolls as we drove along the road. Could we have the pleasure of eating a few, please?"

Then the general and his driver joined us as we all gorged ourselves with the hot rolls and butter. It was an unusual thing. There we were, an inter-service group, officer and enlisted, consuming a delicious thing, made possible only by the bootlegger from the hills of West Virginia. We owed him a lot, and since we were unable to thank him personally, I had Ruiz express our appreciation to him. We kept his whereabouts secret, for he was beneficial to us and not only for his yeast, either.

Following the hot rolls incident, the "Bushmasters" played a joke on one of our good chaplains; the man who kept us spiritually advised and guided us through times of woe, but who had a problem of his own. He liked to take a nip occasionally - like every night for instance, after playing a game of poker with the officers in the mess tent. All wondered where he got his spirits, for he knew nothing of the West Virginia bootlegger operating in the nearby mountain - or at least he said he didn't. We suspected he drank the altar wine he used during communion service. Anyway it was obvious he indulged.

We had a patrol reconning on the north part of the island one day and they found a well-decomposed Japanese body. Only the bones were left; perhaps the unfortunate soldier had starved to death. The mischievous men got an idea and retrieved the skull, bringing it in to camp, where they got a pot, filled it with water, built a fire under the pot, and place the skull therein; shortly, they had it clean as a whistle. Then they painted the skull with aluminized paint and impaled it on a stick. Now they were ready for the final phase of their mischievous plan. The drunken chaplain was selected to be the victim.

It was a warm tropical night, a cool breezing gently waved the palm trees, and as usual the chaplain was playing cards with Pavlich, Hohnhorst, Allen, and Tompkins in the mess tent under the light of a Coleman lantern. The members of the patrol were all alert, knowing the whereabouts of the chaplain, and once they saw him playing cards it was time for them to act. Quickly, they got the painted skull, already impaled on the stick, and ran to the chaplain's tent off on a darkened path, driving the stick into the ground near the tent's entrance. The skull shone brightly in the darkness, the eye sockets and nose showing clearly. The pranksters took position and waited for the fun to begin. Then here, as usual, came the inebriated chaplain. Almost immediately, the chaplain wasn't so inebriated any longer. Seeing the grinning skull near his tent, he froze, looked, turned on his heels and ran screaming that a "ghost" was in his tent. Then the mischievous soldiers quickly removed the skull and took position nearby to await further developments. Shortly, the Chaplain returned, all excited, with a group of men with him, telling them of what he had seen. To his surprise the "ghost" had disappeared and, of course, the followers did not believe his story, accusing him of having too much to drink or maybe he should change his brand of altar wine.

That ended the chaplains drinking from there on. He spoke about the evils of drinking at future sermons after that. He even refused to play poker with the "boys", too. The chaplain was converted for sure. He had been a great chaplain before the incident, but was now even a better chaplain after the fact!

Shortly after the bakers had baked rolls for us to eat (the phrase had been coined since the first discussion with Ruiz), General Krueger, Commander of the Sixth US Army, moved his headquarters from Milne Bay to Goodenough Island. The 1st Marine Division, veterans of Guadalcanal, arrived to stage for the invasion of Cape Glouster and it appeared a major military effort was in progress. We received orders relieving us from all housekeeping and port duties for Goodenough Island and began an intense period of training in preparation for becoming a part of DIRECTOR TASK FORCE. We were to land in Arawa in conjunction with the Marines' invasion of New Britain. The morale increased like a raging prairie fire. Finally, the "Bushmasters", would have the chance to prove their worth in combat. Marine Corps officers, veterans from Guadacanal, were sent to tell us of their experience and describe the combat effectiveness and tactics of the Japanese army.

Training increased along with refitting, performing maintenance of vehicles and weapons, and needed resupply. Morale was high and even the conduct of "Buckhead" Gardner, an "Eight Ball" transferred to us from the 5th Infantry while in Panama, improved. First Sergeant Dixon commented that Gardner was doing much better and suggested, since we were about to enter combat, perhaps I should withdraw pending courts-martial charges against him for his bad conduct, and I did.

During all the commotion, one day I had my second glimpse of General MacArthur. While driving up to the staging area for a meeting concerning the upcoming operations against the Japanese on New Britain, I was forced to stop on the dusty road. Other military vehicles ahead of me had pulled to the side of the road at the direction of a vigorous military policeman. We became restless, waiting to get on the road again. Then we were approached by the military policeman and ordered to get out of the jeep and stand at attention.

"Captain, get out of your vehicle and stand at attention, quick!" the MP said.

"Who do you think you are? An MP ordering us to stand at attention?" I retorted. His remark added to my already bad temper at having to wait unnecessarily in the hot tropical sun.

To my surprise, the MP actually reached for his pistol as I still sat in my jeep, ignoring his threat.

"Captain, I said get out of your jeep and stand at attention immediately. General MacArthur is due to pass by here any second and everyone must be standing at attention when he passes by."

Well, perhaps I should have obeyed the MP, but instead I just laughed at him. What he was doing was against all military discipline, courtesy and customs of the service. I continued to sit as the MP looked at me in a bewildered manner. He realized he had a bull-headed captain on his hands who refused to obey his orders. Why should all of the vehicles be stopped on the dusty road when they should be rolling? We were at war and General MacArthur would have understood anyway. I suppose someone wanted to make brownie points with the Commander-in-Chief, for MacArthur, being a pompous man, liked being groveled to.

Then here he came! In a command car was MacArthur, dressed in his cotton uniform and the his old beaten-up cap he had always worn, even at Bataan, with "scrambled egg" trimming on the bill. With his very picturesque profile, the long-stemmed corncob pipe stuck in his mouth, he was staring straight ahead through tinted sunglasses, oblivious to all who were standing at attention by the side of the road all saluting, except me. After MacArthur passed, the MP gave me a hard stare as I still sat in the jeep. The driver, Woolridge, started the engine, and as we pulled out onto the road the MP saluted me, grinned, and moved on. Perhaps he felt that I had done the right thing even though he was only carrying out orders. The unannounced appearance of the C-in-C certainly did not deserve to disrupt the military effort.

Later that afternoon I had a third view of MacArthur. After he met with the senior commanders who would be involved in the operation against New Britain, we were alerted to be prepared to receive a visit from a V.I.P. There could be no doubt who that was for everyone knew MacArthur was on the island. The "Bushmasters" officers of the battalion were assembled at the flagpole across the creek from battalion headquarters at 5:00PM. Lt. Tompkins and his P & A Platoon had constructed a bridge across the creek, but we were told our distinguished visitor would not cross the creek, but would meet us at the flagpole. As the officers assembled near the flag pole, so did hundreds of the men gather across the creek for a glimpse of the V.I.P., whoever he would be.

Looking up the road we saw a dust trail following a small convoy of vehicles; one vehicle had a flag on each front fender waving rapidly in the trade wind's breeze. The sun was low on the Pacific horizon and the heat of the day was disappearing as the small convoy stopped in front of the assembled officers. Colonel Stofft, the battalion commander, called us to attention, did an about face, and prepared to receive the V.I.P. as the command car with five stars on its flag stopped in front of us. The driver of the command car and a senior officer, perhaps an aide, rapidly dismounted and stood at attention as General MacArthur dismounted. Colonel Stofft, did another about face and commanded: "Present Arms", and we quickly responded. He reported to the general, saying: "Sir, the officers and men of the 2nd Battalion, 158th RCT welcome you and are honored to have you visit us today, General." or words to that effect.

Then General MacArthur offered a few brief words to us: "Thank you, Colonel. I wish you and your fine men the best in your coming adventures against the enemy on New Britain. May Providence bless your arms." His voice was resonant and very regal and, for once, I felt almost sorry for General MacArthur. He was beyond the common man and had to remain isolated from normal events of the day. We all stood in awe. He walked up to Colonel Stofft and offered his hand, then silently returned to his command car and mounted the left rear seat. The little convoy, with its V.V.I.P. (Very, very important person), departed the area in a cloud of swirling dust. We, the "Bushmasters" watched as the VIP's vehicle passed from view. Soon the night would enclose us with our thoughts of New Britain and of our egotistical leader, the most brilliant military commander of all times. We now knew the chain holding us to the stake had been cut, releasing us from the laborious duties of service troops. Would our new-found freedom be a mistake?

MacArthur's visit was electrifying. Colonel Stofft looked at his right hand as if it been touch by the Supreme Being. Then, with the agility of a monkey, he swung himself around the flagpole as we yelled with glee; we knew we would be heading for New Britain. Stevedoring, building roads, laying pipelines, and stringing wire, was over. This was the beginning of the "Bushmasters'" march to glory. They would blaze their way to victory, leapfrogging from island to island, from Goodenough, New Britain, Kiriwina, Wakde-Sarmi, Noemfoor, Luzon and finally Japan itself. No military unit would prove more effective. But the "Bushmasters'" road to glory would be difficult; many names of the regiment's dead and wounded would be listed in historical records before the war's end.

TASK FORCE DIRECTOR was to attack at 6:00 AM, December 15. The initial landings were to be executed by the 112th Cavalry Squadron, with "A" Troop making its landing behind enemy lines. Hopefully, they would prevent the Japanese escape or their reinforcing their front, while "B" Troop would land on nearby Pielo Island, destroying the radar station there. The remainder of the squadron was to land at the jetty, their first objective, then would proceed to the second objective, the high ground just to the northeast. Following this, the squadron would continue to the final objective, cutting off the neck of the peninsula which jutted from the mainland into the ocean, joining forces with Troop "A", which was to land in rear of the enemy near the neck of the peninsula. The whole purpose was to draw attention from the main attack by the Marines landing on Cape Glouster, on the western end of New Britain, on December 26. If our operation was successful, the enemy's barge lines operating between Gosmata on the east and Cape Bushing to the west would be cut, denying the Japanese on Cape Glouster their main source of logistical support.

The operation was to be preceded by a heavy naval and aerial bombardment. The "Bushmasters" would be in reserve and committed later.

The "Bushmasters" launched into severe training with the Navy, practicing climbing up and down cargo nets from Navy's APD ships to LCMs (Landing Craft Materiel) making practice assault landings on the island of Goodenough. We were sharp, ready and eager. We checked and rechecked men and equipment. Again and again, we assembled to be ferried to the Navy's APDs for many practice assault landings on the beaches of Goodenough.

On December 15, we continued training with the Navy, making assault landings as we anxiously awaited the first reports of the cavalry's landing on New Britain. The cavalry's success or failure would determine if we would go to Arawa. We were concerned that the Cavalry squadron, specially trained in recon operations, was not the type of unit that should make the initial landing at Arawa; assault landings were more of an infantry-type operation and we wondered why we were not selected to make the assault. We continued training in order to reduce our landing time from ship to shore. We were transported back to the LTDs time after time. We practiced troop assembly, down the cargo nets to LCMs, bobbing by the ship's side, until finally we accomplished the maneuver in twenty-three minutes, smashing the Marines' records of twenty-six minutes, according to the Navy. "Now we are one up on the 'Gyrenes'", said Major Hornhorst, in jest.

Taking a break from training, we were finishing lunch with the ship's officers in the ornate wardroom when Captain Caffee, the operations officer, excitedly boarded the ship. Rushing to the dining area he made the initial report from New Britain; even before he began we could tell he had bad news for us.

"Colonel Stofft, and Gentlemen, I have a report from the 112th cavalry now engaged with the enemy at Arawa." Caffee, who was usually all smiles and cheerful, did not present his usual self. Quickly, he hung a map on the wall of the ward room. The map showed Cape Mercus peninsula as it jutted out like a finger into the ocean from the belly of New Britain on which Arawa is located.

Then, pointing to Arawa with a ball-point pen, he related the terrible news to us. Troop "A" which was designated to land behind the enemy line had ran into serious trouble.

They were unable to land because their rubber boats had gotten stuck on an unknown reef and never reached shore. Furthermore, they faced a twenty-five foot high cliff on which the enemy had 25mm anti-aircraft guns and blew "A" Troops out of the water. "The extent of the dead and wounded is unknown at this time, but "A" Troop, about 200 men, has been written off as an ineffective combat unit." Then he continued.

"Fortunately, the reminder of the assault landing was successful and the final objective was reached by 12:00 (Noon), but the enemy is counterattacking strongly. There is evidence that the enemy is beginning to move reserve troops from Itna River area in the west toward Arawa which are expected to arrive in a matter of hours. Gentlemen, this is the end of the report; I will keep you informed as more information becomes available. Thank you."

We were dumbfounded. In all of our briefings by the officers from <u>DIRECTOR TASK FORCE</u>, this was the first time we knew of the twenty-five foot vertical cliff at the landing site of "A" Troop. We questioned Caffee: "Did anyone know of the existence of that cliff which would have to be scaled by the troops, and did anyone know of the 25mm anti-aircraft Guns situated on top of that cliff?"

"It seems unreasonable but, to the best of my knowledge, this is the first time we knew about the cliff."

"Murder, absolutely murder," said another. "Those poor bastards didn't have a chance of surviving. They were doomed from the time they scaled down the cargo nets into their rubber boats. Someone should be courts-martialed! What kind of intelligence officers does DIRECTOR TASK FORCE have anyway, Caffee? They should have never sent in the cavalry in the first place; they were not trained for such an operation. Why weren't we sent instead? We would have never gotten caught in such a mess!" The officer raved on about the commanding general, General Shuman, and his inability to get along with people, always threatening officers to get things done. Even though the officer was telling it as he saw it, and it was true, he was being disrespectful and was subject to severe disciplinary action. He did have the courage to state the truth and we all knew it.

Colonel Stofft, seeing the conversation was bordering on a serious rebuff of a sister unit, cautioned: "Gentlemen, let's watch our tongues. We were not there and maybe Troop 'A' was put ashore at the wrong place. Who knows?"

Regardless, we had lost a troop of good men most of whom died while they were hanging helplessly onto the reef as the wicked 25 mm enemy anti-aircraft guns cut them to pieces. The poor devils didn't have a chance to fire a single shot. With the loss of "A" Troop, the 112th Cavalry would not have sufficient troops to hold the line across the finger of land where it joined the mainland near Ditmop.

The "Bushmasters" day of performing the duties of service troops were over, for sure. The pages in the regimental history were beginning to turn; perhaps our baptism of fire was finally at hand. The "Bushmasters" had work to be done - saving the cavalry.

CHAPTER 20

OUR BAPTISM BY FIRE

Captain Caffee's report had its electrifying results. Shortly, we were on the Navy's APDs headed for Finschaffen, New Guiana - a 24 hour voyage across the Solomon Sea. Arriving at Finschaffen, we quickly disembarked and transloaded equipment and personnel aboard LSTs (Landing Ship Tank), combat ready, then crossed the Viatiz Strait to Arawa, New Britain, sixty miles away.

Arawa was desolated. Once a beautiful coconut plantation, owned by a large soap company in the United States, its tall palms trees were now stripped of their limbs, giving it the appearance of a dead planet. This small piece of real estate lay jutting out into the Pacific, churned up by the recent battle; its white sandy road meandering through the tall, twisting, denuded palm tree stumps as if large earth worms standing on end were looking down at us; its many deep shells holes half-filled with stinking sulphur water; the heat of the hot tropical sun reflecting from the sand - this scene certainly did not portray a south sea paradisiacal glory to the "Bushmasters". It appeared that God had forsaken this once beautiful haven and Satan was making it into a hell for us. This was our first impression and even that got worse as we marched to our area in rear of the 112th Cavalry on the Main Line of Resistance (MLR).

Ahead were the Imperial Marines of Nippon. Each Marine was very large, over six feet tall, vicious, and willing to die for the

Emperor (for surrendering was disgraceful). They had already bloodied the nose of the demoralized cavalry, and now stood poised to do battle with the "Bushmasters". Hopefully, the Cavalry would hold while we got ourselves dug in a perimeter defensive posture with 360 degrees protection; the battalion command post, service units, communications, headquarters, aid station, and motor pool would be located in the center of the perimeter. Even though we were not completely dug in we could withstand a Japanese Banzai attack should they launch one through the Cavalry. Since kitchens would not be operational immediately, "C" rations were issued, canteens filled with water, having the taste of sulphur, from shell holes purified by the Engineers water point. Even the military cemetery with its many opened graves could be seen and soon would be filled. Our dead among the KIAs (killed in action), were also in view. Arawa later would prove itself to be a bigger hell then we thought possible, not as much by the vicious Imperial Marines from Japan but by the sun-baked environment, its isolation, its desolation, the lack of palatable food and the terrible-tasting sulfuric drinking water.

Troops were busily engaged under company officers and NCOs preparing defensive positions, while commanders and staff officers went forward to the MLR to visit the Cavalry and to get acquainted with the lay of the land. We were surprised at the defensive positions of the cavalry, for many of their crew-served weapons were too close together, enabling the enemy to neutralize both with a single round of artillery or a mortar shell, nor, often were they mutually supporting. The cavalrymen appeared to be very concerned, knowing they could have done better in defensive preparations, but time did not permit adequate preparations. They also were very nervous for they had lost "A" Troop in its entirety on "D" Day and that it certainly had its mental effects on all. Further, they feared a vicious "Banzai" attack through their position by the Japanese Marines hoping to get the "Bushmasters" off balance before we could properly defend ourselves. It was a good time for such an enemy offensive; it did not materialize, thankfully.

Noting the nervous conditions of the officers and men of the cavalry, I felt it necessary for our officers to go further forward to observe beyond the MLR (Main Line of Resistance), and it was here I also found that we, ownselves, were nervous. Suggesting to Captain Caffee, who was a very close friend of mine since Panama, that we needed more clarity and should go a short distance in front of the MLR for additional information, I was surprised when he exploded. His usual friendly smiles, now registered anger.

"Ben Rod, you are a damn fool! Do you realize we are already in an exposed position and yet you want to go beyond the MLR?"

"Look Bob, we would be in no greater danger there than here for we are already under enemy observation here as well, and we do need more terrain analysis as well as more enemy information. It's better then getting it secondhand."

"Ben Rod, I know you are right, but

let's not go overboard on our first trip up here. Take it easy, huh."

We terminated our tour after visiting the MLR, seeing the excited and nervous looks of the men and officers did not settle our nerves at all. We returned to our own perimeter defensive area, finding the men still vigorously digging in, kidding each other as if they were training back in Australia oblivious of the vicious Jap Imperial Marines not far away who could easily have penetrated the cavalry and be in our area in minutes. But that was the "Bushmasters" trait, a trait that was going to change shortly.

It was the policy that officers dig their own fox-holes, if at all possible. However, there are times, due to official functions, when officers cannot dig concurrently with the men, but they intend to do it later. This has proven disastrous at times for the officer often is caught under fire and has no place prepared for his safety. Such was the case when we returned from visiting the MLR. We hadn't had time to dig our own fox-holes and it was getting dark. However, we were fortunate, for Bandsuch and Richards, often called strikers, looked after me, Colonel Stofft and the staff. They came to our aid and during our visit to the MLR had dug our fox-holes, and we were very grateful. Richards, in his great effort, made my fox hole similar to that of a grave, permitting me to lie flat in the bottom, completely obscuring my body. He had added two rows of sandbags around the top of the dugout, making it even safer.

This is an example of how the men looked after their leaders, realizing they were busy looking after the men's welfare in general, not being able to dig their own defensive positions until much later.

Our first night on Arawa was uneventful, except for the usual single Jap plane from Rabaul the cavalry called, "Washing Machine Charley" that made its usual bomb run. It was only harassing maneuver. Even though it was relatively harmless, we took precautionary measures just in case the bomb should fall in our area. Charley would dropped his single bomb and return to his base. The bomb would have its effect, for the many troops and equipment were so heavily concentrated in a small area that it would be bound to hit something. At times however, they said "Washing Machine Charley" would drop his bomb in the ocean; "Charley" must be a bad navigator, someone said. Regardless "Charley" would accomplish his mission - harassment.

It had been a long hard day crossing the choppy waters of the Strait and, after once more trooping the lines before night, checking the readiness of the men with First Sergeant Dixon, finding them in a good frame of mind, cheerful, and kidding each other, I returned to my fox-hole, or rather a pit dug to accommodate the length of my body - where even a field telephone had been installed, at the head of my dugout. In the event of an air raid I wouldn't have to get up; it would have taken a direct hit for me to get injured or killed. The field telephone would give me contact with the Battalion and Company Commanders, staff sections, and even headquarters TASK FORCE DIRECTOR should the need occur. The pit, with a sleeping bag, had a notch cut in the side for my helmet and pistol, and was, according to Chaplain Gaskins, more like a grave than sleeping quarters. However, it was convenient, for I did not have to get up and run to the nearby fallout shelter when "Washing Machine Charley" from Rabaul made his nightly bomb run or when a RED alert was sounded. Even Colonel Stofft, like everyone else, had to run for the fallout shelter when "Charley" would visit, uninvited. Nightly he and Major Hohnhorst ran for the fallout shelter; I laughed at their sprinting with helmets in hand for the overcrowded shelter. Later, Chaplain Gaskins, feeling my dugout was a good thing, dug his own near me. After that I could hear him saying nightly prayers for us. He was a good man and a comfort to have around. He favorably influenced all around him.

Our arrival on the peninsula had required much effort to get the men prepared, conduct our inspection of the MLR up front and, it had been a long day since leaving Finchaffen, we were all very tired. The moon was full and high in the heavens, and the stars, like emeralds, dotted the sky, blessing us with beauty above even in the war-torn land. The palms trees nearby, with their palm fronds blown away by the navy attack a few days before, looked like tall crooked fence posts sticking upright in the ground without pattern, casting long, eerie, silent shadows in the moonlight, and were a reminder of the enemy presence only a short distance ahead. Hopefully, the Jap Marines would be held in check by the nervous cavalrymen on the MLR, making it safe for us our first night on Arawa. But we were prepared for battle should they break through in one of their fanatical Banzai attacks for which they were known. Artillery, mortar and machine gun final protective fires had been planned and we had registered them on likely approaches of the enemy should they decide to test us, and they might. Further, to keep the enemy off balance the artillery had planned interdictory preparations to be fired occasionally throughout the night.

Removing my helmet and pistol, placing them in the notch in the side of the dugout Johnson had dug for them, still wearing my jungle boots, I stretched my tired body out on the bedding roll in the bottom of my hole. I was tired and in need of sleep and rest. It had been a long day, but yet I was restless. As I lay in the bottom of my grave-like dugout, unable to sleep, I looked upward into the beautiful heavens and wondered just why war was necessary. I couldn't find a reason to justify war. Everyone would be a loser, I resolved.

I was jolted into reality by the ringing of the telephone. It was the switchboard operator: "This is Corporal Searcy at the switchboard, sir. Just wanted a communications check. Do you read me, sir?"

I replied: "Loud and clear, Corporal. appreciate your call. "Are we tied in with all units of the battalion, attached units, and Task Force Director?"

"Affirmative, sir."

"Are you alone, Corporal Searcy?"

"No sir. PfC Riedbig is on the shift with me. Lt Beane is visiting us now checking on us."

Beane was a good officer, I thought. He never left anything unchecked. Maybe he was too conscientious, being a hard taskmaster, but he was an officer and a gentleman, too. I was grateful to have him, I mulled lying in my grave-like dugout. I remembered well his display of excellent leadership during the march over the mountains to the Solomon Sea from Carlieu.

Then, RED ALERT! "Washing Machine Charley" was on the way. There was the sound of rapidly pounding feet and cursing men as they jumped over and ran around my dugout toward the fallout shelter that had been dug and sandbagged after our arrival. It would hold ten men, none of which would be me. And I anxiously awaited for the bomb to drop.

All was silent over the peninsula. My telephone rang again.

"Corporal Searcy here, Captain Jordan. Just wanted to confirm we have a Red Alert in effect, sir."

"Thank you, Corporal. Just be sure you and Pfc Reibig are under cover."Are there others near you switchboard installation. If so have them return to their positions.

"Thank you, sir. We are under cover."

Again silence. Then the drone of a single plane coming from the northeast. Louder and louder the roar of the engine as the plane neared; my pulse rate jumped. I turned over on my belly for some reason. Then I laughed. I could be killed by the bomb whether I was on my back or belly, I thought. It was a nervous reaction. I turned over on my back.

The plane's engines appeared to be over the area, maybe out to the sea a bit. Then came a loud crack of noise, it seemed; the Japanese pilot had opened the bomb bay doors causing the wind to rush inside the plane and making a sharp explosive sound. Then came the swishing sound of the falling bomb. It grew louder and louder as it sped on its way down to us. Again I turned over on my belly, my fingers, like the talons of an eagle, clawed into the bottom of my dugout. Louder and louder; I waited for the explosion. But where? Would any of us be killed!? Why doesn't it impact and explode? Then it happened. The bomb had missed us and landed harmlessly on the edge of the sea. Shortly, Searcy on the switchboard was receiving reports from all units according to procedures. My field telephone rang; it was Searcy to render a status report.

"Captain Jordan, this is Corporal Searcy. All units reports negative casualties, sir."

"Thank you", I replied, and made my report to Colonel Stofft as he passed by my dugout on his way to his tent. The Colonel inspected my dugout and quipped about how a lazy man handles an air raid, laughed and went on his way, with helmet in hand, talking to Hohnhorst, his tent companion, as if they were returning from a late evening stroll. He was calm; a good example, consider the circumstances. Afterwards I made my report to the TASK FORCE DIRECTOR. The TASK FORCE duty officer said no injuries were reported from anyone. Placing the handset of the EE8 Field Telephone in its carrier once again I spread myself on the bottom of my dugout; hopefully, sleep would come.

Saying a silent prayer then, I thought of Wilma and the boys, Bucky and Johnny, back home. It had been so long since I left them back in Charleston and in New Orleans, going on three years now, and the prospects of seeing them soon weren't good. MacArthur had said no one was to be rotated back home until troop requirement for the SWPA was met.

Then I wondered: what peace of mind would Wilma and the boys have if they knew their husband and father was sleeping in a dugout on a Jap-infested island far away in the wide Pacific ocean? Then my thoughts turned to the poor cavalrymen manning the MLR and the poor devils yet further out on the outpost line (OPL), nothing between them and the infiltrating Japanese who could drop a grenade on top of them or stick a knife blade between their shoulders. But my thoughts were interrupted by friendly artillery. The alert artillerymen fired a few interdictory rounds over our heads to keep the enemy beyond the MLR off balance. We could hear the projectiles as they whizzed over us. Then silence. All of this made the bright moonlit night eerie. I wrestled in the twilight of semi-consciousness until finally succumbing to my body's demands for the comforts of sleep in the security offered by my dugout.

It must not have been long until I was awakened, however.

Something was near my dugout. Whatever it was would quietly move, stop and then move again, as if listening, only to continue. Little-by-little the thing came closer and closer. I dared not rise from my grave-like dugout, fearing I would be a defenseless target. Had the Japanese infiltrators succeeded in penetrating the front lines to the rear area, a common tactic of theirs? The full moon lit up the place as if it was daylight, yet, I dared not stand up; all I could see was the starlit, indigo blue sky above, being restricted to looking straight upward. With pistol in hand I nervously waited, making plans to toss out the hand grenade should the Jap drop one in on me; I would have less then five seconds to do so. If the Jap held the grenade for a second or two in his hand after pulling the pin, letting the fuse burn before tossing it, it would detonate almost immediately after he had dropped it on my defenseless body, making me a battlefield statistic.

Trembling, heart throbbing with excitement, I anxiously waited! The stealthy sound had reached the sandbags atop my dugout; my heart and breathing now increased to the rapidity of a machine gun firing on its final protective lines. My eyes were glued upward allowing me to see the hand holding the grenade before it dropped on me. Hopefully, I would have time to wrest the grenade from the Jap's hand and toss it harmlessly away. Then with my pistol, already in hand, I could take care of the mischievous Jap before he could take an alternate action. In my mind I had come face to face with the enemy for the first time. It was a horrible, helpless feeling realizing I would either be killed or I would kill another human; how barbaric!

Breathlessly, I waited, eyes still glued to the top of my sandbagged dugout. Then another move! It must be now! Now! I jumped to my feet, pistol raised, round in chamber, cocked, safety off! Ready for action! Surprise! Even though the bright moonlight lit up the area like the noonday sun, there were no Japs, not a single one! What was it then that had scared me more than I had ever been scared. Something was near! What? My visual search out front revealed nothing, but searching back to my dugout I found the culprit. There it was with it pincers bared, standing on its end looking me right in the eye - a dry land crab! What? Poor crab! In my high nervous state that it had put me, using my pistol I beat the poor thing into the ground; it became a part of the ecology in an instant.

Such was my first combat experience on Arawa. How was I to explain to the men and how would Sergeant Dixon react? It would be hilarious to them, and embarrassing to me. I went to sleep and slept the sleep of a very tired man, for the day had been long and hard, and very exciting, too.

Morning came. I told Captain Caffee about the incident during the night. Splitting his side laughing he dubbed it "Ben Rod's great battle with the land crab", and it stuck. I was given credit for having first "enemy" contact on Arawa. Sergeant Dixon even added to it, saying I had wrestled hand-to-hand in combat with the crab and even won. The experience however, as humorous as it had seemed, certainly was anything but humorous when it happened. No one could have told me it was only a crab at the edge of my dugout for the sounds did fit the exact movement of a Japanese soldier that had infiltrated to the rear and acted in the same way the crab had. Believe me, I was so grateful the crab wasn't a Jap.

At the conclusion of the humorous conversation concerning my "battle" with the crab the sound of battle erupted; it was about 6:30AM. We found this was a daily occurrence. The rattle of MGs and rifle fire would then end as suddenly as it had begun, lasting only a few minutes. Why? Minutes later, daily, litter jeeps would pass through our area carrying dead and wounded soldiers to the nearby underground hospital and cemetery. It was grotesque.

We could easily tell the difference between the dead and wounded as the litter jeeps passed; the wounded would not have their grimacing faces covered by a blanket, while the dead had a blanket over the head, an arm dangling limply over the side, and the toes of the boots shook violently from side to side (the still warm bodies not yet rigid) as the vehicle passed over the war-torn road.

Each morning, as if a ritual, the mini-battle occurred on schedule only to be followed by the parade of the dead and wounded, and the firing would end as suddenly as it had begun. The attacking American force would return to the rear to lick its wounds without accomplishing anything, as we saw it. The terrible scene of the dead and wounded men passing through our area occurred as the "Bushmasters" sat on logs, tree stumps, rocks, etc., having breakfast of the hated dehydrated food. Silently, they peered over the rims of their canteen cups, sipping coffee, at the parade of the dead and suffering wounded soldiers. They wondered when it be their turn.

Greatly disturbed about this seeming loss of men without gain of any kind, the "Bushmaster" commander inquired of TASK FORCE DIRECTOR why this was permitted. They replied it was to keep the enemy off balance and perhaps spoil a planned attack upon the MLR by him. However, the enemy knew the Americans would attack at 6:30AM and prepared to meet them, inflicting casualties we did not need. It was nonsense. We could understand battlefield losses of men when an objective had been clearly defined, but expending the lives of men in this manner was inexcusable. This, in my opinion, was the forerunner of the type of operation that occurred in Vietnam twenty years later when the days' objective was determined by the enemy dead-body count forced upon the military by the political structure in Washington. However, in this case the body count was those of Americans.

A few days before leaving Goodenough Island I received a large knife or a dagger from my brother Doc. It was razor sharp on both sides, coming to a keen point. Encased in a leather scabbard, it was a vicious looking thing and I had no idea how I would ever use it. He probably felt that I was in WWI type operations that raided the enemy trenches, and it could be used to silently dispatch the foe. Even though our men went among the enemy at night at times, we would never have the opportunity to use such a vicious weapon. However, Sergeant Ruiz, of the "hot rolls for us to eat" fame, had different ideas about the use of the dagger and wanted to borrow it. Being Hispanic, he was an expert when it came to using knives and could throw one accurately, and most people would come out second best should they engage him in a knife fight. He would return it to me some day, he said. I let him have the knife, for I certainly had no need for it and had planned to stash it away in my duffel bag where it would stay until the war ended.

It was never intended for the 2nd Battalion "Bushmasters" to remain idle in the rear area of TASK FORCE DIRECTOR. Soon it came. On January 4, we received a warning order: Prepare for combat on January 6, only two days hence. We began hurried preparations. Commanders reported to the command post and attack orders were issued. Whitten was to send out patrols among the Japs after darkness and report back before 6:OOAM on the day of attack, updating us on enemy dispositions, activities, locations of MG emplacements, etc. Men, and individual arms checked; communications procedures, ammunition, medical evacuation, etc. - all were carefully checked.

Then the strangest thing happened. Early on the 5th, the day before the attack, I, as Adjutant, received a call from TASK FORCE DIRECTOR, to provide ninety men to report to the military cemetery to dig graves in which our dead would be buried. Normally, graves are dug by noncombatants, such as the graves registration personnel, but due to most of these being in Europe, very few were available to us. Nevertheless, I balked, for I refused to have men dig their own graves, and the thought of a man digging graves on the eve of combat would certainly have an adverse effect upon him as well; he could be digging his own grave, and I'm sure he would think that, too.

"Major Jones, really you don't expect us to dig our own graves do you? Surely, if we are to do the dying someone else should dig our graves, don't you think?"

"Why not? Your men will be the ones to fill them?"

This was unbelievable; a most callous concern for men who would die the next day.

"Major, even if your Commanding General should issue such an idiotic order, I will not obey it. I will not, nor can I obey such an order. Surely you have non-combatants to do the grave digging! Combatants, never!" And I hung up.

It didn't take long. Colonel Stofft came to my tent.

"Captain Jordan, I know how you feel about our men digging their graves, but there are no others to do it. We must do it some how." I was surprised.

"Colonel, I just don't have the heart to order men to the cemetery to dig their own graves and I know you don't either. Why don't we have the artillery people do it. They seldom have casualties, not like the infantry anyway, Please let's not do this to our men, please!" Then he got very firm with me.

"Ben Rod, we've got to do it. Now let's find a way and quit dragging our feet. I've been given a direct order to have ninety graves dug today."

And so we discussed the matter further. And, after my suggestions the colonel made his decision: "Ben Rod, I want all commanders to have their cooks, clerks, drivers, and any administrative personnel to report to the cemetery immediately, with mattocks, shovels or whatever. Above all not a single combat man will be among them. Major Hohnhorst will supervise this for us."

I called each company commander, personally informing them of the decision, and they all begged to be relieved of it. However, they soon capitulated and sent all administrative people to the cemetery to do the grim job of digging graves they knew would be filled by their friends before nightfall the next day. I will never forget this event. Even though our commander issued the order, he had no other recourse. The graves had to be ready before the attack began the next morning. The Japanese often made American prisoners dig their own graves before executing them, but now here were the Americans making Americans dig their own graves - the difference being that the Japs would still be doing the shooting.

The artillery and 81mm mortars began preparatory fires at 8:00AM. George Nisbeth's heavy machine gun platoon also began delivering overhead fire, bullets splitting the air just above our heads, each making a low, sharp, popping sound as the air filled the vacuum created by the velocity of the bullet. Prior to that I had established the battalion command post (CP) behind the Main Line of Resistance to include communications to the attacking units. The ammunition dump operating under Lt Tompkins, and Doctors Moulton and Beatty were ready to receive the wounded. Their aid station had an operating table and technicians were standing by. On the ground were several stretchers that would be used to evacuate the dead and wounded from the front line by the aid men, a very hazardous mission which they did in a heroic style. Two litter jeeps stood ready to transport the wounded to the underground hospital and the dead to the cemetery. Even though we were receiving our baptism of fire, we seemed to be working well as a team. The battalion commander was pleased with our work. Battle was about to begin; "Bushmasters" were poised.

The attacking elements crossed the LD (Line of Departure); Company "E" of the Bushmasters, and Troop "C", 112th Cavalry, Company "E" on the left, with a trail serving as a boundary between companies, were advancing in good order. The "Bushmasters" and the Cavalrymen went into battle smiling nervously. Some saying they were going to get their Jap as if the foe was a trophy of sorts. To me, personally, it would settle a point I had wondered about since childhood: how would I react under fire? I would soon find out. It was an eerie feeling; men would die, many would be wounded, acrid smoke would fill my nostrils, sound of battle deafening in my ears.

Surprisingly, the reaction of the enemy was slow and we wondered if our preparatory fires had neutralized them. Our support fires continued and the overhead machine gun bullets still cracked above our heads - yet no enemy response. We were thrilled, for we thought the battle was over and we would soon be marching back to our perimeter area.

Then it happened! The entire front exploded. The jungle roared to life. Then the rifle fire, rattle of front-line machine guns, tommy guns, grenades. Cries for stretcher bearers came from Company "E", "many men wounded and killed; have ran into heavy machine gun fire." The machine gun bunker had not been touched by our artillery or mortars. Enemy machine guns had all approaches covered by fire. Snipers in trees delivering deadly fire prevented our men from getting into grenade range of the bunkers; requests for artillery and mortar fires. The enemy is using knee mortars effectively." The voice of Overmyer, commander of Company "E", was alarming.

The evacuation of the dead and wounded began to flow through the Battalion Aid Station. While the Battalion Commander was on the radio to TASK FORCE DIRECTOR, I was called to the telephone and informed by Lt Overmeyer, Commander of Company "E", that Lts. Born and Jensen were badly wounded and their platoons were now commanded by the platoon sergeants, only to become casualties themselves; Lt. McKillip was the only other officer left in the company.

The situation even became worse. The Japanese, being battle wise and tenacious, and this our first contact in battle, only fired, when we fired, so their locations were difficult to pin point. The "Bushmasters" began firing at imaginary targets, becoming what is called "trigger happy". We lost the ability to control our own fires while suffering great losses from snipers. The enemy machine guns bunkers which had laced their fires so perfectly making any advance through them impossible, began raking our forward lines. Major Hohnhorst returned from Company "E" and reported the men were completely demoralized due to the loss of their leaders, killed or wounded, and were without leadership. "The bullets are flying thick as hail and hardly a Jap can be seen; their MGs are laid so that it is impossible to get through the dense final protective fires. Two men are missing." Our casualties became so great that it was necessary for Colonel Stofft to order a general withdrawal and requested artillery and mortars to cover our withdrawal to the original attack positions behind the Cavalry's MLR. It was 1:00PM. We had, however, achieved our baptismal of fire but at a great cost. We had been bloodied, but good.

The beginning of the withdrawal was delayed when the lifting of artillery and mortar fires was requested by Lt Overmeyer, Company "E" Commander, for one of his men, Pvt. Joseph Maza, had been wounded and was last seen crawling back to the rear but could not be accounted for. Even though the company was trying to extract itself from the deadly enemy fire and was in the process of withdrawing, the commander wanted to stay in place until he, personally, looked for Pvt Maza. The Battalion Commander, feeling that such would be suicide for Overmeyer, wisely prohibited him from doing it. Perhaps Maza did clear through the Battalion Aid station, but a check of records revealed that he had not. A further check was made with the underground hospital and no record of him was there, either. Members of "E" Company said Maza had been shot through the chest and stomach and when last seen he was in the enemy's MGs fire lane and could not have possibly survived. The withdrawal continued with our own artillery fires blocking the advance of the enemy, who intended to fire on our rear as we sought security behind the MLR.

The two men missing was a cause of great concern for it was known the Japanese often tortured helpless prisoners, using them for live bayonet practice, cutting off their fingers and then tying their thumbs together behind their backs, making it impossible for the poor victim to help themselves. Later, on Noemfoor Island, evidence supported the allegation that the Japanese practiced cannibalism by cutting away the flesh from the arms and buttocks of both dead Americans and Japanese soldiers. Another torture, maybe a rite, would be to behead the prisoner using a Samurai sword or cutting them to pieces; such was often practiced in the Philippines.

Victory had eluded us; instead, we had to withdraw and lick our wounds, leaving the Japanese still in command of the battlefield. Would there be another day?

While standing on the trail, observing the Battalion's march to the rear, I was impressed by the attitude of the men. Many were laughing and talking about the day's combat, as if they had been playing the Japanese a game of softball, or as if we had won a decisive victory. And it might have been a victory for them personally, for they did receive their baptism of fire, an experience never to be forgotten. But we had lost the battle, if not the war, due to the lack of adequate combat intelligence; nor were we given sufficient time to prepare for battle, having only two days.

The day following the battle, January 7, again we were surprised to receive a very unusual order from DIRECTOR TASK FORCE. We were to clear all the underbrush from the area in front of the Main Line of Resistance. True, a clear field of fire in front of the MLR would be desirable, but in so doing we would be under the observation of the enemy, and he could place fire upon us as we wielded machetes and brushhooks. The cavalry was to provide security to the front and flanks but we knew this would not be sufficient. We tried to reason with the powers to be, but they still demanded we clear the area even though we would be exposed to deadly enemy sniper fire. Lt. Lynn Allen, from my company, was placed in charge, having about fifty men from all units of our battalion. The detail formed at the battalion, armed with machetes, and Allen marched them to the front, scattering them throughout the area.

No sooner had they begun swinging machetes and brushhooks than the snipers began taking their toll. Corporal Pittman from Company "H" was killed immediately and three other men wounded. Then the two men missing from the battle the day before, were seen sitting together against a palm tree as if resting. The brush cutters, overjoyed, rushed forward to them only to be cut down by the deadly enemy sniper fire. The men, already dead, had been placed there as a trap. The cunning, enemy knowing we would find them either while on patrol or as it turned out, clearing the field of fire, covered the bodies with deadly sniper fire and waited in ambush for us. They were effective. Allen, using his head, withdrew the detail, but not before several more men were killed or wounded. What a horrible loss of men! We knew this would happen, and had begged to be relieved of the assignment, but were overruled.

One of the wounded men, Pvt Kacsyskowski, was from my company. He had been hit by a "dum dum" bullet that had entered his right wrist, traveling up the bone of his arm and leaving his arm limp as a dish rag. The bullet, being a "dum dum", not only took out the bone of his arm but his elbow as well, almost removing his lower arm completely. It was the most horrible wound I had ever seen. This type of bullet, having a soft nose, flattens upon impact, becoming a tearing projectile leaving a gaping hole at the exit point, such as taking off the soldier's elbow. Use of such ammunition in war is prohibited by international agreement but the Japanese disregarded the agreement and did what they wanted. But, in spite of his horrible wound Kacsyskowski was cheerful and apologized for some of his mischievousness.

He, a young boy from New York, was one of my "yard birds" and was at times lazy. He usually had his squad leader or platoon leader and me after him for some of his antics, such as being late for formation, or for not keeping his area policed up, etc.; nothing serious, however. Then he would say something innocently like: "Captain Jordan, sir, I'm sorry that I cause you so much trouble, but I don't aim to", just like a repentant son talking to his dad.

"Damn it Addie, if you feel that way, why do you do it?" I would say to him. Meekly he would say that he was sorry and he would receive minor punishment, such as doing extra duty for his derelictions. But he was well liked; a good American boy, he was.

He looked so pitiful lying on the bloody stretcher, almost begging me to accept his forgiveness, and I succored him, telling him how proud I was to have had him in the company and wish him the best. But he would never return to the company due to his grievous wound.

Then I found Sergeant Ruiz among the wounded. Ruiz will be remembered, for it was he who had located the bootlegger on Goodenough Island who had provided us yeast so our cooks could make us "rolls to eat." I went to his stretcher and offered my hand just before they placed him on the litter jeep to take him to the underground hospital. Then he gave me back the long dagger that my brother, Doc, had sent me and which he had borrowed, promising he would return it to me some day. The dagger was now stained with blood; he had gotten his Jap with it, he said, and now I could have the knife back for he had done what had wanted to do. Later, after washing the blood from the blade, I once again placed it in my duffle bag, and there it stayed until I arrived back in the States several months later. Doc, learning the history of his famous dagger, wanted it back and I gave it to him. Today, long after his death, one of his sons,

Harvey, still has it among his most cherished possessions.

Following the battle we alternated with the Cavalry performing Out Post Line duty (OPL), unloading LCMs at the jetty, patrolling, scouting out the enemy positions. Then one night, while Company "E" was on OPL duty, one of their men, Sanford, killed two of his close friends. Unfortunately, for some reason the men had gotten out of their fox-holes on the OPL, in violation of standard procedures. Staying in one's fox-hole during night operations was necessary, for the enemy was always probing our lines by infiltrations and, without asking questions, we fired at anything that moved at night. For some reason these men got out of their fox-holes and Sanford, thinking they were the enemy, using his submachine gun, killed them instantly. Come the dawn, bringing with it the horrible truth; Sanford had killed his close friends. The investigation found him completely blameless, but the poor man never recovered from the shock or his self-imposed guilt and had to be evacuated; he had become a mental case.

CHAPTER 21

THE GALLANT IMPERIAL JAPANESE MARINES

The Fighting Second Battalion, 158th RCT (Bushmasters), still licking its wounds suffered from the battle of January 6th, when 18 medium tanks from the Marine Corps disembarked at the jetty. We watched as the tanks lumbered up the dusty road through our bivouac area toward the MLR (Main Line of Resistance). Those tanks just didn't show up for nothing, we reasoned. Shortly, the Commander of the Fighting Second Bushmasters was called to Headquarters TASK FORCE DIRECTOR. Again, with the tanks attached, we were to attack on 16 January with the mission of "breaking the backs of the Sons of Nippon", or the Japanese Imperial Marines on Arawa. We had received our baptism of fire at the hands of these gallant fighters on 6 January, developing great respect for their tenacity. The enemy marines were much larger then the usual Japanese soldier, and even more fanatical to the Far East Prosperity plan the Japanese had initiated in 1931 against Manchuria and China. We had found them vicious, for they asked for no mercy and intended to die to the last man before surrendering to us. Now, perhaps, with the Marine Corps tanks, on the 16th we would put an end to their existence on Arawa.

Our attack was to be preceded by an aerial bombardment followed by artillery and mortar fire. H-hour would be determined by the completion of the aerial bombardment, hopefully at 9:00AM, so the "Bushmasters" would be in attacking positions by 8:30AM.

In the few days we had left before the onslaught, we prepared diligently. Using foot patrols, aerial photos, and reports from the Navy's PT boats that patrolled the southern coast of New Britain, we had gathered sufficient combat intelligence to make an accurate estimate of the enemy situation; we planned accordingly. All weapons were checked, ammunition resupply procedures rehearsed, and units reorganized where necessary. On the 16th we were ready.

The air attack had to be delayed; fog over the airstrip in New Guinea prevented the planes from taking off said the ALO (Air Liaison Officer). He was near the battalion CP (command post), headset stuck to his ear, having constant contact with the aerial commander.

The delay of the attack was welcome, giving commanders time to further check their men, equipment, communications and ammunition, and for us to settle our nerves. Later, the men began the horse play that American soldiers are noted for when not busily engaged. The company's self-appointed clown, Ricciardi, the bugler, the "jester" as he liked to be called, saw to it that we had no dull moments while we nervously waited for the arrival of the Air Corps. Realizing we all needed "bucking up" and our minds diverted from the possible events of the day, he began by telling his story of "woe".

"Listen, youse guys" he said in his best Brooklyn accent, "I still have to get behind twees to protect myself from the rocks you trow at me when I blow my hone."

"Ricciardi, you have no respect for us. We need our rest but daily you blow your dern horn and wake us up," Corporal Bergeron of the A & P Platoon, quipped. "It's enough to resurrect the dead. Where is your compassion for your brothers-in-arms?" And he was joined by others in laughter, who in jest questioned Ricciardi's claim to fame in bugling.

"Careful", the bugler added with a make-believe threat. "I will send youse guys to visit the honorable Japs if I'm not shown the proper respects I so well desoive."

Marveling at the horseplay, I wondered about the phenomena. How could brave men, facing combat against a very determined and dangerous foe, act as if nothing was happening? It was not a simple thing to understand. Each of these fine men would soon be under deadly Japanese fire; three would die while others would be wounded before the day was over. In a way it was sad. It was the American soldier's psychological makeup.

While waiting for the air column from New Guinea, and after checking the details of the interior arrangements of the battalion command post located in rear of the OPL, I visited the operations tent to see Lt. Whitten, the battalion intelligence office, for an update on the enemy situation. Both of us were from the Wonderful Wild State of West Virginia, so we felt the effects of brotherhood and enjoyed each other's company. I found him and Captain Caffee, the battalion operations officer, standing near the operations map studying the recently posted combat information. They appeared to be concerned.

"Look, Ben Rod," said Whitten, very excited, pointing to the acetate-covered map."You see these enemy machine gun emplacements? Those machine guns are caliber .50s and the BARs (Browning Automatic Rifle) are American weapons captured in the Philippines. These guns are wicked and unless we neutralize them before we jump off today, will inflict excessive casualties on Companies 'F' and 'G'. Then he checked the route of advance of the companies and he realized both would receive fire from the captured American weapons of death in the skilled hands of the Japanese Imperial Marines, if they were not eliminated. "What are we to do?"

"Do Captains Cochran and McGlothlan know of these gun emplacements?" I queried.

"Yes, they do, and they are worried. Also, Caffee and I have coordinated with Peter Hart, the leader of the heavy mortar platoon, and the artillery battalion (LO) Liaison Officer and they will place fire on the guns beginning H-Hour. Maybe, together, they can knock them out before the forward attacking elements arrive in effective range of the Jap-controlled American weapons. Further, Cochran and McGlothlan plan, if the mortar and artillery fire fails to neutralize them, to sneak killer patrols into the enemy's communications trenches and destroy them by grenades or hand-to-hand combat if necessary. We've got to get those guns out of there before they destroy us."

"Maybe the bombing attack will do the job for us, Whitten." I tried to settle him down a bit.

"Well, I don't know, Ben Rod. The Air Corps does wonderful things for us, but they cannot do everything. I doubt they will get a direct hit on those weapons emplacements, but I pray to God they will."

This wonderful person was almost in tears, seeing the possibilities of many casualties that could be inflicted on Companies "F" and "G" unless the captured Americans weapons were eliminated. I tried to calm him down. "Look, Whitten, it appears that you have done all that you can. Just trust Peter Hart's mortars, the Air Corps, the artillery, and the stealth patrols to do the job. That's all you can do, isn't it?"

Captain Caffee entered the conversation: "That is right, Whitten. What else can we do?"

The Battalion Commander entered the operations tent, accompanied by Captain Ed Blocker, the artillery liaison officer. He shouldered his way to the map and pointed at the machine gun emplacements: "Captain, see those gun emplacements on the map? They contain American automatic weapons that could inflict great damage upon us during our attack today; maybe even result in failure if we do not knock them out. Please get with your artillery battalion and have them destroy those emplacements before we reach them during our advance. Think you can do it?"

"Colonel, sir, I have already discussed this with your operations and Intelligence officers and I think we can. However, it all depends how much overhead protection the emplacements have. As you know the Japs are the best when it comes to building communication trenches and gun emplacements.

Sir, we will give it our best, of that you can rest assured."

"Thank you, Captain Blocker."

Having his radioman near, the Artillery LO called his fire direction center, several miles to the rear, relaying data that would place artillery fire on the emplacements during the attack.

A smiling Whitten was satisfied that everything had been done to eliminate the gun emplacements before the attack would begin. Settling down, I returned to my company confident, like on the 6th, that all would be well.

The bantering between Ricciardi and his group was still going on. He was trying to convince his pals he deserved more respect from them, for he was not only the company bugler but also the company jester, too, deserving more respect of his "poisonage". The bantering ceased abruptly. Silence! All eyes turned to the west. The ALO (Air Liaison Officer), with a radio handset stuck to his ear, was the center of attention. With our hearts pounding, we waited for word from him. We got it! The B-24 heavy bombers and the B-25 light bombers from New Guinea were airborne. The dreaded H-hour was only minutes away.

Then last minute orders were barked! Officers, NCOs, and enlisted men nervously checked personal equipment, tightened helmet chin straps, and checked their individual weapons. Lt. George H. Nisbett, commander of the Heavy Machine Gun Platoon, excitedly instructed his NCOs to recheck the dial settings of their automatic weapons. He wanted sufficient overhead clearance while firing over the "Bushmasters'" heads when they crossed the LD. Peter Hart made sure his mortars were set to deliver fire on the enemy's emplacements where the American machine guns that were captured in the Philippians were located. Lt. Beane demanded a radio check on the command net, while Major Hohnhorst chastised a group of "Bushmasters" who had assembled into a small group: "Scatter", he said, for they were a good target for an enemy mortar round. They did. Col Stofft, spartan like, stood on the LD with Captain Caffee and Lt. Whitten; he was the epitome of courage. Looking confident, he wanted to cheer the men as they passed forward to the attack. Many of them would die today, something that was always on our minds. We knew it would happen; hopefully we had planned well and our casualties would be reduced because of this. Would we break the Jap Imperial Marines back today or would it be a replay of the 6th? The knowledge that the bomber column was on its way had caused us to react; it was therapeutic.

Again, our attention become centered on the ALO, with his ear still glued to the handset communicating with the air armada from New Guinea. Then an audible sound, a moaning sound from the southwest, increasing by the second. Louder! Louder!. Our hearts pounded with excitement. The bomber formations were now approaching in elements of three, in column; there were many elements in the column. The beating of propellers, creating a loud din, thundered in our ears. We stood in awe as the mighty air armada approached us. On they came, magnificent, majestic, but awesome!

We had a grandstand view - we thought.

The ALO continued his communications with the lead bombardier, relaying weather conditions, wind directions, velocity, and other atmospheric information; final adjustments would be made before bomb release. On they came, the bombers; it was beautiful but yet, terrifying!

One could not help but wonder and even feel sorry for the poor Jap Imperial Marines who were about to be punished by the terrible air armada; what would it be like to be subject to such an onslaught? One could have compassion for the Jap Marine hovering in his deep cave. Like us, he could hear the angry bombers that would turn his cave into a living hell were almost upon him. He was prepared to die for his Emperor; it would be an honor for him to do that. Would our dreadful enemy be totally destroyed by the air attack, permitting the brave "Bushmasters" to walk to their objectives without even firing a shot or suffering casualties? Would Whitten's and Caffee's situation map at CP have nothing but blue markings, reflecting the presence of only friendly forces when the fight was over? Would the red information reflecting enemy forces be removed, indicating the mighty Jap Imperial Marines were destroyed?

On they came, the bombers! Thundering with all their might! We froze in our tracks and anxiously waited. We prepared for our first aerial onslaught.

The leading element of the air column was over us, bomb bay doors agape. The alarm sounded, why? Bombs were released - hundreds of them! They looked like rungs of a Jacob's ladder stacked and evenly spaced on top of each other, filling the sky! The black projectiles of death were heading for the green plantation - our attack position! Officers screamed: "Take cover, immediately!" an order that was willingly obeyed. No cave was available to us, only the flat ground covered with stripped coconut palm trees. Some men lay flat on the ground, some wrapped their bodies around the palm trees as I did. Everyone took cover, except the ALO who looked in disbelief, continuing to stand. We dug ourselves into the ground to await the terror from the sky, which only recently was an envy of us all. Seconds seemed like hours as I dug into the ground with my fingernails. I felt the extreme agony of helplessness; again my thoughts ran amok.

Eternity seemed to pass; then the earth heaved in torment. My body bounced like a rubber ball responding to the vibrations that raced underground delivering shock waves. The tall coconut trees bent forty-five degrees and then straightened rapidly and flung their fruit-like projectiles as if from giant slingshots. The din of roaring angry engines, mixed with loud explosions from the many bombs made verbal communication impossible, but the deadly bombers, like killer bees, continued their destructive work of death. The ALO, not concerned, was still on his feet, perhaps wondering why the brave "Bushmasters" around him were acting so strangely.

The acrid smoke filled our nostrils and the dense dust churned up by the continuous explosions heightened our fears; the noxious odor and lack of vision added to our distress.

I prayed for deliverance and my thoughts returned to Wilma, and two little boys, Bucky and Johnny, back home. Would I ever see them again? Or would this be the end? Would the terrible agony ever end?

Suddenly, the dreadful horror from the sky did end and we staggered to our feet. Shaking the dirt and grime from our persons, we quickly took stock, and to our surprise, we had only one injury -a man had received a broken arm from a falling coconut, just as had happened in Milne Bay. The ALO, still standing bravely, was amused by the strange actions of his infantry brothers-in-arms. The lead bombardier was right on target; he had correctly computed the bomb release point taking into consideration the wind direction, velocity, and atmospheric conditions. The release point was over us but the impact was on the Jap Imperial Marines. The aerial attack was a masterpiece of air support.

The B-24 heavy bombers had delivered their loads of destruction on the enemy, leaving devastation in their wake. The heavy dust denied us vision and our nostrils smarted from the acrid smoke left in their wake. The heavy bombers, having completed their mission, were followed by the smaller B-25 medium bombers. The smoke and dust had now cleared sufficiently, enabling us to observe the smaller bombers efficient work of destruction.

The B-25s came in at treetop level, belching flames as they fired their 37mm cannons and machine guns mounted in their noses and wings, and dropping their small bombs during their strafing passes. They flew in single file, sufficiently spaced to escape the blast of the exploding bombs dropped from the preceding plane. One by one, time and again, the B-25s, in a round robin fashion, continued making bombing and strafing runs. It was a show I had never experienced before or since. The "Bushmasters" wondered how could the Japanese withstand such an intense pounding and still come out of their caves to meet us in combat? Or even be alive after the terrible, devastating bombardment? The gallant Japanese Imperial Marines, if they did appear from their caves, would meet us not asking for sympathy but death instead.

The B-25s, like the B-24 bombers before them, having done their job, assembled for the return to their respective bases in New Guinea. Now it was up to the "Bushmasters" to finish the job. If necessary, they would enter the enemy's caves, trenches, and MG emplacements, and put an end to their existence. Arawa would be free of the yellow men from Nippon, we reasoned.

During the onslaught by the B-25s, companies "F" and "G", were taking up combat formation, four platoons on line, men abreast. The third platoon of each company was in reserve and would follow by leaps and bounds behind their attacking brothers to exploit a breakthrough or spoil the enemy's counterattack, should he mount a counterattack - and he usually did.

The Marine Corps tanks had met up with the attacking platoons, their engines snorting in defiance. The "Bushmasters" nervously awaited the signal that would cause the line to move forward to cross the LD (Line of

Departure) into "no mans land", or the space between opposing forces - the killing zone.

H-Hour! The signal! The two companies began the advance, with the tanks just ahead, infantry following, firing their machine guns. Nisbeth's machine guns were delivering effective overhead fire, clipping fonds from the coconut trees which fell around us. Bullets were streaking; ever fifth round was a tracer, which created a popping sound as it split the air just above our heads. Peter Hart's mortars and the artillery's howitzers blasted the enemy's machine gun emplacements which had the captured American Cal..50s and BARs (Browning Automatic Rifles).

Nervous commanders awaited for reports from advancing squads and platoons of first enemy reaction. Tanks snorted loudly and continued to fire their machine guns and 37mm cannons at full blast. We hoped to force the enemy down in their caves or fox-holes as the "Bushmasters" advanced. The din of battle was deafening. Colonel Stofft, Captain Caffee, and Lt. Whitten waved greetings to the men as they crossed the LD, for words could not be heard. The "Bushmasters" smiled; they appreciated their battalion commander's concern for them. Initially, like on the 6th of January, the advance of the "Bushmasters" was rapid, maintaining visual lateral contact to avoid gaps in the advancing line. The Company commanders, Captains McGlothlin and Cochran, reported displacement of their CPs to keep better contact with their attacking platoons - a good sign, unless they got too far forward with their CPs. No reports of friendly casualties, but some enemy dead, however.

The coordination of fires from the battalion of 105mm howitzers, the 81mm mortar platoon, and Nisbeth's machine guns, and the Marine tanks placed a wall of steel in front of our attacking platoons, increasing our fighting spirit and confidence. Prematurely, we had a feeling of victory. We would make history! The battalion command post was operating efficiently under fire, as we had done during training in Australia. We had wire and radio contact with the attacking company commanders who reported their unopposed advance. Sergeant Major Sitz continued to check the various sections, the clerks maintained a journal, the message center received reports and sent messages. The ammunition point, with bearers ready, was operating efficiently under Lt Tompkins, and would resupply attacking companies upon request.

What! No pressure? Col. Stofft returned from the LD; he had encouraged the troops as they crossed into "no man's land", creating a picture of confidence. He and Captain Caffee entered the operations tent to await first enemy contact reports from Captains Cochran and Mcglothlin. It was like a training exercise; everyone cheerful. Major Hohnhorst and I again inspected the installation of the CP area and the aid station hoping to find all was in readiness. We wondered if and when the enemy would respond. Our optimism was unbounded.

Suddenly, the Japanese did come to life, sending a mortar shell into the command post area, wounding a radio operator. The blast and concussion stunned me, causing a ringing sensation in my left ear, doing lifelong damage. However, I quickly recovered and was thankful no greater harm had been done even though the ringing in my ear continues even to this day. The advanced elements of Company "F" found the enemy's mortar position, reporting its location, and Peter Hart's mortars effectively destroyed the emplacement.

Captain McGlothlin reported his company had made enemy contact; the captured American-made cal.50 MGs and the BARs, our most dreaded fears, were beginning to deliver effective fire on his leading platoons. The Air Corps, mortars, and artillery had failed to take them out. Now it would be trench warfare, grenades and hand-to-hand combat to eliminate them. Mcglothlin had come under heavy fire and was receiving a counter attack, so he committed his reserve and restored the line. His company was suffering severe casualties and needed medical assistance immediately. Captain Charles M. Moulton, the Battalion Surgeon, dispatched additional stretcher bearers, who pressed forward, disregarding the enemy's grass-cutting machine gun fire ricocheting through the command post area. The report of the early enemy counterattack caused me to take precautionary actions and the Command Post Security, a rifle platoon from Company "E", was alerted to prepare for a possible enemy breakthrough that could be coming our way. The platoon leader of the security platoon, already alert, was checking and preparing his men for the attack should it occur.

Our first casualty was a West Virginia

boy. Checking the identification tags around his neck, I found his name was Whittington, who had no business in the front lines. He was an engineer assigned to the water point located far to the rear. Perhaps he was just curious and wanted a piece of the action. He had made the supreme sacrifice; it was foolish, for he had no business being with us. His arms were dangling over the sides of the stretcher, swaying limply from side to side in unison as the bearers, in silence, carried the body. A closer look revealed an ashen face, half closed eyes, and bluish lips on his very young face. He appeared to be in his late teens or early twenties.

The stretcher, with its burden, was placed on the ground near the battalion aid tent. Because this was our first combat casualty for the day, men of the CP personnel ganged around the inert body. Major Hohnhorst reminded the soldiers they had jobs to do and to stay at their respective stations. The group disappeared. The body was loaded on the waiting litter jeep, covered with a blanket and taken to the cemetery.

The "Bushmaster" commanders reported the front line was now being raked by intense machine gun fire. Cries were heard for additional aid men, key personnel were being killed or wounded, rendering leadership ineffective. Captain Cochran, now reporting, asked for artillery on known enemy machine gun positions that had stopped his advance. He said that Lt. Minor's platoon had knocked out two of the gun positions. Colonel Stofft calmly advised Cochran:

"Cochran, by knocking out the enemy's

machine gun emplacements, you have created a dead space in his final protective fire. Find and exploit that dead space before attempting further advancement. Get men into the enemy's trenches and dispatch him using grenades, gunfire, or bayonets. Use hand-to-hand combat, if you have to, but do it quickly. Should you be successful, the enemy's perimeter defense will be rendered ineffective against us. Now don't get pinned down again by the machine gun fire that is raking the entire front. Use your tanks, Cochran!"

"Wilco (will comply)", Cochran replied in his calm, unexcited drawl. "We will find the dead space and exploit same. Will advise when conditions change." Cochran was a deliberate commander, believing in the principle of the economy of men on the battlefield.

Then from "F" Company: "Colonel Stofft, this is Lt. Perry (1st Lt Robert K. Perry, Tucson, Arizona). Captain McGlothlin is severely wounded in the side and is no longer able to command. The company command Post is completely wiped out by the intense enemy machine gun and sniper fire. There are snipers all around. Men are being shot when they move the slightest bit; casualties are heavy. I no longer have communication with the forward platoons. Furthermore, the company is out of control; we've lost contact with the tanks. The situation is critical; we are no longer combat effective. We expect the enemy to counterattack at any minute, and if they do, they can come all the way to the battalion CP unopposed unless something is done immediately."

The battalion commander then realized what would be the conditions if "F" Company left the right flank of "G" Company exposed as well as his own CP. The Imperial Marines had two options available to them. To roll up the right flank of "G" Company or attack down the boundary line between "F" and "G" Companies directly toward the battalion CP. Seeing what the battalion commander had in mind, I ordered the commander of the platoon of "E" Company that was in battalion reserve, to be prepared to defend the command post should the enemy break through, and placed all battalion command post personnel on full alert to be prepared to assist if necessary. Taking position near the platoon CP, I was now prepared for other actions should the vicious Jap marines head our way. The artillery laid concentrated fire in front of the battalion CP as did Peter Hart's mortar platoon.

Lt Overmyer, the very fine commander of "E" Company, whose company had been badly shaken on the January 6th attack, had joined the battalion commander and was prepared to preempt a threatening enemy counterattack or cover the front in the event Companies "F" and "G" would have to be extracted from the death struggle they were experiencing. The sound of the fierce battle appeared to be only a few hundred yards away. Every soldier, every gun in the Command Post readied for the attack. The Japanese Marines had found the boundary between companies, always the weakest place in the advance, and were actually advancing toward the battalion CP; we were in a dangerous situation. Unless something happened, we, ourselves, in the CP area, would shortly be exchanging fire with the Japanese marines. However, Lt Minor, commander of the right platoon of Company "G", successfully turned his command ninety degrees to the right, and with effective fire, caught the attacking Japanese Marines in the flank. They wreaked havoc on enemy, killing most of them, while the rest faded into the jungle, ending their penetration. The enemy threat to the battalion command post ended, but we remained on the alert.

While Minor dealt effectively with the Japanese Marines, Company "F"'s situation continued to deteriorate. Colonel Stofft was still on the radio talking to Lt. Perry, the acting commander. Lt. Perry's voice went silent. Was he dead or wounded? Now there were no officers in "F" Company, no NCO at hand to try to lead it out of its terrible situation. Something had to be done immediately or the entire company would be among the dead, wounded, or missing.

"Hello, Six." It was the welcome voice of Perry. Six was the code name for Butterfly Six, or Colonel Stofft, during radio transmissions.

"Perry!", Colonel Stofft answered. "What's happened?"

"Oh, hell, Colonel, I'm wounded, too. All of us are either dead or wounded."

"Perry, keep Captain Jordan informed while Caffee and I get some help up to you." He handed me the radio handset.

"Keep talking, Ben Rod. Encourage him. Keep him informed of what we are doing."

Taking the radio handset and trying to act casual to the wounded officer facing death on the other end was tough: "How are you doing, old buddy?"

"Captain, we are in one hell of a mess up here. We need help, but quick!" I could tell his quivering voice was weakening as he pleaded.

"Perry, the battalion will soon be there with reinforcements. Hold on if you can."

"Captain, I cannot hold on to anything now. We are ineffective and at the mercy of these yellow bastards." His voice faded again, then a yell.

"Sergeant Yingling! Sergeant Yingling! Where in the hell are you? Get those men under cover! Answer me, Yingling!" Yingling was a platoon sergeant. Unknown to Perry, Sergeant Yingling had been gravely wounded. His jaw had been completely shot off by an enemy sniper that had been wiping out the Command Post of Company "F".

The wounded officer continued to give me a blow-by-blow description over the radio. His condition was deteriorating rapidly. I was helpless; I was unable to aid the brave man, who could be dying. He said that the first platoon, under the command of Lt. Thomas Bartnicki, seemed to be doing well but he had no communications with it and no idea what was happening to the rest of the company. He described the casualties as they happened around him, calling out the names of the men as they fell while the deadly sniper effectively continued his work of death. It was a nightmare even for me, and I was several hundred yards to the rear; what a terrible thing for Perry and his men. In fact, I could hear the sharp crack of the Japanese cal..25

rifle whose bullet had found its target, then another and another. Then I heard Perry:

"Christ, there he goes again! For God's, sake do something for us, Captain Jordan, please!". It was one of the most pitiful cries for help I had ever heard a man utter. It was as if a big Japanese Marine was upon him poised to put an end to his life as he lay helpless, or at least I felt that way. There was a close friend begging me for help and I was unable to help him. I uttered a silent prayer, the only thing I could do.

"Perry, use your tanks. Quick! Where are they?" I asked.

"I just don't know, Ben Rod. They took off leaving us behind. They are trying to win the war all by themselves, I suppose. They could have knocked out the machine guns but we have no communications with them now. We are in a hell of a mess up here. Help us if you can, please, Captain. Our dead and wounded are scattered all over the place. Can you get the wounded evacuated?"

Screaming to Captain Moulton, the battalion surgeon I said, "Whatever you can do for "F" Company, you must do it now. They will not survive long in the hell they are now under! Hurry! Hurry! In the name of God, please hurry!" I was frantic.

"We have men up there already, Ben Rod, and many of them are pinned down by the intense sniper fire, too!", he said. "They, too, are becoming casualties. We are doing the best we can." And I knew they were.

In the meantime: Stofft to Cochran: "Hold what you have, Cochran. Dig in and be prepared for other possible counterattacks on your right flank. "Fox Trot ('F' Company) is pinned down and suffering heavy casualties. I plan to commit 'Easy' (Company 'E') who will attack down the existing trail on your right boundary, getting in the enemy's rear. Hopefully this will destroy him, relieving the pressure on you and 'Fox Trot' ('F' Company). Be prepared to assist. Do you read me, Cochran?"

"Roger", came the calm voice of Cochran. "Just give me the word and we'll do our best for you." What a display of courage while under fire.

"All officers in 'Fox Trot' are casualties. Send over your executive officer, Lt. Levinson, to take command of the company." Lt. Julian C. Levinson, Denver, Colorado, crossed over the trail to take command of "F" Company at 12:30PM. He found the company pinned down, badly disorganized, mauled and still under intense enemy fire. Levinson immediately received a minor leg wound but continued to reorganize the demoralized company. Adding to the difficulties, Lt Bartnicki, 1st Platoon Leader, was killed at 1:00PM, while leading his men in an attack against the enemy gun emplacement having the captured deadly American cal.50 machine gun. He succeeded in killing many of the enemy, but in doing so he was killed by a blast of machine gun fire in his face. The enemy crew was dispatched by the remaining men of his platoon. Levinson was laboring without designated leaders in squads and platoons and without communications, but the destruction of the enemy's machine guns by Bartnicki had greatly reduced the Japanese's fire upon the company. However, even though the situation had improved somewhat, something still had to be done immediately or else the whole front would cave in.

The determined enemy marines continued to punish us severely. Two of the friendly tanks attached to Company "F" were knocked out while two other tanks were rambling about ineffectively, without communications with the Company "F" command post. These tanks could have been used to knock out the MG emplacement saving the life of Bartnicki and some of his men had communications been established.

The battalion commander committed Company "E", down the trail between Companies "F" and "G", under the effective command of Lt Overmeyer, and the pressure on the front was relieved. In the meantime Major Hohnhorst, a very effective and brave officer, received a minor wound while accompanying the counterattacking force from Company "E" in its move forward. He was able to continue, however. Later he joined Levinson, over in Company "F", assisting him in reorganizing his demoralized and leaderless unit. Together, Levinson and Hohnhorst succeeded in establishing communication with the forward platoons, and evacuated the dead and wounded who were scattered over the area, including Captain McGlothlin and Lt. Perry. Levinson miraculously regained battlefield initiative, got the company on its feet and they continued on their mission dealing death to the enemy who had added many of the "Bushmasters" names to the casualty list.

After the initiative was restored in "F" Company, the battalion commander ordered a general advance. The enemy, as he done in "F" Company area, responded by delivering intense MG fire upon "G" company's forward platoons. But Cochran, a sound tactician, did not suffer the loss of communications and CP personnel that "F" had. Maneuvering his men and tanks expertly, and taking advantage of the dead space found in the enemy's final protective fires, Cochran succeeded in getting into the enemy's rear, destroying the deadly machine guns. The brave "G" men had been effective.

The success of "G" Company was not without great loss, however. First Lieutenant Phillip L. Miner, Wakonada, SD, who had led the vigorous attack silencing the deadly machine guns, preventing an attack on the battalion CP, was observing his front with binoculars when an unseen enemy sniper took aim and fired. The bullet struck the brave officer squarely in the heart. Miner died instantly. The leadership of the platoon fell to T/Sgt William O. Hill, who effectively led it to its final objective even though he, too, was slightly wounded by a shell fragment from a Japanese knee mortar. His demonstrated leadership resulted in his being commissioned a second lieutenant, a battlefield commission.

During this action, and before the unfortunate death of Lt. Minor, two of my men, Clark Bowyer of Tucson, Arizona, and Anthony Ricciardi, Brooklyn, NY, who were almost like blood brothers to each other, attached to Company "G" on a intelligence gathering mission, were a part of the force that silenced the machine guns. These two fine soldiers had succeeded in crawling into a communications trench connecting the enemy bunkers, surprising the enemy. Bowyer killed the first enemy marine, but then a second marine killed Bowyer. The alert Ricciardi killed the second man. Ricciardi later stated it was like a domino game for the few seconds it had lasted. Ricciardi, checking the body of Bowyer and determining that his devoted friend had left this world, bravely continued alone toward the enemy bunker. With his M1 Rifle at the ready, and without concern for his personal safety, he entered the enemy's emplacement. There he found the enemy MG crew had been dispatched, and judging from the condition of the bodies, "G" Company must have used a grenade in silencing them. Becoming accustomed to the darkness inside the bunker he saw a dead Japanese officer with a leather briefcase strapped to his side. Realizing it could contain valuable intelligence information, he removed the case from the dead officer and later turned it in to Lt Whitten, the battalion intelligence officer. Whitten immediately sent it to TASK FORCE DIRECTOR for translating by the Japanese Nise translator. It read partially as follows:

"16 January - 0630 (6:30AM), 9 Boeings and 14 Lockheeds bombed our positions heavily for 40 minutes. At the same time, arty shelled our positions. We were also fired upon by barges from the sea. Noticed active fighting in the front lines. It seemed that the enemy's plan is to cut our rear simultaneously with their frontal attack. 3 men returned along the seacoast from the front lines. They belong to the BIA and MG Co. They reported that the enemy attacked with armored tanks in front and threw lachrymatory (tear) gas in our trenches. Words cannot describe our indignation. Our platoon took up positions amidst the rain of arty shells (Translator's note: the remainder is illegible).

This brave Japanese marine officer, whose name, unfortunately did not appear in the diary, had much to say about the trials the Japanese Marines had suffered before our attack. The Japanese had been on Arawa for some time and even though they had received ammunition and supplies from Gasmada, they had never received food, forcing them to live on what the ground had to offer; thanks to our effective air and naval superiority, we had succeeded in destroying the enemy's supply system. His story was sad and one wonders how they performed as well as they did against the well-supplied US Army.

Death had not only reigned in Companies "F" and "G" but in my company as well. I was shocked by the death of Pfc. Marion R. Howell, Newton, North Carolina and the mortal wounding of T/5 Charles D. Butler, Saratoga, Wyoming, during our darkest hour that day. Sgt Butler was wounded while trying to establish communications with the Marine Corps Tanks that had advanced beyond the infantry protection in the Company "F" Area; he would die on January 18. I visited him as he lay on the stretcher near the battalion aid station while Captain Moulton and Beatty administered to him. Charles was alert and cheerful, and seemed to be beyond the possibility of death. It was than a report came that Pfc Howell had been killed by a sniper while acting as a wireman for Company "F". He was carrying a reel of wire from the battalion switchboard to the Company "F" Command Post. Unfortunately, due to the extreme excitement, he had forgotten to tie into the switchboard and while under intense enemy fire, realizing he had no wire communication back to battalion, rushed back to tie into the switchboard and on his return to Company "F" was killed. His error was most unfortunate; he probably would have lived had he been tied into the battalion switchboard before joining Captain McGlothlan, commander of Company "F", who, by this time, had become a casualty himself.

While thinking of the grievous loss of these two good men, Sergeant Kenneth A. Stokesberry, of the battalion Intelligence Section, emotionally informed me of Clark Bowyer's death while engaging the enemy in Company "G" area. These three men, so dependable, such good soldiers, so loyal to the company and to their work, wiped out within minutes of each other. What a terrible loss! All were key men; it would be most difficult to replace them. The body of Howell had been checked through the battalion Aid station while Butler was being prepared for evacuation to the underground hospital.

"Where is Boyer's body?" I inquired of Sgt Stokesberry. I noticed he had tears in his eyes; the men of the intelligence section were a close-knit group, often going among the Japanese at night, each covering the other, as they stealthily moved among the enemy gathering information.

"Captain Jordan, I hear the stretcher bearers are trying to get up there to get the body as well as other of the many wounded, but the fire is so intense many of the aid men are becoming casualties themselves."

Surprisingly, at that time and for some reason, a Marine Corps tank rambled by with Boyer's body on the back deck. The body was laying on its right side, and from where I stood the death- dealing wound could not be seen. I was heartsick seeing him on the tank instead of on a stretcher, for it seemed to be not befitting for a soldier killed in battle. But, under the circumstances, and since an aid man had been wounded trying to evacuate the body, it was all that could be done. I was grateful the tankers had evacuated the body of this great soldier, yet wondered why the tank was not engaged in the battle raging ahead, instead of evacuating the dead. Medical aid men rushed to the tank and carefully removed the body and placed it on a stretcher, carrying it to the nearby aid station. Later, the body was processed and sent to the rear for interment in the temporary cemetery.

Leaving the heartbreaking scene, I immediately went to the security force protecting the battalion Command Post then being threatened by the rapid advance of the Japanese marines that had broken through the Company "F" front and were rapidly advancing toward us. However, as previously mentioned, the threat was stopped by the rapid and decisive action of Lt. Minor's platoon, which had killed most of the Japanese while the others disappeared into the jungle. The threat over, having time to think of my losses, I wondered just how I would compose letters of condolence to the next of kin of the fine men (see Appendix 10) who had made the supreme sacrifice. Unfortunately there would be more letters.

In spite of the losses the "Bushmaster" battalion was now advancing all along the front. Even "F" Company, badly mauled as it had been, now under the effective leadership of Levinson, still without its officers, but whose NCOs were acting effectively - was on its feet, moving past the destroyed bunker that had housed the American-made MGs and was now cleared, later to be dubbed "Hell's Corner". The enemy in "Hell's Corner" had succeeded in wiping out the company's command post, destroying its communication, and temporarily, its combat effectiveness. Now it was the enemy marines' turn to suffer.

The employment of the US Marine Corps tanks in Company "F" was not as effective as it should have been, especially when the company was being cut to pieces by the captured American machine guns in "Hell's Corner". Perhaps it was because Captain McGlothlin and Lt. Perry had lost communication with them as they had with their own platoons. We do know, however, that the tanks took off on their own, leaving the infantry behind and both suffered casualties as a result. To this day I wonder why the tanks could not have knocked out the MGs instead it required of a frontal attack by Lt. Bartnicki, which cost him his life as well as many of his good men. Even though the company had lost communication with the tankers, there were other means of communicating with them had they remained with the infantry. Each tank had a telephone on its rear enclosed in a bulletproof box accessible to an infantryman walking behind the tank, who could direct the tankers inside to fire at bunkers and MG emplacements, such as Company "F" had experienced in "Hells Corner". However, the truth of the matter is the Marine Corps tanks had sped forward costing infantry their protection and the infantrymen could not get to the telephone to direct the tankers to fire on the MGs. This was a dreadful mistake and it cost us the lives and the wounding of many good men unnecessarily.

The company lost control, lost its officers, and even its command post was wiped out. It appears the company had its command post so far forward that it came under intense MG and sniper fire directed at its forward platoons. If this is so, then the commander had lost his flexibility of command, unable to influence the battle by maneuvering of his forwarding elements, commitment of his reserves, and the application of supporting fires and air support, all critical to winning any battle. Apparently these are the conditions McGlothlin and Perry, unfortunately, had found themselves in; they could not influence the battle and both suffered grievous wounds. We almost lost the battle because of their error.

In contrast to the Company "F" situation, Captain Cochran of "G" Company, just across the trail, did not lose his communications and was successful in eliminating the MGs in his area with a minimum loss of men.

Then it was the tankers turn to cause the battalion commander a problem. It was about 4:15PM and the raging battle had just turned in our favor. The Commander of the

Marine Tank Company, a captain, reported that one of his tanks had gotten bogged down several hundred yards in front of "G" Company. He requested infantry protection to extract his men from the immobile tank. Again, as had happened in Company "F", the tank had moved ahead of the infantry. Trying to cross a small swamp it buried itself up to its belly in mud, losing all traction. Being aware of a similar problem in Company "F", this being the basic reason for the losses it had suffered, the battalion commander exploded.

"Captain, why in the hell did your tanks get ahead of the infantry?"

"I just don't know, Colonel, sir. We do know we have a tank, crew still inside, out there exposed like a sitting duck. If it is captured, the MGs and its cannon could be turned on Company "G", inflicting great damage to it. The crew inside the tank is in great danger and must be extracted without delay; they are helpless."

"What is your plan for retrieving the tank, Captain?"

"Sir, I've ordered my maintenance officer forward with the retriever and maybe he can remove the tank from the swamp, but he will need infantry to cover him while he and his crew remove the tank."

During the strong discussion between the two commanders the Marine Maintenance Officer, a young lieutenant, requested that I point out the location of the bogged-down tank on the situation map. He thanked me, saying little else, mounted his large tank retriever, and ordered the driver forward to the sound of battle, perhaps not realizing the great danger he would face. Within minutes his body was at the aid station, where it was placed on the litter jeep and headed for the military cemetery nearby. I remember thinking: "Life is cheap today." This Marine's life was snuffed out so suddenly and unnecessarily.

Even though an infantry squad from Company "G" was assigned to protect the tank retrieving crew, it was impossible to protect them from the deadly enemy snipers, equipped with scopes, who were tied in the tops of the trees. The young officer had moved his retriever just behind the line of battle and proceeded on foot behind the infantry squad. He was spotted by the Jap sniper, who, like a deer hunter in the forest, took careful aim and fired, as he had done to Lt. Minor few minutes before, dropping the young officer dead in his tracks. The rifle squad reacted quickly and killed the sniper, but it was too late for the young officer. He was dead.

This information was radioed back to the battalion command post and efforts to retrieve the bogged-down tank were abandoned, after we had learned the crew had already made its escape. The tank would remain in the swamp forever.

We were saddened by the unfortunate loss of the Marine Lieutenant, for he, like Minor and Bartnicki and others of the battalion, had bravely made the supreme sacrifice. His life would have been spared had the tankers remained with the infantry. But like Minor, Bartnicki, Bowyer, Yingling and many other good men who died that day in that far away place of Arawa, New Britain, this brave Marine were numbered among our dead; the enemy snipers did not discriminate and their aim was accurate.

The possibility of the abandoned tank being converted to the enemy's use weighed heavily on the battalion commander's mind. We were not sure of the capability of the fierce Japanese Marines even though we knew we had mauled them unmercifully. It was not a time to feel complacent. Colonel Stofft used military procedures in his thinking: could the enemy rally, mount the tank, and turn it against us as they had used the captured American MGs in "Hells Corner?" This was possible, for the careless Marine Corps tankers had deserted the tank, leaving its thousands of rounds of ammunition, its machine guns and its 37mm cannon intact. Why didn't they destroy the weapons? Could the Japanese Marines use the tank's fire power against the left flank of "G" Company, creating another "Hell's Corner" for us? Yes, they could, he reasoned.

The tank must be destroyed! Colonel Stofft directed me to organize my Company's Ammunition and Pioneer Platoon to do it. The men of the platoon were experts in handling explosives and could do the job if they could get to the tank; it would be dangerous. The death of the Marine lieutenant created grave concern for the P & A men's safety while doing the job. However, Sergeant Floyd Abbott, the P & A Platoon Sergeant, having heard the conversation, had already begun preparing demolition charges and readying his platoon for the dangerous mission. Asking for volunteers, he received more men than needed and he selected the most qualified, including Corporal Francis N. Bergeron and Sergeant

Thomas, both trained in such missions. Even First Sergeant Spencer W. Dixon insisted on accompanying the tea party. Considering the unsettled enemy situation in the area, I suggested that an officer accompany the team. Even though the MG bunkers had been silenced, Captain Cochran cautioned us that often the enemy would "play" dead, coming to life to inflict death on those in the rear areas as they advanced to the front.

"Who do you suggest we place in command, Ben Rod? We have no one available."

"Things have settled down here at the CP, I could take the team up. I'm trained in demolition, too." And we both laughed.

"Jordan, you have enough to do around here. Besides, you may have to take command of one of the forward companies, should the enemy mount another attack." Then hesitating: "OK, go up here and get the hell shot out of you. That's what you want, isn't it?"

I was taken aback by this very unusual remark that seemed so callous, considering the great loss of officers and men during the day.

"I'm sorry, Ben Rod, I never meant to say that," he apologized. "You have always wanted to command a rifle company, but I need you here to help. After suffering so many officer casualties in the rifle companies today, you could have been needed to take over command of one of the forward companies." I dismissed the remark as trite and continued to prepare for the tank demolition job. "Good luck," he said.

Sergeant Abbott reported the team was ready to advance. Taking my position in front of the demolition team, with Sergeant Dixon accompanying me, with the wave of my hand and holding a carbine in the other hand, I signaled forward, and we began to move single file through the battle-scared coconut plantation. Soon we were met by a soldier from "G" Company, having a bullet hole in his helmet, which he pointed to with pride, puffing on a half-smoked cigar, a typical Bill Mauldin's Willie and Joe character.

"Stick with 'G' Company, Captain Jordan, and we will get you to your tank." His remark was so casual it was as if he was taking us on a Sunday afternoon tour someplace. He raised his rifle to the port, ready for instant action, and led us through the battlefield as we stepped over the bodies of enemy dead littering the ground around us.

Then: "Get down! Quick!" It was a bloodcurdling scream. "There are two Jap machine guns ahead of you. Quickly, take cover!" and we did, jumping into one of the many shell holes scattered over the battlefield, bare of any vegetation, as the enemy machine gunners sprayed bullets over our shell holes, kicking up dust that filtered down on top of us as we hunkered down inside. When the enemy MGs firing stopped we peeked above the rim of the shell hole and watched as the good "Bushmaster" from Company "G" put an end to the Japs that had played "possum" for the last time. Many dead Japs lay near by. Their faces were ashen gray, their bodies inert and we pumped bullets into them. We watched the bodies shake violently to the impact of bullets ripping through them; we made sure there were no live Japs around. The "G" Company "Bushmaster", still with his unlit, half-smoked cigar protruding from his smiling mouth, ended our vigil: "They are good Japs now," he said.

The battle hardened "Bushmaster" was premature; another burst of MG fire.

"Captain Caffee has been hit!" Another scream.

Looking to my right I saw my good friend thrashing about on the ground. Caffee staggered to his feet, blood gushing from his jaw and covering the upper half of his body. He fell again as he continued to thrash around, clawing at the gaping hole in the lower part of his face that had been inflicted by the enemy MG located to our extreme left, still delivering deadly fire around him. Then, unbelievably, Sergeant Oddennatto of "H" Company ran through the fire, bullets kicking up dust around his feet, picked up Captain Caffee as if he was a baby and carried him to safety. Again the courageous Company "G" "Bushmasters" silenced the "dead" Japs, a job they thought they had done several hours previously.

The sight of my friend, Bob Caffee, blood streaming from his throat, gasping for breath while thrashing violently on the ground, was heartbreaking. In opposition to a longstanding rule never to assist a wounded man on the battlefield, for there were medics to do that, but to keep doing your assigned job, I couldn't help myself, and I ran to him. The lower part of his face appeared to be shot away. Caffee was choking and drowning in his own blood. A terrible gurgling sound was coming from his throat. He was like a brother to me. Often he told me I was too careless and that I should more careful if I ever wanted to see my wife and little boys again. Captains Caffee's death seem to be imminent. Then a miracle happened.

A medic by the name of "Tiny", a nickname for this giant of a man, straddled Caffee's chest, using a penknife to perform a tracheotomy while another medic held Caffee's head, restoring Coffee's breathing saving his life. Captain Caffee was evacuated back to the underground hospital and later to a General hospital in Australia. After the war and after I had resigned from the army, Bob visited Wilma and me in St Albans, West Virginia. The horrible scar, concave in form, had removed the visual identity of the man I had once known, leaving only his voice for me to identify him by, and I remembered. Our meeting was very emotional.

The enemy MGs once more were silenced by the "Bushmasters". The humorous guide remarked to me: "Hell, Captain, these damn Japs have nine lives and we may have to do the job over." We proceeded on our mission to destroy the bogged-down Marine Corps tank in the enemy's territory.

Arriving at the front line, our humorous cigar-chomping guide was replaced by a rifle squad leader whose men had already secured the front area ahead of the tank while we prepared for its destruction. The rifle squad had been in the thick of battle all day but was still in high spirits. The squad leader, a sergeant, was as cool as a summer breeze as he closely checked his squad's position. We would soon get a taste of what they had been going through all day.

Coming to the edge of the swamp, we could see the tank resting on its belly in the soft mud. We cursed the US Marines for getting us into such a dangerous situation. Then our attention was distracted by two shots fired by the security squad from Company "G". The squad leader reported his men had seen two Japanese flee into the jungle and had fired at them. None of his men were hurt. We wondered if the two Japs were on their way to the tank to turn its weapons on us. Even worse: was the tank under enemy observation and would they place fire on us once we began the demolition procedure? Bergeron and Thomas made a final check of the already- prepared demolitions. Nevertheless, enemy snipers were a definite possibility, for it was here Lt. Minor and the Marine Corps Officer were killed only a short time before. Once again our attention was focused on the hapless tank buried in the swamp, a tank that seemed to be begging for its life.

Nearing the edge of the swamp and while under cover, Sergeant Dixon suggested using an anti-tank rifle grenade before Bergeron and Thomas exposed themselves. Taking the rifle from Private Lewis and affixing a grenade to the launcher, he aimed and fired, striking the tank in its rear, but the grenade failed to detonate. We decided against further use of the grenades and prepared to do the demolition without further delay. Again we rehearsed what was to be done. Three charges were to be placed: one on the inside of the tank, one on the rear deck and one inside the engine compartment. All charges were to be connected by a detonating cord insuring sympathic explosions. In all, fifty blocks of TNT would be used to blow up the perfectly good tank abandoned by the Marines earlier in the day. Being familiar with demolitions, I approved the plan proposed by Bergeon and Thomas.

Finally, all ready, the two brave men, Thomas and Bergeron, wide-eyed and nervous, looked to me for the signal to proceed. The remainder of the demolition team, weapons at the ready, took positions to give added security from the jungle's edge. It was a tense moment. All sensed, as I did, that the tank was under possible enemy observation even though the "G" Company rifle squad was in position in front of the tank.

"OK,", I said "let's go."

"Captain, sir, are you going out there?", Dixon asked.

Without answering Dixon, my heart pounding like a trip hammer, I jumped off on a run toward the tank, carrying part of the demolitions, followed by Bergeron and Thomas. Arriving a short distance from the tank we dropped to the ground and scanned the area to the front, especially paying attention to the treetops that may have a Jap sniper. Dixon observed our action, and knowing our concerns, had the men spray all treetops. The rifle squad picked up the cue and did the same thing. We felt our advance to the tank now was safe, so we proceeded.

Like leaping gazelles we sprang forward to the tank. Quickly, I mounted the tank and, to our surprise, nothing happened. Removing the tank's gas cap, I threw it to the ground as Bergeron and Thomas began placing the charges. Thomas was already on the back deck using an ax to cut the heavy screen wire over the engine compartment so Bergeron could place charges directly inside. In the meantime, Bergeron was calmly attaching a blasting cap to a time fuse and then to the detonating cord connecting all three charges. The tank's radio command net was operating and the voice of Colonel Stofft communicating with Cochran and Levison could be heard. He stated fear for our safety and wondered why the tank had not yet been blown. It was late in the afternoon as the sun began to dip below the treetops; he wanted us back before dusk.

"What's delaying Jordan?", I heard him say. Not being familiar with the tank's radio system, I was unable to find the mike to inform him of the status of our work.

Bergeron and Thomas had efficiently performed their work and gave the signal that all was in readiness; the charges had been placed and we were now ready to ignite the fuse that would send the tank into oblivion. Peter Hart's heavy mortars began placing fire in the front of the rifle squad in preparation for our withdrawal, discouraging the enemy from following us to the battalion's rear. Quickly, I jumped to the ground and ordered Thomas to light the fuse.

He did. The time fuse began sputtering immediately after he lit it, using a cigarette lighter. Intermittently spitting red and blue flame, the fuse began to burn toward the detonating cap. Only seconds were left for the existence of the tank whose only crime was being in the hands of the Marine Corps crew that had abandoned it in the swamp. Even though it was metallic, I felt sorrow for it.

Sprinting to the rear to join Dixon and the men, we sought cover to watch the results of our work of destruction. Taking cover, we fixed our eyes on the still form of the hapless vehicle with the burning time fuse inching slowly up its side reaching toward the blasting cap. Using binoculars, I gave a progress report to the men as the spitting fuse climbed slowly to perform its work of destruction. Slowly but surely the flame climbed the tank's side to the three charges placed inside. It all appeared so needless, the loss of the young Marine lieutenant and now the tank itself. All of this could have been prevented had not the Marines tanks rushed ahead, losing their infantry protection in the heat of battle and becoming a burden to us. Now the tank was useless on the battlefield, and perhaps the cause of Company "F"'s horrible losses and Perry's terror.

Everything seemed to be exceptionally quiet. All eyes were fixed on the doomed tank which seemed to still beg for a reprieve from death. The burning fuse inched up toward the detonating cap. I kept the binoculars focused on the tank during its remaining seconds of its life. The fuse is very short now. Only seconds.

Then it happened, the violent end! The loud explosion shook the jungle like a marble in a tin can. The entire battlefront and even those far to the rear heard the explosion, causing TASK FORCE DIRECTOR to become concerned, thinking the enemy had succeeded in blowing up the force's ammunition dump. Black and orange smoke and flames shot into the sky and fragments of tank parts, mixed with flaming gasoline and oil, fell around us forcing us to withdraw further to the rear. Ammunition began to explode inside the tank which added secondary explosions. We watched the tank's agony of death from our covered positions, still feeling sorry for it as if was mortal. Finally, after the smoke settled and flames abated, and fragments of the tank stopped falling we, Bergeron, Thomas, and I went forward to see the results of our work. The demolition was complete. Explosives had dealt the death blow to the once proud vehicle of war.

Satisfied, we reversed our route and headed for the Battalion Command Post several hundred yards to the rear, passing over the now quiet battlefield still strewn with dead enemy marines whose forms were barely visible in the rapidly fading light of day.

The full moon and stars, filling the blue sky, reflected brightly over the western Pacific. No painter could have done a better job duplicating the beauty that was enchanting us as we marched to the rear. How could we reconcile this beauty with the many deaths and the cries of the wounded that had surrounded us all day? Arawa was now at peace, the sounds of war had ended, the cries from "Hells Corner" no longer could be heard. Joy reigned throughout the Bushmaster command post.

The attacking companies had reached their objectives, leaving not a sign of a surviving Imperial Marine. General Patrick from Sixth Army Headquarters, dressed in his bright cotton Khaki uniform, congratulated Colonel Stofft for the fine work the battalion had accomplished. He would report our success to General Walter Krueger, Commander of Sixth US Army, now located on Goodenough Island.

The Japanese hold on Arawa had ended. As best we could tell, not a single one of the enemy was left alive and we took no prisoners. Not that we did not want prisoners, for we did. We needed them for interrogation purposes, but they elected to die for their emperor. It was honorable to die, dishonorable to be taken prisoner. Even though the brave Japanese Marines lost the battle, they won valor.

As if at the end of a hard day's training at Camp Shelby, First Sergeant Dixon formed the company and reported all present or accounted for, reverently calling out the names of the dead and wounded. Taking command, I faced the company to the right and began the sad march to the rear with some now empty ranks. The march route passed by the cemetery and the bodies of our dead were still lying by their shallow graves. The bodies were being prepared for a simple burial, each wrapped in a sheet or blanket, a cord tied around the neck, waist and ankles. Chaplain Gaskins was in the process of saying prayers over the deceased. It was a heartrending sight. It is terrible enough to see one of our buddies killed on the battlefield, but to see him lying by his grave shrouded in a sheet or a blanket, tied at the neck, waist, and ankles, was too much to expect of men after escaping death themselves. Their dead comrades, the brave warriors, like us, the survivors, wanted to live and return to families and loved ones, but fate had determined otherwise.

Wanting to do something in remembrance, I

halted the company, faced it to the left and toward the cemetery. There I gave the front rank a half-right face and ordered three rounds be placed in the magazines of all rifles and carbines, then port arms and commanded: "Front rank only. Prepare to fire three volleys. Fire upon command only. "Ready! Aim! Fire!; Ready! Aim! Fire! Ready! Aim! Fire!" The troops fired a volley between commands. The remainder of the company came to present arms during the volleys. Then hesitating, I ordered: "Ricciardi, blow Taps," and the sound of his bugle reverberated throughout the battalion, over the treeless plantation strewn with the bodies of the Imperial Japanese Marines, and over the now-silent graves of our fallen comrades as the bright moonlight bathed us. Many wept.

The brief ceremony over, we continued our silent march, mindful of our missing friends and fellow soldiers now resting in the cemetery or suffering from wounds in the underground field hospital. We had the gallant Japanese Imperial Marines, whose inert bodies still lay on the battlefield, to thank for this. For some reason we felt compassion for the Japanese Marines as strange as it may seem. But the dead, American and Japanese, had answered their last muster call and Taps had been sounded, a fact that would bring sadness and sorrow to loved ones on both sides of the Pacific. Death in Arawa was no respecter of persons; there seemed to be a brotherhood of sorts existing between us and our enemy for valor was clearly on both sides that day.

A full moon, in all of its glory, surrounded by a swarm of brightly sparkling stars, glowed in the heavens, casting a peaceful tropical magical spell upon us. What a contrast to the awful day of hell we had been through. Those of us in the long, silent marching column tried to find solace and peace to soothe our tormented thoughts, but the terror we had experienced that day on Arawa would not permit that peace to come. But then, we, the survivors, had escaped from the jaws of hell, at least for one day, even though many of our brothers-in- arms didn't.

A PRAYER AT TAPS (*)

Before we go to rest we commit ourselves to thy care, O God our Father, beseeching Thee through Christ our Lord to keep alive thy grace in our hearts. Watch Thou, O Heavenly Father, with those who wake, or watch or weep to-night, and give thine angels charge over those who sleep. Tend those who are sick, rest those who are weary, soothe those who suffer, pity those in affliction; be near and bless those who are dying, and keep under thy holy care those who are dear to us. Through Christ our Lord. Amen

(*) Song and Service Book, Army and Navy, 1942.

CHAPTER 22

THE AFTERMATH OF BATTLE

"Are you the chief "Bushmaster"?" asked Colonel Hooper, the TASK FORCE DIRECTOR Executive Officer.

"No, I'm not." Colonel Stofft said. "Colonel Herndon, the Regimental Commander, who's on Kariwani Island, is the Chief "Bushmaster". Why do you ask?"

"We've heard over the radio from San Francisco that the "Bushmasters" of the 158th RCT., composed of twenty tribes of Indians, have completely wiped out the Japanese on Arawa. Congratulations," replied Hooper.

"Well, Colonel Hooper, the Indians did a good job in combat, but I've only about one hundred of them in the battalion. We have a mixture; mostly white boys mingled with Indians and Mexicans. We are proud of everyone; they all did equally well."

We heard over the radio from London, reading in the Guinea Gold, and other newspaper clippings congratulating the 158th "Bushmasters", for a job well done. Even General MacArthur gave us a little praise; that was very unusual. Also we received a cable from Governor Sydney P. Osborne, of Arizona, the "Bushmasters'" home state:

"I send greetings and congratulations to you and your men on behalf of the citizens of this State. By Executive proclamation, today is being observed as "Bushmaster" Day in the State of Arizona, and we are dedicating this day to the backing up your attack through the purchase of war bonds knowing our jester to be woefully inadequate in comparison with your heroism...."Bushmaster" Day is a proud event in Arizona's annals, and the day of your return will be prouder yet."

Then topping the praise off, we heard the seductive feminine voice of Tokyo Rose over the Tokyo radio. We enjoyed the good American music, but laughed at her attempts to convince us to lay down our arms to end the imperialism of the United States. She said that famous "Bushmasters", murdered their gallant men on Arawa on the 16th, an had violated the international war agreement by their brutal method of warfare. You used knives and machetes to cut and mangled our wounded as they lay helpless. You are butchers of the human race! Should one of you fall into our hands, you will be dealt with accordingly."

"Those so-and-sos", one of the angry "Bushmaster" said as he listened to the radio show: "They are lying about us. They are the ones who butcher and mangle our soldiers cutting them to pieces, soaking them with gasoline, setting them afire, then enjoying watching them run and scream until dead."

Another said: "I will never take another prisoner. One came toward me the other day with his hands up begging to surrender and I fell for it. Then he threw a grenade at me. Luckily it didn't explode and I mowed the yellow bastard down with my tommy gun as I hit the ground."

Reflecting on that, I wondered what effect the war would have on young men exposed to front line combat once they returned home.

They had seen so much inhumanity. Could they ever be normal or would their minds be twisted? Would they have respect for another human being? Would they be fit for society? The "Bushmaster" had killed hundreds of the enemy but yet the enemy was human, too; they seemed to enjoy doing it. Again, I reflected on the cause of war: is war for politicians and the profiteers? Young men die while others back home enjoy the benefit. Could Tokyo Rose be right? Was the United States the aggressor with imperial designs implementing the 1846 Manifest Destiny eventually becoming the leader of the world? Is that what the war is all about? Was the attack on Pearl Harbor permitted to happen giving us an excuse to get us involved the war? We knew the great Japanese fleet was on the move even in early December, but yet we ganged our battleships at Pearl Harbor to be an easy target for them to attack on December 7, 1941. Churchill, Prime Minister of England, they say, jumped for joy, when he heard of the attack for he knew we would declare war on Japan and then Germany would declare war on the United States making us a participant. Time would tell.

All of these unpatriotic thoughts rushed through my mind as we celebrated our victory at Arawa while listening to Tokyo Rose. While I was having these disloyal thoughts, the men continued to enjoy the publicity we were receiving from home, the media, and yes, from "Tokyo Rose".

After breaking the backs of the "Sons of Nippon" on Arawa we fell into a routine of boring camp life while waiting for another combat mission. Life was miserable on the bleak environs of Arawa. However, the Japanese Imperial Air Force at Rabaul had not forgotten. Our air defenses consisted of one AA gun fired with little effect at washing machine Charlie on his nightly raids, and our cal..50 air cooled AA machine guns, stump mounted. Little-by- little the enemy seemed to be concentrating on us - the "Bushmasters". Had they found the hated "Bushmasters" on Arawa? That must be true!

On the morning of 22 January, about 2:00AM, the single Mitshibushi bomber was on its way from Rabaul for its nightly visit. Only the usual harassing single bomb was expected, however, the approach was different. Chaplain Gaskins, who had his dugout near me, and I were very concerned. We heard the usual popping sound as the bomb bay door opened on the underbelly of the bomber. It was much louder than ever before and was followed by the sound of the bomb falling toward the earth, almost whistling, getting louder as it continued to fall. I felt the bomb was about to enter my dugout. Again, I clawed the ground, begging for life as Chaplain Gaskins began to pray. I remembered how grateful I was to have a man of God nearby in my agony of fear. I was in good company, but still felt helpless. The previous air raids, even though feared, were nothing compared to what we were experiencing. Many things flashed through my mind; Wilma and the boys, Lily, Doug, my brothers and sisters. I prayed that I would live to see them once again. Louder and louder the missile of death approached and then it happened. The earth shook with the explosion; one of the sandbags fell on me from atop of my dugout. Gaskins breathed a sigh of relief and thanked the Lord for our deliverance. Then a strange silence followed; only the mournful humming of the lone Japanese bomber on its way back to Rabaul could be heard. What a relief. We checked each other and with the exception of the nervous shakes, we were OK. Not once did we realize the bombs had fallen in our battalion area. The field telephone in the niche of my dugout began to ring. Then I realized something terrible must have happened during the raid. Nervously, I reached for the telephone while still sitting on the bottom of my dugout. Pushing the switch, I heard a cry of terror:

"Medics, medics. Please send the medics to "G" Company!"

It was Captain Cochran in hysteria.

"I cannot get the medics! I cannot get the medics! Do something quick!"

Without further discussion with the hysterical commander of Company "G", I had the switchboard to get me the aid station and informed them to get all medical personnel and litter jeeps down to "G" Company without delay. The medic on duty wanted more information.

"Get down to "G" company with everything you have including Drs. Moulton and Beatty, immediately. Don't ask questions. Hurry!" Please hurry!"

Then I called the field hospital for additional assistance, Col Stofft and the remainder of the staff. Woolwich, my driver, was already standing by and soon, with the battalion commander, and the executive officer, we headed for "G" company area about a half mile away overlooking the ocean near the underground hospital. Disregarding the RED ALERT, which was still in effect, picking up Chaplain Gaskins, we roared out of the CP area heading for Company "G".

Arriving in the devastated area, we ould smell the strong odor of the lingering acrid smoke, torn flesh and blood. Going directly to the company command post, we found Captain Cochran in a state of shock, tears streaming down his face.

"My men could not get out of their hammocks, Colonel! They had gotten in from the Itna River patrol at midnight and did not have time to dig fox-holes and they were so tired." he cried, "I think every one of McGowns' (Alamo Scouts leader) men were killed or wounded!" he screamed.

"How many casualties do you have Cochran?" Col Stofft asked.

"There are five killed and eight wounded, maybe more, we are searching!"

Then from nearby, a weak painful voice:

"Won't someone help me, please?".

"That's Lt McGown", said Lt Ferris Ivy. We rushed to McGown.

"Lift up my legs please; they are hurting so badly." Ivy searched for McGown's legs in the dark.

Ivy lifted up one mangled leg; the other one was missing.

"That's better, Lt., thanks a lot", and McGown returned to a peaceful comatose state. Quickly, the medics placed the unconscious form onto a stretcher and rushed him to the nearby underground hospital. Later we were informed the brave lieutenant, had to have the other leg removed; it was so mangled.

With the wounded now in the hospital, we began to search for the dead, finding several bodies. The condition of the bodies was horrible, some in parts. The men were caught sleeping in the hammocks above ground and the bomb had maximum effect. Near one of the bodies was a purple heart awarded to the person for a small wound he had received during the battle of January 16. One of the his buddies said he was so proud of the award; he took it to bed with him.

After removing the dead and wounded from the area, Chaplin Gaskins shared reverent sentiments with Cochran to calm him. Once the company had settled down we returned to our respective areas knowing the rest of the night would be without harassment from Washing Machine Charley. However, still we wondered if the Japanese were singling us out because we had removed the Imperial Marines on Arawa on the 16th. Was it possible? Only time would tell.

Then again at 4:00 AM the following morning, 23 January, Charley was back in his single plane raid. Our lone AA gun fired sending spots of red glare high overhead without discernable effect. Screams and yells, RED ALERT; the men ran to the air raid shelter, while Gaskins and I hunkered in our grave-like dugouts. Once again our fingers were frantically clawing into the earth, praying, waiting, the awful waiting, a replay of the morning before. Explosion! Where? Seconds later the field telephone in the niche, rang. What sort of a message would I receive. I knew it would be bad.

"Send litter jeeps and aid men," the voice hysterically cried.

"Who is it this time?"

"It hit Company "F" officer's tent."

"Is Lt. Miller hurt?", I inquired.

"Don't know, but he isn't around."

Again, the maximum medical effort was required. We headed for Company "F" located in the opposite direction from Company "G" near the MLR. As we arrived, we faced the distasteful smell of acrid smoke. Inquiring the whereabouts of the officer's tent, a soldier pointed and we rushed in that direction. We found Doctors Moulton and Beatty already at work.

I pushed myself through the crowd of curious soldiers who were wondering what had, once again, happened to their officers. At the dugout that they had used for a common shelter, we found two of the officers stretched out on the ground, the commander, 1st Lt. Kenneth N. Miller, Miami, Arizona, who had replaced Captain John McGlothlan, only a few days before, was still in the dugout sitting on the far end, saying nothing. 1st Lt. Woodrow W. Sanders, Wateree Hill, Camden, SC, and 2nd Lt. Chester Van Ruth, and Miller had recently replaced the officers that had been killed or wounded on the 16th. Miller was registering severe pain and Doctor Moulton was working with him. Then quickly the medics placed him on the waiting litter jeep and rushed him to the underground hospital just down the dusty road.

"What about Sanders and Van Ruth?" Colonel Stofft, anxiously inquired of Doctor Moulton.

"Sandy is dead, Van Ruth is just shook up. He will be OK, Colonel."

The death of the fine and gregarious officer, Sandy Sanders, was a great loss to the "Bushmasters". He had joined us in Panama and had gained the respect of all who knew him. We attended a service for him the same day at 10:00AM. During the service and the interment conducted by Chaplain Gaskins, I reflected upon the losses of officers and men we had suffered in the past few days. Company "F" appeared to be jinxed; they had lost all of its officers twice in less than two weeks requiring replacements. Any officer sent to the company would say his goodby on his way to his new assignment: "Well, so long fellows", and proceed sadly down the road to Company "F", hoping his fate would be more promising than those who had served with the company before him.

The battalion became a case of nerves. The "Bushmasters" did not mind doing battle with the enemy, but there were no escape from the hot tropical sun that had tanned their faces; the terrible tasting dehydrated food, some had refused to eat; sulfuric water from shell-holes, that caused some of us to vomit once we drank the stinking stuff; we had no recreational equipment, only going out on patrols forward of the Main Line of Resistance, looking for stray Japanese Marines who had escaped alive from the battle of the 16th; all enjoyed the patrol assignment; it was a change. They dreaded the nights and welcomed the days. When RED ALERT was sounded we wondered, who would die tonight and felt the presence of death around us. We felt as though we were sitting ducks to be picked off by Charley.

These were trying times for us. Combat missions would be preferable. Morale plummeted. We received word that a few officers and men could be sent to Hawaii on a recreational tour. One candidate was Whitten, who had gone through so much even spending a night among the Japanese marines knowing if he were captured he would surely suffer extreme torture and death. Furthermore, his intelligence section under combat conditions had performed so well I recommended to Colonel Stofft, that he be one of the officers to go to Hawaii and he agreed. Whitten never forgot this and always reminded me that I had done him a favor; he deserved it.

Shortly after Whitten had departed for Hawaii we had a heartbreaking experience. The Japanese were at times using American B-17 bombers, captured in the Philippines in 1942, flying them out of Rabaul against the allies. We were informed to consider any plane that flew over Arawa as the enemy and shoot them down if we could. Because of this the allied fighter and bombers from New Guinea scouted around us on their way to bomb Rabaul. Had they flown directly to Rabaul from Finchaffen they would have flown over us. We had Cal. 50 AA MGs, mounted on tall tree stumps to be used should this happened regardless of the circumstances, fearing, even though the planes were American made, they could be enemy planes, and be attacked by them.

It was late one afternoon, about dusk, when we were alerted that a plane was entering our air space at a very low altitude. Gun crews rushed to their Cal..50s, primed them and was ready for action when the big B-17 bomber appeared, smoke trailing. It didn't take much to imagine the B-17 American crew had flown a mission over Rabaul and perhaps was badly damaged by the Japanese air defenses and was limping it way home, taking the short cut, to Finchaffen. This however, would cause it to fly directly over us. Sadly, our gunners picked up the big plane in their gun sights and began firing at the smoke trailing plane as it flew helplessly over us at about six hundred feet. Firing tracers we could see the effects of our many guns further wounding the helpless plane. It made no attempt to evade the horrible hail of lead that poured from our guns and majestically continued its flight of death over us. Soon it was out of effective range of our deadly fire, escaping being shot down. I often, since then, wondered what happened to the plane's crew, who were only trying to get to their home field in New Guinea, but must have suffered so badly from our so called friendly fire. It was a horrible thing to stand helplessly by and watch our own gunners shoot at one of our own planes regardless of the circumstances. The plane's crew knew this but I'm sure they prayed for mercy but our guns showed them no mercy; we had to follow orders.

Then, shortly after this unfortunate event, and after Whitten had returned from Hawaii, I was sitting in the hot sun on a downed coconut log near my orderly tent. Looking toward the jetty, I noticed a tall and rugged man, dressed in civilian clothes, wearing a broad brimmed cowboy hat, trudging alone up the dusty road toward me. I wondered who would be dressed like that in a combat area. Furthermore, no civilians were permitted in the combat area. Amazed! Was I seeing things? was it John Wayne, the movie star? It was John Wayne, the movie star! The one and only our battalion commander had spoken of often. Why would John Wayne be in the hell hole of Arawa? Then he came within hailing distance.

"Put it there, pal", he said, extending his ham-like hand to me. I pretended to be casual and replied:

"Why, John Wayne, what a pleasant surprise? What are you doing here? Looking for excitement?"

"Nah, Captain, just looking for Fred Stofft." His slanting eyes beamed and a big smile crossed his face. I was amazed; his demeanor was the same off the screen as on. There was no make-believe in him.

Colonel Stofft's tent was just up the hill. It was sparsely furnished with only a folding cot and a chair. I escorted John to the tent. He entered; war hoops sounded in greetings. Like two bear cubs frolicking, the two engaged in a wrestling match. Actually beating each other up, they rolled to the outside of the tent and down the steep hill. I thought: "what a heck of a way to greet people", as I walked down the hill to my tent to get some work done. Finally, their tumbling match over, they stood up, still pounding each others' back, laughing and enjoying recalling the past times they had had together. Then they headed for the tent. John turned to me as they were about to enter the tent: "Captain, please come and join us."

"John, you've come a long way to see a special friend and I don't want to interfere. Thank you anyway."

"Captain, this won't take long, please come."

"Of course, come, Ben Rod," Col Stofft motioned with both head and hand.

I entered the tent with the two good friends, one from Hollywood, the other from Tucson. Both of them had attended UCLA, playing football together there.

John produced a fifth of Scotch and each of them took a swig. Then offered me the bottle and watched as I meekly partook. I hated the stuff but who would refuse a drink with Col. Stofft and his good friend, John Wayne. My throat was burning as if a hot cinder had been placed in it. Thanking them for their generosity, I excused myself, rushed to my tent, leaving the two to celebrate their reunion. Quickly, and in haste, I ran to get a drink of stinking sulphur water from my canteen to cool the burning drink of Scotch that seemed to scorch my throat. "How could anyone drink the stuff?", I thought.

The word got out. John Wayne was in the area! Lynn Allen, the mess officer, somehow found a piece of brightly colored calico he placed on the officers' table. John would have supper with us as we sat on benches made of bamboo poles and table fashioned from discarded wooden boxes, a far cry from John's Hollywood's style of dining. Our menu was white beans, the first we had since arriving in SWPA. What a delight. John, like the rest of us, ate the beans as he enjoyed reminiscing with Col Stofft and telling us stories of their college days together. We were amazed at his ability to fit in and seem at home in our very humble circumstances. John enjoyed the humble meal of white beans as if he were dining in the exotic and sumptuous places in Beverly Hills.

Following our evening meal of white beans, John Wayne and his male entertainers staged a show for us. He had women in his USO-sponsored show but the military in New Guinea would not permit the women to come to Arawa. We told him: "The heck with your men! Where are the women?", and he took the kidding, promising he would do better next time.

We found a natural amphitheater near the battalion headquarters tent. We placed two trucks side by side using the truck beds as a stage. He had no accompanying music. First John sang Minnie the Moocher, the first and only time I had ever heard him sing. We later told him it might be better if he would just stick to cowboy roles instead and he agreed. Then he was followed by a lone unaccompanied vocalist singing Oh What a Beautiful Morning, from the new stage play, Oklahoma. When the soloist got to the point singing the part "when the corn grows as high as an elephant's eye", our artillery located a mile to the rear fired a planned interdictory salvo on the Japanese to the front. The singer, who was not aware of this friendly fire, thought it was enemy artillery firing on us. He jumped off the truck and crawled under it. That was the best part of the show; we all howled and so did John Wayne.

After the show, John sent his companions back to New Guinea on the waiting LCMs, and he bedded down in Col. Stofft's tent under circumstances no more elaborate than any of us, almost on the forward edge of the battlefield.

The Japanese, until then, had given us excitement but they could not compare with the excitement that John inflicted upon us during his short visit. One could hardly imagine the concern even MacArthur would have for the safety of John Wayne, the internationally famous movie star. The problem was that he refused to have an escort; he wanted to just roam around and see the soldiers. Col. Stofft, unfortunately, took John at his word and let him do as he wanted. First, he went down on the beach where we had our artillery liaison plane and talked the pilot into flying him over Ditmop, which could still be occupied by the enemy. Wayne dropped hand grenades on the place. Where did he get the grenades? He would not tell us.

"Damn it, John, are you trying to get me hanged? If anything should happen to you here, I might as well go to the cemetery and start digging my grave." Stofft laughed, not wanting to hurt feelings, but unfortunately, he didn't realized John Wayne was only beginning his mischief.

"John, I want you to stay within sight of me during your stay. I'm serious, even MacArthur's headquarters knows of your whereabouts and that is here with me. God help me if you don't listen."

"Yeah, Fred" he said, "I'll be a good boy. I won't cause you any trouble."

Later in the day we heard a scream from Colonel Stofft:

"Officer's call immediately at Battalion Command Post", Col. Stofft speaking: "Had this place combed from one end to the other. John Wayne is nowhere to be found. Does any one know where he could be? For God's sake, find him soon. I must report his absence to TASK FORCE DIRECTOR and that means the General will probably relieve me of command."

Scattering like covey of quails jumped in West Virginia, every one of us joined in the emergency search for John Wayne. Why would he embarrass his old friend? In the meantime, Colonel Stofft called TF Director, and when we returned to report our findings, there stood Shuman, the commanding general, and the old eagle beak was mad an old wet hen.

"Colonel Stofft, how did this happen? Who brought him here in the first place? Why did you ever let him get out of your sight?" And many other questions he rudely demand of poor Colonel Stofft.

While Colonel Stofft was being drawn and quartered by the CG TASK FORCE DIRECTOR, Whitten motioned me outside the tent.

"Ben Rod" he said in a very low voice, almost a whisper, "we have a boat patrol heading for Itna River to knock out an Japanese outpost there. What do you think? Could Wayne be on that patrol boat?"

"My God, Whitten, where else could he be? This place has been searched from stem to stern and he isn't here! If he's on that boat we might as well put a noose around our sweaty necks and jump off the coconut stump. Our deaths would be less painful than what the general will deal out to us. You better inform Colonel Stofft now, the sooner the better."

"Please, Captain Jordan," I noted he got formal with me, omitting addressing me as Ben Rod as he usually did, "do it for me. I will be blamed for him going on the patrol and I had nothing to do with it. The boat patrol is from Company "E" and I never even saw it leave the jetty."

"OK, but I know the boat is under radio silence. How are we going to get a reply from them?"

"Don't know, Ben Rod. It will take a command decision to break radio silence. Col Stofft, or even the CG TASK FORCE DIRECTOR, may have to do it."

"Are we in contact with the boat patrol?"

"Yes, we receive a signal every thirty minutes on the hour and on the half hour. There is no voice communication until after contact with the enemy on the Itna. It is now 6:50PM; they will give us a beep at 7:00PM."

"What is the approximate location of the boat, Whitten?"

"I figure the patrol has already reached Gilnet on the Itna- its objective, and have accomplished its mission. They have had time to do that, sir."

"That means radio silence may be broken, or soon will be for the attack on the enemy's outpost will have occurred. Quickly, we must tell the colonel and hope for the best. Let's cross our fingers for the bald-headed, eagle beaked, prune faced CG will be there when we tell the battalion commander."

Entering the CP tent, I got the attention

of Colonel Stofft.

"Yes, Captain Jordan, do you have something for us?" he was calm as he usually was under stress.

"Begging the Colonel's pardon sir, but Lt. Whitten suggests that Wayne may be on the boat patrol with Company "E", that by this time has accomplished its mission at Gilnet north of Cape Bushing on Itna River and may be on its way back."

The commanding general, his eyes shooting fire, didn't wait for the battalion commander to answer me. "Is John Wayne on that boat and if so, when will it return?"

"We are not sure, general, but the boat is under radio silence until 7:00PM and then its only a beep - no voice transmission, sir." Whitten said.

Then without further waiting, the battalion commander gave Beane, the Communication Officer, a direct order: "Tell the patrol leader to cease operation immediately and return to base as soon as possible. Instead of one beep signifying contact, tell the radio operator to signal two beeps if VIP is aboard. He should understand who I mean by VIP. Quickly! Get to the radio shack and send the message immediately." Beane, on a run, left for the radio shack. He had only minutes to send the message and get confirmation.

The waiting began. There was silence among the officers from TASK FORCE DIRECTOR and our own. 7:00PM and we waited but not too long. Beane enters the tent:

"The attack on Gilnet was successful and the boat patrol is on its way back to Arawa.

John Wayne is with them and participated in the attack on the outpost. He is OK, a soldier suffered a minor wound. Our attack was a complete surprise. Since the attack is over I have modified communication procedures from silence to clear at any time. They are to proceed to Arawa with haste. The patrol leader informed me he will be at the jetty early tomorrow morning." We all breathed a sigh of relief for the moment but anything could happen to the boat patrol on its way back. They even could be attacked by our own planes, as had happened to Whitten while on a similar mission; he had waved an American flag and the American pilots ceased the attack. They could also encounter a land mine or a Jap water patrol. and many other things could happen.

"Colonel", said the irate general, "I want you and your staff at the jetty tomorrow morning when that patrol boat arrives. Then I want John Wayne arrested. He will go no further than step into an LCM that will be standing by to ferry him across the strait to Finchaffen. Hopefully, we will never see him here again." Than the ill tempered, bald pate general and his executive officer, Colonel Hooper, stomped out of the CP and returned to their own headquarters on the hill. Later Col. Hooper called and apologized to Colonel Stofft for the rude way the Commanding General, had acted in our presence.

We had a sleepless night, waiting for the LCM with its patrol and John Wayne aboard to arrive early the next morning. We wanted to get John Wayne to safety for fighting the Japanese would be easier than fighting the

Commanding General, should anything happen to him. All night we sat at the radio shack tuned in to the boat patrol leader who was standing by advising us concerning the welfare of John Wayne, who was having the time of his life. The men on the boat patrol loved him. His companionship and participation in the attack on the enemy outpost was a masterpiece of a story. (Many years later, and after John's death from cancer, I received a letter from his son, Michael Wayne, BATJAC PRODUCTIONS in Hollywood, requesting I write up the description of this action. They intended to use it in a production featuring John's life. I wrote the article but for some unexplained reason the production never occurred).

Early next morning there we were, the brigadire general, a full colonel, lt colonels, majors, captains, anxiously waiting at the jetty for the LCM bearing the combat patrol and John Wayne. The small craft was making a direct approach onto the beach in front of the group of silently staring officers. Then Colonel Stofft motioned to me to the side:

"Ben Rod, would you please diplomatically handle the situation. I just cannot tell John, my very close friend, that he's under arrest and then send him across that choppy sea in an open LCM to New Guinea."

I agreed and the colonel was happy. The commanding general, was standing near not saying a word. I hoped that he would not speak rudely to John, even though he deserved it.

The LCM plowed onto the beach, lowered its tongue like ramp, and John Wayne led the men off, paying particular attention to the one wounded man aboard. Unlike the day John arrived, there was no greeting. The exception was Colonel Stofft who shook Wayne's hand and chatted with him. The CG never said a word to John. He silently turned, got into his waiting jeep and drove off. I stood by waiting for the greeting between two old friends to be over and then made my approach. John eyed me with some suspicion for he had sensed the dread I was suffering, ordering him away from Arawa.

"John", I said, "it's been good having you with us but it's time for you to return to New Guinea and safety. The commanding general demands you depart now in the waiting LCM for Finchaffen. I hope you are not offended."

"Me offended? Why Captain Jordan, I've had a ball. I would not have missed this if my life had depended on it. I've never experienced such an adventure. Tell you what, Captain, if ever you get to Hollywood, please come to the Athletic Club there and tell them you are my guest. It will not cost you a cent. I'd be honored if you would do that, and bring Fred (Stofft) with you, too."

"Thank you, John. Its been a pleasure, hopefully I can accept your invitation and visit you in Hollywood someday."

John Wayne, the idol of millions, shook our hands, he than grabbed and hugged Col. Stofft, saluted, turned and boarded the LCM. The small craft lifted its ramp, backed out into the stream, and with full throttle, it turned west and headed across the strait for Finchaffen on the north coast of New Guinea. The great actor waved to us as he passed from view. Even though I never saw him again, nor did I have the opportunity to visit the

Athletic Club in Hollywood, we occasionally did correspond for several years until his death. I keep his letters in a secure file for they are choice possessions (see copy of one letter in appendix 10).

Although John Wayne took advantage of the situation and caused great concern to us and the military brass, embarrassing Colonel Stofft, one cannot help but admire him. To me, he demonstrated the brave man that he portrayed on the screen. There was nothing fake about him. He was a credit to his profession.

While thinking about my newfound friend, John Wayne, I also wondered about my nephew and constant companion in my youth, Buss (Leolin V. Landers). I had heard he had entered the Air Corps but nothing else. Years later, his daughter, Marilyn Terry, wife of Dr. Ed Terry, University of Alabama, Tuscaloosa, filled me in concerning his military experience during WWII. I want to include him for he is as much a part of this story as I am. Our boyhood was very close knit as stated in <u>Ben Rod Jordan of Putnam County.</u>

He was in the 20th Air Force, 331st Bomber Group, 315th Bomb Wing, stationed on Guam when the war ended. Inducted March 1944 at Camp Atterberry, Indiana, and later stationed at Shepard Field, Texas, Lowrey Field in Denver, McCook Airbase in Nebraska. He was a crew chief of thirteen planes, a great responsibility. His last duty was on Guam repairing electronics on B-29s. He installed five-hundred-pound Norden Bomb sights aboard the big planes. After the war, Buss built barracks on the island of Guam for the Air Corps. The war had interrupted his thirty-seven-year career in Research and Development at the Union Carbide plant in Charleston. The war separated him from his young wife, Ethel, and beautiful daughter, Marilyn. A son, Barry, was later added to the family.

JOHN WAYNE

1022 Palm Avenue
Hollywood 69, Calif.
August 22, 1962

LTC Keith J. Honaker
2400 Huffine Circle
Johnson City, Tenn.

Dear Keith:

First, let me say that your letter of July 11th reminded me of a very thrilling and wonderful experience in my life. I still see Fred once in a while in Tucson.

As to employment in Hollywood, I just wouldn't know what to tell you. It is practically impossible to get anything in the motion picture business. Television and the government separating theaters from production companies have made such inroads in our business that, while it hasn't gone to pot, it has shrunk so much that there aren't enough jobs to go around. As far as the insurance field is concerned, I don't see how I could be of any assistance.

Thanks again for recalling some exciting memories. I hope something good breaks for you.

Sincerely,

John Wayne

John Wayne

JW:ms

CHAPTER 23

RETURN TO NEW GUINEA

Now that the backs of the Japanese Imperial Marines on Arawa had been broken, our tactical activities were reduced to surveillance patrols. To be vigilant, daily the "Bushmasters" searched several miles in front of the Main Line of Resistance (MLR) to prevent a possible enemy build-up, while the artillery would continue interdictory fires in likely areas of possible enemy concentrations. Arawa was located between Cape Bushing on the west and Gasmata on the east, each having known troop concentrations, perhaps capable of contacting the other and we were to prevent that. The enemy could move by foot overland to Arawa, using the northern route, or they could use barges to haul supplies and replacements from Gasmata to Cape Bushing using the sea. Further, the much-needed supplies could be transhipped from Cape Bushing and ferried up the Itna River to the Japanese army on Cape Glouster, hard pressed by the US 1st Marine Division there, the western part of New Britain. These possibilities of enemy options must be negated or else we could again find ourselves engaged with the fanatical foe, and in conjunction with the navy we took preventive actions. While the "Bushmasters" patrolled to the northwest and northeast, trying to establish any possible enemy contact, the Navy PT base stationed at the jetty on Arawa patrolled the sea lanes on the south, between the above mentioned points, insuring the sea shipping lane was not an option to the enemy.

Then one bright day the Navy squadron commander requested, and the colonel approved, that an army liaison officer accompany his nightly PT patrols. This action would be an excellent means of gathering and sharing enemy intelligence and would be mutually beneficial. Daily, at dusk, the PT patrol left from the jetty and headed for Gasmata, the location of the Japanese supply base. Even though our occupation of Arawa had cut the enemy's sea supply lane between Gasmata and Cape Bushing, the enemy tried to slip much- needed supplies past us until the Navy began patrolling along the south shores of New Britain Island. Wanting such an experience, I requested, and got permission to accompany the navy PT patrol; it was the sort of act John Wayne had pulled on us just to see if it was exciting.

When I reported aboard the small PT boat, the commander, a Navy lieutenant, assigned me a space on deck where I could observe any action that might occur. Soon, with its two powerful Chrysler engines roaring, the boat headed for Gasmata, about a hundred and fifty miles to the east. The small boat looked like a seagoing porcupine with its many machine guns mounted on its deck manned by navy hands. We arrived off Gasmata about 10:00PM. The young commander ordered the engines cut and we began drifting toward the enemy-held shore. I wondered why he was doing this for I thought our mission was only to deny the enemy the shipping route between Cape Bushing and Gasmatta, certainly not to invite disaster. Drifting into shore would only put us in range of the enemy's heavy weapons and we could suffer casualties or even the loss of the PT boat. Since I was only along for the ride and had no authority, even though I was alarmed, I said and did nothing. Anxiously I waited for developments. It didn't take long. Already, the crew was at battle stations and the engineer and helmsmen were standing by for a quick getaway once our presence was noted by the enemy.

We were getting very close to the sandy shore which could be clearly seen, even in the darkness; the crashing of the ocean waves on the sand could be heard. I braced myself for I knew it would be only seconds until the Japanese would discover us and would retaliate. However, the small boat continued to drift closer to the beach. I heard one of the seaman whisper: "Lieutenant!", to the commander, which I took to be a warning to get the heck out of there before we touched bottom. But it was almost too late. Apparently we had been spotted and a large searchlight came on. Immediately the bristling guns on the PT boat opened fire and the light was blasted into darkness. The engineer and the helmsmen went into action, heading the small boat out to sea at full throttle while under fire from automatic weapons of the Japanese shore defenses. Circling, the PT boat again passed near the area where we had been discovered and, with all machine guns ablaze firing toward the enemy's shore, we headed west toward Arawa at full speed. Flashes from the muzzles of the enemy's shore-based automatic weapons could be seen but fortunately the bullets passed harmlessly over our heads.

Later, I asked the commander why he drifted so close-in to shore and had engaged the enemy at such close range. He replied, laughing: "We just wanted to let the Japs know we were there." The bravado was heroic enough, but we could have lost all hands and the boat unnecessarily, proving nothing except that we were a bunch of fools. But I enjoyed watching the Navy working, and they were good at it, if not smart.

In retrospect, nine years later in Indochina, in 1953, I found myself in a similar situation while serving as an observer aboard a French armored boat on a river patrol. Where our navy was overly-zealous, the French were the opposite. The French tied up the armored boat by the Dong Nai River's bank, in enemy territory, and there we stayed all night among the communists, who could be heard prowling around us. In both cases all aboard could have been killed but, for the grace of God, we were spared. What a contrast (see story beginning on page 350, The Eagle Weeps, by the same author).

I would like to explain an unusual situation pertaining to both the U. S. Navy patrol and the French river patrol. The crews and I were exposed to great danger, even death, by the carelessness of the commanders on both occasions, but yet we were spared. However, on subsequent nights in each campaign the boats were attacked and some of the crews were either killed or wounded, and the boats suffered damages. I had been very lucky.

Returning to Arawa aboard the PT boat, I reflected on my past in critical situations where I could have been killed, but was for some reason spared. Examples: in 1933 I almost froze to death; the terrible truck crash and the fire that had killed three and severely burned others; three times, while piloting a small airplane, I was involved in near-fatal air crashes, and for some unexplained reason I was saved. There have been other near death-experiences and I wonder why. All this went through my mind as I returned to the jetty at Arawa riding on the deck of the roaring, powerful Navy PT boat, while the strong wind sprayed us with salt water covering our bodies. My experience aboard the Navy's PT boat was very exciting, enjoyable, and informative.

Our stay on the tropical, sun-baked peninsula of Arawa on Cape Mercus was having an extremely adverse effect on the men. Because there was no escape from the extreme heat and a lack of vegetation which had been destroyed by battle, it was not a pleasant environment. Added to this was the terrible dehydrated food, the terrible-tasting sulfurous water, the lack of athletic equipment and movies. My men began to act like zombies and looked like walking skeletons. They would mope into the mess line formed in the hot blazing tropical sun and, seeing what the menu offered, often would walk away with empty mess kits. We couldn't even have a decent drink of water because our water source was from stinking sulphur holes. Our clothing was ragged; many jungle boots were so badly worn that sockless toes could be seen. One wondered just what was happening in Washington. True, we knew the maximum effort was going to Europe, and we understood that, but why did we have to starve. We could fight the enemy, even with bare hands if we had to, but empty stomachs would only worsen our already deteriorating physical and mental condition. We had food, but because of its terrible taste we could not eat enough of it to sustain our health. Sgt Raybourne, the mess sergeant, almost in tears, begged for something to be done. The company commanders complained, and finally TASK FORCE DIRECTOR did something. One day we received another shipment of dried white beans and Coca Cola, one bottle for each man, along with toothbrushes; we were splurging! What a coincidence; only recently, I had craved cornbread and beans, seasoned well, with green onions and fresh milk that Wilma often prepared for me back home. Now we were having beans instead of the terrible dehydrated food. Great!

While the troops' mouths watered while waiting for the cooks to prepare the beans, we received our bottle of hot Coco Cola, every last one of us. We looked at the bottle as if it were a gem of sorts, not wanting to open it for some reason. We tried to cool it by soaking it in our sun heated sulphur water, that didn't work; we still had hot Coca Cola. Then someone said if we let the water drip on it, that might cool it but that didn't work either. Finally, after finding no means of cooling our Coca Cola, we broke down and drank the Coca Cola, savoring it, enjoying this rare treat we hadn't tasted in over a year.

Then came time to eat and the men ran to the mess line, mess kits and canteen cups rattling. They filled them with the "musical fruit" as Sergeant Dixon called them. Almost hysterical, the men shouted for joy, for they had beans to eat. However, that was only one meal, it was the terrible dehydrated menu come breakfast, but it was a break.

Then came the issue of toothbrushes, something many of the men had not had for some time. They had attempted to wash out their mouths with the terrible sulphur water using their forefingers as brushes. I realized we were in bad shape not only physically but physiological as well. The supply sergeant, Sergeant Billie Dickerson, from Huntington, West Virginia, rushed to see me.

"Captain Jordan", he said excitedly, "we have two men fighting over toothbrushes."

"Sergeant, don't we have enough toothbrushes for every man?"

"Yes, sir, we sure do."

"Why then, are they fighting over tooth brushes, Sergeant?"

"The crazy 'Bushmasters' are fighting over the color of the toothbrushes. We ran out of blue toothbrushes and Jim offered to trade his red toothbrush to John for his blue toothbrush, but John wouldn't trade. Now Jim is trying to take John's blue toothbrush from him and I can't stop the fight."

Even though this was humorous, I realized we were in bad shape; two battle-scarred men fighting over the color of toothbrushes. As it happened, I had been issued a blue toothbrush, so as a peacemaker, I offered to trade my blue unused toothbrush to Jim for his red unused toothbrush. Jim was tickled; the fight ended. Happily John took off with his blue toothbrush, while Jim guarded his blue toothbrush with his life. Now all of us were happy because we had new toothbrushes in the desired colors. The sergeant aptly dubbed the fracas: "The Battle of the Toothbrushes." Sort of reminded me of our "Battle of the Bedbugs" in Panama December 1941.

That was an indication that our mental condition was even worse than suspected. However, there was another indication that linked us to that condition. Late one evening in blackout conditions, while we were sitting on the sand bags surrounding my grave-like dugout, Chaplain Gaskins remarked to me: "You know, Ben Rod, serving under combat conditions is not as bad as this," and I agreed. Then we heard a man crying in the nearby aid tent. Going to investigate we entered the tent; several men were standing under the glare of a dim light, in silence.

"What's the matter here?" Gaskins inquired.

"It's him, sir." The aid man on duty pointed to a man hunkered down in the corner of the tent like a beaten dog.

"What's the matter, son?" Gaskins asked soothingly.

The sniffling man made no reply.

"He got a 'dear John' letter today from his girlfriend back in the states," said the aid man.

The good chaplain continued trying to console him in a sympathic manner. The man was hysterical, saying he had sent all of his money to his girlfriend and they had planned to marry once the war was over.

"I cannot go on without her," he said

between sobs.

Disgustingly! I put in my two cents worth.

"Look, soldier, why did you expect a girl to wait years for you to return, even if you do? True, many of us made plans in good faith at the time of departure into the service, but things change, new people are met. Not having someone to love is a terrible thing to deal with, as we all know. Human nature is fickle and subject to change. For your own welfare, be thankful this happened. You will find another girl when you get back home. Now get out of here and quit being a cry baby."

The soldier got up from the corner of the darkened tent, looked firmly at me, and almost at a run, left. The others in the tent, silent, looked at me as if I were a very hard man. They thought I had no compassion for the poor heart-broken soldier who had just slunk out of the tent.

Later, Gaskins said: "You know, Ben Rod, those words were very harsh for that poor man, but really it probably was the best kind of advice; sympathy would have only added to his deep depression."

Checking later, the next day, I found the man performing as if nothing had happened between him and his girlfriend. He was reconciled to the fact and could now be happy, looking to the future when he would return home.

Often the situation would be reversed. Girls back home were often jilted by their men overseas. They would write to the unfaithful boyfriend and say, once they found out about the philanderer: "What's the girl there got that I haven't got?" and the unfaithful suitor would reply: "Nothing, honey, except she's got it over here." The chaplain and the commanders had a lot of this to deal with during our stay on Arawa after combat ceased and boredom set in.

Then we had a terrible situation in Company "F". They had experienced excessive losses of the company officers; twice in a week all had to be replaced. The battalion, even after sending officers in from other companies, robbing Peter to pay Paul so to speak, even sent staff officers down to the company to spend the night, trying to buck up the men's morale. I spent a night with them once. The following morning a surveillance patrol was dispatched at daylight. The patrol had gone only a short distance when one of the patrol members stepped on an unexploded mortar shell, killing him instantly and wounded another soldier very seriously. The patrol leader radioed the information back to the company command post. With a litter jeep, and accompanied by the company's first sergeant, Sergeant Virgil F. Howell, I went forward to retrieve the body and get the wounded man to the underground hospital. The dead soldier, Sanchez, had recently returned from Sidney, Australia following hospitalization for malaria. He had missed being in combat with his company and volunteered for this patrol to get a similar experience. It was very unfortunate. The patrol reorganized and continued on its mission, while we returned the dead and wounded to the rear area for processing.

Company "F" was really receiving more than its share of bad luck. For example, the following task was really more than could be expected of them but yet they bravely endured it, even though it was not one of combat but rather one following combat: the burial of the enemy dead. The Japanese normally did a good job looking after their dead and wounded, but in the case of January 16, as far as we could tell, not a single Japanese Imperial Marine was left alive. Even our surveillance patrols found none that had escaped. Not having graves registration personnel, we not only had to dig our own graves and bury our own dead, but now we had to bury the enemy dead as well. There were many decaying and bloated dead Japanese bodies in front of Company "F" which must, for health reasons, be gotten underground. It was a monumental problem and the burial had to be expedited; the number of dead bodies demanded more than normal means. The Engineers were called in. Using a bulldozer, they dug a long deep common grave just in front of Company "F", and placed the dead bodies in it. While pushing dirt over the bodies, for some reason they also pushed a stump, roots and all, into the common grave. That was a terrible mistake. The stump created ventilation down to the decaying bodies, and soon the area was permeated with the terribly sweet odor of decaying human flesh. I've never had such an experience. But poor Company "F" had to work, sleep, and eat in this environment until the engineers piled more dirt upon the grave.

The morale of Company "F" did not improve either when two new officers, 2nd Lieutenants, fresh from the states, reported to the battalion for assignment. Looking at the officer status, seeing Company "F" recently had lost all of their officers in a week's time due to combat on January 16 and the air raid on the 22nd, having only two officers present for duty, I recommended to the battalion commander that they be assigned to the company. The commander reviewed the officer status and he agreed with my recommendation to send them to Company "F". The company was still licking their combat wounds, while they lived, slept and until the engineers corrected the situation - ate amid the terrible odor coming from the common grave containing the Japanese dead. This situation certainly did not appeal to anyone, especially not to new officers just reporting in from the states, and who had not yet been under combat conditions. The two officers, one named Boetcher _ and I fail to remember the name of the other one - were escorted by Lt. Van Ruth to their new assignment. Like scared pets, they silently followed Van Ruth. Two hours passed and the field telephone rang. It was a very excited Lt. Van Ruth: "Captain Jordan, Lt. Boetcher committed suicide in his tent!"

"What means did he use to kill himself, Van Ruth?"

"We issued both officers their field equipment, including a carbine, and he used that, sir."

"Have you called the medics?"

"Yes sir. They are arriving now."

I notified Colonel Stofft and together we headed for Company "F" area.

Arriving, we found the men gathered around the tent in which the inert body of Lt.

Boetcher lay upon its back on the ground by his cot. Captain Moulton, the battalion surgeon, was making an examination. He noted a small bullet hole and blood stains over the heart on the officer's jacket. The carbine still lying across the cot. Here, again the "curse" on "F" Company had struck. someone whispered.

"Apparently he was on his knees when he killed himself, colonel", Moulton said. "He must have laid the rifle crosswise on the cot and, while pointing the muzzle toward his chest, he pushed the trigger." Then he said, without emotion, "That would do the trick." It was a cold remark but yet, with the rest of us, he had witnessed so much death, both of the enemy and friendly troops, what else could he say?

Again, the unfortunate death of the officer only added to the jinx of Company "F". Thereafter, assigning officers to the company was a psychological chore for the battalion commander. "Going to Company "F" is a passport to the cemetery", the officer would say, as he left with a forced smile, judging from the company's officer death rate.

In retrospect, it would have been better not to have received new officers on Arawa after combat had ceased. The battalion should have been in an area more suitable for new officer to adjust before being assigned to us at that time, considering the awful environment we were in, and receiving new personnel only would have a terrible adverse effect.

We were in a deplorable state with the terrible food and water adding to our already deteriorating mental state. The battle-scarred area was without a single tree and the tall stumps reflected death itself. The environment certainly wasn't conducive to a secure feeling for the green officer yet to be battle tested. Nor did the stench of death that Boetcher had experienced before his unfortunate suicide add to any secure feeling. It was something no one should have to experience. It was horrible.

What we were experiencing on Arawa was worse than any combat. We felt a terrible feeling of isolation, exclusion, and neglect, and craved a change. Why were we on this god-forsaken place when we could be engaged in combat? The men would say, "No Japs here and sitting here is a waste of time. We need to get going again." I wondered if our minds were being warped; does life have meaning any more? Then I thought of my small family back in the states: do Wilma and my small sons, Bucky and Johnny, really exist? Are they a figment of my imagination? Is this terrible experience real or is it, too, my imagination? I could not imagine that what was happening, was really happening. Had I been killed and gone to hell? Could it be any worse? Was my mind perhaps on the verge of going over the brink? Get busy, I told myself, there's work to be done! And I did. Work was therapeutic. My men needed encouragement and I must act, quickly!

I appointed Lt. Tompkins as the R&R (Rest and Recreational) officer. Without athletic equipment, he organized various games, such as relay races, even kid's games of tag, wrestling, story-telling, and letter writing. It paid off, even though we still ate dehydrated food and drank stinking sulphur water. This little activity was a wonderful therapy. Tompkins initiated physical exercise which we participated in daily.

Shortly after our athletic activity, General MacArthur announced a rotation policy permitting those who had been overseas the longest to return home on a rotation basis providing a qualified replacement was in position before the officer or enlisted man would be released to go home. It was based strictly on time served overseas. Fortunately, I had left the united States on December 23, 1941 with the 150th (Powderhorns) Regiment while the 158th RCT (Bushmaster) left in January 1942. With the exception of Captain Moulton, our battalion surgeon, I had seniority over the other officers of the "Bushmaster" Regiment. Moulton had beaten me out due to his service in Greenland in 1941.

In preparation for the initiation of the rotation program the battalion commander directed me to provide a list of officers and enlisted men of the battalion indicating their order of rotation. This was a difficult task because, except for Moulton and me, most of the officers and men left for Panama on the same date, with the exception of the men who had come to us from the 5th and 14th Infantry Regiments while we were still in Panama and had outdated others in the "Bushmaster" Regiment. On the officers' list, Captain Moulton was first and I was second in the battalion eligible to return to the United States. Once our replacements arrived, were briefed, and could function ready to assume the job, we could rotate home. It had been almost thirty months since I had left the states.

This situation caused strange things to happen in the minds of those who would probably be going home soon. They became very careful about exposing themselves to unnecessary danger. Some actually had a change of personality and became almost withdrawn. They feared at the last minute something would happen to them, so they sought shelter from any danger where previously some of them actually had deliberately exposed themselves to danger. Before, we had to beg Captain Moulton to get into the shelter during an air-raid, for he wanted to see the show. Now he was the first to reach the shelter. Helmet in hand, he sat on the earthen ledge as if he expected the bomb would come into the shelter after him. At the first sound of the alarm, he would head for the fallout shelter with such speed not even an olympic racer could have caught him. We laughed about the humorous actions of those going home as we continued to prepare the rotation list.

Then came good news!

The fighting Second Battalion of the "Bushmaster" Regiment, was to evacuate Arawa and join the regiment in Finchaffen, New Guinea. There we would refit and get needed equipment and replacement personnel in preparation for the Wadke-Sermi operation. We would be a part of General Krueger's leapfrog or island hopping plan. This had electrifying effects. One would think we were going to engage the Japanese in a super softball game. The men cheered and jumped around like small children on a playground. It would be a change from the hellish existence on Arawa. Quickly, the battalion readied itself for a rapid departure. However, my company, and a platoon from each of the other companies, were to follow at a later date. It would be our lot to clean up the peninsula, fill in all of the fox-holes and gun emplacements, pick up every piece of paper, and remove all communication wires. In other words Arawa was to be left as if no battle had been fought there. With the exception of the limbless palm trees that was the way we left it. When inquiring why this was necessary, I was informed that the coconut plantation belonged to a some big American soap-making firm. The army didn't want to be criticized for leaving the plantation in a bad state of police. Furthermore, Uncle Sam was to pay the soap company war damages the plantation had suffered during the battles, the bombardments, and the air strikes. Each coconut tree had to be accounted for, assessed, and paid for. Just like "Tokyo Rose" said, maybe we were engaged in an imperialistic war. Can one imagine what those poor men thought while they were filling in the fox-holes, picking up paper, after having seen their buddies killed and wounded. They had suffered so much, and now we had to pay some one millions of dollars after wresting their plantation from the Japs at the cost of many lives. Were the politicians using Mahan's <u>Manifest Destiny</u> to influence the world by our leadership? Was it actually being played out before our very eyes? Was the war being fought with big businesses being the beneficiaries? Were my thoughts disloyal? It has been said wars are made for the benefit of the rich.

Our mission was completed three days

later. We, the "Battered Bastards" of Arawa, ragged, unshaven, hair like horses' manes, and underfed, departed the peninsula in high spirits. We thanked God. In five LCMs, we headed west on the choppy waters of Vitjaz Strait for Finchaffen located on the Huron Peninsula, a finger of land jutting out from the New Guinea mainland, sixty miles across the open seas.

CHAPTER 24

FAREWELL BUSHMASTERS

We were exhausted, terribly exhausted. As we, members of Headquarters Company of the Second Battalion, 158th Regimental Combat Team (Bushmasters), with attached units from the battalion, lay scrambled as if dead on the beach of Finchaffen. We were a motley lot, our fatigues were ragged and torn, unshaved, needing hair cuts, dubbed ourselves as the "Battered Bastards" of Arawa. Perhaps it was the beating inflicted upon us by the angry salty waves of the Strait that had pushed our small LCMs around like a cork on the end of a fisherman's line. The cold, briny waves of sea water had splashed over the sides of our small boats, soaking us to the skin as we lay in misery in the bottom of our boats, rest being impossible during the rough crossing that night. Further, the loud engines of the LCMs, struggling against the angry sea, hadn't given peace or comfort either. Our energy had been sapped which we had little of, for we were already in a weakened physical condition even before leaving Arawa. Our lack of energy was due to insufficient nutrition for the men, for months, only nibbled at the dehydrated "stuff" the Army called food; they had not had a decent meal in months. Mother earth, made bare by the recent struggles of war, had nothing to offer her malnourished sons on Arawa as she had in Milne Bay or Goodenough. There we traded the dehydrated stuff to the "Fuzzy Wuzzies", the local uncivilized tribes, for taro and bananas and they loved it. There, too, we could climb the coconut trees, gather coconuts, cutting off the ends we could drink the milk therein. But not so on Arawa for the bombardment by the Navy and the Air Corps during the invasion had destroyed the coconuts, nor were there "Fuzzies Wuzzies" around to trade with. Unfortunately, and by inadvertence, the army had become a great ally to the enemy by issuing us the terribly dehydrated food and not realizing it had starved us. Hopefully, that was all behind us now and the menu would be better.

Here we were on the beach swarming with others soldiers. They were from a new infantry division fresh from the states, had just landed. They were dressed in clean fatigues, faces smooth as a baby's posterior, none needed a hair cut, and all were in new uniforms, wore new jungle boots and undented OD painted helmets. What a contrast we were as we lay exhausted and ragged on the sandy beach. But we were proud, we the "Battered Bastard" of Arawa, for we had met the enemy, been bloodied by combat and won the conflict. Their time would come.

I was contemplating my next action - the movement to the Regiment, the location I did not know nor did I have transportation to move the tired troops there. Then First Sergeant Dixon alerted me.

"Captain Jordan", he said almost in a whisper, "there's a Major General approaching us."

Without looking: "Quickly, Sergeant, form up the men and dress them as best as you can!"

Taking position in front of Sergeant Dixon and receiving his report. I did about face as the general stood in front of me.

"Captain Jordan, Headquarters and Headquarters Company, 158th RCT, sir." Emphasizing the "sir".

"At ease Captain and please give your man at ease, too". Doing another about face, I ordered "at ease", and then faced the general again whom I thought would be very critical of us. I tried to explain:

"General, sir, I apologize for the appearance of my men for we have just came from Arawa, New Britain, and we need some attention to our personal appearance."

"Captain, please, you need not apologize to me or to anyone. We have heard, while aboard ship, about the great things you "Bushmasters" did, breaking the back of the Japanese on Arawa. You look like good combat soldiers and good combat soldiers you are, too. I would consider it an honor if you would permit me to shake the hand of each of your fine soldiers." I was surprised.

"Yes, sir! It will be an honor for you to do that for us." And I called the company to attention and ordered to prepare for an inspection. To prepare for an inspection the ranks must be opened to accommodate the inspecting party, and I was not sure the men knew how to do it for it had been so long since we had any close order drill where such things are done on parade ground formation. So I gave the command, after calling the men to attention.

"Prepare for inspection."

And, to my further surprise, the men

responded perfectly. The third rank stood still, while the second rank took two steps forward and the first rank took four steps forward, even aligned themselves to the right. Giving "Ready, front", they smartly faced to the front. The ranks were now opened for the general, and me, accompanied by Sergeant Dixon and the platoon leaders, Allen, Beane, and Tompkins, to pass between. Before the general began greeting the men in ranks I saw a very humorous thing. Private Allen, tall and gangling, needing a shave, helmet dented by combat, the toe of one of his jungle boots was worn away, and I noted one of his big toes stood upright as if it, too, had responded to the general's visit. Trying not to laugh at the comical situation, I accompanied the general through the ranks doing my best to withhold snickering. (Unfortunately Private Allen was killed during the battle of Wadke-Sermi operation according to a letter that Sgt. Dixon sent me after I had arrived back in the states).

While this was going on, and before the general began his individual greeting of each man, I looked at my poor, tired beaten up men, comparing them with the fresh men from the United States. There we stood for the general's visit, uniforms torn and ragged, jungle boots worn so badly that naked toes were sticking out. Their helmets were scared and beaten up, some even having bullet holes in them, faces needed shaving, for we had no razors, and hair crumpled and sticking out from the edges of their helmets, for we had no barbering tools. But it was then I felt the proudest. I realized I was among the best soldiers on earth. They had fought so well against a determined enemy and had suffered so much; and had left many of their comrades in shallow graves on Arawa. They had already blazed their way into the annals of military history. Since that day on the beaches on that faraway place called Finchaffen, and having served in many positions in the military, I've never felt prouder to be a part of anything than I was that day, a member of the "Battered Bastards" of Arawa, the "Bushmasters".

The most considerate general took each man by the hand and told him how proud he was having the privilege of meeting a "Bushmaster" from Arawa. He said that the service and the country would always be indebted for what he did there. The general gave us the spirit we so badly needed and we were made proud. We no longer were dispirited. Regardless of how we looked, we were the best damn soldiers that the SWPA would ever see. So they had proved in Arawa and would later prove again and again as they island-hopped across the Pacific to Japan, they were still of the best - the Indian, the Mexican and the Caucasian, good Bushmasters, all of them.

The general, congratulated us and wished us well. And then he asked if he could do something for the good "Bushmasters".

"Thank you kindly, general, but your visit with us was good therapy and we will always remember it. It's now for me to find my regiment and get my troops transported there."

"Doesn't your regiment know you have arrived, captain?"

"No, sir, they don't. I've tried to reach them on the radio but was unable to do so. I'll find a switchboard here on the beach. I'm sure they must be tied into it and call them to send trucks, sir."

"Captain, stay with your men. Please, let me handle it for you." An aide was standing by and the kind general issued instruction for him to notify the 158th of our present on the beach, and to send trucks for us.

"Now, captain, have your men just lie down on the sand and rest, and you should, too. You must have had a hard time crossing over the rough strait. We will let you know when we have contacted your regiment." The kind general and his aide departed. Once again we laid our tired bodies down to rest on the sands of Finchaffen.

Shortly, the aide returned. "Captain Jordan, we have located your regiment and trucks will soon be on the way to you." I thanked the Captain and once again sat on my pack to wait for the trucks, listening to the kibitzing of the men as they rested. Ricciardi, as usual, was his jovial self, cheering us up with his witty remarks. I wondered just how the death of Bowyer had effected him; they had been so close.

The trucks, all fifteen of them, arrived on the beach. The truck-master reported and we entrucked for our new area and headed out of the crowded beach area under the gaze of the clean shaven, well dressed, yet to be bloodied soldiers as we had been.

On the way to regiment we saw a white woman, an army nurse, the first we had seen since leaving Australia; it had been over a year. Through no fault of her own her appearance was disappointing. She was dressed in cotton trousers and a shirt, a fatigue cap on her head, her hair flared from under it. She looked more like a GI instead of a woman, some said. Riding in a jeep, she paid no attention to the truck-borne ragged "Battered Bastards" of Arawa having recently come from there. It was good that she didn't, for we wasn't much to look at. Hopefully, things will change.

Arriving at regiment, we were surprised to find Colonel Herndon, the regimental commander, his staff, and Colonel Stofft standing in front of the regimental headquarters tent, to welcome us. It was unusual, for Colonel Herndon was not much when it came to such efforts. Maybe the call from the kind general informing him of our arrival at Finchaffen and needing trucks, had alerted him to our condition. He was friendly and asked about the men. Col Stofft, our very impressive and very able battalion commander, said he was glad we were back with him. Members of the regimental staff, including Lt Col Wood, Major Shumaker, Major Day, Capt Allen, and others, welcomed our return to regiment after over a year as a separate unit with the 2nd Battalion; we had left the regiment while at Camp Carlou, near Port Moresby. We felt like we were VIPs by the unusual treatment. Then Col Stofft mentioned a special treat awaited us at the company mess tent. Thanking the Regimental Commander and his staff for their kindness, we left for my company area nearby.

Raybourne, the company mess sergeant and his mess personnel had preceded us with the main body of the "Bushmasters" a few days before, had prepared well for us, he said. I wondered why we were receiving all the attention. Colonel Stofft had his jeep and invited me to ride with him as he escorted us to my company area. We talked on the way, he said the Regiment was getting ready for a big operation - perhaps, Wadke-Sermi. Maybe he could get a few days leave in Sidney before the jump off, he said, hopefully. He needed it. We all did, but he needed it the most.

Then we arrived in the company area, detrucked and First Sergeant Dixon whistled the company into formation. The attach platoons, under waiting guides, departed for their own respective companies. Sergeant Dixon then marched the company in single file, headed for the kitchen tent. Sure enough, there was a big surprise; ice cream! What a wonderful thing; the "Battered Bastards" of Arawa having ice cream!

"We must have died and gone to heaven." Dixon said, as the men stood in awe while Raybourne and his good cooks handed out ice cream as we passed by in a single line.

"Nah, Dixon, just the cooks doing their good thing. Here Sarge, have another helping," said Raybourne. and Dixon gratefully accepted. Then, following the ice cream treat, at the evening meal, we were served a stake dinner.

"Now, I know we have died and gone to heaven. The Army would never give us steaks to eat when they have cornwilly or that damn dehydrated "stuff" for us round." Said Ricciardi. The men relished eating their stakes and marveled at their new surroundings under shady cover. Then we had a hair cutting.

Bergeron, the company barber, got some barbering tools, including hand operated clippers, and we all enjoyed the hair clipping session. We each tipped him all of twenty-five cents. First he refused to accept the tip, but we insisted and he took the twenty-five cents. He deserved it. Cold showers, new issue of clothing, complete with new jungle boots and socks, underwear, and all. Spiritually, if not physically, we were ready and rearing to go on the Wadke-Sermi operation. "God help the poor Japs once we get there." the men said. With our spirits now in high gear we settled into our new environment, which even included trees, enjoying we peace had not had in almost a year. And we were safe from "Washing Machine Charley", too.

Shortly afterwards Colonel Stofft left for Sidney, Australia for a much needed rest. Major Hohnhorst, the Battalion Executive Officer, would command the battalion during his absence. I personally drove the battalion commander to the nearby airstrip and we talked. Both of us seemed to be saddened but I tried to be cheerful; we realized this could be our last time together and many thoughts rambled through my mind. Many things had happened since he had joined us in Panama in December 1942. The battalion, under his command, had been through so much and had accomplished much, welding relationships that appeared to be stronger than that of blood brothers. Then he said to me as we arrived at the airstrip, still sitting in the jeep:

"Ben Rod, I've enjoyed working with you so much and your company performed well. But you know there are times when things and associations must come to an end." and he hesitated. I remained silent and wondered what he was leading up to.

"Ben Rod, you are returning to the states on rotation and probably we will never see each other again. If your departure to the states occurs before I return, I wish you the best of success in your coming assignment. Please remember me and the other 'Bushmasters', won't you?"

Shocked, I hardly knew what to say. I knew a list of officers and men indicating the rotation order had been forwarded to the regiment from Arawa but had no idea MacArthur would ever approve anyone going on rotation, considering the operational requirements that even seemed to be increasing.

Then, choking, I tried to reply without showing emotion. And I expressed my admiration of the man that had led us so ably into combat. Hopefully, some day, we would meet again, perhaps under much more favorable circumstances. Then, after shaking my hand, he picked up his battered bag and headed for the operations tent on the strip. I watched him until he disappeared inside. He had been a good friend, a father image, an example. He would soon become the regimental commander of the 126th Infantry, 32nd Infantry Division, and eventually, after the war, the Adjutant General of the Arizona National Guard, a Major General, later, retiring as a Lt. General. (As of this date General Stofft lives in Paradise Valley, near Phoenix, Arizona. He is ninety years of age).

My thoughts were emotional as I drove alone back to my company area in Finchaffen;

they were mixed. Was I really returning to the states? Could I leave my good men on the eve of a major conflict? While I basked in safety, enjoying the love of my family back home while they would be in combat, against a vicious foe. Many would be wounded while others would die. I was torn. I had been overseas for almost three years and my family needed me and I needed them even more, but could I make the proper decision in my extreme emotional state? Then I remembered seeing Captain Caffee charge a Japanese machine gun on Arawa with only a pistol. He was terribly wounded, loosing half of his face. Why did he do that, when the "Bushmasters" were around that could have and later, did put an end to the Japs machine gun crew? Then there was brave Captain McGlothlin, Commander of Company "F", and all of his good officers were either killed or wounded in less than two weeks. Lt. Minor of Company "G", Lt Bartnicki, Sgt Yangingly, his jaw shot off, and Tiny, the heroic aid man, who was shot in a very private place, and did not want to tell us about it. Then there were Sgt Ruiz, Hodges, Bowyer, and others all dead or severely wounded - but for the grace of God, except for damaged hearing, I never got even a scratch. Haven't you done enough, I reasoned? After all, they need combat experience officers, NCOs, and men to train recruits back in the states. But all of this reasoning still left me in a tizzy. Then finally, as if a small wee voice was speaking: "Get back home, you are in need of your family as they are in need of you. Don't deprive yourself and them any longer. Get back, before it's too late, quick!"

Even that serious talk I had with my self had to be confirmed. Upon returning to the company area, I parked Woolridge's jeep in front of the company's orderly tent, finding First Sergeant Dixon and the company clerk there. I said nothing while I sat at the folding field table, which I used as my desk. Sgt Dixon noted my silence. Perhaps I was brooding.

"Captain, what's the matter?"

Then I told Dixon of my dilemma and he made my mind up in a very firm way.

"Captain Jordan, we have been through a lot together since leaving Panama. You and I built this company from a detachment to a full blown company. We have suffered through thick and thin and we are proud of what we have done. Now I want you to get this straight, Captain. Why would any one not take the well earned opportunity to return to his family? Why would you, of all people, even hesitate. For Gods sake, use your head, Captain! Even on the first day on Wadke-Sermi you or any of us could be killed. What good would that do your family? Get back home to your family before its too late!"

Sergeant Dixon always straight to the point, saying what he thinks, reminded me of my father image, First Sergeant Jim Rhodes. Rhodes, had taught me so much while in Company "D", 150th Infantry from recruit to officer; he had left us in Camp Shelby, Mississippi, with tears in his eyes, in October 1941; I would never see him again. Such NCOs, even though subordinated, are often more wise, at times, than their respective commanders. They were advocates and often were guiding lights in times of a commander's distress; they were and still are the backbone of the Army and the salt of the earth. Such were Rhodes and Dixon.

However, Sergeant Dixon's remarks were poignant and to the point, and I was grateful to him, but I really didn't need him to tell me what I should do, but I did need to be bucked up on the decision I had already made: I was going home; he just made me more determined. It would be tough to give up my company, the "Battered Bastards of Arawa", to another commander, yet unknown. I would feel like an orphan when it would occur, perhaps very soon.

First Lieutenant Roger Norwood reported in. He was the new Commander of Headquarters and Headquarters Company, 2nd Battalion, the "Battered Bastard" of Arawa. Initially, I was almost resentful. Roger, however, was a good officer sent from Regimental Headquarters; I had know him since Panama. However, he still needed seasoning in command; he would soon receive it. First Sergeant Dixon, the other NCOs, and the officers, all experience, would lead him through trying times. He would do well, I was sure. But he had my company, my family, my boys! How could I give them up. But sadly, I had too.

Turning over the company funds, briefing him on the operation of the company's many diverse activities, suggested changes in organization due to combat losses and illness, instructing him concerning personalties of the company and of the battalion, I relieved myself of all operations of the company to Underwood. Now I was a fish out of water. In such cases the new commander usually feels the old commander was in the way, and he wanted to run his new outfit without influence from the former commander. But I did not interfere, devoting my time to visiting with the men and answering the new commander's questions. Little-by-little I emotionally released myself from command and Norwood was very considerate and often expressed appreciation for helping him to get into the swing of thing before I left.

Being sentimental, I wanted my departure from the company to be without fanfare. I never liked this sort of thing, especially now, when I had to leave men who all were like brothers or even sons to me. We had been through so much, but I just wanted to slip away without them even knowing when the time came. It would be emotionally stressful. Sergeant Dixon and Lt Norwood knew of my desire and agreed, but would express my appreciation for having the privilege of serving with them after my departure.

Then, one evening, just before dark, when the sun had settle below the tops of the high mountains of New Guinea, the telephone rang. Sergeant Dixon answered. Following the short conversation he looked at me and in a subdued voice: "Captain Jordan, its time for you to leave. You are to report to the ship Lurline at the pier immediately, it will leave for Milne Bay early tomorrow morning and they want you aboard tonight."

Looking at this wonderful man who had been with me so long and had done so much for the company that I had the honor to command since Panama, I grabbed his hand, I wished him the best and without further word, departed his presence; as with Sergeant Rhodes, I would never see him again.

Woolridge was already in his jeep as I approached with my crammed duffle bag. He stared the engine and soon we were headed up the small trail in the company area, as if I were trying to make an escape.

Sergeant Dixon and Lieutenant Norwood were standing in the entrance of the tent, their outlines reflected by the bright light from a Coleman lantern inside the tent, waving their goodbys and I acknowledged with a salute. Woolridge gunned the jeep and we continued on and just before we left the perimeter of the company area, there they were, many of the men of the company standing by the side of the trail, cheering and waving as I passed. Standing up in the jeep, steadying myself by holding onto the windshield, I waved to the wonderful men who had meant so much to me. I couldn't stop. Like a baby, a grown man, I shed tears. I just couldn't help it! I was only twenty-seven then, much younger them some of the men but yet they were my sons. I often would hear them refer to me as "the old man", a moniker from the old days when the commander was the father image of his men. They referred to him "as the old man" meaning their father. They wouldn't say "the old man" in the commander's presence, but it was an honor to be called that; it was a verbal expression of respect.

Entering the beach road, still standing in the jeep, looking to the rear at the man standing by the side of the trail, whose forms was barely discernable in the darkness, I gave a final wave and they responded accordingly. Taking my seat once again, we drove silently the few miles to the pier. Only the hum of the jeeps engine spoke; we didn't answer.

There it was! The Lurline! This was a luxury ship that had plowed the Pacific Ocean between San Francisco and Hawaii before the war. I was to be a passenger on the wonderful ship back to San Francisco! Soft comforting lights from the great ship reflected on the still water from the portholes and the wide door with a gangway leading to the pier. It looked like the a tropical paradise seen in dreams of the palm trees, the trade winds, and one could even imagine the beautiful Hawaiian music, beautiful girls dancing in grass skirts, bodies swaying while arms and hand made graceful movement in tune with the soothing music. My spirits was immediately lifted and I had no further desires to be a hero. I just wanted to go home now to be with my beautiful young wife, Wilma and two young sons, Bucky and Johnny. The Lurline was a good place to begin.

Woolridge helped me go aboard. "Gee, Captain, what are they doing to you?. A 'Bushmaster' will be ruined on a thing like this. How can you hope to survive?"

"Woolridge, I will manage somehow to endure the terrible hardships. We all have to have our trials and tribulations and we must be strong." And we laughed at our bantering. Woolridge, had been my driver since Panama, and I found it hard to leave him, too. He was a loyal and devoted member of the company. He was my last contact with the outfit. We had developed a brotherhood type relationship and had learned to look after each other when the need occurred.

The steward meet me at the gangway.

"Captain Jordan?"

"Yes, I am."

"Follow me, please."

"Thank you."

Biding Woolridge last farewell, as I followed the steward down the hallway of the luxury ship I reflected upon Dixon's remarks the day we returned from Arawa: "We must have all died and gone to heaven," when Raybourne served us ice cream after months of eating dehydrated "stuff" - I won't call it food. And now here I was aboard a luxury ship that would carry me across the wide Pacific to my young family. It just had to be heaven; I had just came out of hell.

The steward took me into a very orate lounge furnished with overstuffed furniture. Sitting there were three field artillery captains, looking beat up just like I was. One of the captains, Ed Blocker, had been our Artillery Liaison Officer on Arawa.

He had, January 16, placed his artillery fires on the Japanese machine gun emplacements having the deadly American made Cal.. 50 machine guns and BARs they had been captured in the Philippines. But these guns did terribly damage to Company "F", wiping out most of the company's officers and many of the NCOs and men as they tried to maneuver around them and finally did knock out the deadly weapons. Sgt Yangling had his jaw shot off here as his squad engaged the emplacements.

"Greetings, Blocker and Gentlemen. Quite an improvement of quarters since I last saw you, Blocker," being cheerful.

"Quite an improvement, Ben Rod", and he introduced his companions, also from his battalion. The waiter, in his white coat, approached and offered us cold Coco Cola, served in goblets; gratefully, we accepted. We sat in the comfortable overstuffed chairs and sofa, enjoying each others company; naturally, our discussion turned to our trip back home. Being only recently from the barren hell of Arawa, we were now enjoying the unbelievable comforts of the luxury liner which hopefully would carry us home. Again, we were approached by the steward, note pad in hand.

"Gentlemen", almost reverently, said, "dinner will be served soon, is there anything you like for us to prepare for you?"

This blew our minds. We had talked of getting the works once in San Francisco, already had concocted the unbelievable meal of "T" bone steaks, french fries, apply pie, and ice cream and having all the other trimmings. We, jokingly, gave the steward our order for what we expected have once in San Francisco. Politely, the steward wrote on his small pad the order as we had given it, as if it wasn't no unusual thing. He left, saying he would return once the table was prepared and ready for us.

The four of us looked incredulously at each other.

"Now that's peculiar", said Blocker. "He acted as if he would have the food we ordered right on the table for us."

"Nah, that impossible, Ed. How could he have such a menu over here? They eat what do. We'll be lucky to get 'C' rations tonight.", said another. But we still anticipated.

We dismissed the subject of the dreamed-up menu and continued discussing the upcoming operation, thought to be in the Wadke-Sermi area. We felt we were lucky to be on our way home, even though we had guilt feelings; our friends would be going in while we basked on our way home in luxury. Why were we so lucky? Our names, especially mine, just happened to be second on the rotation list, just because I had left the states a few days before hundred of others did. Was it poetic justice? Was it fair? It would be a long time before they would be home, if ever. What a difference a few days made. God help them! Then we went silent, perhaps in prayer for our brother-in-arms who, once more, would face a deadly and an unforgiving enemy, known to practice cannibalism and torture on dead and defenseless prisoners of war.

We were aroused by the reappearance of the friendly steward.

"Gentlemen", he said very formally, "dinner is being served. Would you please follow me?"

"No doubt we have steaks and french fries, apple pie?" asked Blocker.

"No doubt about it, sir." Again, we looked with wonder at each other and followed the steward to the dining room in silence.

We stood agog. Entering we noted the white linen table cloths, the unattended lighted bar, the thick rug, the ornate surroundings befitting the very rich that had been guest before the war changed things. We were escorted to our table, which was set with the best silver and china. The steward individually pulled out our chairs and invited us to sit. Then poured ice water into our clear stemmed crystal goblets. Making us comfortable, he departed, leaving us to drink the first glass of good tasting water in almost a year, savoring it to the last drop and hoped there would be more. Then the steward returned with four waiters each having a tray, one for each of us. Thereon were the "T" bone steaks, french fries, salad, coffee, rolls as we had ordered in jest, thinking such would be impossible. Yet there it was as we had ordered. We sat in silence, the four of us, thinking only days before our menu consisted of the hated dehydrate rations on the sunbaked, denuded of vegetation placed called Arawa. I noted a tear in one of the Artillery captains's eyes; probably tears were in all of our eyes.

Gobbling the steaks and french fires, we relished the surrounding under the glare of the chandelier and the thought of home, yet far away. "Are we really going home?" one said. Another said: "This is not real, I think we are dreaming, soon we will wake up standing in the mess line, the cooks dishing out that damn dehydrated food to us on Arawa, or some other God-forsaken place!, Would someone pinch me. I want to see if this is real." Blocker pinched his Artillery brother on the arm. "Ouch! Well, I'll be dammed. It is real", the officer laughed and we too thought it funny, laughing as he did almost hysterically.

Our joviality interrupted. The waiter appeared with another tray. On it was the apple pie and ice cream, the steward had promised us. We were like small kids when their Mommy's gave them candy. For it had been so long since we had such sumptuous food under such ornate surroundings. Then came coffee, the final course. And we still sat around the linen-draped table, with only the bare bone of the "T" bone steak remaining on the plate. Leisurely, we sipped the coffee and the others smoked their cigarettes, which Blocker offered me. I declined, but enjoyed the conversation, as the waiter cleared the table. We closely observed as we talked for even the work of the waiter was interesting, for it too had been so long since we had such service.

Again, the steward approached as we sat around the table enjoying the exquisite surroundings.

"Gentlemen, you must be tired. May I escort you to your quarters for the night?" He led us out of the ornate dining room and down the halls of the luxury Lurline; we followed with great anticipation.

Coming to one of the state rooms, he said: Captain Jordan this is your state room. Enjoy your rest. Call if you need anything."

And I entered the room with bunks already prepared with clean sheets, a soft pillow. There was a private bath, complete with tub and shower, porthole, giving me view of the sea. All this was just for me alone. It didn't take long; enjoying my first hot shower since Australia the year before, I was soon asleep between clean sheets, head on a soft pillow; under circumstances I thought would never come true. It was a far cry from the grave-like dugout with sandbags around its top on Arawa. Truly, I was sleeping the sleep of a king in his palace.

CHAPTER 25

I'M GOING HOME! THANK GOD, I'M GOING HOME!

The big powerful engines of the Lurline throbbed. It was early and I still fought for sleep. The engines energizing the big ship, made me aware there were interesting things to see and that I should get on deck to observe them; maybe doing this would be more interesting then lying in my comfortable bunk in the very luxurious stateroom. Quickly, I dressed in my fatigues and jungle boots, shaved, brushed my teeth, (using the red toothbrush I had received in a trade with Jim on Arawa; he had wanted a blue one), and went out on the deck. The great ship was turning its prow from west to east and soon would be on its way to Milne Bay with the happy "Bushmaster" from Panama and his artillery companions. One by one I was joined by Blocker and his artillerymen. Could we really be on our way home, I asked myself in silence? We continued to watch as the mighty ship continued making its turn, for it had to make a 180-degree turnabout before taking its eastward course. It was a majestic maneuver.

The sun was now directly ahead as the ship plowed the Pacific toward the horizon, leaving a widening wake behind. Our curiosity satisfied, Ed Blocker and I went for breakfast in the ship's ornate wardroom with the ship's officers and a few other military passengers. They, like us, were jubilant, for they were also on their way home from the Asiatic hell. The shipmaster said our stay in Milne Bay would be short; we were to take on additional passengers for home there. Then we would head northeast on the bounding main for Hawaii and on to San Francisco, our destination.

We were traveling in a dream world, the blue sea under us, the blue sky above us, the bright sun ahead of us - it was a beautiful sight; it was exotic. What could shatter our dream world? Surely, angels were hovering! Arawa, the forbidden land and its hell, was behind us forever; the nightmare was over!

The great ship traveled eastward for several hours, still leaving a spreading wake in its trail. Several hours later the Lurline began to arc to the right and continued until the bright morning sun was glistening in its wake. It had completed a 180-degree turn, heading into Milne Bay, with its almost continuous downpour of rain. It was at Milne Bay the year before when we, the "Bushmasters", were dumped off a ship and told to build our camp in a swamp knee-deep in water as the rain pounded us. It was here we ate, slept, played, and guarded the perimeter in the continuous rain. We had lost the affable and cheerful Col. Lee from Philadelphia when his plane crashed in the nearby mountain. Later the pilot of the crashed plane, a young Australian, had cried for his mother during his last minute of life. And it was here our clothing, shoes, and beds became mildewed from the continuous rain and humidity. We had only six days of sunshine during our eight weeks stay here before moving to Goodenough, an island of paradisiacal bliss compared to the water-hole of Milne Bay.

In many ways, Milne Bay was even worse

than Arawa. Was our entry into the rain-soaked Milne Bay an evil omen? Would we continue to be blessed and leave with the Lurline that hopefully would take us to our loved ones far beyond the horizon? We were depressed - we did not know why, but we were depressed. Why? Maybe it was the rain, the almost continuous down-pour of rain, the heavily rain-laden clouds, pouring from the darkened low hanging clouds obscuring the mountains tops; horrible memories continued to depress us.

The big ship dropped anchor late in the afternoon. The anchor chain thumped and rattled as the big anchor attached pulled it out, splashing down, causing waves to ripple from its center of impact in the rain-swept waters. Shortly, a small harbor boat approached and the big ship's steps were lowered to accommodate the port officials. They had a firm and disdaining look as they boarded. The homebound passengers were alarmed for they had a premonition. Later, we were assembled in the ship's ornate lounge and given the bad news. The Lurline, the luxury ship we had hoped would provide our happy return home, had its mission changed, they said. It would transport combat troops in the new leapfrogging attack method (skipping from island to island) operation of General Walter C. Krueger's Sixth Army. All passengers were to immediately disembark and would be quartered at the local replacement depot for only a short time, they said. Instead of returning to the states on the luxury liner, Lurline, we would be traveling on an even more luxurious ship, the SS America, the flagship of America, already anchored in the harbor. We had never seen the flagship, but had heard of its size, luxury, and its speciousness. How lucky can we get, someone said, but few echoed the sentiment; we were at the point where only seeing was believing. The disappointed officers from Arawa packed again and, with heavy duffle bags slung on shoulders, descended the ship's rain-drenched ladder to the small harbor boat bobbing on the choppy water of Milne Bay.

The billeting officer at the Milne Bay assigned us to a cot in a tent having a wooden floor. The rain pounded the canvas tent, unmercifully, giving a monotonous but comforting tone, conducive to good sleeping. Sleeping would be all we would have to do while waiting to board the SS America, the queen of the seas. We were encouraged to remain in the vicinity, reporting daily, for our departure on the SS America was imminent. Daily, even more often, we rushed to the beach, still in the rain, assuring ourselves the America was still at anchor. It was a beautiful sight, serene, majestic, the flagship of the United States was in all its glory; we were mystified by it. Then one morning, rushing to the beach, we stood agog; the great ship was disappearing over the horizon without us. We were heartsick. After a touch of heaven while on the Lurline, now, we were, once again, back in hell. Was Milne Bay good enough for us? Had we earned our rewards of Milne Bay? Sadly, we wondered why we were being treated as we were? We were not in condition for much more of such treatment; up to glory and then down to hell. Would we ever see our families? One man didn't; he found peace in death, committing suicide.

Rushing back to the headquarters tent, we demanded to know why we were not on the SS America. Again, we were told the ship had a change of mission. It was returning to Australia to take aboard army nurses bound for home in the states. Why, then, were we not aboard the ship? We could have traveled with the nurses. Then we were informed that the ship was traveling under direct orders of General MacArthur's headquarters in Brisbane, Australia. We understood more troops were needed in the SWPA and perhaps MacArthur used the incident to discourage the rotation policy of returning troops back to the states. Was it a ploy to discourage us? Would we request cancellation of orders returning us home? Would combat be better than rotting in the replacement depot for a ship that may never come? The fact that General MacArthur, commander of the SWPA Theater was living in luxury with his wife and son in Brisbane, did not make him a popular figure with us at that time. Then Blocker said: "It's very obvious General MacArthur did not want the soldiers, just out of combat, aboard the luxury liner with the nurses. Therefore, even though there were only a few nurses that would travel aboard the SS America, for the great ship had sufficient space for thousands of troops aboard, there would be no soldiers among its passengers. We reasoned, in our emotionally charged minds, that the Commander-in Chief of SWPA had little regard for us as we rotted in the waters of Milne Bay. As a result our short stay at Milne Bay turned out to be six weeks, a total loss of time of hundreds of combat-experienced officers, NCOs, and soldiers. These highly trained and combat experienced troops could have been back in the states training urgently needed troops, and they themselves, could eventually be returned to combat duty.

The terrible continuous rains added to our worsening depression, and being casuals, waiting for assignment, we had no duties to perform; we slept away our lives in boredom. The rain, the continuous rain, poured; mentally we were slowly drowning. We were tent-bound only going to the mess tent for heated "C" rations and to the wash house that sat over a mountain stream that carried away the leftovers into the bay after we had sat on the commode. We thought how unique it was that no plumbing was needed. The pattering of the rain on the canvas just above our heads was monotonous and, with time, it, too, became our punishment. Someone found a book; it was passed around once read, then reread; there were no others. We wrote letters but received none, since the mail system failed to keep up with our change of address.

Then we visited the base hospital, for we heard that some of our friends, wounded at the Wadke-Sarmi operation, were there. It was a mistake, and we felt the severe pangs of guilt; it was a combat wound for which no decoration would be received, being mental, but nevertheless, a wound. Further, our mental wound was infected by an increased guilt. Here we were stuck in the rain-soaked Milne Bay, whining to go home and basking in safety, while our friends were locked in deadly conflict with the vicious enemy and were suffering and dying. While at the hospital we tried to cheer up our fellow wounded "Bushmasters", and they were glad to see us; the more we talked to them, the more depressed we became. Finally, I said to Captain Norvall, as he lay wounded on his hospital cot, that perhaps I should cancel my orders home and rejoin my unit at Wadke-Sarmi. He, like Sergeant Dixon had said before I had left Finchaffen:

"Ben Rod, you have lost nothing over here. Only death, or even worse, a life-disabling wound, awaits you here. For God's sake, stick it out here in Milne Bay. They can't keep you here forever. Get home to your wife and boys. You have done your share, you shouldn't feel badly about going home. Now quit your belly aching and do what you know is right. Go home while you can."

Then he described the battle of the Lone Tree Hill. The jungle-smart Japanese would lie in wait, rush into the attack and then fade back into the jungle after dealing death or wounding many of the "Bushmasters". The "Bushmasters" had suffered from the deadly effects of the many Japanese sniper bullets, just as they had in Arawa, as they cut their way through the heavy jungle growth, he said. Colonel Herndon was relieved of command of the Regiment at the battle of the Lone Tree Hill on Wake-Sarme for withdrawing the RCT "Bushmasters" in the face of a numerically superior enemy. Even though events proved Colonel Herndon right, the Army never recognized its mistake of relieving him after 22 years as commander of the 158th Infantry Regiment. Had Herndon continued to attack the numerically superior enemy, his casualties would have been extremely heavy, and without victory. Instead of being relieved, Colonel Herndon should have been promoted and decorated. He was relegated to a desk job at Finschaffen.

Our visit to the hospital only added to our already deepening depression; we returned to our rain-soaked tent at the Replacement Depot to lick our psychological wounds.

Like Dixon, Norvelle was right. My place was at home, if ever I could get there, and my experience gained in the SWPA could be applied to training recruits back in the states preparing them for combat. We lay in our bunks waiting for something to happen and it did, but not for us. The Normandy invasion occurred on June 6, 1944 and we shouted with excitement; the Wadke-Sarmi operation ended in victory for the "Bushmasters". They would continue on to other victories in Neomfore, Luzon, and finally, Japan itself, but without us.

Gambling, big gambling, rampaged among those waiting to go home. Many had a lot of money and no place to spend it. Fortunes were lost and won. One evening I observed, with many others, two gamblers playing stud poker, both going for broke. One would raise and the other would call, raise again and again the call. This kept going on until over three thousand dollars was in the pot. The final raise and the final call. The cards were shown, four aces by the caller, four kings by the loser. The interesting thing about the game was not the money won or lost, but the reaction of both gamblers; neither batted an eye as the winner nonchalantly raked in the stack of money he had won. "Professional gamblers", someone said. I never gambled; could never see the benefit of taking someone's money or losing mine. Didn't make sense.

The rain continued to pound Milne Bay and we slept. We read when we could find something new to read and wrote letters home telling our loved ones of our disappointment and of our boredom and begging them to be patient. Time was wasted by the hundreds of troops in the replacement depot, all waiting to go home. We despaired, some cursed, another committed suicide. How long! O how long will it be?

Then late one afternoon we received the message.

"Get your bags and go to the pier immediately to board ship. You are going home," the Staff Duty Officer informed us. His poncho glistened with the heavy rain that had poured down on him from the dark-low hanging clouds while on his way from his orderly tent to give us the good news. "Transportation is waiting in front of the orderly tent," and he darted back out into the rain. We never saw him again.

Quickly, we assembled our belongings, closed our duffle bags, put on our ponchos, and headed for the jeeps that would take us to the pier. No let-up in the rain, but for all we cared, it was sunshine, maybe liquid sunshine! The jeeps took off and splashed through mud-holes that filled the poorly-maintained graveled road, which, ironically, we, the "Bushmasters", had helped to build the year before. Jubilant, we arrived at the pier.

It wasn't the Lurline nor was it the SS America. It was a tub, called a Victory ship, the name I don't recall, made of concrete, they said. It didn't have an ornate wardroom with expensive linens, nor were the tables adorned with silver and crystal, for there were no tables. There were no stately cabins with clean sheets and a private bathroom as we had on the Lurline. Rather, my stateroom was a small prisoner-of-war cell, which I shared with five other officers. The bunks were stacked three on each side. Our dining facility was an open space in the bowels of the ship, no seats or chairs; the diners stood shoulder to shoulder while eating; the menu - heated army "C" rations. This unpretentious, unadorned vessel, would however, provide me a bunk which would be my haven, my home during the slow voyage home, as the "tub" slowly crawled across the wide Pacific taking me back to reality. It would take me out of rain-soaked Milne Bay, an inlet hemmed in by high, precipitous mountains on the eastern tip of New Guinea. We would sail into the broad open space of the blue Pacific Ocean across the distant horizon, and home. With that I was satisfied; hopefully the ship would withstand the seas until we got to San Francisco thirty days later, maybe longer.

Thirty days! That's a lifetime! Day by day, the ship would be taking me home, a home I had left more than thirty-three months ago. This should never happen to a young family, but it had. Would I be accepted with my malaria-infected body, a disease which had been held in check by the attabrine tablets that had pushed the terrible monster back into my spleen, turning my skin a sickish yellow? The fever would surely lay me low once I was back home and the attabrine effects had worn off. I was told to expect as much. This terrible disease had almost killed me in 1941 at Camp Shelby. I had contracted it during the Louisiana maneuvers. When I left Milne Bay, I was down to 140 pounds, for I could not eat the "stuff" the army called food on Arawa. Would Wilma be disappointed with me for being so skinny and yellow-looking? Would the boys know me? Would they adjust to me, the father, whom they probably didn't remember? I would be a stranger to them. Why is he here, Mommy? they could say. My thoughts weren't encouraging, nor was my imagination.

Boarding the tub, we registered, received instructions and occupied our crammed quarters, all six of us. The space between bunks was so narrow only one officer could stand in the space between bunks. The others had to remain outside or get into our respective bunks, while the other brought in his duffle bag and squared himself away. So it was when going to bed or getting up during the long slow voyage across the wide Pacific Ocean.

We received a message from the troop commander. All officers were to attend an Officers Call at troop headquarters at 8:00PM. It was only a few minutes until then. We wondered why the call was so soon. The troop commander, a Major Ross from Toledo, Ohio, told us he was a passenger like us, going home, too. By virtue of his rank, Ross was designated troop commander, a very demanding and tiring task. Being the next senior officer, I was designated Executive Officer, responsible for all administrative functions during the trip. We organized the troops according to troop compartments and assigned officers to be in charge of each. Under Ross' direction we had an excellent organization even before we lifted anchor. Later, each officer went to his respective compartment and informed the troops who he was and that he would be responsible for the operation of the compartment. Then he selected NCOs and assigned certain responsibilities, appointing an acting first sergeant, who actually ran the place under the officer's direction. Then we worked out a mess schedule, indicating two meals to be served daily at 10:00AM and at 4:00PM and had it posted in each compartment. Another schedule was developed for exercise since we had little space on deck for such activities. Immediately we were concerned about the inactivity during the slow voyage and realized we must do something about that. We had a chaplain aboard, who took on the religious and recreational activities, including movies. He proved to be very effective and the troops enjoyed what he did for them. There were doctors and medical technicians among us and they set up a medical facility; a duty officer was always on duty in troop headquarters. There were also a Charge of Quarters and an acting Sergeant Major. Troop compartments had to be inspected daily by me or Major Ross, accompanied by the officer in charge of the compartments; we were concerned about sanitation problems in such cramped quarters if we became careless. We did not want to harass the men; there was no need for that. Before we left dockside we had formed into an effective organization and hopefully, this would keep down boredom during the long trip beyond the horizon. The NCOs, the backbone of any organization, were impressed with our organization and they would carry out all instructions from troop headquarters. They liked to do that without officer interference and we saw to it there was none.

All was in readiness by daylight. Under a heavily-laden sky, rain splashing the decks of the sluggish Victory ship, with its load of happy casuals, most of whom were combat veterans of the Buna and Gona, and the Owens Stanley Mountain campaigns, turned its prow eastward, its screws churning the waters, creating a turbulent wake behind; we were on our way!

The welcome sunshine was awaiting us at the mouth of Milne Bay; it was like turning on a light switch, turning darkness into light, for we had escaped from a dense downpour of rain to an immediate sunshine. Finally, we had escaped the wall of continuous rain. And now only the broad open space of the Pacific Ocean was ahead. We were no longer prisoners. We were escaping from other hells of Arawa, Buna, Gona, Owens Stanley Mountain and now from Milne Bay.

Major Ross's troop organization aboard ship served us well. The compartments were kept clean; the NCOs saw to this. Daily we made our inspections - not only for sanitation reasons, but to keep the men, who were in casual status, alert which would reduce boredom, an enemy of the worst kind. The chaplain held services on Sundays, provided games, showed movies, and got some reading materials from some source aboard ship. He gave me a book, a large book, The Sun is My Undoing, I believe that was the title, but the name of the author escapes me. There were no deck chairs, or any chairs aboard the ship. Unable to remain on my bunk, I found a quiet place under a lifeboat, held in place by its davits, to read as I lay underneath it. The lifeboat provided shade from the hot tropical sun and prevented interference from other activities of the ship. Reading and walking the decks for exercise, watching the chaplain's movies and attending his services were my main source of escaping the boredom during the long slow voyage across the Pacific.

Slowly, we continued to crawl across the wide ocean. Time seemed to stand still and became a major source of punishment for us; there were no escaping from it, and our impatience increased; many withdrew into their shell of isolation to brood; boredom and impatience increased. Then LAND! - it was the United States! The troops yelled, some cried, others just stared. Were we really home?

Arriving in San Francisco Bay, we passed under the Golden Gate Bridge. As we observed the skyline of San Francisco, we saw automobiles and people as we stood in awe on the deck of the slow Victory ship that had finally arrived after many weeks at sea.

This was our first sight of civilization since leaving Brisbane, Australia in March the year before. We would disembark at Angel Island and be quartered there, where we would be fed and processed for crossing the country on a troop-train. We would be permitted to cross over to Fort Mason, adjacent to San Francisco, to buy needed clothing. Our moldy, thread-bare fatigues were not fit to be seen in would soon head for the trash bin. Eagerly we disembarked, and we of the ship's troop command were relieved of our responsibilities by the navy commander of Angel Island. They had a good meal prepared for us, a far cry from the heated "C" rations we had been eating for almost thirty days aboard the slow Victory ship. Then a small boat took us over to Fort Mason where we purchased new uniforms and accouterments. Among the clothing I bought was a gabardine summer uniform with blouse. I wanted to wear it when I would meet Wilma at Fort Benjamin Harrison, Indiana, our agreed meeting place. One cannot imagine our feelings while buying new clothing, preparing to meet those whom we loved so much. It had been almost three years since I had left her in New Orleans for Panama.

After purchasing our clothing, we rushed back to Angel Island, took showers, dressed in our clean and new cotton uniforms and marveled at ourselves in a mirror. But we were taken aback; our appearance was anything but complementary; we looked as if we had escaped from a bone yard some place - we were so skinny! We headed back to San Francisco to get the "works"; a visit to the barbershop. We would demand a facial, a haircut, and a shave, a pleasure we had not experienced ever since departing Panama almost two years before. Our barbering needs had been provided by a soldier barber, who took the job as a volunteer, trained or untrained. His tools were carried in the first sergeant's field desk. He was very popular, getting all of twenty-five cents for each haircut. The barber's chair was most anything from a wooden crate to a jungle log and a neat hair cut was only a secondary consideration, providing the stubble was no longer than an inch, or even shorter. Getting a GI haircut reminded me of when I was a kid in Putnam County; Leonard Harrison would cut my hair as I sat on a split-bottom chair under an apple tree in his front yard, and he didn't charge me anything, either - a tow head boy who didn't have a penny, let alone twenty-five cents. Leonard was good to me and he always gave me a haircut when I needed one. I thought of him each time the company barber cut my hair; with Leonard, also, appearance was only a secondary consideration. Each of those men performed a very important mission.

Colonel Cronk wanted to get "the works", too, but along with it, a manicure. A manicure! Can you imagine a soldier right out of the jungle getting a manicure job? Well, we wanted to see how this big man, just out of the jungle, a veteran of Buna and Gona, would act when the lady manicurist worked with his rough ham-like hands, with nails on the ends of his fingers like the talons of an eagle. It was said he had killed a Jap without benefit of a rifle or knife, with just those big hands. So Major Ross and I accompanied the colonel as he walked down the street in search a barbershop featuring a very attractive manicurist.

We found one. She was working with the tools of her trade, while she sat in the big window of the barbershop across the street from where we stood. It was obvious she was a drawing card. But that didn't deter the excited colonel.

"Hot damn", he said, "that's for me." He took off like a stallion running in the Kentucky Derby. We followed to see the show that was sure to happen.

"We sure don't want to miss this, Ben Rod. Let's go watch," Ross said. We eagerly raced behind the sprinting Cronk to the barbershop.

The barbershop, crowded with battle-tested jungleers from the New Guinea area, required us to wait our return to get "the works". Cronk, unable to keep his eyes off the beautiful girl still sitting in the barbershop window, waited with obvious anticipation.

Time passed. Cronk finally spread himself in the barber's chair and demanded "the works".

"Give me 'the works', he demanded, "including a manicure job."

The colonel's remarks attracted the attention of the soldiers from the battlefields of the New Guinea area, waiting their turn, to look at their companion, who was lying spread-eagle in the barber's chair, demanding attention to his unkept fingernails. They laughed, but the big colonel laughed the loudest.

"You guys don't have the guts to get a manicure, do you? Just watch, if you dare; I'm getting one," he said with an eager voice. He laid back to await the attention of the beautiful girl. Her attention was now directed at the colonel who had perhaps hadn't been near a woman in almost a year. She probably felt more space between them would be cogent and continued to sit in the window without further notice of the big man in the barber's chair, who occasionally glanced at her with anticipation and eagerness.

The barber reminded the overzealous colonel that he had to cut his hair first, and would he mind sitting up in the chair? Later, he said, he would see to it that he would get the remainder of "the works". Reluctantly, the big colonel permitted the barber to raise the back of the chair and begin cutting his hair. That job completed, the barber once again reclined the chair and began to apply the facial, placing a hot towel on Cronk's moon-shaped face after massaging his shoulders and neck. This put Cronk almost in a twilight world.

The manicurist arrived by his side. She took his big unkempt hand in her dainty one and began a slight massage. We could scarcely imagine what was racing through the big jungleer's mind. The barber continued to work with his customer spread out on his chair. Then, the facial was completed, the barber jerked off the hot towel. Cronk looked at the manicurist, who had been working tenderly on his big hands with nails that looked like bear claws, realizing she was not the pretty and dainty girl sitting in the window, who now was nervously watching, but a much older woman. She was attractive but certainly without the appeal of the younger girl. Quickly, Cronk evacuated the barber's chair and, not saying a word, stomped out of the barbershop under the guffaws of all. Later he returned to the barbershop and paid the barber ten dollars, twice the amount that the barber usually charged. He didn't even wait for the change, so the colonel never got "the works." Later, at Camp Robinson, Arkansas, he became the executive officer of the 75th Recruit Training Regiment, and I commanded Company "A" of that Regiment. He said to me over coffee in my company mess hall one morning: "Gee, that old woman must have been seventy years old." Then he continued, "Ben Rod, if ever you tell anyone about that, I will never speak to you again." But I did tell it and the word went all of over the regiment. Cronk laughed with all of us about the incident. Many would say to him, "Get your manicure today, colonel?"

"None of your d______business." he would reply and then laughed. He was a great guy and a great sport, but the manicurist in San Francisco really got his goat. He never lived it down, and added to the story each time he told it, until finally, he convinced everyone that it had been a national event of some sort.

CHAPTER 26

I'M HOME! THANK GOD I'M HOME!

The veterans from the New Guinea area left San Francisco within three days. Our departure for the east was a joy, yet there seem to be an unusual calm that prevailed over the battle-scarred jungleers. It was as if the troops were dreading something. This worried the troop commanders, for we wanted the trip to Fort Benjamin Harrison to be a happy one for them. Hopefully, we would find a remedy and make their meeting with loved ones a most joyous one.

We were traveling on two troop-trains. Our train took the northern route under the command of Major Ross. The second train was on the southern route under the command of Colonel Cronk. I was with Ross, still his executive officer. Again, we used about the same organization aboard the train as we had on the Victory ship while crossing the Pacific. We placed an officer in charge of each railroad passenger car and they selected NCOs to help. As on the ship, we insisted the passengers cars be kept clean and would make car inspections twice daily without harassment, keeping an eye on the men for personal cleanliness as well. We knew our appearance would be very important once we met our families and friends at Fort Benjamin Harrison three days hence. We wanted to look our best, but our bony frames and yellow, sickly-looking skins, weren't very masculine; we needed all the help we could get to be more presentable.

It was a long train, having ten or more passenger cars, carrying about four hundred troops. Each car had built-in bunks, stacked one above the other on each side, with a narrow aisle in between; the hard seats certainly weren't meant for comfort, either. The troop kitchen personnel served us as we sat in our uncomfortable seats, ladling food and drink into our mess kits and canteen cups from mermite cans carried along the aisle by KPs (kitchen police) designated from the troops. A complement of cooks and a mess officer, provided by the army, were permanently assigned to the train. The kitchen cars, always prepared and stocked with food, could be transferred from train to train depending upon the need. Needless to say, we were not traveling in luxury by any means. It was a miserable way for troops returning home to travel, but the great expectation of seeing our families and loved ones exceeded the inconveniences and the lack of creature comforts.

Since then, I have wondered why the army could not have had the train stop in towns along the way and have concessionaires to serve us in a decent manner. The method being used to feed the veterans was a reminder of how I, as a boy, used to slop hogs in the pig-sty on my father's farm in Putnam County. Making things even more miserable, the windows throughout the long train had to be raised for ventilation to try to escape the stifling hot July heat, but then we suffered from the invasion of cinders, ash, and dirt, adding further to our misery. Reflecting back to the beginning of the trip home, it appeared one thing after another had happened, creating lasting bad memories, beginning with our being dumped off the Lurline in Milne Bay. The terrible crowded conditions for the men on the Victory ship were bad enough - but now in the final link of travel, we were eating cinders and dirt in our food, as well as sleeping in debris. Normally this would tear down the morale of any troop unit. We understood the necessity of austerity while in combat, but once the combat was over, or between campaigns, we really did expect better treatment, especially when we were to meet our families for the first time after months, even years of separation. Well, just like the officer of WWI vintage told us while we sat on the damp cold ground in January, 1941, at Camp Shelby, Mississippi, "Soldiers will live miserably and they will die miserably," and I had witnessed both. But why should this be now since we had gone through so much hell in New Guinea and New Britain, the first US Army troops to engage the Japanese, being treated like second-class citizens; the misery should be over, at least for a little while. Now the veterans were malaria infected, sick and depressed and worried how they would be accepted by their families. How could they prepare for this most important event traveling under the most substandard conditions the army could provide? Really, considering the condition of the men, we all should have been on a hospital train, with the best of medical care and food available. The only good thing about it was that we didn't realize how sick we were and wouldn't know until we had arrived at our next duty station.

Most, including me, would become quite debilitated by the dreaded malaria fever, a residue from the Southwest Pacific jungles. Sherman said following the Civil War: "War is hell", and we certainly had had our share of it.

Were these disloyal thoughts? Maybe, and they would not have occurred had it been me alone, but when I saw the condition of the troops, and how the army was handling them under such horrible conditions, my heart cried out for them. Their trial would soon be over; they would be among their loved ones. Hopefully, the misery of the trip since Milne Bay would be forgotten while in the tender loving care of their families.

"Look, men", we encouraged them, "have on a clean uniform, be shaved when we arrive at Fort Ben. Your families will be there." Some just smiled, but most didn't. Did they dread the occasion? One man said he had no one to meet him at Fort Ben. How sad! We wanted them to be clean, yet we had no showers aboard; but we did have water, cold water, to wash and shave. We had lived under similar conditions for many months in combat. But we're going home now; we must look our best! Why didn't the army take us off the train and let us clean ourselves up after the dirty train trip. Then we could meet our families in a lounge, so we would be half decent in our appearance. That wasn't to be; we must be accepted as we were and the army could care less, we thought. But we were concerned about the situation and Ross called an officers' meeting with each passenger car represented. We discussed the situation as the train with its homebound soldiers sped eastward.

"Gentlemen", Ross said, "we have a problem. We know there is no complete solution, but we can try to do something about it. The men are under stress for some reason, and we must buck them up some how. In fact, I'm not sure what we can do. What will our families think of us once they see us after all these many months? In my opinion, many families will be strengthened while others will be broken up, unfortunately; many of us have changed and may never be the same again. The change will be traumatic to many, especially to the wives and children. Now let us encourage the men to look their best for the event of their lives. Even the best will be pathetic in some cases. We have lost weight, our skins are yellow, and our newly acquired ill-fitting uniforms do little to enhance our appearance."

Major Ross was right and I reflected on his comments. Here are over four hundred battle-scarred, seemingly sick soldiers, who needed all the tender loving care a family could give them, and their attitude would be most important to them and to their families. So I added to Ross's remarks.

"May I suggest a thought. Why not encourage the men to try to be eager to see their families, making sure they look their best once they leave the train. They could pretend they were just returning from a short trip, rushing to their loved ones, giving them a hug of a lifetime. I'm sure the response will be gratifying. Let us not dwell on the negative for this is a very important occasion. What we do once leaving the train will have lasting effects."

"Good idea, Ben Rod," Ross agreed. "What do you gentlemen say to that?" and they all agreed to encourage the men to try to look good and be cheerful when meeting their loved ones. They would remember their loved ones as they had left them, but would they be the same? What change would be noticed?

We settled down to a routine, mostly sitting on hard, uncomfortable seats listening to the clickety-clack of the train wheels on the steel rails. It was monotonous, like the pattering of rain on the tent in Milne Bay, but in silence we sat and listened to the clacking sound of the wheels on the steel rails as the train rolled eastward, taking us to our loved ones at Fort Benjamin Harrison, Indiana; memories rapidly recalled. Frequently, I walked the long length of the train to the last car. Since there was no platform, I stood in the doorway, leaning on the gate, looking down at the crossties blurring past from under the car. The sound of the whistle, the constant clickety-clacking of the wheels, talking to the men, and coordinating details with car commanders did help to pass the time.

The train had a scheduled stop in Carling, Montana. Many people came aboard with food, candy, and soft drinks. It must have been a sacrifice for these good people for it was during a period of rationing. Their gifts of food included fresh milk in quart glass bottles. The men, not having milk for so long, drank it down without stopping. Even I drank a quart. Silently, the men sat in their seats as the food and milk were being passed out. Major

Ross thanked the good people of Carling for their generosity and the train pulled out for Ogden, Utah. At Ogden we took on additional passenger cars of troops going to Chicago, and during the hookup the American Red Cross came aboard, serving us coffee and doughnuts. One of the young girls, cute as a button, with beautiful brown shoulder-length hair and sparkling eyes, wearing a neat, clean Red Cross uniform, caught the eye of the men. She responded with a big smile and they swooned. They talked about that smile all the away to Fort Benjamin Harrison. Apparently they had considered her the typical girl they had left behind when they left to fight in the war.

Arriving in Chicago two days later, we watched the skyline of skyscrapers on the way in. After the crew had serviced the train we departed Chicago. Soon we were nearing Fort Benjamin Harrison; it would be only a matter of hours now. We sent word to all car commanders to prepare for disembarking the train. Major Ross ordered all passengers cars to have a last-minute cleanup and inspection. Furthermore, car commanders must check each man for personal cleanness, making sure he had on a clean uniform, was clean shaven, and shoes shined and wear a necktie for the occasion. A liaison officer from the Fort came aboard at Lafayette, giving us disembarkating instructions. The men, with their baggage, were to be formed in four ranks on the left side of their respective cars. Car commanders, after the formation, were to report when the men were all accounted for. Major Ross, once he received the report, was to turn the formation over to the commander of the Fort.

Then all officer would be released from their assigned duties. We were ready for the change.

The troop-train began to slow; the whistle began to moan. Ft. Benjamin Harrison was all around us. The passengers, eagerly, were looking out of the windows, hoping to get a first glimpse of a loved one, a family member, or a friend. Personal baggage and dufflebags were gathered; the veterans were now silently smiling, something we had hoped for during the long trip from San Francisco. The long train moved even slower, then came to a temporary stop, shifting, then crawled slowly forward. Another stop, with the screeching of brakes, and the long train from San Francisco, with its hundreds of troops, quivered and came to complete stop. It seemed to sigh warily from its long journey. Officers ordered the troops, with their baggage, off the train, and to form in four ranks immediately. The troops, carrying their heavy and bulky dufflebags, moved single file through the aisle and down the steps of the passenger cars to the station platform. While the troops were disembarking I, too, looked out the window and was surprised, for only a few families were there to meet the train; to make matters worse they were on the wrong side of the train. Why did the army permit this to happen? The families should have been in place to meet their loved ones. Where was Wilma? Was she there to meet me? I eagerly searched the group of waiting wives and again I was unable to find her. Is it possible she had failed to come; could there have been an accident or something beyond her control? With great concern I got off the train with Ross and he, too, seem to be worried.

"Ben Rod", he said, "have your seen your wife? Thelma was supposed to be here; wonder what's happened?" He was concerned; the veterans continued to form up on the station platform under command of their respective NCOs and officers.

"Major Ross", I said, trying to hide my great disappointment, "I'm sure they're here some place. Let's turn over the troops to the officers of the Fort and they will show up, I'm sure. They've got to be here."

"Major Ross", said the station officer, a major, in charge, "we have officers and NCOs prepared to take over the troops immediately. Please find your wives and don't worry about the troops. We will see to it that they, too, will join their families."

Receiving reports from the car commanders that all troops were present or accounted for, which Major Ross reported to the representative of the post, we were relieved of command, and with some apprehension, started walking toward the front of the train, hoping to find our AWOL wives.

And to our surprise, there they were! Running towards us with open arms from around the big black locomotive. For the first time in almost three years I held Wilma in my arms; it was my return to glory! The hell of Arawa was far behind; I had paid my dues for this indescribable moment of joy, my return to glory! I crushed her within my embrace, the moment I had dreamed of. She was dressed in white, and I loved her in white, her flowing dark, auburn shoulder- length hair, her beautiful happy smile, her soft skin touching my face, her sweet tender kiss telling me of her love. What an occasion it was; the long separation of thirty-three months was over; the jungle hells of Panama, New Guinea, New Britain and Milne Bay, too, all nightmares, were over; the nightmare was over! Truly, it was if I had arrived from hell and entered into Paradise with all sins forgiven - my angel had come; heaven couldn't have been any better for me. For a few minutes we were in a world of our own, oblivious of others around us.

Finally, after settling down, and returning to earth, I introduced Wilma to Major Ross, who had enjoyed his own reunion with Thelma, his wife, and he introduced her to me. This was the beginning of a wonderful relationship lasting until his death several years later.

Then again my attention was directed to my beautiful wife, my sweetheart. Here I was, all 140 pounds of me, down from the 170 pounds I once weighed, my leathery yellow skin caused by malaria suppressive tablets; still in each others arms, we wept with joy. Many cries of happiness were heard from others. Once we settled down, an escort suggested we retire to a more suitable place to complete our reunion and we departed for the lounge in a large building nearby. Then I looked, for the last time, at the tired and weary troops, veterans of Bona and Gona, the Owens Stanley mountains, Arawa, and other areas of the Pacific, and I said a silent prayer for them. We had hoped that all would go well with them when they met their families. Would it be a joy like ours had been? And they, too, watched as we swooned in our lovely wives' arms. Had we been overly concerned while traveling with them on the train from San Francisco? They were now marching away under control of the Fort Benjamin Harrison officers to a designated place to meet their own families. I've often wondered about these fine men who were still suffering from the rigors of war, malaria, and fatigue. They certainly, like me, needed much tender loving care - something we, like children, needed badly, for such had been denied us for so long.

The terrible nightmares were over, so was life in the grave-like dugout, surrounded by layers of sandbags in far-away Arawa, that my faithful friend, Johnson, had dug for me while I, with others, were inspecting the MLR the day we had arrived there. So were the nightly air-raids that had killed and maimed many of the "Bushmasters"; gone was the terrible dehydrated food and the horrible-tasting sulphur water from shell holes that had starved us into ill health; gone was the extreme isolation that had turned men into almost zombies, who found joy engaging the Japanese in the game of death, as if it was a form of recreation for them; gone, too, was the hot tropical sun that had scorched the finger of land on which we were isolated; we suffered from the intense heat, making Arawa into a place of mental hellish torment. As Sergeant Dixon said: "We must have died and gone to heaven", when we returned from Arawa when served ice cream in Finchaffen, for it was like that - our meeting at Fort Benjamin Harrison.

Were we fit to be among civilized

people? Some said we weren't. They said we were trained killers and could be dangerous until we went through some sort of rehabilitation. We knew how to kill, that is true, but only to kill those who, like us, were trained killers, too, and who wanted to kill us, also. But we were no threat among our kind, be it Americans or others who were on our side. We were also trained to be kind and considerate to others, even to our defenseless enemy. Our wives and families would have difficulties while we adjusted, but we would. Hopefully, they would understand. Many didn't. I was most fortunate. I was honored and respected by my wife, friends, and extended family. I couldn't have been happier had I went to heaven that day at Fort Benjamin Harrison, while holding my wonderful lovely wife in my arms, enjoying the wedded bliss that I had so long desired and needed.

The happy officers, with their wonderful wives, went into the lounge and took another good look at each other. It was a beginning of adjusting and updating. We looked at each other almost unbelievingly. Was it a mirage, was it really her? Occasionally hugging her, reassuring myself that it wasn't a dream, her tender loving response confirmed her reality. Finally, the army provided a bus, taking us to our hotel in Indianapolis. A big dinner was served at the hotel to us as a group; we had formed a bond that would last for many years. Later we would say goodby to our new friends but would again meet at Camp Butler, near Durham, North Carolina at the end of a thirty-day leave, before departing for our next duty assignments.

Hand in hand, like courting couples, Wilma and I walked the streets of Indianapolis, still filling each other in about the many events that had occurred during the many months apart, especially about Bucky and Johnny. Would they remember me? I wondered, and Wilma said she was sure they would, for they jumped with joy when she told them she was going to get daddy and bring him home. I remembered when I had left them crying after me as I boarded the C&O train in Charleston for the return trip to Camp Shelby and on my way to Panama. That was a terrible day, and I still remembered it too well. I could hardly wait to get my hands on them!

* * * * * *

WILMA TELLS HER HEARTWARMING STORY

Finally, after almost three years, Ben Rod was coming home from the war in the South Pacific. He phoned me from San Francisco, telling me when he would arrive at Fort Benjamin Harrison, Indiana. After his long absence from us, he was finally coming home. The sound of his voice brought tears of joy. Would he remember me? Would he have changed? Had I changed? My family encouraged me to leave the children with them and meet Ben Rod alone, feeling we needed that time to be together alone. I told Bucky and Johnny that I would bring their daddy home.

I boarded the train in Charleston and arrived in Indianapolis the evening before Ben Rod's scheduled arrival. There I checked into a hotel and the anxious waiting began. I was unable to sleep, for my mind was running a mile a minute in anticipation of our meeting.

I thought of all the things I wanted to say to him, how I missed him and how much I loved him. I prayed that he would feel the same way about me. Finally, I fell into a peaceful sleep, waking up as the bright sunlight filled the room.

Hurriedly, I put on the pretty white eyelet dress that I had been saving for this important occasion. Ben Rod always liked me in white. Placing a white gardenia in my hair (it was the custom in those day for young women to wear a flower in their hair), using very little makeup, only a touch of lipstick, trying to look my very best, I was ready. When I left my room and entered the lobby, I ran into a young woman whom I suspected was there for the same reason - to meet her husband. I introduced myself to her and she told me she was Thelma Ross from Toledo, Ohio. She, too, was there to met her husband, Major Harry Ross. Quickly we became friends and over breakfast we told our life histories to each other. We had about two hours before the train was to arrive and we could hardly contain our pent-up emotions. We went together to the army depot and inquired about the time of the arrival of the troop train. Anxiously, we asked the railroad personnel on duty which track the train would be coming in on, but he wasn't sure. He said jokingly, "If you place your ear close to the track you can hear the train coming even though it is several miles away." We did this and, to our surprise, we did hear the train as it rumbled on the tracks. We realized it was almost upon us. The distance that had for so long been many thousands of miles between Ben Rod and me was now reduced to only a very few minutes. In our excitement we had forgotten to inquire how the troops would leave the train and found ourselves on the opposite side of the track.

It was coming! The big black locomotive, flags waving, steam spurting from the sides, black puffs of smoke exploding from the stack, was pulling many passenger cars loaded with soldiers waving from the windows. The train began to slow down and gradually stopped with screeching brakes. What was happening? Immediately we realized our big mistake; we were on the opposite side of the train from which the troops would be getting off. A bit shaken, we started walking briskly past the many passenger cars toward the engine, heading for the other side of the track. By this time most of the troops had left the train and were forming up under the direction of their officers. We rounded the big locomotive and looked down the line of troops on the platform, feeling sheepish. There we saw them, and, at the same time, they saw us. We started running toward each other. And for the first time in almost three years we were in each other's arms. We realized at last our dreams had come true, our prayers had been answered. Then I looked at him; the once robust man of almost six feet, who had weighed 175 pounds was now a mere skeleton. His skin, once a healthy tan, was now a livid yellow. His eyes were sunken into his head; the malaria fever that was running in his blood would soon bring him down to his bed. Neither of us realized it then, but he was a sick man in need of much tender loving care. His eyes reflected the strange things that had happened to him somewhere in the Pacific. I had him with me now and I was eager to get him back to Charleston to nurse him back to good health.

Ben Rod's attention quickly turned to thoughts of his two young sons. He wondered if they would know him after his long absence. His worries were unnecessary, for I had read his letters to them, told them stories about how proud he was of them and that he was trying to make a better and safer world for them to grow up in. I often showed them pictures of him, telling them: "This is your daddy". Often I would take them to visit their Aunt Della, my brother, Paul's, wife, and their cousins, Steve and Lois, who, too, were missing their daddy, who was in Europe. We talked of the many fun things we would do when their daddys would return home. Happily, now these wonderful plans were about to happen.

* * * * * *

On to Charleston and to my sons, brothers, sisters, nieces, nephews, Wilma's family, friends and all. What a joyous occasion awaited us! The next morning we departed Indianapolis for Charleston on the C & O passenger train. The train was painfully slow. I fretted because of the frequesnt stops made on the way, and Wilma tried to settle me down and to be patient. Finally, stopping for a short time in Huntington, West Virginia, and realizing that our families and friends were not aware of our exact arrival time in Charleston, but not having time to make a call myself, I gave a total stranger twenty-five cents and requested him to call Wilma's parents in Charleston, only fifty miles away, giving them our arrival time.

The eagerness and anticipation increased; it would be only a short time until the big reunion. Wanting to look my best, just after departing Huntington, I changed into my new gabardine tans uniform complete with blouse, bill cap, new shirt and tie, shoes shined, decked out in the few ribbons I had earned in the Pacific; Wilma admired me in my new uniform; we were eager and waiting. I'm grateful to the stranger, whoever he was, for he did make the call and when we arrived, many were there at the C&O Depot to greet us. The Guthries, the Honakers, the Jordans, brothers, sisters, nieces, nephews, and friends. My loss of weight was not even mentioned. Immediately, I found my sons who were holding on to their Grandmother Guthrie and Aunt Helen; being very shy, they regarded me strangely. Perhaps they were wondering why so much fuss was being made over a stranger who had arrived on the big train with their beautiful mother in tow. It was a wonderful occasion. They were as I had imagined; Buck, age six, and John, age four, who looked like the mischievous characters out of Tom Sawyer or Huckleberry Finn, would soon wrestle with me once we got reacquainted. Now, finally, the four of us were together as a family as I had often prayed to happen, even though at times I wondered if I would ever see my loved ones again. Now the terror was over, the killing fields were far away, as was "Washing Machine Charley"; I was in domestic bliss, such happiness I had never experienced before, but had hoped for since leaving Charleston, December 8, 1941. At times it had been hell indescribable, but not always from the enemy's bullets.

Returning to reality and taking the boys by the hands, with Wilma beside me, I circulated among the people that had come to greet us at the depot. All were in tears of joy. It was if the heavens had opened up to welcome us home. There were Lily and Doug, my beautiful sister and handsome brother-in-law, and their two wonderful teen-age daughters, Christabell and Jewell (Boggie). They, and my brother, Doc, had been the cause of so many of the good things that had happened to me. That day I remembered and expressed my love for them. They seemed to be so proud of me as I returned from the war, for only few veterans had returned up until that time; everyone was so patriotic then.

Finally, after greetings and expressions of welcome from many, the people began to leave, and we returned to the home of Wilma's parents to relax and enjoy my young family once again and be with my brothers and sisters and friends. Hopefully, I could forget the war and put the hell of Arawa behind me, but that was difficult, for I still remembered my "boys" of the "Bushmasters", now engaged with the vicious enemy on the away place called Nuomfor Island.

The thirty days leave passed rather rapidly. However, before we departed for Camp Butler, North Carolina, I paid a visit to my sister, Grace, and her daughter Norma, who lived on Bream Street, in Charleston, and mt sister Fern and her husband, Willie Kinser, and their large family in Putnam County. Their farm was near our old home place, now owned and occupied by the Ranson Sigman family; we knew Ranson and Lottie Sigman well. I also visited Bonny and Homer Kelly, another sister and brother-in-law, my brothers Bill and Willard and their wives, Chris and Boots. Unfortunately, I was unable to see my older brother, Doc and his wife, Lou, and their large family, for he was away working in a shipyard on the east coast. In Putnam County I managed to see Guthrie Casto, Ed Harrison, and the Fisher family down on Hizer Creek. However, I was not able to see Denver, Leonard, Earl, Virgie, Mable, Gertrude, and others of the family, who had been so close to me during my boyhood at the little one-room schoolhouse of Mt. Etna. Finally, I went to the cemetery at the Center Point Chapel to visit the graves of my mother, Clementine, my father, Rosser, and my sister, Alma. My father had died two years before and I had not had the opportunity to visit his grave. As I stood over the graves of my loved ones I realized I must say something. In reverent silence, my head bowed, I said: "Mother, Dad, Alma, even though I've walked through the valley of death, I'm home. Thank God, I'm home! here in Putnam County." I think they would have liked that. Their youngest son and brother, if but for a short time, was home with them.

CHAPTER 27

CAMP ROBINSON, ARKANSAS

It was a long bus ride through the green hills of southern West Virginia and Virginia to Camp Butler, North Carolina, near Durham. Wilma had accompanied me and we would stay in a hotel in Durham during processing. Later, I would depart for Camp Robinson, Arkansas, my new duty station. I would get settled, and hopefully, find quarters in Little Rock and send for my small family.

We were happy to find many of our friends also being processed at Camp Butler. Not only were Major Ross and his wife, Thelma, there, but many of the old 150th Infantry (Powderhorns) boys, who were inducted with me in 1941 were there, too, many whom I had known for many years even before the war. They had gone to Panama with the me and then, a year later, after I had reported to the "Bushmasters", had been reassigned to Europe. Some had made the D-Day Invasion, June 6th. I was informed by Lt. Thomas (Tack) Jones of Lt. Frank Corley's death; he had been killed during the invasion. Both Jones and Corley had been sergeants, but had been commissioned as 2nd Lieutenants and had proven themselves under fire in Normandy. Both were decorated.

Daily, after a short time spent processing at Butler, the officers and their wives would meet in the restaurant of our hotel for breakfast, lunch and dinner. We had time to talk of the past, renew acquaintances, and had a great time in general. We bowled, went to the movies, toured Duke University

Campus, and enjoyed other recreational activities, all in beautiful surroundings so far removed from the places of hell we all had recently been; I suffered mental torment even thinking of them; they were places of no return.

My processing complete, and with orders in hand assigning me to Camp Robinson, Arkansas, we said our goodbys to friends and returned to Charleston. Needing an extra day's delay enroute, for I wanted to take Wilma back to Charleston, I requested and received approval, supposedly, for the delay.

Getting Wilma settled in Charleston, and plans made for her and the boys to join me once quarters were found in Little Rock, I took the train to Little Rock and then a bus into Camp Robinson, arriving about 11:00PM. Reporting to the staff duty officer I was assigned to a small wall tent with a GI cot for the night. I reported to the Camp's Adjutant General Section the next morning and was given orders assigning me to the 75th Recruit Training Regiment. Since I had reported in one day late, I was expected to give an explanation to Colonel Davis, my new Regimental Commander, who would report his actions for my lack of punctuality, they said. Both the Lt. Colonel and the AG said nothing probably would come of it since I had gotten approval for the delay. Had the delay not been granted, I would have gone directly to Robinson from Camp Butler and Wilma would have returned to Charleston on her own, but I wanted to be with her.

When I reported to the regiment, the adjutant, Captain Kelly, immediately ushered me into the presence of Colonel Davis, the regimental commander. Colonel Davis was a small, balding man with a mustache, appearing to have a crippled leg, but seemed friendly. He was cordial and welcomed me warmly.

"Captain Jordan," he said, "I welcome you to the regiment. We need combat-experienced officers and NCOs to train recruits for fillers over the world. The recruits have confidence in returning officers and NCOs who have had combat experience, for they know you will serve them well. But, first, I feel that you need an administrative assignment for a short time until you have completely recovered, physically, from your experience in the Southwest Pacific Area. You really need more time to recover from the malaria that could be running in your bloodstream. Captain Kelly, the adjutant, is leaving us soon and I would like you to take his place. What do you think? Would you like the assignment?"

Based upon my experience as adjutant for the 2nd Battalion of the "Bushmasters", being responsible for so many administrative functions, even though I had enjoyed the duty, I politely declined.

"Colonel Davis, I love to work with troops, training them for combat. Even though I've done my job well while serving as an adjutant in my former battalion, I'm really not much of an administrative man. If you don't mind, sir, I would like an infantry company where I can mold the men into a fighting force and be proud of them. Sitting behind a desk is not my forte. May I have command of one of your infantry companies?"

"Certainly, you may, Captain Jordan. But I must inform you the companies train long hours, often requiring you to be present in the area early each morning, even as early as 4:00AM and very late at night. I really feel you should reconsider."

I didn't. I should have, maybe. Ever since leaving Company "D", 150th Infantry in Panama, I wanted command of a rifle company, but because I had experience as an adjutant in the 1st Battalion, 150th Infantry, I was considered an expert in administration. Efficient administration is a dream of any commander and is crucial to command functions. Even Col. Stofft, the most capable commander of the 2nd Battalion of the "Bushmaster" Regiment, refused my pleas for command of a rifle company for the same reason. I still remained as his adjutant, a very important duty.

"All right, Captain, if that's what you want, that's what you get." And he called in Captain Kelley, the regimental adjutant.

"Captain Kelly, prepare orders assigning Captain Jordan to command of Company "A", replacing Captain Carter who will be leaving for Europe soon."

"I thought Captain Jordan was to replace me, Colonel. As you know I must leave for Europe soon, too. A replacement is needed to understudy me to learn the ropes."

"Yes, I know Kelley, but Captain Jordan does not want the job even after I informed him of the demands a rifle company places upon its commander. Perhaps, Lt. Anderson, your assistant, can handle the job until someone is willing and capable to take over the job. Have

Colonel Cronk come in, please."

Colonel Cronk? Could it be the Colonel Cronk who wanted "the works" in the San Francisco barbershop include a manicure job?

"Yes, sir", said Kelley as he left to get Colonel Cronk, glancing at me suspiciously. Shortly, he returned with the big Colonel who was the size of a brick wall, one and the same who had demanded "the works" in the barbershop to include the manicure job. He was wearing a helmet on top of his big head, reminding me of a pea on top of a doll's head. It was comical, and I burst out laughing, not about the helmet that sat on top of his head like a pea on a doll's head, but about the barbershop incident. Cronk begin to laugh, too.

"Now look, Jordan, a word about San Francisco and I'll break your neck. That's top secret. Do you understand?" We both laughed, our sides splitting, while the tiny helmet on top of his big head shaking only added to my uncontrollable laughter.

"Would you gentlemen mind telling me what is going on? I suppose from all the hysterical laughing you must have known each other before today, right?"

"All right, Jordan, tell Colonel Davis, if you must. If you don't, he will give you a direct order to do so anyway."

"Yes, Captain Jordan, better tell me, for if you don't I will always suspect you two are harboring a top military secret of some sort."

I told him and Kelley about our arrival in San Francisco and about Cronk getting "the works" at the barbershop. They joined in the guffawing with Cronk laughing the loudest.

"Well, that's enough of bantering", said Colonel Davis. "Colonel Cronk, take Captain Jordan up to Company "A". He will replace Captain Carter as commander. I want him to understudy Carter for at least two weeks. He will be surprised at what goes on in a training company, but that's what he wants."

We left Colonel Davis's office and Cronk buttonholed me outside the regimental headquarters building. "Ben Rod", Cronk said, "do you know what you are getting yourself into? These companies work around the clock. I wouldn't take one of these companies for love nor money. After what we've been through in SWPA, we are not physically able to handle it. I still can fix things for you to remain in a relatively easy job here at regiment. Now, for gosh sakes, use your head for once." But I still wanted my rifle company.

Captain Carter was a strict disciplinarian with a very cold personality, a demanding officer. He could care less about high morale, something I always hoped for and usually achieved. He ruled his company using threats like, "you do this or else." I could tell the men were uncomfortable around him, even his officers and NCOs. Many of the NCOs and juniors officers took on his demeanor, and at times, I wondered if Company "A" trainees were slaves instead of trainees while undergoing training preparing them for combat. Biting my tongue, I managed to keep my mouth shut and to do so until the day I became the company commander. Then things changed.

During my "breaking-in time", free to do

what I wanted, I participated in all company training activities including the infiltration course, known distance (KD) range firing, machine gun and mortar live firing, road marches, physical training, and bayonet training, etc. The recruits, NCOs, and officers wondered why I had engaged the infiltration course which required me to crawl under barbed wire, through dust and mud while machine guns were firing live rounds only inches above my head. This was certainly not expected of me, a returned combat veteran. But I didn't have the experience, except in combat, and I needed it to prepare me for the command of the company. The trainees enjoyed my participating with them, giving them confidence, for it was a nerve racking thing for a young kid of eighteen years to do. Should a man become hysterical and attempt to run from the course, the machine guns would cut him down before the firing could be stopped. Even for me, a combat veteran, crawling under the barbed wire through thick dust and mud holes, with weapon and equipment strapped to my body, demolitions exploding, bullets splitting the air just inches above my head, was very trying. One could imagine the terror that the young recruits, recently school kids, were experiencing. They would feel better seeing me among them.

Updating my training was necessary for it was more demanding than it had been at Camp Shelby in 1941. Basic training at Camp Robinson was even more demanding physically than combat. Training was from early morning to late at night often terminating in night classes or field exercises until 10:00PM, even later. It was not unusual for me to be in my orderly room (office) at 4:00AM, have breakfast with the men and on the road march by 6:00AM. The colonel's admonitions came true. It required every ounce of might I had until I regained the strength that had been sapped by service in Arawa. However, unknown to me, the latent malaria fever was beginning to have its effects.

It was during a Sunday dinner, after a hard week of training recruits, shortly after Wilma and the boys had arrived, I felt a sudden weakness and dizziness. Following dinner I took a nap to rest a bit, but was aroused by a knock on the door. It was a local preacher who came to make a call on us. I opened the door and the next thing I knew, the Reverend and Wilma were standing over me. I had passed out. They rushed me to the camp hospital. It was the dreaded malaria fever and again I had to suffer as I had in Camp Shelby in 1941.

After two weeks in the hospital and bed rest at home, I returned to my company to continue training my men. I was still in a very weakened condition. Lt. Kindick, my executive officer, had commanded the company during my absence. Little-by-little I regained my strength and knowledge of SOP (Standard of Operating Procedures) that would give me a handle for effective operations of the company.

After Captain Carter's departure, I found myself in command of two hundred trainees plus six officers and about thirty permanent cadre. Further, I would have not only training operations but also mess and supply administration as well. Individual records were required for every hour of training for each trainee resulting in much make-up training missed due to sickness, KP, and other administrative duties performed in the company area. I couldn't imagine why each of the poor trainees were prepared to continue under the threat process of command which they had been exposed to by their former commander. While undergoing basic training, troops must be dealt with firmly but in an understanding manner, and recognized for their accomplishments, never under threat of punishment for unintentional failure. Command must be tempered with compassion and understanding, and soldiers expect and demand that, too. Often I would throw the book at a soldier who purposely messed up, but when it was over, the offense was forgotten and the soldier had learned a lesson which from that time forward he remembered and obeyed the rules. He realized, under these conditions, he would get his just dues, be it recognition or punishment, such as extra duty or restriction, or praise. I had learned years before some soldiers will go as far as a commander will permit and it's up to the commander to haul in the reins if he expects to have discipline, something a good outfit wants. Troops don't like a "soft" or a "mother" type commander, rather one with both firmness and knowledge; a feeling of brotherhood must exist among the men. Discipline promotes elan and morale, a spirit of belonging to a good unit. Otherwise, your organization will become very ineffective. I had no problem administering military justice, for the men knew my policy:

intentionally mess up and you would get called up on the carpet. I had the authority to restrict a man for fourteen days to the limits of the company area and to administer extra duty for minor violations. I could prefer charges, courtmartialing a man for more serious offenses, the courts being handled by the regiment. I had to do little of this; most problems were handled by interviews and encouragement. The man's dignity was never removed unless it was the last resort. It was necessary to back up your officers and NCOs in their decision-making, but only if they were right. A soldier in the ranks must never suffer from injustice. To some old NCOs and officers this may seem to be "mealy-mouthed", but I never pulled the punches when severe discipline was needed. Often this was for the good of the offender and certainly for the good of the company. The men knew where I stood and they knew disciplinary action would be forthcoming if they intentionally violated policies.

There were several derelictions that were unpardonable as far as I was concerned. One was a soldier who would not keep his person clean and another was a "yardbird" or a malingerer, who rode the sick book, falling out on road marches, making excuses. I had no sympathy for such soldiers, for they placed an additional burden on others who would have to take up the slack. The soldiers either performed or took the consequences. Usually the NCOs took care of much of this on their own, unknown to me. Often, when I did know, I turned my back, unless such action threatened to get out of hand. The NCOs knew their limits and were usually right. Even the men in the ranks brought the "deadbeat" or "yardbird" back in line; they were proud of their company and did not want such people around messing things up.

This was the spirit the company rallied to. Relying on the squad and platoon leaders, we progressed. Our morale was high and our training effective. We marched, we paraded, we fired on the KD (known distance) ranges. All company officers and NCOs did what the men did, displaying to the trainees how it should be done. There were no more threats, but recognition instead.

During all of this activity, and when I had time, I was house-hunting, for I missed my family so much. In the meantime I lived in a tar-paper shack near the officers' latrine and officer's mess on post. I had a cot and a shelf for my personal gear; my quarters were anything but luxurious. I needed my family badly. Then I found a house, a nice house at Oak Park in Little Rock. It was owned by a lady who was glad to rent it to me furnished at a reasonable price. I also needed an automobile and found a white 1940 Nash, paying cash for it.

"Come quickly to Little Rock....immediately! I've got us a house and a car, too," I telegraphed Wilma.

How wonderful it was when I met them at the train station in Little Rock! Wilma's mother, Mrs Guthrie, was with them; eagerly I took them to our Nash parked near by and with great pride, chauffeured them to our house in Oak Park. The boys shouted with glee and Wilma smiled. We were happy, once again, to have our own place. Groceries were already on the shelves and in the refrigerator so Wilma fixed a good breakfast the next morning. I took a day off to be with them to enjoy our home and our car.

It was the beginning of a new life, a happy life. Wilma's mother, after staying a few days, tearfully departed for Charleston. It was hard for her to give up the boys whom she had been so close to for almost three years, but she knew she had to do it. Her departure was sad for her and for us.

Even though gas rationing was in effect, by using our Nash sparingly and doubling up with others riding to work to save gasoline, we were able take short recreational rides to nearby Hot Springs and other places of interest. We made good friends, especially with my executive officer, Lt. Kindick and his wife, who often came to visit us. Having no children of their own, they especially enjoyed our boys, often bringing gifts and candy to them. The other officers of the company, Lts. Downey, Matthews, Ceretti, and Horn and the NCOs, all, became a close knit family. The trainees, now in their eighth week of training, were doing well and worked very hard for it wouldn't be too long before they would be fillers in the ranks of combat units in Europe or Southwest Pacific Area. The officers and most of the NCOs were combat veterans either from the Pacific Area, Aleutian Islands, or North Africa. All of them realized the importance of our training. Perhaps we would save many lives if we trained the young soldiers well, and we did.

Then one morning, just after reporting

in for duty from overseas, I entered the main gate of Camp Robinson dressed in starched fatigues. It was about 4:30AM. I was stopped by the Military Police on duty at the main gate, who shined his flashlight inside the car.

"Captain, are you dressed in fatigues, sir?"

I told him I was.

"Do you know you are in violation of post regulations?"

"Why?"

"Fatigues are considered to be inappropriate dress for off post."

"Having just arrived, I'm not aware of this. However, I will comply hereafter."

"Sorry, Captain, I must make a DR (Delinquency Report).

"Do what you have to. It's your duty."

I gave the MP the necessary personal information and continued to my company, had breakfast with the troops, and left the area for KD rifle firing at 6:00AM, marching to the ranges about an hour's marching time.

Due to our heavy training schedule, often working far into the night, I had completely forgot about the DR, considering it of little importance. During the week following the incident we fired the troops on the known distance ranges, beginning at first light and until 5:00PM, had instruction during the late evening and in general, we worked hard. At night, sessions were held to improve scoring and other matters. Then one morning, just before marching my company to the training area, I received a call from the adjutant, Lt. Anderson, said for me to report to Colonel Davis without delay. I couldn't imagine why.

"Good morning, Captain Jordan. I must congratulate you for the fine job your company is doing on the KD ranges. Your officers and NCOs are doing a fine job. Please express my congratulations."

"Thank you, sir. They'll be pleased."

What's this guy got up his sleeve, I thought.

"Captain Jordan, I got a DR on you from the division concerning your dress coming on post the other morning. Fatigues are considered inappropriate attire off post."

I stammered. "The DR is correct, sir. Being newly assigned to Camp Robinson, I was not aware of that regulation." I explained my fatigues were clean and starched, my boots shined and I was ready to march with my company to the KD Rifle ranges.

Colonel Davis smiled and said, in what I considered to be in jest, "Well, I will ask the division what's the appropriate punishment for a combat officer from New Guinea coming on post at 4:00AM wearing fatigues." He pitched the DR into his out basket, again congratulating me for the good work of my company, and wished me well. I left to join my company already in formation to march to the training area.

Two weeks later, again I was called and instructed to report to Colonel Davis. "Captain Jordan, because you violated post regulations by coming on post dressed in fatigues, you are hereby notified that your punishment is being restricted to the regimental area for a period of two weeks," said Colonel Davis. I was dumbfounded. Was I being treated like a recruit after the hell in the SWPA?

It was necessary for Wilma to bring my toilet articles and clothing to me for I could not leave the post to get them. Wilma and the boys came to see me on the weekends, but the rest of the time I spent with the company night and day. So what, I reasoned, I had violated post regulations and the punishment was justified. I thought nothing more about it. However, I did have to reply by endorsement the reason why I was one day late reporting in to Camp Robinson, even though I requested a day's delay in transit. It had been approved, but the final paper "fell through the cracks" and no record was ever found. Apparently my record was not inviable by the pencil pushers at division and regiment. Then I took myself to task as if I were Colonel Davis speaking to me as I felt he would like: "You had better straighten up, you former "Bushmaster", recently from the hellish place called Arawa. Even though you spent almost three years away from your family, you will spend the next two weeks restricted to the regimental area anyway. To hell with your combat record; you can't come in on post dressed in fatigues ready for work, nor can you report in a day late even if we did approve your request and it got lost in the mill somewhere." My reasoning set the stage during my stay in Robinson; I had lost the spirit I wanted so much to have. Even though Colonel Davis was friendly, often visiting me in the field and in my orderly room, I was still bitter and never forgot the injustice.

This was the attitude of the brass at Camp Robinson, having little personal regard for combat veterans, I think simply due to jealousy. They had been behind their desks since the beginning of war, never leaving the safety of the United States, and now the combat veterans were returning. It would be no time at all until they would have the easy jobs and they, the "desk flyers", would be on their way overseas to the jungles. The army was still tugging at my sensitive strings. I must hold on, I thought. I would get over it. What those pencil pushers need is a tour in the jungles where the Japs will change them greatly and they see men die and suffer in ragged fatigues. Having seen this, I'm sure no DRs would be issued to anyone wearing fatigues while in their personal car coming on post at 4:00AM. Silently, I talked to myself. Yet, I took it, for now. Both were minor incidents, but my skin had been pricked. Later I would make a drastic decision in anger and in disgust, based upon these incidents. The decision would be a terrible mistake.

While my feathers were still ruffled, we had to move. The landlady wanted her sister to move in for she had no place for her to go. Luckily we found an even nicer house at Cammack Village, located on a high hill in North Little Rock; a turning and twisting road led to it. One morning, just before Christmas, and while I was on my way to camp, very early, the radio warned of ice on the roads. Paying little attention, I began the descent of the steep hill and about halfway down I hit a patch of ice. The car went out of control, spinning completely around, ending up heading in the opposite direction sitting on the edge of the road. I was only inches from a steep ledge and could have easily crashed down into the creek bed far below. I sat stupefied. Still later on the same road, while driving alone home late one night, about 11:00PM, just over the top of a hill, two cars were stopped, one in each lane, blocking the road. In terror, traveling very fast, I jammed the brakes and, to my horror, the pedal went to the floor without pressure. Such will happen if air is in the brake lines. Being unable to stop, I headed off the road to the right. There again I was aghast. Another car was parked just off the road there. All I could do was aim between the two parked cars, the one in my lane and the one parked off the road to the right. I closed my eyes, for I was sure I would take off the fenders of both cars, but, surprisingly, instead I made it through without touching either car. It was a miracle. When I told Lt. Kindick about my narrow escape, he made a classic remark that I've used it since to describe the situation. He said, "Captain, had there been an additional coat of paint on those cars, you would have had one of the biggest car crashes around." In both cases, death could have been the result. Again, I reflected upon my charmed life. I've been sheltered, for some reason.

Being a sympathetic person as a commander of troops, I get very attached to my men. Often times, they look to you, their commander, as their father image - and rightfully so, for there is none other who can help them in time of need. In WWII, when they came to you for training they were still just kids. They were homesick, having never been away from home before. They were living under strange circumstances, and scared. The company NCOs and officers, by necessity, must order them around firmly. Group living with about two hundred other men, whom they had never met, in an open barracks, standing in mess line, formations, run, getting into uniform, getting issued armloads of equipment, weapon; the poor devils, until they get situated and know each other and their leaders, must have wondered what sort of a hell they were in.

The most common fear that new men have is the loss of privacy. Back home they usually had a room of their own and the bathroom was used in privacy. In the army, the bathroom (latrine) was to accommodate mass production of use. The GI latrine (bathroom) usually had eight commodes all out in the open, no enclosures. At times all eight commodes were busily occupied. Like robots, there would be a man on each one, nature in full blast. To some new recruits it was traumatic to use a commode in the presence of other men. To some it was most difficult to perform acts of nature in the presence of others and they just couldn't do it. They had to be encouraged to use the latrine. Some even went for several days without using a commode and, needless to say, they were in bad shape. Finding out about this, I ordered the latrine closed for a few minutes, placed a guard outside the door, and ordered one poor fellow, who was in great pain, inside. In a few minutes, he came out a greatly relieved man and a grateful one at that. He had done the thing he had wanted to do for several days; he never forgot the incident, nor did his buddies, either. This appears to be funny, but to that man, closing the latrine for his private use was one of the best things that ever happened to him, he confessed later. He soon got over his timidity and, like the rest of his barrack mates, used the commode right along with the best of them.

The demand for use of the latrine, especially when troops returned from training, reaches the maximum when the first sergeant "dismissed" the company. Like a herd of cattle, the race to the latrine is on; privacy is out of the question. However, it is only a matter of time before the young recruits, by necessity, become veterans, using the "comfort station" with its eight "thrones" giving them relief, and without timidity. It is the beginning of a new way of life and discipline, the likes of which is beyond their imagination, initially.

The recruit must be first untrained. One concept of this, and probably why this is so, the recruit must be untrained from his causal civilian ways and then trained to meet the military needs. He would know nothing else until his military service was over. His life would be changed forever. Some men will never get over it, good or bad, applying it to their vocations or avocations following their military service.

They came to us in all shapes and sizes. Their clothing ranged from dress suits to ragged attire. Some men had hair down to their shoulders (the long hair being a target of some NCOs who feel hair longer than an inch was just cause for a trip to the GI barbershop). The barber, under the supervision of the stern NCO, can satisfy his, the NCO's, demands in less than a minute, after which time the recruit's locks of hair are usually on the floor surrounding the barber's chair. Then the NCO proudly marched his clipped recruit back for all to see. It was a trying time for the recent recruit just out of civilian life.

While all of this was going on, I watched from the sidelines, feeling sorry for the confused, bewildered, scared, and yet homesick recruits as they stood in platoon formation at rigid attention while being inspected by their demanding NCOs and officers. They would see me around, aloof, and perhaps wondered, I'm sure, just how I would fit into the scheme of things. Later, I gave them the opportunity to learn how I did fit; beginning with the mess line. The mess line is a good place to begin after the uniform and clothing issue, bedding, equipment, the haircuts, and getting into uniform, has been accomplished. There I talked to them, telling them who I was. I welcomed them to the company. Until that time, the poor devils wondered if anyone would say such encouraging things to them after all the harassment that they had been through. Perhaps they thought no one even cared for them any longer. In the mess line and in the mess hall, often eating with them, the bonding began. The officers and NCOs saw what I was doing and followed my example. Soon the stubble-haired recruits began to feel at home. The good feelings were carried forth in training, on the rifle range, on long road marches, or during bivouacs. A competitive spirit was generated and morale soared. When the twelve weeks training period was over we were like a bunch of brothers. Then they were shipped out and would never be seen by us again. It was hard for me and it was hard for them. Soon another group of 200 recruits would report and the cycle would begin all over again.

It was just before Christmas 1944. We had just completed a cycle of training. It was one of the best groups of trainees we had ever trained. They were looking forward to going home on Christmas leave before shipping overseas. Then it happened: The Battle of the Bulge. The VIII US Army Corps in Germany had been almost destroyed by the last thrust of the German Army as it attacked toward Liege, Belgium. Fillers were needed immediately. In fact, we were alerted to prepare to move as a unit to Europe by air, and we would go into combat as a unit. We had not yet heard of the battle and wondered what was happening. The alert was called off, but the recruits, now trained for combat duty, were shipped out immediately by air, and without Christmas leave, to become fillers in the decimated VIII Army Corps. They arrived in time to help restore the ruptured front. Many of the poor kids died within days after they had arrived. After the battle some of the men wrote to us about the cold and freezing weather, the vicious Germans, but above all, they thanked us for the good training they had received while in Company "A". They had applied their military knowledge on the front line. We, as well as they, were grateful that our training procedures had been successful.

Just as Colonels Davis and Cronk said, training recruits was difficult and demanding. Many long hours were spent with the men in the cold, rain, sleet, and in even snow. We trained under all conditions, for combat would not show mercy under these conditions. I enjoyed it, for I liked to do things with the men. We made a game of it, kept the men informed, and tried to make life easier for them. I often remembered the old WWI officer's statement to us while we, as second lieutenants, sat on the cold damp ground in Camp Shelly in January, 1941: "A soldier lives miserably and he will die miserably". That remark still haunted me. We, the officers and NCOs of Company "A", tried to train our men well, while at the same time treating them as brothers, trying at least to make life less miserable for them. The trainees appreciated this. It was a sad day for us of Company "A" when a cycle of training was completed, for, with the exception of a few, we would never see or hear from any of the good men again. It would have been a terrible mistake for me to have heeded Colonels Davis and Cronk's advice to take a desk job when I reported in at Camp Robinson. There was no joy sitting behind a desk when good men needed to be molded into good combat soldiers. To me this was a sacred responsibility.

CHAPTER 28

VICTORY! END OF WAR! A CIVILIAN?

The defeat of the German Army by Eisenhower at the Battle of the Bulge insured the defeat of the Axis powers in Europe. The war in the Pacific was progressing very favorably; secret plans were being made to use the atomic bomb on Japan. Victory in Europe found the nervous Americans on the River Elbe in Western Germany facing the mighty Russian army. Patton, the famous, illustrious American general, chomping at the bit, was ready to spring to the attack to "kill the SOBs, the real enemy", as he faced the Russians, nose to nose. "Let's do it while we have the army over here," he said, advice fortunately ignored, even though, as events later proved, Russia or Communism, which we had made strong, was our real enemy. Then Eisenhower fired Patton when he declared the Nazis were only a political party just like the Republicans and Democrats. Again he was right, but the politico did not like the comparison. They squawked until Eisenhower fired Patton, one of the best combat generals we ever had, "Old Blood and Guts", they called him. "Yeah, his guts and our blood," said a veteran of the famous Third Army. But we did cause Communism to grow after the war, creating a monster that almost destroyed us, inflation from which we are suffering today due to the military and industrial complex that President Eisenhower had warned, that is sapping our economy.

While all the confab continued over Patton, Company "A"'s mission never changed;

we continued to make good soldiers out of good men, weeding out the worst, turning out 200 every twelve weeks. With the war over in Europe, the allies began the gargantuan effort of moving armies from Europe to the Pacific Theater of Operations to bring Japan to her knees. All resources, men and equipment in Europe and in the United States would be used. It was felt an invasion of Japan itself would be necessary and perhaps we would lose over 500,000 soldiers killed and wounded. It would be a terrible price to pay, but it would have to be done. There would be no let-up in training regardless of what had happened in Europe.

Looking to the future, the army visualized that once the war was over military personnel would leave the ranks and files. They needed to keep prepared and so they requested reserve officers to apply for Regular Army commissions. My battalion and regimental commanders suggested that I submit my application. They thought I would do a good job. I considered it but wanted to wait, for I was not altogether happy with what was going on in the Regular Army. Many crazy things had happened during the war. But my forte was working with men and, if I received a Regular Army commission, I would be subjected to some of the crazy things that I had seen going on. It appeared that I had a natural compatibility with soldiers, but I could not understand some of the strange orders that came from higher headquarters. Many officers felt the same way I did and wanted no more of it. They intended to get out of the army after the war. I was ambivalent, but a certain event, unfortunately, made up my mind for me.

An officer, Lieutenant Whipper, a retread from the Army Air Corps, reported for duty at Company "A". Being a blabbermouth, he said he had escaped from a Japanese PW camp in the Philippines, joined the guerrillas there, killed many Japs, and then escaped from the Philippines on a US Navy submarine. Whatever he did in the Philippines he certainly wasn't fit to lead men in Company "A". His stories impressed us at first, but he continued to tell them to all who would listen. Those who had not heard them would gang around and he poured out his heart, especially at parties. He was a hero, self-made hero. Usually, a military person with combat experience, because of the terrible gore and the terror of the battlefield, will say very little of what he saw. If they do discuss it, as Whipper did, it is considered a concocted story by those who have been there. Sometimes, however, the stories of many were true and relating them was therapeutic to the person that had experienced them. But this was not so with Whipper. He was the joy of the regiment, except for Colonel Cronk, me, and others recently returned from the jungles in SWPA. The Colonel, a very big man, had the courage of the devil and was afraid of nothing. He was a great leader at the battle of Buna while with the 32nd Infantry Division, some said he had killed a Japanese soldier with his bare hands. One day he said to me:

"Ben Rod, there's something fishy about Whipper. He says things that don't ring true with me. In my opinion all of his stories are fakes, I think." Many of us agreed with him.

But Whipper supposedly continued to relate the terrible things that had happened and what he had done in the Philippines. Those of us who had fought the Japanese in the jungle doubted him, but remained silent, leaving when he began vociferously telling his "heroic" stories. His performance of duty was less than desired; he was a deadbeat officer. It was necessary to assign him duties even a private could do better.

It was then the atomic bombs were dropped on Hiroshima and Nagasaki, bringing the Pacific war to a close. MacArthur signed a peace treaty with Japan aboard the Battleship Missouri - the Big "MO", they called the great battlewagon. The world once more enjoyed peace, or it was thought peace was at hand. This wishful thinking was short-lived, however, for Russia had entered the war against Japan only three days before by invading Manchuria and demanded her share of the spoils of Japan. Later MacArthur told Russia to go to hell, the only language they could understand. Shortly thereafter the cold war began; Russia sealed off Berlin, leaving only the air space for the allies to supply the western part of the city.

Again the idea of a Regular Army commission came to the forefront, for the Army realized there would be an exodus of officers, which in fact was already beginning. It took no military expert to realize a large standing army would be necessary to counter the Russian threat. Still I demurred. Then it happened. It was Whipper.

We continued to train as if the war was still going on and one evening when we formed for night training, Lt. Whipper was missing. I had Kindick, the executive officer, to report him as absent without leave (AWOL) to the regiment. The company then was marched to the training area to engage in compass and map training under condition of darkness. I would take on Whipper in an appropriate manner once he returned to military control, I thought. It didn't take long for things to happen. First Sergeant Bacaum rushed out from the barrack area with an urgent message from the battalion commander, Major Hill.

"Captain Jordan, the battalion wants you to come in immediately. Whipper has taken the battalion commander's jeep and drove it off post according to the MPs at Main Gate. They say he is drunk."

I jumped with joy. Now, I thought, I could get rid of him for his many various offenses, breaching all military discipline the Army ever had on the books.

"It will be good riddance," said Kindick as he heard me expound about what I was going to do to the SOB. We had enough of the braggart and his self-imposed heroism and lack of dedication to duty.

The battalion commander, was furious. "The SOB stole my jeep, and I cannot get out into the field tonight to be with the companies. I have arranged for you to take a jeep from regiment. Go after him and, once you find him, arrest the SOB. Put him in the stockade and throw the key away. He's spent his last day with us." I laughed at the very disturbed major, a good friend of mine.

Knowing Whipper had left the post and must pass through the Main Gate, I proceeded to locate the wayward officer. Interviewing the MP on duty, I was told that Whipper, even after being threatened that he would be shot if he took the jeep off the post, drove out the gate, ignoring the three MPs. Losing his nerve, the MP did not fire at the fleeing drunken officer.

I chased Whipper all night over Little Rock, from one beer joint to another, but never caught up with him. Returning to post at sun-up and going to search his quarters, I found him passed out in his bunk. His clothing was a mess soaked with spilt beer and rancid vomit. Dragging him out of his bunk, across the floor of the shack and down the three steps, and across the ground into the bathhouse, I threw him down on the concrete. When I turned on the cold shower, Whipper began to struggle, but I held him down, both of us getting soaked to the skin.

"Hell", he slurred, "it's raining. Get me out of here." He continued to struggle but I held him to the concrete. Other officers came in and wondered why I was holding him down, not knowing why, they tried to interfere, but backed off when I told them what had happened. The struggle under cold water shower continued until he began to sober up. When he became coherent, I ordered him to get to his quarters and get dressed. Then he would accompany me to the regiment to see Colonel Davis. Still soaked, he staggered out of the bathhouse, down the narrow concrete walk and into his tar paper shack. Later, he reported to me. His condition was anything but presentable, but I, with haste, took him to regiment as he protested.

"Captain Jordan," the adjutant began, "Lieutenant Whipper will be taken by the regimental commander to see the division commanding general. You are not to accompany them. Leave Lt. Whipper in my custody and the regimental commander wants you to return to your organization. He will let you know of the results of the meeting between Whipper and the division commander."

"It's immaterial, but I want this guy out of my organization, even out of the army. He's not fit to be an officer!" Colonel Cronk, the Executive Officer, sitting in his office nearby heard the remark, called me in and invited me to have a seat. He spoke frankly.

"Damn it, Ben Rod, watch what you say here. You are bordering on disrespect for a fellow officer. This could get you into serious trouble. Officially, you are making judgement only a courtmartial can make. Now shut up and maybe together we can get rid of the SOB." Colonel Cronk, only very recently, had cautioned me about my strong attack on the Army system of handling cases similar to Whipper's and I did respect him for it. But Whipper was different, and must be drummed out of the Army. I reasoned.

Returning to my company and finding that it had already left for the field, I began walking to the training area. My mind wasn't on training, but what was happening to Whipper in the division commander's office. Why was the case being handled by the division commander himself? Why not the regimental commander? Something was not right. Returning to my office during the noon break, I walked into my orderly room and there sat Whipper behind my desk. I exploded.

"Whipper, get out of my office and ask permission from the First Sergeant to enter into my presence immediately." This was the procedure used when a private asks permission to see the company commander, certainly not for respectable officers or senior NCOs. Silently, he complied leaving my office.

Soon there was a rap on the door. It was First Sergeant Becaum, who entered and said: "Lieutenant Whipper requests permission to see the Company Commander, sir." Baucum had heard the conversation between us and had a big smile on his face, for he knew what was about to happen.

"Permission granted, Sergeant."

Whipper entered and he stood rigidly at attention.

"All right Whipper, what happened at Division?"

"Nothing, sir. I was told to return to the company for duty. Here I am, sir."

"Whipper, you have performed your last duty, if we can call it duty, with this company. I want you out of here this minute. Please report to battalion for your new assignment," And he left.

"Colonel Cronk," I called. "What in heavens name happened at Division with Whipper. I thought we were going to kick him out of the Army!"

"Just getting ready to call you, Ben Rod. Colonel Davis wants to see you in his office immediately. You had better come now. He's waiting."

My anger must have been showing as I

entered Colonel Davis's office. "Captain Jordan, the division commander feels that due to the terrible experience Whipper has had in the Philippines, he should be given another chance to redeem himself and wants him to continue under your direction, feeling you are more knowledgeable of his condition, perhaps aiding his rehabilitation."

Unbelievable!

Anger overpowered me. The memories crushed through my mind like a stream of water rushing over a waterfall. I remembered having received two weeks restriction for driving to work in clean starched fatigues while in my car at four o'clock in the morning prepared for work. This after having recently returned from a combat area and not yet familiar with post regulations prohibiting wearing inappropriate clothing off post. Furthermore, having to reply by endorsement for being a day late, even after a verbal approval had been granted. I compared that with what Whipper had done and he wasn't even reprimanded. Was this justice? Hell no!

Returning to my orderly room, and while in a rage of temper, I prepared and submitted my resignation from the army effective immediately, knowing full well I was making a terrible mistake. A person in the state of mind I was in that day was not capable of making a sound decision. After many pleas from my officers and NCOs, the battalion commander, Major Hill, and from Colonel Cronk, the regimental executive officer, even other officers of the battalion urging me to reconsider and withdraw my resignation, I unfortunately ignored their pleas. In spite of my better judgement, Wilma and I packed, and with our two sons, Bucky and Johnny, was on our way to Charleston and to a new future. Hopefully, it would be adventurous. A Civilian! How would I adjust to the placid life of routine civilian surroundings after Arawa and Camp Robinson, poles apart.

Ironically, my efforts to rid the army of a deadbeat backfired. Because of my over-zealous action, Whipper was the victor. He was in while I was out. I had acted unwisely, even realizing at the time I was doing it. Ten years later, after I had returned to active duty, I met Whipper at Fort Campbell, Kentucky. He was a master sergeant in the Air Force. He was a member of a C-119 aircraft squadron that had arrived to drop paratroopers of the 188th Airborne Infantry Regiment, an operation I had planned. It was during the orientation meeting between the pilots and me, coordinating the details of the jump, that he recognizing me as I conducted the meeting. Whipper made himself known; he was very friendly and did not even mention Camp Robinson. Whipper had gained weight, looked sloppy, had a mustache, and had less hair, otherwise recognizable. Again, our meeting was ironic. Unknowingly to him, I had him to blame for making the rash decision taking me out of the army that had adverse affect upon my Army career. Three years later after making the rash decision, I would return to active duty and I know, for sure this rash decision m,ade in 1945 had cost me a rank in promotion, which is a considerable in computed retirement pay.

CHAPTER 29

EPILOGUE

Having three months accrued leave with pay, I took my time finding a job in Charleston. In the meantime we bought a modest house on Cunningham Street in St Albans, just west of Charleston. After a few days of doing nothing, I become very restless and I began in earnest to find a job. Was I ready to take up the life that I had left behind almost five years before? I was sure that I was. Many veterans then could receive up to six months "rocking chair money", but I wanted none of that for I had always worked for my money and "rocking chair" money wasn't for me. It was time to establish a home and seek a sound future for my family. My old job at the glass bottling plant was available but stacking bottles in a dark recesses of the warehouse no longer appealed to me, even though later, they told me, I could be considered for the position of assistant manager of the shipping department.

William McTeer, an insurance supervisor, whom I had known and respected before the war, suggested that I consider the insurance career. He took me to his office where I met Denver Bird and others of the staff and the other salesmen. I ended up having lunch, as his guest, at an underwriters meeting at the prestigious Daniel Boone Hotel. McTeer introduced me to the members, as Captain Ben Rod Jordan, recently out of the Army and made a big to-do over me as if I had won the Congressional Medal of Honor. Many of the members later introduced themselves and wished me well.

McTeer's Home Office offered me a position as a salesman, suggesting I sign a contract, but I delayed. We had just completed moving into our home and the house needed some work, and the boys were ready to enter school. We met new neighbors and soon all was ready for neighborhood living. Wilma, again, became very active in her church, the Church of Jesus Christ of Latter-Day Saints, the Mormon Church, on Indiana Ave. in Charleston. The church was very family oriented, and she wanted our sons to have a good spiritual background as well. She was wise. Each Sunday we attended church services and lasting friendships were forged. The church was tolerant of my religious views, even though at first I wasn't tolerant of theirs. They always made we welcome and I met some of the finest people I had ever known. They were true and loyal to their church, neighbors, community, and country, and very patriotic; many of the local Mormon boys, members of the 150th Infantry, had served with me in Panama. I was impressed by their dedication.

It was time I settled down and go to work. Eventually, I did sign a contract with the insurance company and they suggested I specialize on returning servicemen who would soon be married and have responsibilities - then they certainly would need the coverage. This was the beginning of the baby boomers and they would need our attention for many years to come. I found that to be so and they, the veterans, looked to me with confidence and trusted my advice in insurance matters.

McTeer and I had wonderful experiences together in the insurance business. He was very knowledgeable and taught me a lot. We enjoyed each other's company. We did a lot of good and I was sold solidly on the business. It is a type of business where everyone benefits, especially the beneficiaries. Oftentimes, when death occurs to a breadwinner, the money from his insurance policy was often the only means of family support.

On one occasion, when Mcteer and I were checking into a hotel in Ripley, West Virginia, we encountered a receptionist who said she didn't believe in insurance any more. We asked her why she had such an opinion.

"My husband died a few years ago and, even though we had carried the policy for several years, we were unable to pay the premium a year before his death, so we could not collect on the policy."

"Do you have your policy here?", ask MaTeer.

"Yes, I do."

"May I see it?"

"You may."

To our surprise our company had issued the policy in 1934.

Taking the number of the policy and giving it back to the lady, we went immediately to our room and called the Home Office. After checking we found the insurance policy, had a face value of $5000, was actually in force under the extended coverage provision due to the cash value at the time of the insured's death but no claim had ever been received.

"Send death claim immediately," was the response.

We prepared the death claim within minutes, took it down to the wife of the deceased, asked her to sign it. At first she refused, perhaps thinking we were frauds. Then people around, who knew McTeer, convinced her we were sincere. She signed the death claim and we placed it in the envelope we had already addressed, sealed it and had her mail it. A few days later, while we were at the office in Charleston, her check came and we hurriedly went to Ripley to deliver it to the beneficiary.

Still we had trouble making the lady believe we were on the up-and-up. Not until we took her to the bank and the teller shelled out $5000 did she believe us. Then she shouted for joy, showing people in the bank her handfuls of money, her recent fortune. From that day on, that lady was one of our best contacts in Ripley. She sang our praises to everyone, saying we were the best insurance men around.

This is just one example of the many happy experiences we had. We had gained the confidence and trust of the people. We never oversold a young client starting out, but we did build a recommended program for his future consideration and he added to his program as his needs changed or his income increased. As in the army, the returned veterans trusted us, and not once did we knowingly violate that trust. We made things right when there was a misunderstanding. Often people consulted us on the most confidential family matters. We made ourselves available at times of deaths, often attending funerals of family members of our clients and they appreciated that. We tried to deliver the insurance check on the day of the funeral, for there were always times of financial needs. The bereaved appreciated that, too.

But it wasn't the Army. Why of all things the Army? After Arawa, Milne Bay, Camp Robinson, disloyal brass? Yet I missed the Army. The opportunity presented itself for me to join the West Virginia National Guard, which was being reorganized in 1946. Brigadier General Charles R. Fox, the Adjutant General of West Virginia, whom I had known before and during the war, requested that I assist him and others to reorganize the National Guard. My old regiment, the 150th Infantry (Powderhorns), had been deactivated in Panama and returned to state control. It would be in the southern part of the state while the sister regiment, the 149th Infantry, would be in the north, the same as it was before the war. Working with the S-3, Operations and Training, I assisted in the publication of training schedules and policies. Later I became the Executive Officer of the First Battalion of the 150th Infantry, with headquarters in Saint Albans, West Virginia. Lt Col Brandy Gatens, the battalion commander, whom I had known even before the war, and had served with in the Panama Canal Zone, was grateful we were together again. Many of the old members of the Guard joined and it was like a reunion. Later I was called to General Fox's staff as S-3, Operations and Training, a position I held until I returned to active duty later in 1948. I held this position during the summer encampment of the West Virginia National Guard at Fort Knox, Kentucky in 1948. However, my position in the National Guard demanded so much time it interfered with my insurance business. It was then I decided to return to active duty with the army reporting for duty at Fort Benning, Georgia, and was assigned to command Company "B", 325th Infantry, a rifle company. Finally, after many years, I got my rifle company and I was happy. Later, I would join the 82nd Airborne Division at Fort Bragg, North Carolina, commanding Company "L", 325th Airborne Infantry Regiment, where I would jump out of perfectly good airplanes in "fright". With First Sergeant Barry, many other good NCOs, Lts. Hazeltine and Hutchison, we forged an outfit that blazed itself into history. We trained very hard, made many parachute jumps, participated in "Exercise Swarmer" in 1949, an exercise patterned after the German parachute jump on Crete in WWII. It was then I met Lt. Col. (later General) William C. Westmoreland, the Divison Chief of Staff, commander of all forces during the Vietnam War, and later the Army Chief of Staff. Company "L" was recognized for its good work and the then Colonel Westmoreland sent the company to Camp Stewart, Georgia, in 1949, to support the summer national guard training. This was almost a vacation for us, since it was a separate operation from the division and regiment.

Before taking command of Company "B", in Fort Benning, Georgia, and while still in limbo, I was temporarily assigned to escort duty working out of Atlanta Army Depot but still stationed at Fort Benning, traveling in between. Even though it was an interesting assignment, it was yet a sad duty. I escorted the remains of officers killed during WWII to their families, and at one time escorted many remains at once via rail to Memphis. Each casket had an escort and I had a casket to be delivered personally to the next of kin; the escort had to be of equal or higher rank than the deceased. The escorts were instructed and understood how the procedure operated, how meticulous the Army was in caring for the dead, but it was still sad delivering remains to a family; it was really a heartbreaking experience. Until then the family had hoped that their loved one was still listed among the missing and would return to them some day; their hopes was shattered.

The escorts were given very detailed instructions describing the procedure from the interment of the body, its exhumation, and how the remains were prepared and placed in the casket. Depending upon the desires of the next of kin the remains were either returned to the family in the United States or else reinterred in a permanent cemetery in Arlington or overseas. We were told never to voluntarily reveal the procedure of preparing the body for delivery to the families of the deceased unless it was absolutely necessary; what was in the casket was anything except what the family expected. Once the casket was returned to the family they perhaps felt the body was intact, beautifully embalmed as if it had came out of the undertaker shop. But it was anything except that. However, once we had turned the remains over to the family representative the United States government no longer exercised control. Should the family insist the casket be opened we were to used all our influence and persuasion to prevent it. It would be a tragedy, for the once beautiful-image of their loved one would be lost forever. The undertakers also knew the conditions of the remains and they did all they could to persuade the family from opening the casket. However, during the Korean and the Vietnam war the caskets were opened for viewing, for the deceased remains were on their way home within hours after death. In contrast, the remains of WWII soldiers were in the temporary graves for as much as three years before being returned back to the next of kin. One can imagine the condition of the remains once exhumation had occurred.

The reaction of the families most of the time was deep appreciation for bringing their loved ones home to them. However there were times when the families of some enlisted men killed in battle blamed the escorts for the death of their loved one; this was not a very pleasant experience for them. Fortunately, I never faced this terrible situation, but was always received with the warmest of regards and appreciation. Usually the escort stayed for the funeral, but only upon request of the family. If not invited to stay we would return to the depot immediately after delivering the remains. With the exception of one, I attended the funerals and presented the flag to the next of kin, expressing gratitude from the President of the United States. Departing the cemetery at the conclusion of the services, the family surrounded me, expressing their deep appreciation and often there were tears as I departed. It was unusual, but the family seemed to feel I was by the side of their son when he was killed and wanted to know all the details. The family, and friends attending the service, felt a very close kinship to me. I fondly remember these incidents and the families of each.

My last assignment while escorting the remains of officers killed in battle was most interesting. I departed Atlanta Army Depot with about thirty Army ambulances late one afternoon, each having a casket. Also, each casket and an individual escort, but I was responsible for the complete procession and had a casket for which I was also personally responsible. The caskets were place aboard a train at the Atlanta railroad station with the final destination being Memphis, Tennessee, arriving about 10:00AM the next day. All through the night we traveled across Georgia, Alabama, and finally into west Tennessee, dropping off caskets at various places along the way. I was present at each drop-off point and always there were many people present, regardless of the time of the night, and each time the mother or wife of the deceased would bend over the casket and weep; it was a sad scene. Then we would continue to the next place, doing the same thing along the way. Finally arriving in Memphis with about ten caskets of remains, there were hundred of people waiting at the station, including newsmen, and radio reporters. All the caskets were placed on line by the funeral directors, each was immediately surrounding with grieving families members. It was a very sad occasion and a memorable one, too.

There was one funeral I didn't attend, however. Not even a family member was in attendance at the station to receive the remains of their loved one. Shortly, the funeral director came to me and stated the family wanted me as their guest and that a car, with driver, was awaiting my pleasure at the entrance to the depot. The director accepted the remains in the name of the family, and being relieved of my responsibilities, I went to the car - a stretched black limousine.

Arriving at a palatial home somewhere in Memphis, I was warmly received by the mother of the deceased captain, a very dignified and gracious lady, perhaps in her middle age. Even though she discussed the past life of her son she showed no pain of sorrow nor did she express any. She had the servant to serve us tea and cookies and invited me to stay in her home during my stay in Memphis, if I so desired. Not wanting to inconvenience me, she said it was not necessary for me to attend the funeral. With that I thanked the gracious lady for her hospitality and requested to be returned to the railroad station for passage back to Fort Benning. She rang for the butler and instructed him to inform the uniformed chauffeur to return me to the railroad station, thanking me for bringing her son home. This was the end of my escort duty, and I was grateful.

Escort duty over, I was glad to take command of Company "B", located at Fort Benning, Georgia. Even though we lived in a splinter village (converted army barracks) on the post, not far from the golf course, Wilma and the boys were happy with the arrangements, enjoying the fellowship of the other officers, their wives, and the many children that bounced around the area. You never meet a stranger while in the service; the bonds are strong. Later we would move to Fort Bragg, North Carolina, living in another splinter village, known as Smoke Bomb Hill. The Army would demand much of us once again.

June 25, 1950, the Korean war began; Truman called it a police action. Then our politicians made another blunder by organizing the MAAG Indochina in 1950 in an effort to assist the French to continue their cruel occupation of the land - a land whose people were gracious and gentle, but which she, France, had raped for almost a hundred years. Then I was ordered to Saigon to become a part of the situation that eventually created the disastrous Vietnam War, a war that would become the longest war we have ever fought, but yet, in spite of what they say, we never lost (see the book The Eagle Weeps by the same author).

This ended our living in "splinter villages" (converted WWII army barracks). Our living accommodations, during the remainder of my service in the army, often consisted of a more specious and acceptable quarters to include villas staffed with servants, provided by the host government (in Indochina), and Europe, to spacious quarters on Beltzell Avenue, Ft Benning, near the world renown Infantry School, having amenities such as the officer club, swimming pool, tennis courts, nearby golf course, and the post chapel. Then too, at times we lived off-post in quarters, even though not spacious, but more acceptable than the "splinter villages" of "Smoke Bomb Hill" at Fort Bragg, North Carolina, or at Fort Benning, Georgia. While we lived in Saigon the French provided us a household staff for the three story villa in which we lived. Wilma, never before having had the luxury of having a household staff, and being intimidated at first by all of the attention she was receiving, had difficulties adjusting to and supervise the non-English speaking servants, but she finally managed. Usually one of the household staff member could converse in English and she issued instructions through him to the others for performance of daily activities and chores.

The end of the Saga, until...?

APPENDIX 1
ROSTER OF COMPANY "D", 150TH INFANTRY (RIFLE) INDUCTED INTO FEDERAL SERVICE JANUARY 17, 1941 HOME STATION, CHARLESTON, WEST VIRGINIA

CAPTAIN
Charnock, John N.

FIRST LIEUTENANTS
Johnson, Dale K.
Wright, Carles E.

SECOND LIEUTENANTS
Hanshaw, Woodrow W.
Honaker, Keith J.
Robins, William

FIRST SERGEANT
Rhodes, James

SERGEANTS
Adkins, Elisha E., Corley, George F. (KIA), Knowles, Robert D., Painter, Garland, Thompson, Gordon W., Thompson, Harry J. Vorholt, Alvin A.

CORPORALS
Blake, Russell R., Burns, Clarence B., Mckee, James W., Mckinney Jr, John H., Price Jr, Frank S., Spradling, Calvin P., Wallace, Bobby A., Warrington, Harvey A.

PRIVATES FIRST CLASS
Bernatowicz, Sixtus L., Harrison, Harry A., Heitzman, Harry M., Hendricks, Albert A., Hoffman, Wilbur F., Hunt, Lyle C., Jarrett,

Dewey W., Jones, Dorsel R., Jones, Elvin A., Jones, Leondras L., Jones, Thomas E., King, James A., Lane, Powell W., Markle, Ancle, Martin, Harry J., Mellinger, Bernard H., Miller, Earl E., Minear, Lloyd W., Pauley, Elsworth D., Pauley, James M., Peters, Ira P., Pierce, Paul R., Rabel, Russell H., Bryant, Chester J., Cunningham, Phillip J., Elliott, Kenneth G., Fortuna, Henry R., Hicks, Hoyte, E., King, Jack; Munday, Woodrow W., Sites, Eston, D., Summers, Forrest.

PRIVATES

Adkins, Ernest, Adkins, Joe H., Brecker, Bennie; Buckland, Harry S., Chapman, Kenneth; Crouch, Herman; Craft, William B., Cross, Charles E., Daoust, John; Davis, Homer D., Dent, Garland C., Dye, Cecil E., Gandy, Lacy C., Gatens, Hugh L., Gentry, James L., Goddard, Jess W., Goddard, Milkton, W., Griffith, David, W., Hamilton, Stanley C., Hammond, Jack N., Rankin, Wendell E., Ray, Aubrey; Roseberry, James B., Shaffer, Clifford J., Shearer, James D., Silman, Virgil H., Silverman, Abe W., Smith Cecil; Smoot, Herbert; Stevens, George B., Spradling, Wade; Strickland, Holly F., Taylor, William D., Thompson, McKinley, Turner, Donald J., Wahl, Theodore C. (Chet), Walker, Charles K., Waybright; White, Ernest E., Williams Jr, Arnold S., Young, Estil R.

APPENDIX 2

HEADQUARTERS COMPANY, SECOND BATTALION
158TH REGIMENTAL COMBAT TEAM (BUSHMASTERS)
ARAWA - NEW BRITIAN 1944

CAPTAIN
Honaker, Keith J.

FIRST LIEUTENANTS
Pavlich, John
Whitten, Jennings B.

SECOND LIEUTENANTS
Allen, Lynn
Bean, James W.
Tompkins, Chester G.

FIRST SERGEANT
Dixon, Spencer

STAFF SERGEANTS
Cochran, Sidney D., Dickerson, Billie W., Higginbotham Alvis E., Kring, Rollyn B., Mendez, Jose M., Raybourn, Russell T., Stokesberry, Kenneth A.,

SERGEANTS, GRADE IV
Bauters, Clarence A., Chapo, Joseph J., Gomez, Raul V., Lewis, Perley G., Ruiz, Ernest C. (WIA), Sheilds, Willard H.

TEHCNICIANS, GRADE IV
Deeds, James E., Drevo, Stanley, Gonzales, Jess S., Swenson, Arthur P.

CORPORALS, GRADE IV

Andreas, Dixon H., Bergeron, Francis H., Bredemeyer, Fred A., Cecchetto, Angele; Crum, Jay; Jogoda, Max; Johnson, Thomas R., Kiernan, Thomas F., Luchetta, Fred; McKiernan, Vincent T., Searcy, Thomas H.

TECHNICIANS, GRADE V

Butler, Charles D. (KIA); Doyschen, Murray; Leger, Avie; Newby Jerry O., Otero, Edward J., Touchberry, Jackson; William, John J.

PRIVATES, FIRST CLASS

Archer, Lester M., Bandsuch, Michael E., Brown, Joseph E., Burt, Charles F., Cook, Thomas C., Dodson, Floyd L., Feck, William L., Ford, Richard S., Garcia, Manuel G., Gluch, Stephen; Grimes, Thomas R., Hanley, Timothy P., Howard, Willie; Howe, Edwin W., Howsell, Marion R., (KIA); Kibbie, Patrick A., Kepler, Floyd W., Kosinsky, Phillip; Leedom, Samuel W., Lukomski, John A., Matheson, Edgar, B., Moore, Willie E., Morceau, Raymond C. Oviatt, Harold L., Parrill, Virgil F., Powell Melvin C., Ricciardi, Anthony L., Richards, Robert L. Riesbig, Rudy J., Roberts, Sherman B., Roupa, Eduardo F., Ruehling, Arnold T., Singhass, Walter F., Springle, Charles F., Swindall, Arthur L., Taylor, Gene; Wooldridge, Daniel M., Wright, Thomas F.

PRIVATES, GRADE VII

Allen, William E. (KIA), Alvina, Vincent J., Block, Harold U., Boyer, Clark J. (KIA), Byoskowski, Henry; Campbell, Baxter F., Coulter, Thomas C., Craft, Harold J., Davis, Ora M.,DeArmond, Robert E., Depriest, Lee A.,

Ferguson, Walter, S., Ellison, Lawrence M., Gelongo, Alfred C., Giammenco Jr, Salvatore, V., Glendening, Leo D., Hennon, Charles P., Hill, Herman H., Hinton, Clarence E., Hodges Jr, Robert; Holoch, Wade H., Huskins, John B., Karagiosis, Vesilies; Kelley, Patrick V., King, Milton, L., Knight, William E., Ksayczkowski, Edward (WIA); Leaton, Jack; LeClaire, Adelard E., Lewis, Martin A., Lungaro, John; Marfia, John; Martin, James, S., McClung, Donald S., Miller, Arthur W., Minyon, James M., Osoba Jr, Frank., Palma, Joseph E., Rogers Jr, Clinton; Rogers, Earl W., Ruff, Walter R., Serati, Robert H., Smith, Edgar M., Starnari, Anthony; Stevens, Tommie E., Surico, Pasquale F., Tackett, LeRoy, Taylor, Troy A., Varnado, Cary W., Willaert, George C., Zavec, Joseph H.

APPENDIX 3

HEADQUARTERS SECOND BATTALION
158th Infantry (Rifle)
A.P.O. 323

11 February 1944

SUBJECT: Commendation

TO: All Officers and Enlisted Men, 2nd Battalion, 158th Infantry

1. The Commanding Officer takes pleasure in transmitting the following message to all Officers and Enlisted Men of the 2nd Battalion, 158th Infantry, from Governor Sydney P. Osborne of Arizona, and William R. Branson, Chairman, Arizona State War Finance Committee:

"I send greetings and congratulations to you and your men on behalf of the citizens of this State. By Executive Proclamation today is being observed as "BUSHMASTER DAY" in the State of Arizona, and we are dedicating this day to backing of your attack through the purchase of War Bonds knowing our gesture to be woefully inadequate in comparison with your heroism. One of Arizona's fourth war loan drives has already been met. "BUSHMASTER DAY" is a proud event in Arizona annals, and the day of your triumphant return will be prouder yet."

2. The Commanding General, Sixth Army takes pleasure in transmitting this message to the Officers and men of the 158th Infantry from Governor Sydney P. Osborne of Arizona, and William R. Brenson, Chairman, Arizona State War Finance Committee to Colonel Herndon.

For the Commanding Officer:

Keith J. Honaker
Capt., 158th Infantry
Adjutant

Appendix 4

NORTHERN EDITION (AMERICAN)

"GUINEA GOLD"

In The Field, Thursday, January 20, 1944

RED INDIANS OF UNITED STATES ARMY GAIN SPECTACULAR SUCCESS AT ARAWA

It was revealed yesterday that Red Indians (2nd Battalion, 158th Regimental Combat Team (Bushmasters) United States Army and important part in the recent fighting at Arawa (New Britain). Known as "Bushmasters," the Indians put the Japanese to flight in one action and in a rapid advance of 1000 yards, capturing 28 machine-guns and a field battery.

In addition, 139 Japanese were killed. Yesterday's GHQ Communique which reported the Red Indians' success, also disclosed further heavy blows at Japanese shipping, barge traffic, and supply bases by Allied aircraft from Ambonia (west of Dutch New Guinea) to New Britain.

NOTE: The 2nd Battalion consisted of about twenty-five percent Indians. The rest were a mixture of Caucasians and Hispanics. We did not put the Japanese to flight-rather we had to kill them to the last man. They refused to surrender. We either had to kill them or be killed by them, but not before they had killed or wounded many of our men. The Author.

APPENDIX 5

HEADQUARTERS SECOND BATTALION
158TH REGIMENTAL COMBAT TEAM (BUSHMASTERS)
APO 3470, SWPA
5 August 1943

ROSTER OF OFFICERS

LIEUTENANT COLONEL
Stofft, Frederick R.

MAJOR
Hohnhorst, Henry C.
Stelman, Henry (MC)

CAPTAINS
Caffee, Robert C. (WAI)
Cochran, Orville, A.
McGlothlin, John A. (WAI)
Francis, Clarence W.
Honaker, Keith J.
Barton, James E.
Moulton, Charles W (MC)
Deutsch, Albert (MC)
Reaney, Burnell V (MC)
Barnes, Earle E (MC)
Gaskins, Steve P (CH)

FIRST LIEUTENANTS
Overmeyer, Charles F., Brown, LeRoy (WIA), Parrish, James W (KIA), Perry, Robert K (WIA), Pavlich, John; Miller, Kenneth N (WAI), Sanders, Woodrow F (KIA), Hart, (Peter) Bayard W., Hunter, John W., Sackrider, Frank S., Whitten, Jennings B., Ivie Farris; Nesbeth, George; Feagan, Robert R., Beatty, William R.

SECOND LIEUTENANTS

Hatch, Walter E., Levinson, Julian C., Williams, Effron A., McGowen, John R. C (KIA), Postel, Clarence C., Allen, Lynn, Bean, James W. Thompson, George S., Born, Richard W. (WIA); Geweinner, Mrcus N., Miner, Phillip LeRoy (KIA), Bartnickia, Thomas C. (KIA), Van Ruth, Chester D (WAI).

LEGEND: KIA - Killed in Action
WIA - Wounded in Action

APPENDIX 6

MOVEMENT FROM PANAMA TO AUSTRALIA
BILLETING OF OFFICERS AND NCOS
ABOARD THE HERMITAGE
JANUARY 1943
"C" DECK

CABIN 102
Colonel Herndon, J. Prugh

CABIN 104
Captains Allen, Ross N., and Day, Boyse E.

CABIN 106
Mjor Young Jr, Clarence E., and Captain Emrie, Matthew H.

CABIN 110
Majors Colvin, George T. and Shoemaker, Paul

CABIN 112
Captains Erb, Herbert B., Barta, Edward J., McGlothlin, John A., Mudge, Orville D.

CABIN 114
Captains Martin, William R., Wright, Travis G., 1st Lts. Zieg, Donald G., Dwight, Travis

CABIN 116
Captains Honaker, Keith J., Tarrance, William N., Barnes, Charles R., Caffee, Robert C.

CABIN 118

S/Sgts. Numkena, George P., Co F.; Patton Ernest A., Co A; Leithmeyer, Frank T., Ser Co; Stout, Harry M.., Ser Co; Wange, Clayton G., Ser Co; Styles, Ivan L., Ser Co.

CABIN 120

S/Sgts. Robertson, Jack L., Ser Co; Sanders, Milford N., Hq Co; 1st Sgt Michelback, Frank L., Hq Co; T/Sgt. Hussy, James P., Hq Co; T/Sgt Schornich, Rusell A., Hq Co.

CABIN 124

S/Sgt. Gilorease, Dan N., Med Det; 1/Sgt Sennett, Frank E., 1st Bn; 1/Sgt Patton John O., Co A;1st Sgt Steger, Emil O., Co B; 1/Sgt Rice, Harold R., Co C; 1/Sgt Lewis Frank E., Co D.

CABIN 126

S/Sgt Dickerson, Billie W., Hq Co 2Bn; 1/Sgt Root Drydend, Co E; 1/Sgt Howell, Virgil F., Co F;1/Sgt Hall, John C., Co G; 1/Sgt Anderson Calyton, Co H; 1/Sgt Wanger, Harry J, Hq Co 1Bn.

CABIN 119

Lt Colonels Gibbs, Edwin N.,Wood, Wilson B.

CABIN 121

Lt Colonel Stofft, Frederick R., Major Hohnhorst, Henry C.

CABIN 123

Captains Hutchinson, Robert H., Veluzzi, Joseph F., Welch, Helmar L., Moulton, Charles W.

CABIN 125

S/Sgts Hammond, Stinson T., Co A; Bodkin, Claude W., Co B; Mason, Elmer E., Co C; Miller, Merl C., Co D.

"A" DECK

CABIN 210

1st Lts Bennett, Erwin R., Long, Ellsworth M.

CABIN 212

1st Lts Greenwald, Martin S., Daily, William

CABIN 214

1st Lts Beatty Jr, William; Welke, Joseph R.

CABIN 216

1st Lts Wilson Jr, William C., McCVlain James M., Cotellessa, Paul.

CABIN 218

1st lts Somes, John W., Bland, Robert B., Durban, Frampton W.

CABIN 220

1st Lts Gerson, Seymour; Curley, Wallace S., Ruewer, Frank H.

CABIN 222

Captains Cochran, Orville A., Francis, Clarence W., Barton, James E.

CABIN 224

Captains Cump, Percy W., Cogan, Thomas V., 1st lt Douthett, Seth H.

CABIN 226

1st lts Whitten Jennings B., Pavlich, John.

CABIN 228

1st lts Millr, Kenneth N., Sanders, Woodrow F., 2nd lt Born, Richard W.

CABIN 209

1ST lts Perry, Robert K., Brown, LeRoy C.

CABIN 211

2nd lts Gweinner, Marcus C., Williams Jr, Effron A., 1st lts Burnett, Don E., Hunter, John W., 2nd lts Ivie Farris.

CABIN 215

2nd lt Levinson, Julian; 1st lts Hart, Bayard W., Webb, Beekman L.

CABIN 217

1st lts Parrish, James W., Nesbett, George N., Sackrider, Frank S.

CABIN 219

WOJGs Bartlett, Floyd H., Rolfe, Ralph E

CABIN 221

S/Sgt Faltis, Steve J., Ser Co; T/Sgt Wilson, John W., Ser Co; 1/Sgt Dixon, Spencer W., Hq Co 2Bn.

CABIN 223

1st lt Cole, Charles E., 2nd lt Feagans, Robert R.

1 room - 12 Berths - 12 Lockers:
2nd lts O'Hanlon, Jerome O., Cartledge, James O., Cook, Charles H., Thomas Rudolph, Brake, Ralph W., Boyd, George L., Braun, Harold; Parks, William G., Burbey, John H., Hunt, Reed E., Bean, James W.

1 room - 12 Berths - 12 Lockers:
2nd lts Lockard, Edward D., Hatch Walter, E., Clack, Robert P., Thompson, George S., Postel, Clarence C., Curfman, Ralph H., Thompins, Chester H., Allen, Lynn

Appendix 7

HEADQUARTERS CO 2ND BN
ONE HUNDRED FIFTY-EIGHTH INFANTRY
ARAWA, NEW BRITAIN ISLAND
APO 928
5 February 1944

COMPANY DEFENSE PLAN

1. Headquarters Company has been assigned a defensive mission in the Battalion sector to organize and defend in case of an enemy attack.

a. Information of the enemy operation at Gilnit on the Itna River and areas to the North indicates that a hostile attack could be launched from the North and Northwest, making the area the MLR. Recent reports from Gilnit states the enemy is in large numbers and have prevented our patrols from proceeding up the Itna River.

b. The adjacent and supporting units consist of the following:

(1) Companies H, G. and F, on the right in respective order and Service Detachment, 29th Evacuation Hospital, 59 Engineer Combat Company on the left. Company E located on the Kaurakubin Point to the west.

(2) Supporting units consists of the following:
a. 148th FA Battalion prepared to fire on targets of opportunity to the North.

b. 490th AAA to repulse any air attacks on our position.

c. The mission of this Company is to organize and defend the high ground south of the swamp and to prevent enemy break through attacking from the North.

d. Areas and missions of each platoon are as follows:

(1) The Anti-Tank platoon will develop the company left sector from the right boundary of Service Detachment over the left flank of the A&P Platoon making suitable individual emplacements, and assigning each section an area to defend coordinating with adjacent units.

(2) The A&P Platoon will defend and organize the area from the right flank of the AT platoon over to the left flank of Company H and assigning each squad a sector of the defense and coordinating fires on each flank with adjacent units.

(3) The A-T and A-P Platoons will establish a four man listening post at the edge of the clearing in their respective areas consisting of one NCO and three enlisted men to be manned from 1800 hours to 0600 hours and two men awake at all times. Each man is to be armed with his individual arms and ammunition and two hand grenades. Uniform will be steel helmets, fatigues, leggings, shoes or jungle boots with side arms.

(4) Company Headquarters and Communication platoon will be held in reserve to be deployed on order of the Company Commander to counter any enemy penetration of the defensive sector.

e. Location of AT Guns will be present location and to use canister ammunition when firing during enemy attack.

f. Engineer tools can be secured from the Engineer Company, Ammunition and supply point remains as it is.

g. Location of the Battalion Aid Station: rear of HQ Co.

h. Command and Observation posts will be in the shell hole to the left of present C.P.

i. Signal Communication will be by C-11 telephone from Platoon listening posts to the Company CP and EE 8-A from CO CP to BN CP. Communication net work will be operation from 1800 to 0600. Listening posts will have ground projector and white parachute flares used only in case of a large disturbance illuminating the Company sector for night observation.

KEITH J. HONAKER,Capt.,
158th Infantry Commanding

Guthrie Blair Castro
(1913 - 1995)

Murdered by thieves while trying to protect his son's home. April, 1995

NOTE: Due to the nature, the circumstances, and to maintain the flavor, and local lore intended in appendix 8, very little editing have been performed on the document. This is especially desired since Guthrei Casto, a contributor, a school mate of the author at the old Mt Etna School, even though advanced in age, disabled, having to walk using a walker that he had made using bicycles wheels, was brutally murdered while attempting to protect the home of his son being robbed by a bunch of thieves.

Appendix 8

Legends of Guthrie Casto

STORY 1
THE MORMON PREACHERS

In the early 1900 there came to Valley Bell school house on 18 mile creek two Mormon Preachers to hold a revival meeting. Large crowds came because there was no other place to go.

They were unable to hold the attention of the crowd. Finally, the Mormons gave up and one of them got up on a table and told the crowd to listen. He told them there would come a great deluge (flood) and when they saw the school house go down the creek they would remember the two Mormon preachers who had tried to save them.

The school house was a long way from the creek. However, in a few days it rained and the creek got up and the school house, and as the Mormons had said, went down 18 mile creek with the bell ringing as it bumped against the trees along the bank.

When the creek went down the bell was found in a sand bar; all that was left of the Valley Bell school. The bell was hauled up by Charley Rush and it remained with him for several years.

STORY 2
THE BOY AIN'T LOST

One day a man traveling on his horse asked a little boy, who was sitting on a rail fence by the road near the old Mt Etna schoolhouse, how far it was to Red House. "I don't know," the boy replied. Than the stranger asked the boy how far it was back to Plymouth: "I don't know," again was the reply. The man said: "You don't know much of anything, do you?" The boy replied: "Nope, but I ain't lost either."

STORY 3

THE SCARED HORSE AND THE LUMBER TRAIN

During the years from 1900 to about 1930 there was a railroad in this community that hauled out timber for barrel staves, cross ties, and lumber. Men came from everywhere to cut timber and we loved to see the train loaded with cut logs once they were cut and dragged from the forest by the horses to the railhead. Seeing the big engine, puffing its black smoke and blowing its whistle, was good entertainment for us boys. We had no other entertainment except what mischievousness we could get into when not working in the field ourselves.

In 1920, I Guthrie, was riding on a horse behind my father, Avril B. Casto. We met a log train coming down Black Lick hollow and the horse got scared.

They stopped the train and a brakeman got off, took me from the horse, carried me around the train. My father got the horse around the train and the man put me on the horse and we continued on our way.

STORY 4

About a quarter mile from Center Point Knob and Sigman Post Office, on the McClain Turnpike (Route 34), there was an old slave farm. In later days it was owned by Pleas

Davis.

There in old cemetery there in the woods are some slave graves with rough stones as markers. It has not been cared for in several years.

The old rail road grade is nearby.

STORY 5

A LITTLE GIRL ASKS AND ANSWERS

One little girl at Mt Etna School asked her teacher how many months in the year had 28 days. The teacher replied February. The little girl said she thought all twelve had 28 days.

STORY 6

THE CHRISTMAS TREE

Christmas time at Mt Etna school had a special meaning to us. One Christmas our teacher, Thresa Ranson, sent us boys, we were about ten to twelve years of age, to bring in a Christmas tree and we came back with one about 6 feet tall. She sent us back to cut a larger one.

We cut another one; it was about 20 feet tall and about 10 inches at the bottom. We planned on the way back to the school house just how we would get it inside the building. So we planned: while one boy would open the door, three or four of us would pull while the rest would push. Even this great planning of ours did not work. When we got the tree about a third of the way in we ran out of power. Then we could not get the tree in or out of the door. We spent some time chopping it up and getting it out of the door. You will have to guess what happened next. It makes me hurt yet to think about what happened to us. Our teacher was very mad at us.

STORY 7

THE BOY WANTED TO BE A PREACHER

One of our teachers at Mt Etna School asked us one day what we wanted to be when we grew up. One boy said he wanted to be a doctor, another said he wanted to be a fireman, while another a steam boat captain. Another hesitated a while and replied that he wanted to be a preacher. The teacher asked him why. The boy replied: "I would only have to work one day a week and could get a lot of chicken."

STORY 8

A BELL FOR THE CENTER POINT CHURCH

In the mid 1920 the people in the community decided to raise money to buy a bell for the church. It was decided to piece a quilt and asked for donations from people and their names then would be on the quilt. When it finished they had collected about $105.00 to purchase the bell. About everyone's name in the community was on the quilt. The quilt is still in the community to this day and the bell is still ringing.

STORY 9

THE OLD WATER MILL

Down on Painters Fork Creek there was an old water mill that was used to grind corn meal for the settlers in the community. They would hand strip the kernels of corn from the cob corn and take it to the mill to have it ground into meal. Often they would have to wait some time for the water to fill up enough to turn the old mill wheel. The mill was owned and operated by a Mr. Riley Higginbotham. Later, the Joseph's in Paradise, having a grist mill powered by a one cylinder gasoline engine and we could get our meal ground much faster.

STORY 10

CHESTNUT HARVEST TIME IN THE FALL

About every farm in the neighborhood had one or more chestnut trees. The old native chestnut tree grew to about 100 feet tall and produced a bountiful supply of chestnuts. Not like the present day chestnuts; they were smaller and sweeter.

Brady Boggess, owner of a grocery store at Sigman, paid five cents a paint for them (chestnuts). With this incentive every boy in the community was out early each morning, during the fall, picking up chestnuts before the turkeys did. Each family had turkeys and they, too, the turkeys, knew where the trees were and would travel from tree to tree gobbling down each and every chestnut they found on the ground. However, the chestnut trees died out in the late 1920 and early 30s.

The chestnuts served as snack during school which we ate when the teacher wasn't looking. When she did see us our chestnut was removed from our pockets and deposited in the pot bellied stove or the nearby coal bucket.

STORY 11

THE COMMUNITY WASH AREA AND SPRING

Route 34 (McClain Turnpike), which runs from Red House on the Kanawha River to Divide Hill in Jackson County, was sometimes a very dry ridge and water often became very scarce. Some women would carry their clothes a long way to find water to wash them.

Scott Ridge, a very long ridge, entered Route 34 about one half mile from the Village of Paradise. On this ridge, about one fourth mile from Route 34, was a spring by the road side. Near the spring was an old iron kettle. The women used the kettle to boil their clothes. While their clothes boiled they would gather dry wood to leave under the kettle for the next person. There were always water and dry wood for the next person.

Also, at the intersection of Route 34 and Scott Ridge, was an old coopers shop where they made wooden barrels and wooden kegs. I have some of the old tools used by the coopers.

STORY 12

THE COUNTRY STORE AND POST OFFICE

A country store and postoffice was owned and operated by Brady Boggess in Sigman, located about a mile from Center Point Church on the old McClain Turnpike. In the late 1920 and early 1930s some of the prices were as follows:

Can sardines, $.05 each. If you ate the sardines at the store he would furnish crackers, vinegar and spoon. A water bucket, with dipper, was always on the counter for everyone to use.

Raisins $.10 each box

Remington knives, $1.00 each

Shot gun shells, $.03 each

50 twenty-two caliber rifle shells, $.15

Men's horsehide shoes, $2.50

Flour, 24 lbs, $.39

Watches, Ingersol, $1.00 each

Brady also bought our rabbits for $.20 each, also our furs such as fox hides, skunk, Opossum, weasel, and mink. We traded eggs with him at $.08 per dozen. We could not get cash but traded the eggs for groceries.

STORY 13
THE DEPRESSION

In the 1930s, during the depression, work and money was very scarce. Farm labor was ten cents per hour; if you stopped to rest your pay was docked; you were not paid for resting. Labor for a man and 2 horses and farm tools paid from $2.50 to $3.50 per day or eight hours of work.

We were always on the lookout for snakes, rattlers, and copperheads. If you were bitten they would make a poultice from chopped up onions and salt and bind over the bite then pour kerosene on the poultice.

STORY 14
MISGUIDED

One of the local churches had a business meeting to see what could be done to improve the church. They ask the pastor to make the first suggestion. He replied: "The church needs a new chandelier."

"I object." said a lady member in the rear.

"Why?"

"We have no money to buy it with and no one to play it if we had it. What the church needs is more light."

STORY 15
ROY FISHER AND HIS HORSE

Dora Blake was our teacher at Mt Etna school in 1922. There was a cripple boy by the name of Roy Fisher who rode a horse to school to school. He brought ears of corn to feed his horse. Once the horse ate the kernels, leaving the bare cobs, we would take the cobs and break them into small pieces of about two inches long. We soaked them in water making them heavy and play war with them. The boys were divided into two teams, each team having the same number of pieces of corn cobs - about six pieces per boy. The war began: a boy was out when hit with a piece of corn cob or when he had thrown all of his pieces of corn cobs. This game lasted one week or until I, Guthrie Casto, peeped around the corner of the school house one fine day looking for a victim. However, being spotted by an enemy, who let go with a piece of corn cob striking me in the temple knocking me out cold. The teacher took over, there were no more war games with corn cobs. This actually happened.

WHOA, MULE, WHOA, as sung by Anna Casto, mother of Guthrie, Wayne, and Gaynell Casto Folden:

WHOA MULE, WHOA

I am the owner of a mule
The greatest mule I know
He's ring-boned and spare-ribbed
And a very good to go.
He'd kick a fly off his left ear
He never could stand still
I'll have a match for the fool mule
If it cost me a dollar bill

Chorus
Whoa. mule whoa
Why don't you hear me "holler"
Tie a knot into his tail
Or he'll run through the collar
Why don't you put him on the track
Why don't you make him go
Every time I stop that mule

It's Whoa, mule whoa

I took my girl out riding one day
That mule began to balk
He threw her out upon the ground
And he tore her Sunday frock
She swore she'd get revenge of him
And stopped to pick up a brick
That mule let go with both hind feet
Oh! you bet that gal was sick

Chorus
I carried her home upon my back
And I placed her on the bed
Put a mustard plaster on her feet
Another on her head.
The doctor came and felt her pulse
And said she's very low
The last words that poor girl said
Was whoa, mule whoa.

Chorus

Liza Jane, contributed by Gaynell Folden Casto:

LIZA JANE
Don't you hear the sleigh bells ringing? The snow is falling fast
I've got an old mule and a horse my honey, and I've got them hitched at last
Miss Liza put your bonnet on, climb in and take a seat
Gather up the robe you are sittin on and cover up your feet
And its whoa I tell, whoa there mule I say
Just keep your seat Miss Liza Jane and hold on

to the sleigh.
We're going to the preacher, Miss Liza you keep cool
I haven't got time to kiss you now, I'm busy with this mule
Miss Liza don't get frightened at anything you see
For I'll stay with you Miss Liza Jane if you will stay with me.
And its whoa I tell you, whoa there mule I say.
Just keep your seat Miss Liza Jane and hold on to the sleigh.
When I got him to the ferry he swore he'd never cross
So I put a blindfold on the mule and another on the horse
Roustabouts gathered around him with baseball bats, a gig
They hit him on the head, they beat him on the back
And they punched him in the ribs
And its whoa I tell you, Whoa there mule I say
Just keep your seat Miss Liza Jane and hold on to the sleigh
I put him on the pavement stones, the street he would not tread
I took the bridle off him and hammered him over the head
I tried in vain to make him go, but strength would not prevail
When a hobo spoke up and said to me, Why don't you twist his tail?
And it's whoa I tell you, whoa there mule I say
Just keep your seat Miss Liza Jane and hold on to the sleigh

The old mule got mad, he ripped and he tore
and I hit him with a rail
I told a silly hobo standing by to twist the
old mule's tail
The silly hobo gave a twist and the mule's
face swore a grin
He shut both eyes and he kicked straight out
and that took the hobo in
And its whoa I tell you, whoa there mule I say
Just keep your seat Miss Liza Jane and hold on
to the sleigh.

Memorial, by the Upper Vandalia Historical Society:

AVRILL CASTO MEMORIAL
(1876 - 1982)

Avrill Casto is gone and with his passing the Society has lost a good friend, a charter member, and the foremost authority on Putnam County history.

Averill Bond Casto died September 26, 1982, only a few days before his 96th birthday. He was born on Jim Ridge, Putnam County, on October 9. 1876, the son of William M. and Louvisa (Parkins) Casto. He is survived by his wife, Sara Anna (Cartmill) Casto; daughter Mrs. Gaynell Folden of Kanawha City; sons, Guthrie B. of Poca and Wayne G. of Nitro; sisters, Mrs. Louis Gibson of Poca and Mrs. Ruby Hill of Red House.

During his long and productive life, Averill Casto was many things; farmer, carpenter, mechanic, blacksmith, and surveyor, but always he was an historian. No matter what his vocation was, he managed to find time for his avocation which was local history. Not only did he acquire a remarkable knowledge of putnam County history, he accumulated an extensive collection of historical records, relics, and artifacts pertaining to our local area.

For his outstanding contribution is preserving the history of putnam County, the Upper Candalia Historical Society presented Mr. Casto with their "Heritage Award" in 1971. The Society joins with the family and many friends in his memory.

Memories of Mt Etna School (1936-1944) by Wayne G. Casto

I became a student at Mt Etna School in 1936 (6 years old Nov. 18). My teacher was L. O. Jeffries. I was born and raised about 200 yards from the schoolhouse.

Some years we had two or more teachers, but my grade cards are signed as follows:

Primer	1936-37	L.O. Jeffries
Second grade	1937-38	Eugenia Parkins
Third grade	1938-39	L.O. Jeffries
Fourth grade	1939-40	H. Estel Lewis
Fifth grade	1940-41	H. Estel Lewis
Sixth grade	1941-42	Ruthana Parkins
Seventh grade	1942-43	Dorothy Ford and L.O. Jeffries
Eighth grade	1943-44	Effie Clark

The school day started with the flag raising, weather permitting, and the pledge of allegiance. Some teachers had us sing hymns along with patriotic songs. Some schools had each student read a verse from the Bible, but I only remember doing that at the Lincoln school when I went there one half day.

We got our drinking water from a spring south of the schoolhouse in Polcyn's hollow. Usually two of us would go after the water. When wintergreen was ripe we would run down the hill to gain time enough to pick teaberries from the hillside across the creek. We had a good water cooler and many used hand-folded paper cups for drinking. Some had cups or glasses, but most of the boys preferred bottles. It was a thrill to get away using as half-pint whiskey bottle instead of a soft drink bottle.

We had a few minutes recess in the morning and in the afternoon, but the noon dinner break was the time for real play. One lady teacher always rang the hand-bell about five minutes early to allow last minute rushes to the outdoor toilets. Returning to class and after we were all settled at our desks, she, the teacher, would maker her trip (to the toilet). One day some of the boys went across the road into my father's field and caught a buck sheep. Just before we went in the schoolhouse following the noon break, they put the buck in the girls' toilet to surprise the teacher. She was not very happy with us the rest of the day.

It was not too unusual for the teachers to find a blacksnake or greensnake in her desk drawer or an owl or another kind of a bird in the bookcase. Our bookcase was a wall-hung cabinet about sixteen inches wide and about twenty inches high with a solid door. There were not many books in our library and they were well worn. The library books had been available for the students even when Ben Rod

Jordan went to school at Mt Etna. Most of us bought our own textbooks from older students. The books were not changed every year and some had four or more names of previous owners in them. The county furnished books for those who could not afford to buy them, but those books had to be returned at the end of the year.

Our athletic department consisted of a softball and a bat and some years we had a volleyball and net. We played hard and rough and there were occasional fights. Most of the girls were accustomed to hard work and as a result did not tolerate much lip from the boys. Some of the girls could swing a pretty hard fist.

In early years I was not much interested in the girls except as equal playmates. In later years I joined some of the other boys in the goal of kissing every girl in the school. Usually we got by without too much fuss or slapping. There could be no exception, one miss kissing a girl and you were considered a failure or a coward.

School was never stopped because of weather. We had no carpet on the floor to ruin with chewing gum (we seldom had chewing gum) and there was no air conditioning. The windows were opened in hot weather, with no screen to keep out flies and wasps. Pupils sitting by the walls would unplug the bullet holes in the walls to let in more air. In winter we re-plugged the holes with paper wads, but cold air still whistled through the cracks.

One winter we had a teacher who spent more time teaching the girls to sew then she did teaching the boys. We boys cleared a corner and played marbles inside the school most of the time. My thumb got so sore shooting marbles. I learned to crochet and made my mother a little Mexican sombrero that held about four for five thimbles. It was a work of art!

Speaking of marbles; one fall there were many fights over marbles games. Our teacher, Opie Jeffries, wanting to put an end to the fights, played with us winning all boys' marbles and put them in a five gallon bucket. The whole school went with him out on the ridge behind the schoolhouse where he threw the bucketful of marbles into a briar patch and outlawed marbles for the rest of the year. He was a good teacher, but he had to keep control.

We had one teacher that was a fair teacher, but too temperamental to earn respect. When someone was to be whipped, she sent me with my sharp knife to cut three or four good switches. If they were not as big as my forefinger, she promised to use them on me. Therefore, I cut the specified diameter but also managed to "ring" the switches so they would break after one or two whacks. No one got hurt enough to justify the amount of crying and yelling that went on. We were all pretty good at acting, except in the Thanksgiving and Christmas plays.

Back to Opie Jeffries. In good weather he would plan something special for us about once a month to inspire us to study harder. If we studied and did good on our tests we would get off on Friday afternoon. We would go on a field trip exploring the woods and flowers, learning about bugs, worms, leaves and anything we came upon during the outing.

On one of our trips to 18 mile creek in a large truck, we had a pretty good string of fish when a game warden came by. He asked Opie if we had any luck and Opie said: "No we were just playing around." Just then one of the girls pulled the string of fish out and showed him what we had. He, the warden, just laughed and went on down the road.

On one such outing we gathered dozens of cattail flowers. When we arrived at school the next monday we found the cattails bloom all over the schoolhouse floor. Every movement of the broom sent white clouds in every direction. Finally, someone solved the problem by tossing a lighted match in the doorway. It was a spectacular flash and very little residue (of the cattails) was left to be cleaned.

In winter the snow covered the road below the school making a perfect track for riding sleds or fence rails. An eight or ten foot fence rail about eight inches wide and three or four inches thick would hold at least four of us and soon the snow was packed. It would be as slick on the top as it was on the bottom. There were splinters, of course, but I don't remember anyone getting hurt in the short, but wild rides "on the rails".

Sometimes after a bad snowstorm, I would have three or four overnight guests. Many of the students walked over a mile to school and another mile back home. That was rough in bad weather. My parent always found room for a few extras. They were well repaid when I started high school at Poca. I found a warm bed and good meals with various families that saved me long walks and from missing school.

During the late 1930's and early 1940's local residents were expected to donate one day of labor per year working on the dirt roads. That was a day of fun for us, getting out of school to pick up nails and glass from the road and drain water from mud holes. Than it seemed funny to drop a rock in a deep puddle to splash someone with muddy water.

Of course, the sour came with the sweet. Once a year the health nurse arrived and those who had not received all the required vaccinations were in for a sticking.

Since the schoolhouse was a general meeting place for he community, many events were held there. During World WII the teacher registered families and distributed the ration books for the neighborhood. I got to help Ruthana Parkins register the first ration books when I was in the sixth grade. Local women and older girls took a course in Home Nursing Care one year, taught by a Red Cross volunteer.

One night some boys hid in the bushes below the road to scare the girls walking home after the class. The boys began screaming like cougars, but the trick backfired. Fay Harrison threw so many rocks into the bushes that the boys were glad to escape. That was their first and last attempt to scare the girls. Some of the boys got revenge by pouring some of my skunk "essence" in a window of the school house one evening and the class had to canceled. The next day I had to air the building and burn corn meal to help neutralize the scent. I was the janitor for my lasts two or three years at Mt. Etna.

Only about two other boys knew where I had buried the bottle of "perfume" that I had collected when skinning the skunks I had trapped. If one of us was desperate for a day out of school, they would put one two drops of the "perfume" on his shoe-sole. After being marked present at roll call he would then get close to the stove to get warm. Before long the "perfume" would be so strong the teacher would send him home.

It was not unusual for parents to visit the school to observe the teacher's methods and the way their child responded. Some parents did not care about their children's progress. Sometimes the older students, who were done with their lessons, would be assigned to help younger students with problems. It was a hard job for a teacher to cover all eight grades in all subjects and have time to devote to one or two pupils that were having trouble.

One day my father notice a cloud of dust all around the schoolhouse. My mother got our binoculars and found the answer. Donald and Sally Plycyn had brought a sturdy old baby buggy to school and we had the teacher (Opie Jeffreis) in the buggy. After fifteen or twenty trips around the building, we went down the hill to the Mt. Etna road where we rally made the dust fly.

Never let it be said that Mt. Etna was a dull school.

Attachment 5, Contributed by Virgie Fisher Morton

It was April 1st, all was out on the

playground of Mt Etna School when our teacher, Professor Smith, came walking up the path to the school. Keith said: "Look, see all them black cattle.", Professor Smith looked, Keith said: "April Fool!" The professor being a non-sense person we feared Keith was due a whipping but he escaped the professor's wrath for some unexplained reason.

I think Kay Kessell was our teacher when a debate was held: Slaves vs Indians. I was captain of the Indian team and Keith Honaker was captain of slave team. We had such a heated argument. Really I don't know who won, but we never had no more debates.

It was just before Christmas, about 1927, Professor Smith said he wasn't treating the student for Christmas, as always the custom. We were all very upset. So on the day before Christmas eve, the boys all decided they would roll the teacher in the snow, if he didn't. So we were all watching when the Professor came walking up the road; the boys ready to spring upon the hapless teacher. Some one said: "Oh Look, he has a sack on his back." Later we were given candy and oranges and the Professor was saved from a rolling in the snow. However the boys, Denver, Leonard, Leonard, Earl Fisher, Bill, Willard (Buck), and Keith Honaker, Leolin Landers, Roy Creasy, Edgar Harrison and Guthrie Casto and others, were disappointed for they had looked forward to doing honors to the Professor.

One time Bill Honaker, during school session, asked permission to see Denver Fisher as if to whisper something to him.

Permission granted, and Bill proceeded to visit Denver at his seat and pretended to whisper in his ear, but instead bit Denver's ear. Denver, being alert, caught on quickly and went over to Ed Harrison and bit his ear, the domino effect was working. Ed went over to Guthrie Casto and bit his ear and so on. And finally, Guthrie bit Leonard Fisher's ear. Leonard being unawares of the prank going on, yelled. The teacher then got into the act and asked Leonard the cause of the matter. "Guthrie bit my, teacher." Guthrie said: "Ed bit my ear, teacher." and Ed said: "Denver bit my ear, teacher," and Denver said: "But Bill bit my ear." and so on until all the boys were identified of committing the crime of biting ears. All the culprits were lined up on the raised platform, in front of the school, and given a good switching by the teacher; that is all except Leonard.

IN MEMORY OF GRACE

by

VIRGIE FISHER MORTON

She, Grace Honaker, was an inspiration to me. At school she helped in school programs; Christmas time, Thanksgiving and Halloween. At church they would have Epworth League Young Peoples meetings and Grace would put on some of the best church plays with just a few of us kids. Often she would work up very big plays and I remember in one play I had four parts. She was a wonderful person.

JOHN WAYNE

1022 Palm Avenue
Hollywood 69, Calif.
August 22, 1962

LTC Keith J. Honaker
2400 Huffine Circle
Johnson City, Tenn.

Dear Keith:

First, let me say that your letter of July 11th reminded me of a very thrilling and wonderful experience in my life. I still see Fred once in a while in Tucson.

As to employment in Hollywood, I just wouldn't know what to tell you. It is practically impossible to get anything in the motion picture business. Television and the government separating theaters from production companies have made such inroads in our business that, while it hasn't gone to pot, it has shrunk so much that there aren't enough jobs to go around. As far as the insurance field is concerned, I don't see how I could be of any assistance.

Thanks again for recalling some exciting memories. I hope something good breaks for you.

Sincerely,

John Wayne

JW:ms

APPENDIX 10

HEADQUARTERS COMPANY, 2ND BATTALION
ONE HUNDRED FIFTY-EIGHTH INFANTRY
APO 928 c/o Postmaster
San Francisco, California

19 January 1944

Mrs. Bessie J. Boyer
116 N. 1st Avenue
Tucson, Arizona

Dear Mrs. Boyer:

Your son, Clark, who is a member of Headquarters Company was killed in action while engaged against the enemy on Arawe, New Britain on 16 January 1944.

You have the deepest sympathy of the officers and men of this organization in your bereavement. Clark was held in high regards by all members of this command. He was a splendid soldier having an outstanding character and devoted to the country's cause. His loss will be deeply felt by his many friends and by me personally.

You may rest assured that a proper military funeral and burial was conducted. Among the words the Chaplain read from scriptures were two passages to which you might like to turn: 2nd Timothy 4:7-9 and John 11: 25,26.

I wish to express my own personal sympathy in your great loss. Please feel free to call upon me for additional information you may desire. I shall write you as soon as possible if there are further arrangements yet to be made.

With the kindest of regards and with my deepest sympathy,

Yours Most Sincerely,

KEITH J. HONAKER

Capt., 158th Infantry
Commanding

NOTE: A typical letter of condolence sent to the next of kin of those killed in action. It was a sad duty that I had to perform. Once the letters were received by the families, the next of kin would often write for additional information concerning details of how their loved had died. It was difficult trying to explain satisfactorily for death on the battlefield is gruesome and would only cause the family additional grief; commanders made their explanations brief.

Appendix 11

September 1948

To: Whom It May Concern:

It is with much pleasure I recommend for a Commission in the Regular Army Captain Keith Jewell Honaker, Infantry, 0407834 NGUS. Captain Honaker was a Major in the West Virginia National Guard both as Executive Officer of the First Battalion, 150th Infantry and later as S-3 on my staff. During the recent field training period at Fort Knox, Kentucky, Captain Honaker was in command of the Advanced Detachment, responsible for opening the camp, drawing and issuing supplies and similar functions. During the encampment he was S-3 on the Staff of the Commanding General West Virginia National Guard. In this latter capacity, he was under the direct daily supervision of the undersigned and results of his work in the former capacity were observed upon arrival at Fort Knox.

The Staff Officers at the Armored Center, Fort Knox, Kentucky who were associated with Captain Honaker were highly complimentary in their praise of his amiable personality and the efficient service.

Captain Honaker is an officer of superior efficiency in his grade, is amiable, trustworthy, completely dependable and is highly recommended for Commission in the Regular Army.

Charles R. Fox
Brigadier General
The Adjutant General

CRF:vt

A certified true copy:

Keith J. Honaker
Lt Col USA (Ret)